MW00884661

THE ARDWELLIAN CHRONICLES
BOOK SIX

BREATH
BY
BREATH

BY
DENNIS YOUNG

EDITED BY
JENNIFER FRONTERA

THANKS MICK

Dennis Young

ISBN-13: 978-1983581298
ISBN-10: 1983581291

First published 2018

The Lancer Captain nodded. "I am honored. Go to your crèche, tell them I have said you are to have wine and bread. Then rest, as I may need you further in the day."

She bowed and took her leave as two soldiers came, saluting. "Sorcerers and priests have searched the Dark Queen's sanctuary for clues. Her servant-guard was slain, and blood of humans found throughout the chambers."

The Lancer Captain shook his head. "Her guardian was human, captured and charmed many moons ago. His blood, surely."

The soldiers traded glances. "Our thought as well, yet the priests say nay. Another human, and female. Long dark hair was found, perhaps torn from the assassin's head during the struggle."

"One only? Surely sorcery was used."

"Death was by the sword, cleaving the Dark Queen in two."

The Lancer Captain had no words to say. Iy'lly'eth had been known as the greatest of the great, not only in her piety and service to *Mother Darkness* and *The Abyss*, but adept in the Dark Arts as well. *One assassin only? Wielding only steel?*

At last he spoke again. "What of her body?"

"Taken by the clergy, to prepare her passing to the Hands Beyond This Life."

"Take me to them."

The soldiers saluted once again, and the Lancer Captain marched away beside them in the silence.

* * *

Venic had been woken by the sounds of soldiers running in the passageways. He lay abed in quiet, wondering if it were a challenge of some sort, set by the hierarchy to keep soldiers on alert, not playing dice in darkened corners.

He started as a voice roared, echoing beyond the way. Not a dark elf voice, but something else, and his eyes opened widely as he came to know it as a dwarf.

In Ma'li'vil? Perhaps a prisoner escaped? Or have dwarves invaded and Drow fight them in the darkness?

He rose quietly, donned a robe before padding to the door, opened it a finger's-width and peeked beyond the threshold. All was quiet again, then a column ran quickly by, toward the stairway down, boots heavy on the treads, shouts and curses fading as they descended.

He stepped away as the door burst open, and Archane came into his arms. She trembled, fists beating softly on his chest, and he felt her tears trickle down his shoulder.

"Iy'lly'eth is dead... slain in her sanctuary, her guardian killed, and the living altar destroyed. All prophesied has become as truth, and now we face the future without the Dark Queen's guidance." She raised her face. "I must take the task, and as her Chosen, cannot let this fall to power struggles in our time of victory." She met his eyes with strength. "I need your aid, but still, as you are human, I cannot be seen reliant on your abilities."

He bit back a harsh reply, breathed deeply, and held her closer. The beating of her heart and the scent of woman all about her roused him quickly. He lifted her in his arms, carried her to the bed, and without a word, ravaged her until they both were spent. He lay aside basking in the afterglow, watching as her breathing calmed, the rise and falling of her breasts as music to his soul.

Archane rose before him, worry on her face. "There are duties I must perform. Once Iy'lly'eth's spirit is ascended to *Mother Darkness* and the land at last subjugated, there will be war within the Race."

Venic's eyes opened wide as she continued. "There are families who have waited a thousand years for opportunity such as this. Iy'lly'eth left no children, no line of succession or instructions in the clergy. Therefore, not only will the families fight for power, the priesthood itself will seek advantage."

"My abilities grow each day with your tutelage," he replied.

She grinned and took his maleness in her hand. "And other things about you."

He gasped as she roused him once again, yet gently pulled her hand away. "We must make a plan for escape, should it be needed. You cannot rule the Race alone without allies at your side."

She rose, washed her face in a bowl of scented water, and drew a dark robe about her slenderness. "I have planned well and will need you in the shadows, should time come. Therefore, planning for escape will be your charge, but quickly. Once the Dark Queen's immolation and prayers have been seen to, assassins will roam *Ma'li'vil* with impunity, seeking those who oppose their masters." She shuddered, turned away, silence drawn about her.

"Tell me of them," he said gently, rising to take her in his arms again. "I have studied years beside you, the Dark Arts deeply in my soul with your teachings." He chuckled. "You are the harsh taskmistress, tho' I would have it no other way."

Her ruby eyes glowed with heat. "I will teach you more, once this crisis passes, and we will set our way. But for now…" She knelt, kissed his belly, then her sensuous mouth engulfed his manhood, and she drove him into ecstasy again.

* * *

The Story of Venic and Archane…

Iy'lly'eth's rule of the Drow had been forever, said the tales, since Time began and the Race was born by blood of *Mother Darkness*. As *The Abyss* spewed forth formless Chaos, and the world was split into male and female, to propagate the Race and give pleasure in its doing, the Dark Queen took it all in hand to bring Order.

Through ages of the Drow, none alive could speak of knowing another leader, nor a consort who sat at Iy'lly'eth's side in ruling. Lovers there were many, male and female, some who stayed long years, others only for a night… and others, still, who gave their hearts not only to the Dark Queen in admiration, but on the altar in sacrifice.

Only once had Iy'lly'eth conceived, but that child emerged stillborn, and mourning lasted a rounding of the sun or more. Never since had the Dark Queen been with child, and stories began to rise of a pact; that for whatever life she chose, as long as it was wished, Iy'lly'eth would rule the Drow, yet no successor to her reign would emerge from her womb.

Then came war for all the land, elves and humans rallied against the dark elves. For near two hundred years, elves kept to the plains and forests while humans congregated in the cities. Then came the *Grhayvhald*, and the secret of mithril in the mountains called Ariannias, where Drow had never ventured. Iy'lly'eth sent envoys to learn the secret, and a pact was made; not for gold or jewels, but life for the duchess there, as her only daughter was a half-breed of elf and human Joining.

Iy'lly'eth considered this, and wondered of its doing, for never had she contemplated joining of any Races. Here, in the fortress of *Ma'li'vil on the Mountain*, secreted from the prying eyes of elves and humans, Iy'lly'eth would test this in her own way, that perhaps the Drow and humans could bring forth offspring. Surely, she surmised, the land could then be subjugated without its own destruction. Through intrigue and conspiracy, by careful plans and influence, the world would fall to her. Therefore, she sought a temptress, one whose pleasures could not be resisted, and set

11

the plan in motion. The chosen was one of her own, an acolyte and favorite of the Dark Queen, beautiful nearly as Iy'lly'eth her own self.

Her name… was Archane.

* * *

Venic had been a captive, one whose heart was soon to rest in the hands of Iy'lly'eth's priesthood, for the glory of *Mother Darkness* and *The Abyss*. Captured in a skirmish in the mountains near the abandoned fortress of *Tophet*, he was seen by Iy'lly'eth's Lancer Captain and brought before her, though stories said he was reluctant to stand before the Dark Queen, thinking his mortal time was done. What she saw in him was far beyond his dishevelment and wounds. Taller than the tallest of her soldiers, broad of chest and shoulders, hard eyes and unkempt beard… still, there was a power about him, one she had never felt within a human.

"How desperate are you to live?" she asked, then smiled at his reply, that he would not betray his trust of humans or of elves. "All say the same, before they lay upon the cold obsidian of the altar." She smiled again at his resolve. "I have a plan," the Dark Queen continued. "To unite our people and find a way beyond war and desecration of the world. Might you have interest in knowing of it?"

"Parley may be used as deception, while armies march and assassins find their way within chambers of the leaders," Venic replied.

Once more Iy'lly'eth smiled, knowing his mind sharper than many she had seen. "I speak not of uniting with parley and procedure, but of the flesh itself. Yours to… a female of our kind."

"Abomination!" Venic shouted, and now Iy'lly'eth laughed.

"Not so, for it is said in whispers of the Forest Lord himself, joining of elves and humans has been done."

Venic shook his head. "I know nothing of such sorcery."

Iy'lly'eth nodded to the door, and guards opened it and passed word beyond. "Let us see your manner with her before you. Let us test your calm and your resistance to a life of pleasured nights."

Archane entered, draped in crimson gown and headpiece, bright hair flowing from beneath her scarves and gold tiara. She bowed to Iy'lly'eth, then turned to Venic, facing him unflinching.

"He is large," she said, her voice as music. She stood closer, her face only tall as his upper arm, and ran a slender hand about his chin. "He needs of a sharp dagger on his skin," she crooned, stroking his forehead, lifting away the hair about his eyes. "I will have him at your command, Dark Queen, yet only after his wounds are tended and his body bathed."

Venic, for his manner, stood stoic, yet could not move his eyes from Archane's lithe and slender figure as she circled him. At last he nodded slowly, her fragrance in his face and in his mind. "Tell me what I must do to live. Yet know I do this only for my people."

Archane stood before him once again, looking deep into his eyes. "That, my dear human, will change."

* * *

Venic was led away, servants given orders to prepare him for Archane's pleasure. Four guards followed closely, and when the chamber doors were closed, Iy'lly'eth turned to Archane with a question.

"Are you prepared to bear a child, should this succeed?"

Archane bowed her head, then met the Dark Queen's eyes with a wry smile. "Does this preclude enjoyment of the pleasures, My Queen? Surely you have noticed of his power."

"Ah…" Iy'lly'eth nodded slowly and returned the smile. "You seek more than your duty, and I cannot say nay. Do as you will and speak with me on the Dark Moon Sacrifice. May *Mother Darkness* bless your fertility, and his." Her smile faded, and her face took on a look of mild reproof. "But do not let this man, this human, take your impetus away from needs of the Race."

* * *

The servants ushered Archane into the chamber where Venic had been taken. She stood aside, watching as he bathed, his chest and shoulders showing signs of battle, bruises, small abrasions, and a cut across his arm.

He paused as she walked his way, then spoke. "I would ask your indulgence to my privacy for a moment. Surely you do not wish to see me unclothed."

Archane met his eyes with boldness. "Yet our purpose is to test the Dark Queen's scheme, yes? How else may we do this, clothed in garments head to toe?" She grinned salaciously.

Venic thought for moments, then stood and stepped from the bathing tub. Servants scattered, tittering, as Archane's eyes widened. As she had said, he was large, yet now she saw her words were true of all his form. He met her grin with one of his own.

"A testing of many things," he said boldly. "How may a sword fit a sheath made too small? Or is there magic in the fitting?"

Archane lifted a towel from the chair nearby and dried him slowly. "We shall take the time necessary, and find the magic, should it exist."

* * *

In the moons that followed, Venic became not only Archane's consort, but her student. His mind was sharp, quickest she had ever seen, even in those of the Drow. And the Dark Arts suited well his manner, though his human arrogance would test her temper every day. Still, she stood fast beside him, and when asked by Iy'lly'eth of her true task would answer only that *Mother Darkness* showed a different way.

Iy'lly'eth gave her time, reasoning the gods knew better than did mortals, yet her patience showed its limits, and after a year or more of 'prenticeship, the Dark Queen called them to her presence.

"I would know your success or failure," Iy'lly'eth said, as she laid a hand on Archane's belly. "Might we raise an army of half-breeds to fight alongside our soldiers?"

Archane and Venic both nearly bristled at the Dark Queen's coarse words. At last Archane spoke, not with subservience, but near-defiance in her tone. "There are other ways, Mistress, than of bearing children who only die in service to the Race. Perhaps a different way is needed. Plans often must be changed when success of one is not achieved. Other ventures may show fruit and give us pause to reflect."

Iy'lly'eth eyed Venic standing silent beside Archane. "You hold your tongue well for a human." She nearly smiled as he raised his face, yet held his peace. "Archane, as well you know, is my favorite, and as a child sometimes given leeway, speaks when she should listen. I hear her words, and they are not without merit. What have you to say in this matter? Speak plainly, and know your heart is not at risk."

Venic and Archane traded glances before he spoke. "Dark Queen, your wisdom, while thought at first a worthy venture, has yielded something not considered. As I learn of Drow, your manner and devotion to the Race, I see the failings of my own people. We bicker, fight, and speak falsehoods to each other, playing games of power and position that, in truth, do not exist, or are only fleeting. We kill each other, and when too many humans die, we turn on others, such as the Drow. There is little I see of worthiness in humans of this world."

He took Archane beneath his arm. "This lady, in her teachings, has shown the power of the Arts she commands, and bids me learn each day.

While still we seek success of your command…" he showed a sly grin, as did Archane. "As said, other ways and successes come to light."

Archane's hand tightened on Venic's arm as Iy'lly'eth watched in silence. At last she motioned servants forward, a golden tray with three crystal goblets set upon it. She chose one and drank, then offered the tray to Venic and Archane. "It seems we find a different path, as you both have said." She sipped dark wine. "Have you pledged to each other in the presence of *Mother Darkness*? Is this your wish, to become mated consorts and serve the Race as needed?"

Once more Venic and Archane looked to each other, then nodded to the Dark Queen.

"It is," said Venic, and Archane smiled.

* * *

After Iy'lly'eth, and the Rising Tide…

So'lauf'ein, the matriarch of House Hovenethra, had called council a day beyond the Final Fires of Iy'lly'eth. Deep in the great mountain fortress *Avernus*, the family elders gathered, to speak the way and plan the new rule of the Drow.

"Dark Mistress, our spies tell us of Iy'lly'eth's allies drawing close about each other." The messenger stood within the Circle of seven dark faces watching, listening, all the while their minds thinking how best to cause the downfall of the House of Iy'lly'eth, now leaderless. "Their priesthood seeks aid from the Caste of Sorcery as their soldiers march the halls, listening for word against the continued rule."

"Warinethra sorcerers, most likely," said Briza, the Second Elder of the House. "Many ages they have served the Dark Arts way, surpassing all others save Iy'lly'eth's own necromancers. As our own mages fume at disassociation, how may we find a way beyond Iy'lly'eth's clergy and their maneuverings?"

"What of the soldiers?" asked So'lauf'ein. "Who of the Great Houses might they ally with?"

"Unknown at this time, Dark Mistress, yet we suspect Modennethra," replied the messenger.

"Soldiers may unbalance everything," said Jar'laxle, youngest female of the elders. "They are loyal to one thing only, *Mother Darkness*. While mouthing words to the Houses, they think only of the life beyond this world."

15

The council chamber was quiet as the elders passed looks between their number. The messenger waited for word to glean more knowledge, or return to her crèche and rest.

So'lauf'ein struck her staff upon the Echo Stone, the sharp sound ringing in every ear. "Seek a Lancer Captain who will speak with us, one whose words you know do not favor Iy'lly'eth's House. Offer whatever he may ask for his attendance."

"What of this Archane?" Berg'inyon, the only male of the elders, raised the question.

Briza snorted. "What of her? An acolyte, one of many chosen to warm Iy'lly'eth's bed." She showed a wry grin. "Shall we deliver her to your chambers for a dalliance?"

Berg'inyon ignored the barb. "Whispers say she is more, and was tutored by Iy'lly'eth for years. She may be more formidable than thought." He paused, his voice lowering as the others gathered near. "Gor'wath is dead, and there are those who say it was by her command."

The elders passed looks about once more.

"She has a suitor," said Jar'laxle, and the others turned to listen. "A human male, said to be highly skilled in the Dark Arts."

"You know of this... man?" Briza shook her head in wonderment. A human in *Ma'li'vil*... and not a slave?

"Little, tho' I would know him by sight."

Berg'inyon laughed. "Yes, as his skin is light as day and likely his height a head taller than our own. You have acquaintanced him? When and where?"

Jar'laxle paused to think. "A birthing of a minor priestess as I recall, perhaps five moons past. In a private ceremony, and Archane's impertinence to bring him. Rumors there rose nearly to a din."

The elders chuckled, all but So'lauf'ein. She raised a hand for quiet. "Might we parley with him, or is he within her spell?"

Jar'laxle nodded in respect, then spoke. "Never would I trust a human. But I must ask, what is our purpose in this gathering of knowledge? Simply to keep our enemies closer?"

"That, and prepare our way into the leadership." Briza traded glances with So'lauf'ein. "Now is our best time, with the House of Iy'lly'eth leaderless and the clergy preparing for a struggle. This Archane has favored us, unknown to herself, as Gor'wath is dead and one less there is to deal with. Should we be vigilant and move with care, Hovenethra may at last take its place as rulers of the Race."

She lit a red candle before herself and the other elders did the same, chanting lowly. "For *Mother Darkness* and the good of Drow, we must see it done."

* * *

Archane's Ascension…

A moon passed, and at the first all was calm, as *Ma'li'vil* mourned and the fortresses of *Avernus* and *Necroman* sent tribute to the House of Iy'lly'eth.

Archane, in that time, garnered allies, in the clergy, sorcerers from House Warinethra, and the Lancer Captain seen in the harem, who soon became her secret lover. And while her loyalty was to the Race as she yet was Drow, her true affections were for the human Venic, his tutoring of the Dark Arts and their power, to say nothing of the satisfaction found with him, that still Archane could not reason. Yet she was wily, and had learned for years at Iy'lly'eth's side how many hands could be appeased at once, and favors gathered as flowers upon the mountainside.

* * *

The council chamber in the House of Iy'lly'eth echoed with anger, as the clergy squabbled over leadership as scavengers about the bones of prey. Archane sat at the High Place once occupied only by the Dark Queen herself, and that, in part, was what had led to half a moon of near-violence. Still, the brace of soldiers in the corners, and those arrayed before Archane, kept matters in control, that chaos did not lead to blood upon the carved stonework of the floors.

The Lancer Captain watched from the main entrance, his gaze locked with Archane's as she waited for the room to calm.

"We will have order, and none with words to say will not be heard." Archane raised a hand for silence, and slowly voices quieted.

T'sa'brak, a male of the clergy inner circle, and a confidant of Iy'lly'eth in her reign, cast an eye from his place beside Archane. "If you hear them all, we may well be here a moon or more." He chuckled lightly, then drew his face more serious as Archane speared him with her gaze.

"They cannot see beyond their own ambitions," she said softly. "If this House cannot stand together, others will take advantage, and even as we speak, are doing so."

T'sa'brak's brow furrowed with a question.

Archane nodded gently to the doors at the chamber entrance. "Two there, alone and watching. Who are they, not raising voices as the others? Who among the priesthood would hold their tongues as they?"

"From where, Dark Lady? Who would be bold enough to set spies in our midst?"

Archane showed a wicked smile. "They were allowed in at my command. The Lancer Captain knows and will see their leaving halted. Perhaps we will learn a bit from them, should they have knowledge of their master's intent."

T'sa'brak nodded slowly. "What then?"

Archane's smile grew. "Perhaps a gift to the leaders there."

"Gift?"

"Hearts, of those brash enough to seek our manner. Surely it would give pause to such a foolish thing happening again."

They watched as the Lancer Captain sent soldiers among the throng, and the way in which the priests and priestesses, acolytes and servants, parted before them. No words were said, no threats intoned, only were there glances from beneath polished helms at those railing in their words.

Quiet soon descended, and as Archane rose to speak, the two standing in the corner drew small crossbows and loosed their bolts. One struck T'sa'brak, the other Archane's seat. The old dark elf priest fell, blood upon his shoulder and breathing labored in his chest. Two healers rushed to aid him, but before the bolt could be removed, T'sa'brak spit blood and bile upon himself as the wound bubbled with a stench. He coughed, spasmed heavily, and died at Archane's feet.

The assassins ran for the doorways, met there by soldiers waiting. The Lancer Captain shouted to take them alive, but before his soldiers could respond, blades were drawn by both and plunged deep into their own chests.

Archane marched to the writhing figures on the floor, rolled one to his back and pulled the knife away. "Watch, as the Dark Princess of Iy'lly'eth takes your heart," she hissed.

She drew the dagger down his chest, reached beneath the ribcage with her empty hand, then followed with the dagger closely. The assassin screamed as Archane cut away his heart, blood spraying everywhere. She pulled the pulsing organ free and held it there before his dying eyes. "This is your ending! This is your fate! You are but sacrifice to the glory of the House of Iy'lly'eth! I will find your mistress and do the same to her!"

* * *

18

Two moons, and the land yet shuddered with Archane's bold move. Though she knew not who had sent the assassins, and only with the rising of the Dark Moon did she call coven with her priesthood.

Haelris, Second Priestess of the Black Web, motioned Archane aside and bowed before her. "Dark Lady, word has come of the Houses asking council to be called. Some are worried they will be blamed for the attack, or made a sacrifice without cause."

Archane raised her face at the bold words, yet knew Haelris had been trusted by Iy'lly'eth herself. "Who asks this boon? Shall I guess it to be Hovenethra leading, the rest following as attentive dogs?"

Haelris bowed again. "Nay, for Warinethra has sent envoys this very night, saying they pledge to the House of Iy'lly'eth and seek only calm within the Race."

Archane pondered hidden meanings and covert treachery. "Your thoughts on this? Iy'lly'eth found Warinethra useful in our war against the elves and humans. Their mages kept the Forest Lord at bay as the campaign against K'ron'iss wended to its end."

Haelris paused before her answer. "Perhaps a private meeting with their elders would give you confidence. Surely words between yourself and their leaders would be less… guarded."

Archane nodded. "See it done. We will speak with them ten nights hence. See to their comfort and the grand hall is prepared. Advise the Lancer Captain his guards are to be present, yet unseen."

Haelris bowed and took her exit as the priest Ha'd'rogh stepped to Archane's side and spoke softly in her ear. "You suspect her, Dark Lady? Might she be the one admitting the assassins where T'sa'brak died?"

"We know only by our scrying we were betrayed," whispered Archane, watching as Haelris passed beyond the doors, jewelry on her wrists and ankles tinkling brightly. "The Lancer Captain has orders to have her watched, and I have acolytes observing her discretely. Soon enough we will know, and if confirmed, she will become a sacrifice to Iy'lly'eth's memory."

* * *

It came to Archane as she lay abed with three concubines, two females and a male. She watched, amused, as the male ravaged first one, then the other female, throes of passion heard late into the night. As Archane drifted into sleep, the question arose in her mind; might one of

19

these be an assassin? How might she protect herself from such a threat, therefore, other than bar them from her bed?

How best to use such a thing against her enemies, should need arise?

* * *

A Planning for the Future…

Archane lay in Venic's arms, the blankets skewed and passions spent, wondering, once more, who might be a spy or assassin waiting for the moment. *Surely not Venic, for I would know, would I not? Nor the Lancer Captain, as I have probed his mind as he lay satiated from our joining. Who then lies in wait, to take my heart and hold it before the enemy?*

"What troubles lay about your mind?" he asked, caressing her shoulders gently. "I feel the angst within your spirit, the dread upon your thoughts. Speak, and I will listen."

She nestled closer, wondering now of feelings for this human, and how they came to be. "The Race must survive, and as One. I pray for Iy'lly'eth's wisdom, yet it seems to abandon me in most desperate times. How to proceed? How to insure our survival?"

"Do we share love?"

Archane paused to consider. *Love is a human thing, and one the elves have taken up. Love brings thoughts of selfishness and poor decisions. Love brings confusion of the mind, as the heart seeks rule and emotions fight against stark reason.*

"A better question," he continued, knowing her reluctance to answer. "Do you hold trust in me?"

Archane let go a breath. "As much as any." She raised herself to her knees, and put a finger to his lips before he could reply. "In this time, trust is paramount, yet difficult to find. In truth, I say yes, but no matter. You have no power in the hierarchy, therefore…" She took his hands to her dark and glistening breasts. "I am yours in the ways we share… but only those."

"Then allow a word, if you will, Dark Princess. Be bold in your newfound leadership, for enemies will sense your hesitation. Give them no time to act against you. Take the battle unto their presence, as done against the elves and humans. Therein is the wisdom of Iy'lly'eth you seek."

She lay herself upon him, warm, dark skin against his lean, pale maleness, and smiled contentedly. "You would have me lay waste to the Great Houses of our people? Only for threats imagined, not true attempts?"

"Attempt was made, yes?" He rolled atop her, pinned her arms above her head, and held his face a breath away from hers. "Now, my princess, how would you escape should I be here for your heart?"

For a single moment, fear was seen in her face, yet he caught it all, then nodded. "Therefore, you cannot take the chance. Your entourage, your priests and priestesses, even the Lancer Captain you keep as your secret toy. How can you trust them, with none about to trust?"

Her eyes widened at the Lancer Captain's mention, speaking at the last. "You seek a place beside me, yet without the formal trappings and responsibilities."

"I have no ambition for the Drow, nor would I be accepted in any manner of official status."

She slid her wrists from his hands and wrapped her arms about him. "My bodyguard, one disinterested in gain or place."

He moved his knee between her legs, parting them slowly, and found her warmth again. She gasped, then smiled, and drew him deeper in.

"I have my place," he whispered, as they rocked in ancient rhythm, and lost themselves in pleasures once again.

* * *

Beyond that day, Venic always was in Archane's entourage. Garbed in crimson cloak and hood, his face was seldom seen, and only then might others of the Drow pretend his human presence was not noticed.

There was a power about him, a quiet malevolence, enough to raise the hackles of the soldiers round, and even Archane's own priestesses showed deference when he came into the chamber. In whispered words they named him *Culis, Red Moon*, for always did he hover near Archane as in protection, his human paleness hidden beneath garment folds and trappings.

And as rumors spread throughout the fortress of the dalliance with the Lancer Captain causing of ill feelings between Archane and her protector, the Black Web let it be known; such words were treasonous, and always did the sacrificial altar wait for hearts, warm and beating, given to the glory of Iy'lly'eth's memory and *Mother Darkness*.

And Archane's own hand to wield the dagger, and harvest them as needed.

* * *

"**D**ark Princess, the envoys from House Warinethra await your pleasure in the grand hall."

Archane glanced to the servant, then attendants round preparing her for the conference. They primped and coifed her regally, heavy vestments of crimson and sable, bracers adorned with a hundred rubies, and a golden tiara set upon her glowing silvery hair. Archane stood as Haelris and Ha'd'rogh entered from a room aside, bowed, and took their places. Together with a dozen guards they passed beyond the doors and through the passageways of *Ma'li'vil*.

Warinethra's entourage rose and bowed as Archane entered the meeting hall. Their guards stood at the table side, watching as Archane's soldiers took places at the entrances.

The tallest of the Warinethra trio laid back her hood and bowed again. "Talice, Dark Princess, and I present Dark Mages Imbros and Vhurd'aer. We speak for Era'kasy'ne, Matriarch of our House. How may we serve the House of Iy'lly'eth?"

Archane only nodded, listening carefully to the near-whispers of the female Talice. She was as those Archane had met before of Warinethra; fine-boned, lighter-skinned than was Archane, eyes nearly black throughout and slanted deeply. Talice was slender even more than most of Drow, hair fine and light, and somewhere within Archane's bosom came a twinge of deep allure.

Servants entered, setting food and drink upon a sideboard, scented candles lit, and the fire stoked to warm the room.

Archane gestured to the pillowed chairs. "The House of Iy'lly'eth welcomes our colleagues of House Warinethra." She was careful to use words neutral in their meaning, showing nothing of alliance or approval. While Archane knew this might be thought ill-timed or insulting in some way, vigilance was warranted.

Again, the Warinethra envoys bowed, sat themselves and partook, after Haelris and Ha'd'rogh had done the same, and only from the portions chosen by both parties. Archane knew trust was something fragile in this time, and sipped slowly from the cup offered by Talice herself to the Dark Princess.

Time passed, Haelris speaking of the conclave's purpose and agenda. Ha'd'rogh inquired of status of Warinethra's soldiers and sorcerers, as many had participated in the victories against the elves. While mages and apprentices had been sequestered after driving the elves into a trap, hundreds of Warinethra soldiers had fallen in the battles.

"I say in strictest confidence," said Talice, peering o'er her cup and into Archane's eyes, "we ask a boon of your great House, that ours does not fall prey to greed of others."

"What others, if you will say?" asked Ha'd'rogh, as Archane listened.

"Two, Dark Lord, and surely you may guess. Always has Hovenethra sought power in the Race. Now word comes of support, perhaps even an alliance, by the House of Modennethra."

Ha'd'rogh traded glances with Haelris as Archane held her peace. He drew from his cup, then continued. "Such an alliance would be powerful and bold. What fortunes does Modennethra seek?"

"Perhaps the place Hovenethra now occupies," replied Talice.

"And what is that place?" asked Archane, her voice sharp in the quiet hall.

Talice blinked twice, swallowed wine, then looked to Imbros and Vhurd'aer before she spoke. "Dark Princess, is not Hovenethra thought to be a power in the Race, second only to the House of Iy'lly'eth itself? Forgive me if I misspoke, yet it is only knowledge passed among the other Houses."

"And this knowledge, is it accepted by your Mistress?"

Imbros raised a hand for pause. "We mean no disrespect. We seek only parley and frank discourse. No claim of truth is made for these… rumors."

"Rumor may be accepted as a truth, should advantage be desired," said Ha'd'rogh.

"Our point," replied Talice, bowing in her seat. "And should Modennethra desire a higher standing, alliance becomes their key."

Thoughts raced through Archane's mind as a plan began to form. "For the nonce we will accept this as suspicion only, and we thank you for the news." She paused, then rose unexpectedly. Warinethra rose as one, and quickly Ha'd'rogh and Haelris followed. Archane locked eyes with Talice. "Come with me, as I have private words to share."

She turned, soldiers falling in around her, and Talice glanced to her own soldiers, shifting nervously about. The Warinethra envoy shook her head, nodded to the mages with worry in their eyes, then fell in step with Archane's guards. All remaining traded looks of apprehension, knowing not what to say or do. At last Haelris motioned to the chairs and they sat.

The silence in the grand hall was deafening in their ears.

* * *

Archane led Talice to a private chamber and set the guards outside the door. Once within, they faced each other, only an arm's length apart, and Archane spoke in quiet tones.

"Have you a trusted concubine, male or female?"

Talice dropped her dark eyes away. "Dark Princess, you ask of very personal things."

"Speak freely, as these words hold urgent meaning. If you speak for your Mistress Era'kasy'ne, with whom I am acquaintanced, I ask Warinethra's aid in finding truth within your accusations."

Talice clasped her hands to mask their trembling. "We do not accuse, only inform, Dark Princess. We seek to support the great House of Iy'lly'eth."

"And in doing so, increase the power and prestige of Warinethra. Play no games with me, as the future of the Race is in the balance. Times are, alliances will show the way."

"The House of Iy'lly'eth holds the power," whispered Talice, eyes averted.

Archane tucked a finger 'neath Talice's chin and raised her face. "Have courage, if Warinethra seeks my favor. I ask again of a trusted concubine, one who may find the way to Hovenethra."

Talice held her words for breathless moments. "A… spy?"

"An informant. One whose loyalty is without question. One whose talents would be coveted within the hierarchy of Hovenethra."

Once more Talice paused, then nodded slowly. "I may know of such, Dark Princess. Yes, and I see now your wisdom." She bowed. "Iy'lly'eth's spirit smiles within your own. Warinethra will aid you as we may."

* * *

Hovenethra…

"Word is, Warinethra has traveled to *Ma'li'vil* at behest of Archane." Berg'inyon had begged entrance to So'lauf'ein's private chambers even as the Matriarch was bathing. He waited with impatience beyond a silken curtain as attendants wrapped a heavy cloak about their mistress. "Should the House of Iy'lly'eth gain alliance with the sorcerers of Warinethra, it may cause great upheaval in the ruling clans."

So'lauf'ein emerged, her face hard upon the old male elder. "You interrupt my bath to impart words already known? Where have you been these last two days as issues of importance made way through the hierarchy? Shall I speak of it to you?"

Berg'inyon stepped back, So'lauf'ein's wrath nearly as a blow. "I have taken leave, as much has been heavy on my mind, Mistress." He shrugged and showed a nervous smile. "A bit of respite is known to clear the spirit."

So'lauf'ein huffed. "You have a new concubine, a female found waiting at your very door, I have heard. One not of the House and unknown to any here, yet you allowed her into your bed! Have you not enough to keep your interest? Can you not realize what may well be in our midst?"

Berg'inyon pondered. "I swear by the spirit of Hovenethra, she is naught but a pleasure toy. Unique, yes, and satisfying, but nothing more."

"Fool! We sent assassins to the very hall of Archane, and nearly did we succeed. Do you not think this princess and her Black Web would do the same?"

Berg'inyon bowed. "We have seen no assassins, true? Our soldiers keep those felt a danger or undesired away and probe deeply for treachery."

"You, yourself, are probing deeply into your concubine, crude tho' my words may be. Have you searched her mind, her heart, for the treachery you say soldiers keep away? Is she a spy, listening as you mumble secrets, laying satiated in her arms?"

So'lauf'ein stepped closer, her face a hand's-width from Berg'inyon's. "Find the truth of her. If she is as you say, perhaps your ending will be one of pleasure, nothing else. Should she be sent by Archane or any of her ilk, or somehow by alliance with Warinethra, learn of it, and now. Bring her to me, should she be a spy!"

* * *

The Hand of Archane…

A moon passed. The great Houses of the Race sent tribute and emissaries into Archane's presence, pledging loyalty to the Dark Princess. From Hovenethra came Briza and Berg'inyon and Ath'a'vul, elders known for centuries to Iy'lly'eth herself, and warned of by the Lancer Captain for their shrewdness. From Warinethra came Talice with the matriarch Era'kasy'ne and her mated one, Hadrogh, the only male of elders in that House. From Modennethra and Karachitthra came Byrtyn and Ulitree, and soon enough, *Ma'li'vil* was filled with the highest of the high.

Yet never did So'lauf'ein of Hovenethra come forth, and Archane noticed of it. The Dark Princess knew it was an unsubtle slight, respect withheld and warning of Hovenethra's intent; that So'lauf'ein herself sought to become leader of the Race.

And with word now of Warinethra's concubine discovered, Archane began to plan the way for Hovenethra's ending.

* * *

The grand hall of *Ma'li'vil* rang with voices raised in anger. Ten days and more, and late into the nights, the great Houses of the land debated, demanded, threatened, and deliberated the future of the Race and how it would be led.

Warinethra pledged loyalty once again to the House of Iy'lly'eth, the Matriarch Era'kasy'ne baring her own breast before the council, offering her heart in tribute to Archane.

Modennethra's entourage brought captives from the city of K'ron'iss, soldiers and those of the Pale One's own bedchamber. Yet more, Modennethra's leaders spoke in favor of Hovenethra, saying new leadership was needed after ages of Iy'lly'eth's stern rule.

Voices rose from every side, those in favor, those opposed, as soldiers gathered quietly at the entrances. At the last Archane stood and struck her staff upon the stonework floor. "Enough! Debate is warranted, yet there will be no threats, else I will have those threatening removed!" There was little doubt within the chamber what the Dark Princess spoke of, as guards about drew weapons.

Slowly the mood was calmed, as sconces on the walls were refilled and incense lit, and servants placed food and drink before those in the chamber. At the last the emissaries set attention to the meals before them.

Archane motioned Byrtyn, matriarch of Modennethra, to a private chamber. Guards followed and blocked the doorway as Modennethra clergy followed, protesting loudly. The door was closed and latched, the Lancer Captain himself taking place before it, assuring those of Modennethra their matriarch would not be harmed.

Within the room, Archane paced as Byrtyn struggled to arrange her garments and set her headdress straight. She waited as the Dark Princess found rein upon her temper. Archane turned away, encircled by her acolytes, and gave a prayer for composure. At last she faced the Moden matriarch.

"You speak in favor of Hovenethra. Why so? Has your House not prospered through the ages, favored by Iy'lly'eth herself? And now you wish to see her rule abandoned?"

Byrtyn turned her eyes away, breathed deep, then faced Archane again. "Times change, Dark Lady, and with it fortunes of the Houses. Hovenethra sees the House of Iy'lly'eth weaker now, the Dark Queen gone, Gor'wath dead, and only those untested at its lead." Her eyes found Venic standing silent in a corner, watching. "You treat with humans who are our enemies. Some say you lay with them, disgracing the Race and making mockery of our victories."

Archane's face deepened further, yet she held her tongue, seeking solace in the silence. She chanced a glance to Venic, and at the last, faced Byrtyn once again. "Your words are heard and are worthy, as Modennethra always has been wise, with bold candor. Yet if you stand with Hovenethra, do you not see their true intent? They want not only leadership, but domination. Has Modennethra not been given leave to rule the mountain fortress *Avernus* as seen fit? Do you not command a legion of soldiers victorious at the Cross-Plains River battle, and your priesthood harvesting elven hearts by scores? What more might Hovenethra offer, with the land now subdued and our will enforced?"

Byrtyn said nothing for moments, yet did not look away.

She has courage deep, I must give her that, thought Archane. *Still, if Modennethra turns from the House of Iy'lly'eth, who will follow? Who, then, will remain?*

"There are rumors of great magic in the elven emperor's city," began Byrtyn, then she paused as if wondering what to say.

"I know of them," said Venic, and the dark elf women turned, aghast.

Byrtyn sneered. "You are a foolish human whose heart should long ago have been offered to the Darkness. You know nothing."

Venic stepped forward boldly, no deference seen to Byrtyn, no bow or nod of recognition. His eyes were hard upon the elder priestess. "Rumors of a way beyond this world, where K'ron'iss himself and many of his faithful escaped to. The manner unknown to nearly all, save a story of a 'window' to another place beyond the one we live in, yes?" He chuckled. "Those stories have been heard for many years among the elves and humans. The emperor himself could not keep his boastful manner quiet when drink was in his mind."

"What is this?" Archane's question nearly was a whisper, filled with accusation at both Byrtyn and Venic.

"A fable, likely, Dark Princess," replied Venic. "Yet as Hovenethra's army scoured the emperor's city once it had been secured by Iy'lly'eth's Black Guard, they also searched for truth." He nodded to Byrtyn, listening closely. "It would seem their House has shared knowledge with the Modennethra matriarchy, yet not with you."

Archane turned her gaze slowly to Byrtyn. "For your life, you will say what you know of this to me."

The old priestess swallowed hard and nodded. "As said, and Hovenethra's claim is by the finding of that legend. So'lauf'ein herself gave these words to me."

"You held a secret from this House, favoring another. Tell me why I should not have you on the altar this very night!"

Byrtyn trembled and tears began to fall. "I have no answer, Dark Princess. I did only what I thought best for the Race and future times."

Silence hung heavy in the room, then Archane motioned to the door. "Take your entourage from this House. Do not presume my mercy a sign of weakness, but rather to keep the Race you seem to think you know of well intact. Hovenethra's duplicity will be their downfall. Go."

Byrtyn bowed quickly and departed. Archane watched the door close quietly, then turned to Venic, eyes blazing. "You will tell me all you know of this, or by the spirit of Iy'lly'eth herself, I will have your heart out!"

* * *

Archane dismissed the council, and guards quickly ushered all beyond the grand hall amidst protestations of ill-mannered treatment and respect ignored. Venic trailed behind her, guarded by soldiers with hands upon their weapons, eyes sharp and watching the human closely for any sign of treachery.

Archane led him to her private chambers, waved the guards beyond the door, and faced Venic once more. "Speak."

She gestured, and Venic sat in a simple chair, though it had been his wish to stand.

He knew it was Archane's will that placed him there. He thought to say a fable of his own, yet found his tongue unwilling to speak other than the truth. It came to him in a flash of insight, Archane now controlled his very words. "Dark Princess, I know little other than tales told for many years of the Window. Yet with your teachings, I have scryed beyond what is known, seeking the hearts and minds of those very elves and humans knowing of the tale."

Archane waited without reply, and Venic continued. "Some I cannot see, others thrash about in agony or despair. Yet a few know in certainty of it."

28

"Of this Window? You speak of K'ron'iss, emperor of the elves, and his self-named city, yes?"

Venic fought against his own reply, yielding at the last. "An emperor with little recognition, a fop and lecherous elf, if ever was there one. Still, clever and resourceful, shrewd in dealing with humans who are corruptible when fortune and position offered."

"Yet this Window! Speak of it!"

Venic's throat caught, and he heaved a breath, face pale and sweating as he fought against Archane's power. "A… construct of great magic, surely garnered in ancient times, but I cannot say from where. Yet only Drow have the knowledge, I swear to you! Elves and humans do not believe the Dark Arts power."

"Then from where and whence did it come? Who but Drow could conceive of such a thing!" Archane turned away, pacing angrily to a prayer fountain, knelt and laid her forehead to the cold and soothing stone. Music of the waters slowly settled in her spirit, and at the last she rose, closed upon Venic once again, and looked into his face. "Might the Dark Queen herself have made a pact with this elf? Surely, she would not treat against her own kind, and if so, for what purpose? Where does this thing, this Window, lead?"

Venic shook his head, for truly he did not know the answer. Tears trickled down his cheeks, and at the last he spoke again. "Moons I have studied ancient texts and sigils, and my search at last bore fruit. The artifact is likely hidden by Hovenethra's clergy, tho' doubtlessly beyond their knowledge. They sought to use its discovery as their final play against the House of Iy'lly'eth."

Archane knelt before Venic, a sly smile upon her lips. "Might you find this thing and speak its place? Is your ability grown, that we may see it for ourselves?"

Venic slowly nodded. "Dark Princess, for you, the world, or any other we may find."

She stood, releasing him from the chair and her spell of truthfulness. "Then do so, and know reward shall be yours again. Yet do not fail me, nor hide your findings ever, or your heart will be mine, not only in desire, but warm and bloody in my hand."

* * *

Moons passed. Hovenethra took refuge in its fortress of *Necroman*, drawing close about itself. Modennethra, strong in

Avernus and sequestered, kept away, until upon the Dark Moon Sacrifice, their clergy elders were summoned by So'lauf'ein.

Byrtyn sent her Second Priestess Mizz'rym, and the priest Qendass in her stead, seeking safety in her bower and posting guards in all the corridors. And when word came both had been sacrificed by So'lauf'ein's own hand, she knew Hovenethra was aware of her words to Archane, and the Dark Princess now apprised of the treasure held by So'lauf'ein. Therefore, and as expected, *Necroman* barred all not known, and Modennethra kept apart, hidden deep in *Avernus*, subject to the whims of So'lauf'ein and her priesthood.

And with secrecy secured, Byrtyn began to plan the way beyond the eyes of So'lauf'ein.

* * *

Hovenethra...

The elders of Hovenethra met once more, the small chamber deep within the cavern complex and known to no one save those of the ruling clan. No servants, no guards, only six attending, they spoke of deeds to come against the House of Iy'lly'eth.

"We cannot meet them on the battlefield, as our armies lay depleted," said Ath'a'vul, a male who, in his younger years, had been a soldier of the House and lived through battles too many now to count. "Their war leaders are incorruptible, loyal to a fault not only to the House but Archane herself."

He chuckled, and So'lauf'ein looked his way. "You find humor in this doing? We speak opposition against the House ruling of our people for a thousand years. Share your thoughts of humor or cease them."

"Ath'a'vul only says of rumors that Archane shares her pleasures to keep soldiers in her favor," replied Briza.

So'lauf'ein huffed a breath. "Then she must receive them dusk to dawn, and even then, allow them to ravage her as she sleeps."

"Tho' there is a grain of truthfulness," said Briza, as Ath'a'vul nodded in agreement. "We know she favors a certain Lancer Captain, and if him, why not others? Archane shows no shame, as she lays with a human. War leaders surely are more welcome."

"We have learned something of this Venic, her consort," said Jarlaxle, youngest of the females. "He studies at her side and has done so since his capture some years ago. His mind is sharp, and he shows a talent for the Arts. We know he scries upon us, yet we have kept our secrets."

"Still we did not think to keep the artifact a secret from Modennethra," said So'lauf'ein, with warning in her tone. "And therefore, we are betrayed by one we thought an ally. And Archane becomes aware, not by this Venic's ability, but lack of our own."

Silence sat heavy on the council circle as glances passed around and candles burned softly on the table.

"What is your wish, Dark Mistress?" asked Briza, deference heavy in her voice.

"What choice have we?" Ath'a'vul raised the question others feared to ask. "The purpose of this council is how best to proceed against the House of Iy'lly'eth, is it not? Therefore, there is but the answer no one wishes to propose."

So'lauf'ein stirred in her seat, looking round, meeting every gaze with hers. "Archane must die. With Gor'wath gone and no others strong enough to challenge her, she alone is the key for Hovenethra's coming into power. We must lead the Race, or surely war will be our ending."

"The land about is subjugated, Dark Mistress." Briza spoke in quiet tones, again respect showing heavy in her voice. "How may we gain allies of the Houses as Iy'lly'eth's armies crushed the humans and the remaining cities sit powerless?"

"Then Hovenethra will lead," replied So'lauf'ein. "Find a way, and it must not be by sacrifice, or she will become a martyr. Archane must die, and perhaps at the hand of one she took into her bed. This Venic would be most likely, yes? A human, neither trusted or admired by any? By his hand, a dagger in her heart, perhaps some sort of human ritual killing. Humans are known for their cruelty to one another. If Archane's anger were unleashed upon him, for whatever reason, perhaps in his revenge he would kill her brutally." She looked to Ath'a'vul. "Perhaps even defiled and dismembered. Yet dead, and with no trace of Drow involvement. Kill Archane, and make it seem as the worst of human rage."

* * *

Lost in Shadows…

Venic sequestered himself deep in the catacombs of *Ma'li'vil*, finding quiet in which to scry upon Hovenethra and the artifact. Six moons he stayed from Archane and her entourage. Six moons without her charms or pleasures, without the feel of her skin against his own, or her womanhood swallowing his maleness deep and snugly, and the ecstasy of their climaxing together.

He had lost himself in studies of ancient texts, searched scrolls and books and spoken with sages in their darkened niches, seeking knowledge to replace his thwarted lust.

More time was spent in a chamber hidden by a fallen wall, collapsed so long ago there were none alive who remember the event. With soldiers' aid, he cleared the rubble, though it took nearly another moön to do so, and at the last he was chastised harshly by a sergeant who did not know his face. Nearly was he taken captive there and then, yet on hearing of the ruckus, the Lancer Captain came and calmed the matter quickly.

"Take word to your mistress," Venic had told him, "we have found a place more ancient than any known within the fortress. I will keep it all intact and reside here as I learn." He waited for the Lancer Captain to reply, yet he only glanced about, then nodded. "Should she feel of interest, offer her my best regards, and tell her Venic would be honored by her presence."

It was three days later, by his estimation, Archane entered the chamber, saw his plain and simple bedding on the floor, and took him to it, where she pleasured him as never she had done.

* * *

"I have come to some success with the sigils." Venic laid a scroll nearly fragile as a winter's leaf on the rough table and held the lantern closely by. "There are incantations relating to the summoning of daemons, others dealing with turning the very rocks to gold." He turned the pages of crumbling tome, dust scattering in the dimness of the cavern. "Others I still have yet to learn the meaning of, yet here…" He tapped gently on a slender book aside. "There are words within I suspect are of necromancy and the dead."

"What words?" Archane's bare hip pressed to his, hair askew and robes wrinkled with their exertion. Never had Venic seen her in so plain a manner, and it roused him, only moments past their encounter.

He chuckled. "Words I cannot yet pronounce, nor would I say them aloud until I know their true intent." He turned to her, concern within his eyes. "Dark Princess, I know your lust for power of the Arts, and would beg you, tread not into these treasures until my studies are complete."

Archane's ruby eyes met his, unflinching. "You say I cannot know them until they give their secrets unto you? I am the power here, and will take what is wanted, human." Her face softened as he looked away and her hand wended slowly beneath his simple tunic. "Tho' I give you leave to continue, for you have brought this to my sight. Therefore, teach me as you learn yourself." She glanced about the gloomy earthen room. "I will see to better comforts for the both of us."

Archane ordered formal bedding, a separate space curtained for a bath, and wardrobes for both she and Venic set within a corner. Then lanterns were hung about the walls, a small prayer fountain bubbling in a nook, and a sideboard laid with food and drink. All the while Venic studied deeper in the chamber, and only when Archane or a servant interrupted did he pause to eat or speak or sleep. He was consumed, nearly as by Archane's own charms, and tales began to drift beyond the hidden passage.

In time, when a year had passed, an entourage from House Hovenethra came to the gates of *Ma'li'vil*, asking audience with Archane.

Venic barely noticed when she left his company to tend her duty.

* * *

Murder Most Foul...

It began with a mistake of recognition.

Briza led the contingent of Hovenethra to the gates of *Ma'li'vil*, allowed entrance by the gate captain from the heavy snow and wind. They waited in the entryway, the inner gate yet open and guards watching as the entourage passed by. It was then Briza distracted the gate captain and his soldiers, falling to her knees and feigning illness as three hooded figures from her party slipped past and disappeared into the caverns.

The gate captain called a healer, who tended Briza carefully, knowing Hovenethra less than welcome, yet worried if she succumbed to whatever it was that ailed her, the wrath of Archane would be the least of worries. At last, after ministrations of a warm compress upon her forehead and a simple cantrip of curing, Briza slowly rose and thanked the healer for his work.

The gate captain, in the tumult, had lost count of the Hovenethra delegation, and as his soldiers and the servants led the visitors away, he quietly ordered other guards to search the hallways fairly. They reported nothing found, yet as the gates were sealed once more, the captain called a messenger to advise the Black Web of the incident.

The Hovenethra assassins followed the honor detail, cloaked in garments made to mimic the earthy walls and shadows. Their orders were to wait until after meetings were concluded, seek Archane alone and kill her, by whatever means available. And, if possible, kill the human with her, to cover their existence and create a scene of terror.

The priestess Briza did not know she also was a target, should it be necessary for a body of their own to be found, as though the plan was thought against all the Houses, not only that of Iy'lly'eth.

* * *

Archane waited with little patience in the grand hall as servants set the table and guards took places round the room. The Lancer Captain ordered six to the entrance, four more at Archane's seat, and a dozen placed about the table, three paces back from chairs where the entourage would sit. All the guards wore light armor and held ceremonial spears, yet short swords hung at their belts, weapons that would pierce the toughest heavy leather, should need come.

Hovenethra entered, the old priestess Briza at the fore and a dozen others following, then the honor guards and Archane's Lancer Captain at the end. Archane watched from the head of table as Briza bowed and took her seat. The others followed carefully, each pausing before Archane and showing deference, then sitting one by one. The honor detail took exit, yet the Lancer Captain stayed, and Archane caught his nodding gesture from the corner of her eye.

Wine was poured around from a crystalline carafe, and Archane drank to show it was not poisoned. Quiet voices murmured round the table, and at the last, the Dark Princess raised a point. "The House of Hovenethra has not been seen in *Ma'li'vil* nearly for a year. What is your business, as last you were within our walls, insurrection seemed to be your purpose?"

Briza shushed the others of her party, holding tight her own anger at Archane's harsh words. She bowed in her seat. "Dark Princess, we seek amends and hope to gather once more the great Houses of the Race. While we feel intentions were... misrepresented or perhaps misunderstood, we only wish to clarify our thoughts to you."

"Then do so," replied Archane, "for I have little time for posturing. This artifact taken from the elf emperor's city, speak of it and spare no words. I will not tolerate further deceit or fables."

Briza glanced about, the guards attentive and alert, then bowed again. "We extend invitation to yourself, and whomever you wish to accompany you, to *Necroman*. While words may explain our findings, to see it with your own eyes would be the best."

"And if I choose to send an emissary at the first? Will they be allowed to see this thing and return safe with words? Or do you only seek to hold me in your power, away from *Ma'li'vi?* Again, speak, and know a lie will not be tolerated."

Briza glanced about, many of her priestesses only shrugging or nodding in agreement. She faced Archane again. "Dark Princess, we offer safety, and extend invitation to whatever guards or soldiers you wish to travel with. Our only thought is the Houses stand in agreement on this matter."

Archane considered. Once more she traded glances with the Lancer Captain, now standing at her side. She looked to her priest Ha'd'rogh and the youngest of the elder priestesses O'lorae. Both showed concern, and Archane rose and led them to a corner.

"I hear no lies, Dark Princess," said O'lorae, "and sense only deep concern, in part for their own lives here in our chambers."

Ha'd'rogh nodded softly. "I agree, yet if accepted, we should decline to travel until weather clears. Else an... incident along the way would be seen as only that, no fault of Hovenethra's. I have wondered of their coming in such a storm."

"Still, they will not leave until clearing skies," said Archane, "giving time for them to poke and prod about our doings. Perhaps a rumor has made way into their ears."

"Dark Lady?" O'lorae gave a questioning glance.

Archane shook her head. "Nothing you must know. Therefore, we will accept, yet wait for snow and wind to lessen before considering our visit."

They took their places once again and Archane nodded Ha'd'rogh to address the Hovenethra elders. "We will accept your gracious offer, yet not travel until weather clears and trails are safer."

Briza nodded curtly, then servants set a feast before them all. Archane sipped wine, partaking only lightly, then motioned the Lancer Captain to her side. "Bring Venic to the hall once Hovenethra has been shown to their sequestering. I would speak with him of this venture."

"Dark Princess, it may be difficult to draw him from his studies. Nearly for a year he has lived only in the secret chambers."

"Make it so. Tell him Archane desires his company and seeks his wisdom on this changing of events."

The Lancer Captain bowed and took his leave. Archane called for servants to refill the goblets of the visitors, then her own. She drank again, watching shadows in the room, seeking movement.

* * *

35

The hall was quiet and empty of Hovenethra visitors when Venic came, bowed before Archane and found a place at the table where servants filled his plate. He ate quickly, drank two goblets of dark wine, then sat back, exhausted from his work. Archane waited in the silence, pacing before the great fireplace, thinking of words to share and words then to withhold.

"The Lancer Captain says of enemies in our midst." Venic poured another goblet full and drank again.

Archane looked to servants at the sideboard and guards waiting at the entrance. She sat closely by, her voice nearly as a whisper. "Briza of Hovenethra and an entourage, come to offer passage to their domain. This Window, the artifact in question, is in their keeping. They wish to tout their holding of it, display it in our presence, but what then? Surely they will not release it." She coughed a bitter laugh. "Thinking I would travel in the heart of winter and perhaps an accident of dubious sort would occur along the way."

Venic pondered, then shook his head. "Surely they would know the better. Why then are they here?"

"As said —"

"Nay, for this invitation might have been delivered by a messenger, or lesser elder than Briza her own self. Surely, they flaunt their power and their treasure, yes, but why an entourage of such size in weather? Two moons and snows would lessen, the danger passed." He drank, thinking once again. "Something is amiss."

"They sought to have us leave now, yet we declined."

Venic nodded. "And well you should. Yet still… how many?"

Archane motioned to the Lancer Captain, who bowed as he approached. "Seek numbers in the entourage and where they are now. See Ha'd'rogh and others of the Black Web are guarded well. Double guards in the corridor where Hovenethra is sequestered."

He bowed once more, retreating through the doors. In moments, another dozen guards entered and took places round the room.

"Are we now prisoners in our own House?" asked Archane. She shuddered and drew closer to Venic. He looked about, noting firewood stacked and the sideboard still with food and drink upon it. Near three dozen guards and six servants now were in the chamber.

"We are safe for three days herein. In that time, you may wish to order the passages cleared and searched carefully."

She showed a salacious grin. "Where then shall we bed? Alone, or together?"

Venic looked away and took a breath. "It has been many moons since I tasted of your charms." He turned to her and moved closer. "Would you prefer your private chambers? A bed and bath await, I am certain. Surely a dozen guards would ensure safe passage."

She touched his knee and smiled again. "Only if you will accompany me. Perhaps that taste will be renewed."

* * *

Briza knelt before the fire as Jarlaxle watched aside. The younger female elder held her peace as Briza shivered, the room not cold, but depressing, and nearly dark.

At last Jarlaxle took her mentor's hands and led her to a pillowed seat. "Dark Lady, calm your spirit, I beg you. Surely soon our matters will be done, and we may leave this place."

Briza sat, head in hands, and let go a scornful laugh. "I worry of our safety."

Jarlaxle shook her head, not understanding.

Briza leaned closer, her voice a trembling whisper. "Archane dies, we are killed as perpetrators, and So'lauf'ein proclaims the Age of Hovenethra, thereby removing not only the House of Iy'lly'eth as a rival, but those who may oppose her as struggles ensue within the House."

Jarlaxle sat back, aghast. "Surely not, as the Dark Mistress yet needs of allies." She looked round the room, eyes probing deep shadows and wondering if their own assassins waited there. "I cannot believe one of So'lauf'ein's wisdom would be so callous of our lives. Might we leave this place now, or are we prisoners?"

Briza rose and paced once more. "Go to the entourage, only those of the clergy. Say we are calling counsel in this room and be quick about it. We must find escape before the deed is done and Archane's blood flows. The assassins will waste little time finding of their goal now negotiations are concluded."

* * *

A dozen guards escorted Archane and Venic to the private chambers, closed the door and took places in the corridor. What had not been seen were shadows in those very corridors as Archane entertained and debated with Hovenethra's ministers. Though two guards were at Archane's chamber door, even as the Dark Princess was away, the shadows found manner to divert attention, with a servant from Hovenethra's contingent running naked in the hallway. One guard had followed, and she led him to a darkened passage where she pleasured him completely, then bade the second follow. And in the moments in between, as the guards passed each other at the corner, three shadows slipped into Archane's sanctuary.

They had set a simple trap with a cantrip in the entryway, that should the human attend into her chamber, both might be captured and there dealt with. Then they read a scroll of silence on the doorway, that once Archane had entered, nothing could be heard beyond the chamber.

They hid within the wardrobe or behind heavy draperies at the bath, and there they drew weapons quietly, waiting for Archane's arrival. Their orders were to spill her blood and see her body was defiled, kill the human, and set the scene as though Archane had died defending her own life. Then find Briza and kill her and the attendants if they could, and finally seek escape, or give their own lives for Hovenethra.

* * *

Through the corridors and darkened passageways Briza and the clergy of Hovenethra hastened. Down the multitude of stairways, passing guards in numbers they had not seen before, they carried packs filled with food and drink, heavy garments rustling as they hurried to the central gates of the fortress in the mountain.

They were paused by guards, more than a dozen, who queried them of leaving at such a time, with weather worsening in the day, and snow gathering about the trails. Still they insisted they must leave, citing urgent news from *Necroman* and orders from So'lauf'ein herself.

At last the guards acquiesced, and opened the gates. Briza nodded thanks, and the Hovenethra entourage passed quickly beyond the entryway, knowing had they stayed, worse than blood and death would have found them all with certainty.

* * *

The private chamber doors were closed. The cantrip trap sprang quickly, and before they could even breathe, Venic and Archane were captured in a web of magic threads, legs bound, and bodies tightly wrapped. Heavy silken cloaks from Archane's own wardrobe flew about, encircling the Dark Princess and the human, as the assassins leapt from their hiding places with weapons in their hands.

Venic freed an arm, called a charm and broke away the ties, drew his sword and charged. Two of the assassins paused, as they had not considered a defense from a man they did not know. Yet Venic had been a soldier, training ingrained deeply in his manner. He took them both to the floor, then rose swinging wildly with rage, holding both at bay.

The third assassin closed on Archane, still held within the cantrip. He slashed across her body, cutting through her flesh. She screamed, blood soaking through her garments, and fell to her knees. The assassin raised his sword again.

Venic turned, parried the assassin's second blow, spun and took him down with a thrust into his belly. The others fell upon him, and he fought them back again.

All the while Archane lay on the floor, bleeding out her life's blood, then rolled aside and called a blazing column from above. The assassin taken down flashed into oblivion, screaming as he burned.

The others drove Venic to a corner, cut him on one arm and in a leg. One shouted out a spell, and the wardrobe collapsed upon the human. The second turned to Archane and drove his sword into her side. She choked a gasp, collapsed, and then was still.

Venic fought his way beyond the fallen wardrobe, drove his sword point through the nearest assassin's hip, then brought the third to his knees with a slash across his back.

He crawled to Archane, both covered in blood—their own and of their enemies. He took her in his arms and began to chant. "I have studied nearly for a year of the necromancy arts and will not let you die! Yet if you die, you will return and live again! Live! Live always as you were, in strength and beauty, power and fortitude, your body whole as before! Do not die! Live! Live by the power of *Mother Darkness*, by the enchantment of this spell! Live! Forever live!"

The third assassin rose, wounded though he was, as did the second. Once more they laid upon Venic as he rolled away, and drove the sword from his hand. He backed away, backed away, scrambling for his life. He watched in horror as the third assassin's sword came down heavily, cutting Archane's head from her shoulders, her body twitching in its death throes. Venic found his sword, parried the attacks from the second, then screamed as the other hacked Archane's chest apart, split away her ribcage, and cut her heart to shreds.

Venic willed his body up, slashed his attacker 'cross the throat, leapt upon the other, and drove his sword deep into his side, both rolling on the floor now slick with blood and entrails.

He collapsed atop the body, fear and hate and deep remorse dragging him into the darkness. His wounds yet leaking and pain in every part, he let it take him.

Archane was dead. He had failed in his attempt to save her, as the ancient tome and incantations did not serve. Before he faded into darkness, he realized the words spoken were of a spell he had studied only once.

* * *

Time passed. How much time, Venic did not know. He woke, then drifted once again, pain sometimes in his body, others not. He knew he would die soon, and wondered of its doing. He could feel the hands of death upon him, the cold within his arms and legs, the deep numbness in his chest, the slowing flow of his own blood mingling with Archane's. He could not see; barely could he feel. He knew death closer than ever it had been, even when a soldier fighting Drow in the mountains or at the Cross-Plains River. Close. So very, very close.

* * *

Archane woke. Where was she? Was this the death at last, and did she dwell now where Iy'lly'eth her own self had gone? Yet the stone on which she lay was cold, her body naked, whole, and breathing. Why so? She thought back.

Pain... a flash of steel across her chest, a sword point driven into her side. Blood, so much blood, then a heaviness upon her throat. Then nothingness, dark and empty.

Now alive. Yet how?

She rose to sit, breathing deeply, and looked about. Her own bedchamber met her eyes, yet from the entryway, a sound. Was it assassins, come to kill her? Yet did she not recall dying at their hands, moments ago? A dream? A vision? Once more, how?

She rose, moved her hands about her body, intact, fresh, filled with life as young and growing. She took a simple robe from off the hangar and peeked around a corner. The scene before her brought a wave of grief, horror, and revulsion. Bodies, five of them, upon the floor. Three were Drow, dressed in simple black, Venic bleeding from a dozen cuts, and the other...

Archane collapsed, retching, tears flowing freely, screams filling of the chamber, resounding in her ears. She buried her face into her hands, cried for *Mother Darkness* to keep her sane as she sorted through her memories. Slowly she calmed, clarity at last coming to her mind.

She crawled to Venic, felt him breathing 'neath her hands, and called a charm of healing to him. He choked, gasped, thrashed within her arms as the spell sought to make his body whole once more. She held him as he cried, and her tears mingled there with his, his blood covering her arms and hands, as he breathed deeply without pain.

"How…"

She placed a finger on his lips, her eyes moving from one body to the next. "We will speak, yet there is duty to be done. Somehow, some way, you have returned me to the living."

Long moments passed as Venic calmed, then nodded. "The necromancy… I was afraid… I did not know it well."

She showed a wry look to him. "Well enough, it seems. Yet…" Again, her eyes drifted to the dismembered body. Her own. She looked into his eyes. "As you rise, do not fall to madness. What you will see, I cannot explain, yet we will find answers together. Rise, and see your work."

* * *

It took more time, and once again Venic did not know the passing of it, except as a horrific nightmare. He had knelt at the shattered remains of Archane's own body, then looked to her as she stood in life before him. He touched her cold corpse, then knelt before her living form. The warmth of her hand upon his brow brought his tears once more, and he held her fingers tightly within his. Nearly did he faint away, not understanding what had happened.

"Tho' I live again, and surely this is the power of the spell," she said, kneeling at his side, cradling his face. "Worry not, for I am no specter, but alive as you have wished me."

He shook his head. "I wished you alive in the body there before us, to be healed and saved. This…" Nearly was he afraid to meet her eyes.

She stood. "No matter, for still I am Archane and lead this House. And work there is to do, before any see the truth of it."

She looked to the fireplace, incanted words, and the flames rose to a roar. "The bodies, all of them, into the fire. Quickly! Still if Hovenethra is within *Ma'li'vil*, I will have them on the altar by the Dark Moon!"

Venic stood with quaking legs. "Yours… as well? How…"

"Yes! Then we must cleanse the stench and the blood from the chambers." She gave him a hard look. "Do you not understand your doing?"

He shook his head. "If you die… you rise again? Are these your words?"

She gave a wicked grin. "Immortal, tho' surely it is not as I would wish. Pain of death, yet rising once again. Contemplate the implications to the other Houses."

Venic closed his eyes and muttered words too soft for her to hear.

They took the cantrip trapping down with minor spells and tossed the bodies into the fire, Archane's the last, then cleaned away the blood with magic servants. Then bathed together, washed away the stench of death and near-madness, and held each other closely. At last they sat, silent in their company, sipping wine and private in their thoughts.

"We must find this artifact, this Window of K'ron'iss, as you say it is called." Archane peered over her goblet, waiting for his answer.

Venic could only nod, still unsure what had been seen was real. At last he cleared his throat to speak. "I must return to the hidden chambers and investigate this... happening. I must understand what has indeed occurred."

Archane considered. "And then?"

"Return to you, Dark Princess, so I may impart the truth of it. Both of us must know how the incantation has progressed. And its future effect upon yourself."

She set aside her goblet. "I will go with you. I wish to see these tomes with my own eyes."

He looked away for moments before answering. "Perhaps you should see to Hovenethra first, then come to me. I will hold the answers until you arrive."

She nodded slowly. "Yes, your point is taken. Therefore, I will meet you once I have seen to our guests." *And their demise,* she thought, knowing Venic was no part of her planning thereof.

Venic rose, bowed, and without another word, took his leave. Archane's eyes drifted once more to the fire, the bones within it slowly falling into char. She shuddered, then drained her goblet, shivering.

* * *

Venic stumbled out the door, strode quickly as his weakened legs would carry him, and found a darkened passageway aside. He leaned against the cold, hard earthen wall, begging silently for his pounding heart to calm. He breathed deeply, the musty smells of dirt and rock and dampness laying hard upon his mind.

How long since I have seen the sun, or the golden moon itself, he wondered. *There was a time, those years ago, when I sought solace in the forest with elves and men, keepers of the plains and tenders of the world. Now the call of magic has held me here, and I see its price for learning. Sorcery in its basest form! To change that which is natural, death, however it comes to us! Now Archane lives again, and should she die, will she not rise once more?*

He glanced around the corner, saw only dark-clad figures walking slowly about the halls of *Ma'li'vil*, guards at intersections, yet none showed signs of agitation. He forced his hands from shaking, and walked with purpose to the stairway.

Down and down and down, to the lowest levels, passing guards once more, and fewer others as he descended. Into the hidden chambers at the last, and he sat, shivering of cold and fear and terror. He poured a goblet full, drank it down and poured another. He looked about the chamber, seeing nothing had been disturbed since his leaving.

Quietly and with purpose, he collected books and scrolls, items he knew would be necessary for his planning. He wrapped cheese and bread, slipped two wine bottles into a heavy bag, and stuffed his pack to bursting. Then he sat once more, looking round, assessing what else he might need for the future.

Few places I know are safe beyond this fortress. Still, no longer will I betray my kind, as I have done the worst of everything. Archane alive, immortal, and no matter what I do, it will not change my sin.

He rose, took a walking staff in hand, tossed the pack across his shoulder, and began an incantation. Colors flew before his mind, sparks and clouds racing quick behind his eyes, as he faded from the room.

Into a void where time and space and matter were no more, and as the astral wind tossed his hair and swept his cloak about, his thoughts were only of his task.

With study, he had surmised, and war between the Houses, the artifact would be closely kept, buried somewhere in the depths of whatever House might hold it. Until any of the leaders were certain it could not be taken from them, it would remain so, never seen, never probed, else scrying from the others would lead them to its place.

Now all had changed, and he chuckled grimly at his own doing in a rage of lust and anger. Should Archane truly be immortal, nothing would stop her until she possessed the Window. Not even fear of death, or the pain there caused. For she would rise again, taking up the battle, until none were left but her and those who followed. She would become a goddess, never relenting in her pursuit, never letting go of the Race she now commanded.

The Drow must be barred from where the Window led. For Venic had not told all the truth to Archane or others, and none had followed the link within his mind. He knew Hovenethra held the artifact, yet surely did not understand its power. Nor, in surety, did Venic. Though with time he would learn; however, that, for now, could wait.

He only knew he must find the Window of K'ron'iss and keep it from Archane.

PART TWO
AND NOW, THE PRESENT

Dennis Young

BOOK TWO
A BLINK OF THE EYE

"Locked together for all eternity,
a loveless embrace neither may break.
Is this your wish?
To spend forever with me before you,
as time passes in our former world?
How may you do this thing?
More, what may I offer to entice your... aid in seeing us free?"

Mors'ul'jyn to Chitthra
While trapped in *Dag'Niar Calidrii*

Dennis Young

Somewhere on the plains of Ardwel, after the fall...

Chitthra woke.

The summer sun of Ardwel's plains beat down upon her. Bruised and aching, she slowly rose, naked but for a tattered tunic round her shoulders and scraps of breeches hanging from her hips. Limping her way into a copse, she shed the ruin of clothing and huddled 'neath the overgrowth around a great oak tree.

Tho' when last I saw the land, winter approached. I cannot know how time passed within the Black Blade's prison. Moons, at the least... if not years.

She knelt in meditation, cleared her mind and glanced beyond her sanctuary. No villages were seen, no sign of Telveperen, the city-states, or even roads upon the hills. It might have been as ages past, before elves and men came to Ardwel, unspoiled, untouched, free of hate and war.

Her eyes swept further, catching glints of brightness in the grasses. She tied the scraps of clothing round her waist and took a covert path back into the clearing. She knelt, and knew then what had happened.

Shards of the Black Blade! Somehow, some way, Mors'ul'jyn held the power to break the spell! Yet as she was truly Re', it was created all those years ago by her own self. Might she have set the way, knowing even then a manner of escape? If so, where is she? Dead, nearly as I was? Or loose once more upon the land?

Chitthra gathered up the shards, returned to the copse, and laid them out before her. Fitting pieces carefully, she knew she had them all.

I must find Sheynon and warn him the mad woman has returned. I cannot break my vow of his family's protection!

She gathered stalks of heavy grasses and wove a basket, ignoring pangs of hunger and aches within her limbs. Hefting the shards and studying the sun, she set out west, thinking her location surely east of Telveperen, and said a silent prayer.

Din'daeron'dae guide me well, for as I live, I must find allies. Surely this is Ardwel as I know it, and I pray my findings are not too late.

She walked as the sun preceded her to the horizon, topped a rise and saw a road below. In a valley set a village, and she gave a smile and made a sign into the air.

* * *

The village, as it turned, was Drow, and she wondered how far from the western coast it lay. She held the basket high, covering herself, yet none paid her mind as she walked the road leading through the town.

A stable caught her eye, horses being tended in the evening, and she saw a worker lay aside her over-tunic. Chitthra slipped between the barn and fences, quietly slid the garment from the post, and disappeared into the shadows. Once hidden, she donned the tunic, tied the lacings, and let go a guilty breath.

Never would I do such a thing in past times. Still, should I be able, I will make atonement along the way, once I have found answers to this time and place.

She hurried west, taking refuge in the forest once again, and as she passed an apple orchard, she paused to collect fruit on the ground. Disappearing in the waning light, she found a rocky overhang and settled for the evening, devouring three apples quickly, hungry as she was.

She nested in the undergrowth covered by low-hanging limbs and heavy branches, knelt and gave a prayer to *Din'daeron'dae*, then sat and watched as *Grand Selene*, half-full, brightened the summer sky.

I must find Telveperen or another village, to know how time has passed. And Mors'ul'jyn, where has she gone, and what mischief will she cause? But for this night, rest, and come sunrise, I will seek answers. Tho' I may rue the truth of what has transpired in my absence.

* * *

The hard-packed road was weary on her feet, but Chitthra walked it briskly. Before the sun had risen, she collected dew from leaves and grasses, quenched her thirst and ate the two remaining apples in her basket. She knew, should she not find shelter in the day, she must catch her supper or seek a stream the forest creatures might frequent.

A cloud of dust upon the road appeared, coming from the west, and she paused, set down her basket, and waited. Standards in the air brought great relief, for they were of Telveperen, yet she wondered for a moment how a dark elf might be thought of on the road.

We will see, and with time passing no less than six moons, the angst of murder and martyrdom may have faded. I pray Sheynon has found peace within his heart for the passing of Galandria.

The riders were a company of soldiers, and they paused before her, ten circling with spears lowered, points gleaming in the sun. Chitthra held her hands empty at her sides, as the captain motioned to her garb.

"You have lost your breeches." The company round laughed softly, yet his face showed no humor in it. "Tell me what a half-dressed Drow seeks beneath the hot sun of summer."

Chitthra gave a nodding bow. "Good captain, I am Chitthra, friend to Earion Calidriil and Aeren Grey. I know of the happenings at the

50

fortress and the tragedy therein. Pray tell me, are Lord Sheynon and his family safe? Has the mad woman Mors'ul'jyn been seen or, gods willing, killed for her crimes against Elvenkind and the land at large? I beg you, give warning to your lord if she still stalks him and his children."

None spoke; not the captain, nor his soldiers, yet glances made way between them all. Chitthra waited, fear growing in her belly, not for herself, but Sheynon. She knew the creature calling herself Mors'ul'jyn would not stop until her vengeance had been slaked, or death stopped her in her tracks.

Perhaps not even then, she thought wryly, *for knowing her ability, she was the greatest of human mages, save Veniculis himself. She escaped the prison of the Black Blade. Perhaps she set ways beyond death as well. Steffyn Foxxe would know, tho' dare I say his name?*

The captain dismounted and drew near, a look of disbelief upon his face. He spoke in quiet tones. "I cannot know your manner, yet you speak names truthfully. Should I answer, will you then seek Sheynon your own self? Are you this Mors'ul'jyn, perhaps?" He passed his gaze around. "You cannot slay us all, regardless your power. So I ask you, as *Yarhetha'an* watches us this day, who are you? How do you come to know these names, and what else might you say to convince me not to take your tongue for lying?"

Chitthra thought briefly, then nodded. "Earion... he has but one arm, taken by a brute named Kaul, tho' it was the Black Blade's doing, not his. Stokar in Jeseriam saved his life, and Earion found acceptance in his wounding." She swallowed and bowed. "He was my friend. He, and Aeren, and even Drakkon, for his pompous nature, there was a goodness in him I could feel."

The captain watched her face with care. "I am Arnien, captain of the guard in Telveperen. Much has happened in these last years —"

"Years, my lord?" Chitthra wrapped her arms about herself and nearly did she weep. "How many... since the Lady's passing?"

Arnien's lips drew a hard line across his face. "More than five, and changes now abound. However, for the nonce, I will take your words as given. We will escort you to the fortress, and there you may tell your tale to Earion himself. For your spirit, I hope it is a truthful one."

* * *

Chitthra was not allowed beyond the gates, left standing in the sun with twenty guards about her. Yet in only moments, a figure burst from within the courtyard, ran to her and embraced her tightly, yet with only a single arm. "Chitthra!"

"Earion! How I have prayed for your safety!" She nearly screamed, then held him, caressed his trembling shoulders, his tears mingling with hers. Arnien nodded with a grin, dismissed the soldiers and waited as Earion and Chitthra whispered into each other's ears. At last they turned to him together, faces red but smiles bright and beaming.

"She is as a sister to me," said Earion, "standing fast in honor through my wounding. I love her as few others." He sniffed, wiped his nose against his sleeve, then hugged her once again.

"Good captain, I thank you for your courage," said Chitthra. "I feared you would cut me down and leave my body for the scavengers, yet you did not. My thanks."

Arnien nodded. "Earion, I am sure, will see to your comfort now, my lady. He may well scrub your back for you while in the bath, he is so happy."

Chitthra winked at Earion, who grinned. "I would let him."

"Come, we have years to speak of and more tales to tell than any bard," said Earion. "And yes, a bath and meal for you. Then you may speak of... this." He pointed to the basket with the shards.

Chitthra's face grew serious. "Much there is to speak of, but only with those trusted. Sheynon?"

Earion waved his hand. "Later. First, bathed, then fed... and dressed. Then we may talk of secrets held for years."

* * *

Chitthra sat in the garden shade, Earion beside her and attendants at their call. She had bathed, two of Galandria's own waiting ladies tending to her needs, dressed in a fiery silken tunic, and fed sumptuously. Then retreated to the evening's cooling calm, a glass of elven wine in hand. She was oblivious to the looks between the attendants, that Earion, now Steward of the castle, would treat with Drow.

"So many changes," Chitthra whispered. Earion's words had been frank and full, leaving no details unsaid. Of Galandria's murder, of the complicity of the Guild of Learned and the deaths therein by Mors'ul'jyn, of Crysalon's disappearance, and Aeren's rise to power in the City-State of Truth.

"And Archane," he concluded at the last. "Not seen, nor heard from in years. The Drow retreated from Vichelli, now DragonFall, as named by Kaul. And the brute has barred elves and men from his table, saying only when he decides will he parley."

Chitthra chuckled. "And this surprises us, my friend? Kaul's agenda is his alone. Tho' I do not think he will stay behind his walls forever. Too restless is his spirit, too wanting of adventure. No administrator is he, but driven by his lust… for power, for pleasures, for gold." She grinned fully. "Too easy to read is Kaul, as an' open tome."

A silence came upon them until Chitthra looked again to Earion. "Tell me… why did you not seek healing, once the world had calmed again." She motioned to his missing arm.

He sipped wine and blew a breath. "The land has changed, and in that changing, I became aware of how small my part there was. Not of what came after, but my wounding itself." He raised the stump of his arm. "I keep it as a reminder, to humble me when this life becomes too gentle."

Chitthra nodded after a quiet moment. "You have changed, as you say the world has, but for you, the better. Always did I know the strength of Calidriil lay within your spirit."

Earion grinned sheepishly. "My lady, strength comes in many ways, and only with your guidance, and that of Aeren, did I find what little I may have. Sheynon set me to the task of Telveperen, and I have some success, but it takes many in support. Galandria's own seneschal, Lady Mal'geilir, who nearly took her own life as you recall, gives no rest to me when I seem to waver. Arnien and Duienain, her captains, lead in Galandria's memory. This castle, for the horrors it has seen, becomes stronger. What part I play is little." He raised his stump again. "Humility, and never does it leave my mind."

More silence passed, more wine was poured, and at last Chitthra broached the subject she dearly needed answers to. "Sheynon… is he well? The children?"

Earion shrugged. "He takes the task of protection seriously as he may. For the children, for Telveperen, for Elvenkind at large. Galandria's spirit tends him well."

"Yet Mors'ul'jyn…"

"Not seen for years, nor heard of. Neither she nor Archane, and Kaul hiding behind his gates. Coronis, even, is tempered, still mourning the loss of Galandria."

He drew near, and his voice dropped to a whisper. "It is tho' her death has sobered the land as not before. Might she have seen this? Her Sight was a rare gift, and Galandria would do whatever in her mind was needed for the protection of our people."

Chitthra began to speak, then held her words for a long moment. "I cannot say, for I knew her not, but from others. Yet if your words are true, and I have no reason not to believe them, then yes…" She thought of Daeron Foxxe, *Din'daeron'dae*, the one she prayed to. "There have been such wonders in this world. And Galandria Telveperen's spirit was among the brightest."

* * *

A night of peaceful sleep and breakfast at the rising sun prepared Chitthra for what she knew was needed, lest her spirt would become too quickly accustomed to a gentle life. Speaking with the stable master, asking the kitchens to prepare ten days of provisions, she met again with Earion.

"First to the City-State of Truth, then, in honesty, I know not where to go. Yet I feel I must see Sheynon with my own eyes and know him safe."

Earion took her hand gently into his. "I would offer you a place here, for whatever time you desire, my lady. Telveperen would be honored."

Chitthra took him gently in her arms. "I know," she whispered, "yet I cannot feel the land is safe from Archane, her followers, from Mors'ul'jyn. Still evil hides in wait. I must see it does not set upon the land again."

He drew slowly away and kissed her cheek. "Then go in peace and strength. Should you pass this way, our gates are open."

She bowed, took her saddle, and rode beyond the great oaken gates. Before they were opened in her path, she saw the stains of martyrdom still upon them.

* * *

Hidden beneath the ruins of Drakenmoore…

The chamber was dark. Not the dark of night, or as the bed when sleeping, but the darkness of a cavern. It was kept that way, for Archane was far too cunning to be allowed to see her prison.

Five years she had been kept by Mors'ul'jyn, allowed beyond the darkness for meals, or light fitness times, that her body did not wither. And in those fleeting moments she was mute, unless Mors'ul'jyn wished to hear her voice for gentle conversation.

Stripped of her powers, without a voice to summon aid, and having no knowledge of where her prison lay, Archane, the Dark Princess and ruler of the Drow, held little opportunity.

Carried beyond the City-State of Truth after her battle with Crysalon, ruler of the humans, Mors'ul'jyn had seen Archane back to health. Her wounds were great, and moons it took for her to heal, mind and body, spirit and emotions. Mors'ul'jyn thought to make a pact, for the good of both. But Archane knew her well, not only as Mors'ul'jyn, but first as Reena, the girl whose body Mors'ul'jyn had stolen in Castle Drakenmoore.

Mors'ul'jyn was not Reena in her mind, but the wizard-woman Re', Teresa Drakenmoore, and with incantations older than was she, had stripped away Reena's spirit from her body, took it for her own, and proceeded to wreak havoc on the land.

Vengeance against the elves, Calidriil by name, and the first victim was his own wife, Galandria Telveperen, murdered brutally by Mors'ul'jyn's hands. But on discovery of Archane, nearly dead from her fight against Crysalon, Mors'ul'jyn had sought another way. One with power she had never thought, at the side of the Dark Princess, to rule the Drow together.

It was not to be. Far too clever was Archane, and Mors'ul'jyn herself knew her for her cunning.

An impasse. Neither could be trusted by the other. Both would seek the other's death, should it be to her advantage. A harsh reality for such brilliant minds.

Archane then became a prisoner, her existence kept from others. But soon enough, Mors'ul'jyn began to realize, she, herself, was as much a prisoner as the Dark Princess.

And with that recognition, a different plan began to form. One needing an accomplice, known and wielding power now his own.

Kaul Morg'ash, King of DragonFall. Mors'ul'jyn's past compatriot and lover.

* * *

The chamber door swung aside as heavy hinges groaned in protest, sharp sounds in the silence of the hall. Archane stood and closed her eyes against the brightness, awaiting Mors'ul'jyn to enter. Yet it was not her, but two armored giants, gleaming in the light. One motioned her to follow and the second fell in line. Neither spoke, and with what vestiges of power she had left, Archane knew there was nothing living 'neath the armor.

They led her through the passageway into a well-appointed chamber, offered her a chair at a table set for two. A suckling roast steamed on a platter, greens fresh from the garden, bread from the ovens, and a pot of scented tea; all were there before her. The armored figures took their places at the doorway.

Archane sat. Her mouth filled, for a feast lay there before her eyes, and she knew then something now had changed. Something urgent. Something dangerous. She smiled.

"You tempt me. Why so? Why should I not decline, and return to my chamber? There is little you may do not already done."

Mors'ul'jyn approached from a second doorway that vanished as she came before Archane. "Yes," she crooned. "I have kept you alive these years, and that is your bane, is it not?" She poured tea for Archane and then herself. She carved the roast and took a bite, ate a bit of greens, and motioned to the table. "Partake. Little do you have to fear of poison. What would be the pleasure in that doing?"

Archane served herself daintily, took tiny bites and sipped her tea, all the while eyes locked with Mors'ul'jyn's. They ate in silence, and soon the table cleared itself and a fresh pot of tea appeared, cups refilling of themselves.

"You need of sunshine," said Mors'ul'jyn, then chuckled. "Or at the least, the air beyond this place. Might you wish to see the world again?"

Archane did not answer as Mors'ul'jyn continued. "I have reasoned your past. Shall I tell you of it? Tales say you are immortal, tho' may suffer pain of death. How is this so, I have wondered." She drank, then set away her cup. "When I found you, you were nearly naked from the battle with Crysalon. No armor, no robes or cloak of power, no staff or other accouterments one of your stature and position might possess. Naught but a simple robe and cloak of linen, nearly burned away by holy fire." She paused, leaning forward, elbows on the table. "You, dear lady, were a breathing corpse, half your body burned away, your beauty gone."

A mirror appeared before Archane, and she gasped, looking into it.

"I gave you this!" Mors'ul'jyn said. "I returned your beauty, your allure. Tho' I thought many times to leave you as you were, scarred and hideous, I relented, for I know…" Mors'ul'jyn's voice broke and she rose, pacing away.

Archane only watched, curious now of why her beauty had been spared.

Mors'ul'jyn turned back to the table. "I kept you alive, for I found the truth of it. You died upon the road to the City-State of Truth, killed by mercenaries. Not by Crysalon, not by his army or his guards, but ruffians and outlaws! Then rose from the dead, took your vengeance on the city-state, and nearly died again. How many times, I wonder, in all the years and centuries, has your body suffered pain of death? How many bodies has your spirit manifested in? How is it you are sane, or are you? And what will you do to regain your rightful place as leader of the Drow?"

Archane sipped tea, cold now, and grimaced. "What would you have of me?" She gestured to the now-empty table. "You only wish to gloat and beat your chest for my survival? Very well. I thank you for my life. Yet we have had this conversation more times than I can count, tho' not so… enticingly. Therefore, I ask again. What is the price for my freedom? Or is this but another form of abuse?"

Mors'ul'jyn sat once more. "I have taken vengeance, and yes, it was your handmaiden Reena who became my saving way." She gestured to her body, ran her hands over her face and figure, smiling. "This youthful body, this wonderment of feeling, lust, and energy I had not felt in more than thirty years, became salvation." She looked Archane in the eye, deeply. "Do not think I have not considered taking your very place. What was done once may be done again."

Archane raised her face. "I would end my own life before allowing that to happen."

Mors'ul'jyn laughed. "And then? Return again?" She looked about the room. "Where, dear lady, would you return to? My thought is, you must know your surroundings before your body reconstructs itself. Whatever hand has done this to you had little knowledge and less ability. They erred, and greatly! This is little more than a curse!"

Archane swallowed and said nothing, knowing there was truth within the words. At last she spoke. "Very well. A pact between us, this is what you seek? How may we seal it? How do we find trust enough to carry out this plan? Shall we bond ourselves together in the eyes of *Mother Darkness*, One, as the elves say?" She frowned. "Or as said by humans, marriage?"

Mors'ul'jyn grinned wickedly. "Humans frown on those of same gender joining in any way, save for simple pleasures and silver. Elves… are more enlightened, yet I hold no interest in them. Dark elves, as you taught me, handing me from male to female in your harem, care little of the difference. But no… this is not my thought."

Archane glanced to the cleavage showing beneath Mors'ul'jyn's robe. "I know those pleasures well."

Mors'ul'jyn shuddered. "Enough of this. Pleasures will be no part. I have agenda, as do you. We will work for the betterment of both, nothing more. Or do you prefer the darkness of your chamber once again?"

Archane considered. "More. I must know your plan, part by part."

"That will come in time. For now, only know we will entice another, one known well to both of us. An old... friend."

Archane shook her head. "We need no others. I have power, as do you." She motioned to the chamber round.

"You have no power, dear lady. Five years have passed. Do you not think the Drow have moved on without you? This will take a different form of ability."

Archane scoffed. "Ability of whom? Surely the humans and elves have moved on. Rebuilt, regrouped, and hold the land again."

"And your people war among themselves for power. The void left by your disappearance brought the dark elves to their knees."

Archane pondered once again. "Likely true. Therefore, what?"

Mors'ul'jyn paused before her answer. "As said, an acquaintance of the past. One named Kaul. I believe you know him."

"Kaul? The brute?" Archane laughed.

"He holds the city you claimed as your own, now called DragonFall. And yes, power is in his hands, yet more." Her grin widened. "I know him well. Should you be willing, we may both drive him mad with lust. Kaul, for all his scheming, is not the sharpest dagger in the sheath."

* * *

The City-State of DragonFall...

Once known as Vichelli, the City-State of DragonFall nestled in the central plains of Ardwel, a crossroads for those traveling the land, north and south, east and Western Isles. The birthplace of the *Rising Star*, dominant religion of humans in the land, it now was held by Kaul Morg'ash, taken as a prize for his aid in routing of the Drow.

Kaul was naught but a carouser, lecherous and crude as one would think someone of his lineage might be. For Kaul was human, Drow, and orc, issue of a violent conception, or more likely, several.

The city had become a den of iniquity, of debauchery, of lewd men and loose women, of dealings done in dark alleys, and murder not uncommon. What law there was left no witnesses, for the Brood Squad was no less violent than the ones they dealt with. In practice, they were more so, with armor, weapons, and base attitude given them by Kaul.

Still, the city drew from the land about, farmers, merchants, cutthroats and thieves, for there were none of rules, and tax collectors, once more sent by Kaul, would have their due of all.

Kaul, himself, had taken residence in the palace grounds, safety there provided by a thousand guards and numerous assassins, all loyal to Kaul, for he was not only of their kind, but more brutal than the rest.

Yet there were times he showed a decent side, or more so than at others. His harem was as he, mixed and varied, and in five years of rule, had brought him no less than fifteen children. This, Kaul knew, would become a problem, for as they grew, children such as his would look for power their own. How to deal, was one of his concerns, and in a time of peace throughout the land, one could not send his offspring out to war.

Or might he?

* * *

The messenger bowed before Kaul and passed a small parcel to his minister. The lackey cut the ties and unfolded a note inside, then passed it to Kaul's waiting hands.

"What is this?" Kaul growled, drinking from a tankard of morning ale. He handed back the parchment. "Read it to me. And refill my cup."

The minister bowed, motioned servants forward with the morning meal and a pitcher, then cleared his throat and perused the writing on the page. He mumbled words to himself and paused.

"Is the hand illegible?" asked Kaul. "Or is it a secret?"

The minister drew a small box from the parcel and opened it. He paled, even more so than he was, then passed the box to Kaul.

"Read it," repeated Kaul as he took the box in hand.

"My King, it says only, 'We wait'."

Kaul sneered and withdrew the items. "Hair? Tied in a ribbon?"

Two clippings were withdrawn. One, short and nearly white, the other longer and glowing as fresh-fallen snow. Kaul examined them both closely, the short hair tied with a ribbon of many colors, the longer with a bow of sable. He drank again, and placed the items back into the box.

"Is there a messenger with this? If so, bid him wait." He drank once more as guards escorted the minister away, then nodded to himself. "Clever, and with subtlety. It will be amusing to see my old lover once again."

He rose, calling for his armor.

* * *

They met beyond the gates of the city, for Kaul would not allow entry to any he did not trust. A day tent kept the scorching summer sun at bay, but the swirling wind drove dust about them.

Mors'ul'jyn had thought to appear as last he saw her, dirty, disheveled, nearly nude in little more than rags. Yet this would only pique his interest in ways she did not want, and therefore clothed herself modestly in summer garb.

Archane had been allowed only a simple robe and cloak, as worn when she was found nearly dead of wounds. Mors'ul'jyn held little trust for the Dark Princess, and thought once to bind her hands and put a spell of silence on her lips. Yet she relented, knowing Archane's sultry voice would soothe the beast in Kaul.

Fifty guards stood only paces behind the Mongrel, and fifty more with crossbows at the gates. Kaul stood before them, a giant of a creature, and drank from a flagon filled with bitter-smelling brew. His eyes narrowed at the sight of Archane, for when last seen, she had been a corpse, bloody and beheaded. He drank once more, then spat upon the ground.

He grinned at Mors'ul'jyn, showing points of teeth, a look she remembered well. "You bring a concubine? Very well, I accept the gift. I have only one Drow in my harem, and she no longer gives her pleasures to me." He laughed as Archane raised her face, eyes sharp as daggers.

Mors'ul'jyn returned his disparagement. "Soft living has made you more a man." She gestured to his belly, now round and bulging 'neath his armor, and his heavy face. "You are not the beast who ravaged me in the dungeon." She sighed, sarcasm heavy in her voice. "A pity. I had told such tales of you to Archane."

Kaul lost his humor quickly, drank, and spat again. "What is your purpose, woman? I have a city to rule and little time for reminiscing."

Mors'ul'jyn glanced to the guards, all ruffians as Kaul, no discipline among them as they shifted nervously and muttered to each other. "We would speak in private with words only for your ears. No treachery, on my word." She smirked. "We were companions once, and tho' not of a mind, were honorable to each other. I offer that pact once more." She glanced to Archane, mute beside her. "For the both of us."

Kaul mulled the words, then motioned the guards back to the gates. He called servants who set a table, poured wine before the women, then refilled their liege's tankard. Kaul motioned them to eat. "You both are too skinny for my liking in this day. Fill your bellies, then we will speak. I have business and will return before the sun reaches the horizon."

With that, he turned and walked away, disappearing through the gates. Half the guards followed in his steps, the other half remaining, watching, drawing no closer, nor showing weapons.

60

Archane nodded to the table. "Do you trust him not to poison us and laugh about it?"

Mors'ul'jyn thought for moments, then nodded. "We have his attention. Therefore, yes, I do. Feed yourself. This may be a lengthy parley."

* * *

Kaul returned as the sun began to set, and in that time Mors'ul'jyn and Archane said little to each other. The table had been cleared, fresh tea and wine brought from the city, and at last, the Mongrel sat before them once again.

"You have a plan, one you hope to gain my approval of, yes? This says you cannot see success alone."

Mors'ul'jyn sipped tea and paused before her answer. "Have you the power wanted, here, in this city? By my knowledge, it was granted to you by the elves and men, once secured from… usurpers." She glanced to Archane, who did not react. "Yet tales tell you wanted more, and Vichelli was but a stone on which to step. The City-State of Truth was your desire, was it not? Or might something larger catch your eye?"

Kaul drank. "You have a way into the City-State of Truth? How so? Might you entice the skinny girl, Aeren, to return north, to Audrey Vincent's court?" He chuckled. "Doubtful that will happen."

Mors'ul'jyn caught Archane's flashing eyes at the mention of the name Audrey Vincent. She thought to ask of it when away from Kaul's presence. "We come bearing an offer, yes," she continued. "One to harken back to your days of adventure. You have grown soft, Kaul, and your spirit needs a calling, does it not?"

Kaul shifted in his regal seat. "I am not the brute I was. I have concubines, children, a city needing still to be tamed. Who will do these things if I am absent?"

"We may set a warden," said Archane, before Mors'ul'jyn could answer. "Chosen only by our agreement."

Kaul laughed. "A dark elf? We drove them out, killing as they ran! You cannot think—"

Mors'ul'jyn held a hand. "As said, and by agreement. This is not to be decided now." She held her cup, and a servant filled it once again, then she nodded to Archane.

"My people suffer in my absence," said the Dark Princess. "I have been… held away by circumstance for five years now, as my trusted priesthood holds the great Houses from each other's throats. Aid is needed in support of them, and one disinterested in the politics of Drow."

A silence fell as the sun dipped low and stars began to wink into the sky. *Selene* rose full and ruddy in the east, color falling on their faces.

At last Kaul spoke. "If your priesthood is yet loyal, why are soldiers needed? Five years is too long, and my thought is, your lackeys sit now in your stead. Why should they give up such a place?"

"Loyalty," replied Archane, and Kaul laughed aloud.

"Loyalty? You ruled through terror, and the fear of other leaders becoming a sacrifice beneath your blade! Recall, oh *Dark Princess*, I lived among you." He drank again, emptying his tankard. "I was party to Skaan's plan of vengeance for what happened there to Reena. I was chased out, fearing for my life, and Reena saved me! Took me into Drakenmoore, gifted me with *NorthWind!*" His eyes looked hard upon Mors'ul'jyn, "Yet it was not Reena, for you had taken her body by sorcery!" He turned again to Archane. "Skaan wanted only truth of what happened to her daughter, yet you, *Dark Princess*, refused! When you were gone, the Drow fell to war within the Houses, is my thought, to cleanse your name from their minds and start afresh."

Kaul rose and paced, then closed on the women, leaning closely to Archane's face. "I held your severed head, I saw your body burn," he hissed. "Tales said of your immortality and now I see the truth of it. Should I kill you here, will you rise and seek vengeance on me?"

He turned away, cursing 'neath his breath, then faced them once more. "Why should I be a part? How to trust enough to see the matter done? Give me assurance or depart!"

Moments passed before Mors'ul'jyn spoke, keeping a tremble from her voice with effort. "Very well. You have put your mind to this, more than I might have thought."

Kaul laughed. "What more did I have to pass the time, in a city I did not want, held from the prize truly I deserved!"

Mors'ul'jyn nodded. "We shall find another way. We leave in peace, as we arrived." They rose and turned to go.

"Wait," said Kaul, and he approached them, then slowed, showing empty hands. "I will consider your request for aid, but I will have my due." He cast a roguish eye upon the women. "I have soldiers and this city's treasury at my call. Tell me what you offer for my aid regaining of your fortunes."

* * *

Ung'gu'wi…

The servant rushed through the darkened passageway and into Mor'i'jil's chamber without consent. "Dark Lord, awaken! The Seers say Archane is found!"

Mor'i'jil pulled the blanket tighter, mumbling in his sleep. The servant dared not touch him, but stood in a corner, imploring the ancient priest to wake, as guards entered. They pushed the servant to her knees and drew their weapons.

Mor'i'jil rolled aside, waking slowly. "Do no harm, I hear her." He sat, disheveled in his bedclothes, the concubine moving 'neath the covers and rolling to her feet. She bowed quickly and ran beyond the bed chamber. "Tea, scented and strong," ordered Mor'i'jil, "then return and say your message."

The servant bowed and took her exit, the guards following quietly. Mor'i'jil rose, his knees protesting, and hobbled to the wardrobe, donned breeches and a simple tunic. Other servants entered, stoked the fire and set a table with the morning meal. One brushed his hair as he sat, sleep still within his mind, thoughts turning as he ate.

If Archane is yet alive, how will it play with the Houses? Five years I have done what I may to keep them from each other's throats, praying to Iyllyeth she would return. Now it may come to pass. Who will suffer for it? Dare I speak this news to the other leaders? To the priesthood? The army?

Ung'gu'wi had become a place of danger; tunnels, warrens, chambers, all lying far beneath the Black Forest. The home of Drow within the land of Ardwel, it had grown for centuries, and now its passageways lay north and south for many marching days. East of the Silver River, it was a place shunned by elves and humans, and from which dark elf villages had spread. But with their military now in shambles following defeats at Castle Lahai in the north and Vichelli in the central plains, the Drow had drawn into themselves once more.

Human, elf, and Drow, all had lost those most venerated, souls and spirits needed for the Races then to prosper. Now gone. Archane. Galandria Telveperen. Crysalon. In only days, three leaders had met their fates. Never had the land, or the Races there within it, suffered such.

And with those losses, dissention rose within the dark elf society. Voices kept silent for a thousand years rose at last. It was all Mor'i'jil could do to keep the passages of *Ung'gu'wi* from running dark with blood of Drow.

The servant returned, placed the pot of tea before the priest, then bowed and stood in the corner once again.

Mor'i'jil drank, savoring the rich taste, his mind at last moving in a semblance of order. "Speak your words and spare none. Tell me all you know."

The servant bowed again. "The Seers spoke in the mid of night, saying Archane's spirit lives. Within the land, and closely by the city she once held, still only briefly was she seen. Yet she lives!"

Mor'i'jil shook his head, not understanding. "She is no longer there, yes? Where, then, has she gone?"

"Dark Lord, the Seers cannot find her again. They suggest the priesthood offer prayers for guidance."

Done and done, thought Mor'i'jil. *Prayers, sacrifices, offerings for moons beyond Archane's disappearance. Soldiers scoured the land, unseen by elves or men. We knew her place and then did not. Heartbeats, weak and injured, then nothing. Nothing from one who we thought immortal, or so said the tales. Now she returns? Yet only fleetingly? What sorcery is this?*

"Dark Lord, shall I—" The servant paused her words at Mor'i'jil's raised hand.

Sorcery? Might this be the cause? Found by someone of great power, taking her away, hiding her from our searches? Why have I not thought of this before? Who might be responsible? Drow? Elves? Surely, tho', not humans...

Mor'i'jil nearly paled in revelation. He rose, knees protesting once again. "Summon the Lancer Captain, then go to your crèche, say you are to be fed and rested. *Iyllyeth* grants you thanks for your message."

The servant beamed, bowed, and hurried out. Mor'i'jil sat again, knowing now what must have happened. He cursed his ancient mind for taking years to see who the guilty party was, now keeping the Dark Princess from her people.

* * *

The Lancer Captain listened Mor'i'jil paced before him. He knew the old priest as a confidant of Archane, and knew he held power as few others in the hierarchy. Only heads of Households in the Drow society demanded deference as he, but with growing age, Mor'i'jil was feeble. The matriarchs of the Great Houses only waited, for his death at assassins' hands, or simply for his ancient heart to cease its beating due to time. It mattered not to them which was the cause.

But the Lancer Captain, as Mor'i'jil, was faithful to the Race itself, and knew Archane's rule had been one of power and prestige. Until defeat came at the hands of Thalion Lahai at the castle north, and armies of Crysalon and the elves on the gates of Vichelli. For that, he had seen others executed. Not sacrificed, nor dead of honorable combat, but simply killed for poor decisions, their bodies left in the Black Forest for scavengers. He had escaped the wrath of leaders only because… in truth, he did not know. Perhaps his association with the priesthood, and the knowing of the leaders there he was a favorite of Archane.

Therefore, he gave attention to Mor'i'jil's ramblings. Of the girl called Reena, of Drakenmoore and the conflagration of Ma'chen'der, the mage thrown into the fires of *NorthWind* Forge, and the rumors of what Reena had become. He shivered in his cloak. Hideous sorcery. Reena's spirit torn from her body, replaced there by… a human. One with the power to do so. He considered the implications.

"Dark Lord," the Lancer Captain said, when Mor'i'jil at last paused to take a breath, "your words are worthy as they always are, and I stand ready for commands as necessary. Yet if the Dark Princess once again has vanished, where shall we seek her? This… Re', this human necromancer, powerful as she is, where might she hide Archane? How may we find her? And what shall you say to the Great Houses of this event?"

He drew closer, and guards about shifted nervously. He backed away a pace. "They wait, as well you know, for you to pass from this life. By your hand alone have you kept our Race whole in the memory of Archane. If she lives, I foresee blood-letting greater than we have ever seen."

Mor'i'jil considered. "We will say nothing until we have confirmed the Seers' visions. We will not allow… panic, as was seen when it was found the Dark Princess was missing." He looked carefully to the Lancer Captain. "You will see to this, yes? I trust your discretion in this matter."

The Lancer Captain bowed. "As you say, Dark Lord. We will see calm is maintained in *Ung'gu'wi* for the nonce. Your commands will be obeyed."

* * *

The City-State of Truth…

Three days across the land, and Chitthra at last looked upon the edifice of the greatest city in all Ardwel. Home now to the religion of the *Rising Star*, taken by Shiva Lahai on his search for Crysalon when kidnapped, the City-State of Truth was that and more. It was where Crysalon had set his rule and vanished from in his battle with Archane, where Aeren Grey, now Greywald as Chitthra had learned, sat as Warden of the City, with support of clergy such as Thalion Lahai, ministers of Crysalon who survived the devastation, and a Letter of Marque, signed and sealed by Her Excellency Audrey Vincent, Baroness of the Eastern Marches, Aeren's liege and mentor.

Chitthra paused, dismounted before the towering gates, and was approached by three guards in livery of the city.

"What business has a Drow in the city this day?" asked one roughly. He looked her slender figure up and down. "Come to sell your pleasures or seek a back to stab?"

The others chuckled, one circling behind Chitthra, and she tensed a moment, then relaxed. She bowed to the guard who spoke. "My name is Chitthra, friend of Aeren Greywald and Sheynon Calidriil. I would ask an audience with the Lady Greywald." She slowly drew a parchment from her cloak, bound with a ribbon in the colors of Telveperen. "From Earion Calidriil, Steward of the Fortress Telveperen. Please see this to the Lady Aeren's hand."

"What is this?" A voice from the gates, and Chitthra watched as a column paused within the passageway. An elf of stature dismounted his horse and quickly walked to Chitthra's side.

She bowed. "My lord Drakkon, it has been… some time."

Drakkon only stared. "We thought you dead years ago. We had no knowledge of your whereabouts, if you lived or died. Pray tell…" He paused as Chitthra held a hand.

"With all respect, I have ridden three days from Telveperen." Chitthra motioned to the parchment now dangling from the guard's hand. "I beg you, take me to Aeren if you can. I bear urgent news."

Drakkon turned to the guard and motioned more from the gate. "See her in safety to the palace grounds. She is a trusted compatriot of battles past and a dear friend of the Warden. She has my trust completely."

The guards about cast glances to each other and mumbled apologies, which Chitthra ignored. "My thanks. And you?"

Drakkon showed a tight grin. "Liaison between Coronis, Telveperen, and the City-State." He shrugged and chuckled. "It seems none may take my manner long, so they send me on errands of dubious importance."

Chitthra held a laugh of her own within. "Tho' we did not share closeness, always were you truthful. I see you now and am happy for it."

Drakkon motioned to the guards around. "Take her quickly to the palace." He looked to Chitthra once again. "We will meet again, I am certain. Until then, fare thee well, and know you are remembered with great fondness."

* * *

They escorted her to the palace grounds, through the gates and up the stairs to the palace proper. Through the halls, bootsteps echoing through the marble passageways, and people, humans all, watching as the dark elf woman walked with guards around her, headed for the throne room.

They paused at the great oaken doors and a woman came from within. She was human, tall and dark hair streaked with gray, eyes dark and intelligent. She took Chitthra's measure with a glance. "I am Arna, Sage to the Thrones and Historian of the Lands About. I now serve Lady Aeren Greywald, Warden of the City-State of Truth." She smiled warmly. "And I have heard tales of you for many years. Welcome."

Chitthra did not have words, so she only bowed. The doors opened and Arna motioned her to enter. It was the grandest hall Chitthra had ever seen, the room dressed in summer colors, guards in every corner, a sideboard set with a light meal, the fragrance of wine drifting in the air. At the center of the room were two thrones, vacant, and a single seat apart. In the seat was another woman, and she rose as Chitthra approached, squealed nearly as a girl, and ran to embrace her deeply.

Once more memories flowed as they held each other tightly. Chitthra drew slowly away and gazed into Aeren's face. If now she needed further confirmation years had passed, she was convinced, looking at the woman in her arms.

Aeren was no longer the lanky girl Chitthra had known. The curves of womanhood had, at the last, set upon her figure, though she still was tall and more slender than was Arna. Yet her face! Eyes verdant as they ever were, hair darkening with age and hanging well below her shoulders, lines of worry beginning now to show upon her forehead.

Yes, this now shows the time has passed, thought Chitthra, *for Aeren is become a woman, and I see it in her soul.*

Aeren held her tightly once again, taller by a hand, and crushed herself, breast to breast, against Chitthra's lean frame. Chitthra felt herself responding, a longing deeply felt, and gently forced herself away, looking once more into Aeren's emerald eyes.

"We must speak," she finally managed, "and if you will, a meal, as I have not eaten all this day. My thought was to find you quickly as I might."

Aeren only nodded, grinning ear to ear, and motioned to the sideboard. They took a seat as cool water was poured before them, then ale or wine as they would choose.

Chitthra drank, refilled her glass, and drank again.

All the while, Aeren only watched. At last she spoke. "I have dreamed of you nearly every night of your absence. I prayed to *Jhad* for your safety, that I would see you with my eyes once more." She signed herself and shed a single tear. "Welcome back, my lady. We have so much to speak of now you are safe again."

* * *

They spoke until the throne room darkened and sconces on the walls were lit. They walked arm in arm through the palace garden, sat by fountains and listened to the music of the waters, as words were shared, and feelings flowed.

Returning to the palace, they paced the halls, for neither sought a chair, only wanting closeness as shared those years ago.

"Hawk..." Aeren's voice nearly broke, and Chitthra paused to take her hand again.

"I did not broach the subject, for I feared he was gone. Else he would likely be here at your side."

Aeren nodded and wiped away a tear. "Raven brought the news, returned to Kaul a moon or more. She came to the City-State on my invitation and stayed two years. Yet she was restless, a fighter as you know, and in time the guards would not spar with her, as her temper took her senses."

They shared a quiet laugh, then Aeren spoke again. "She missed her brother even more than I, tho' for different reasons." She shrugged with remembrance. "The only lover ever I have known, and I miss his touch greatly, Chitthra. I know not of Raven's fate, and pray for her safety."

"She wanted not to be safe," replied the dark elf woman, "but to follow in his footsteps, honorable combat her demise. There are few like her in this land."

They walked on, the hallways quiet in the evening, then Chitthra spoke again. "Therefore, tales of Archane's immortality are true. Dead by Hawk's own blade, yet risen to seek Crysalon and lay blame at his feet."

Aeren nodded. "All true, yet it was not Crysalon's doing, but that of Kaul and his mercenaries. What armies could not do, a band of ruffians accomplished, and brought peace to the land-five years and more."

"Earion says the same, my lady. That with the leaders gone, Ardwel's factions draw into themselves, seeking comfort and a chance to mourn. It is... strange to think in this manner, that without the leaders present, peace returns, unencumbered."

Chitthra paused and faced Aeren once again. "And your part, that you have taken the task herein… they have come to know you as a wise and wondrous woman, one worthy of your title." She smiled. "Your mentor would be proud."

Aeren showed a self-depreciating smile. "I pray only I may aid them as I can. I did not seek this, yet accepted as I knew it necessary."

Chitthra touched Aeren's cheek with gentle fingers. "Of all the memories of times together, do you know what it is I miss most of all?"

Aeren shook her head.

"The bathing house, and our closeness in the waters."

Aeren's face lit with an idea, and she took Chitthra's hand in hers. "Come with me, and we may find that closeness once again."

* * *

They drifted in the warm and scented waters of the palace bath, the night late and none around attending. Candles burning on the mantel and flower petals in the water gave a fragrance nearly sensual in the air.

"We were trapped by Anon Gûl, together for eternity within the Black Blade, and its name I will not utter." Chitthra sat, shoulder to shoulder with Aeren, water lapping gently round them as they spoke nearly in whispers, telling secrets in the dimness.

"I recall," said Aeren, "the one taking Earion's arm, and Kaul's denial."

"Tho' it was more than a blade," replied Chitthra. She shivered, though the water warm and restful. "Made by Re' herself, it held a place … an existence away from our reality. And I have not told you, but Anon Gûl was not the true one, for she is yet within the Western Isles."

"Chitthra?"

The dark elf woman nodded, frowning. "In truth, she was Steffyn Foxxe, the elf grand sorcerer, friend of Sheynon Calidriil. Yet it was his errors, his misplaced belief in his own abilities, that caused the death of Galandria Telveperen. He is complicit as is Mors'ul'jyn."

Aeren moved to face Chitthra squarely. "I cannot believe it. Why would a dear friend not only of Calidriil, but my liege as well, do such a thing? Say no more to me of this."

Chitthra dropped her gaze away. "I saw him change before my eyes. He admitted poorest judgement. He could not bring himself to kill Mors'ul'jyn, the wizard-woman Re's soul and essence within her, for he knows magic fades and those who hold the power are few."

69

Aeren studied Chitthra's face, then kissed her cheek. "I know you would not lie, and accept your words. Yet what now? Do you seek vengeance on him? Does Sheynon know of this? Surely he is aware."

"If not, I shall find Steffyn Foxxe and take him before Sheynon to beg forgiveness. If he will not go…" She looked to Aeren. "Galandria Telveperen was a Knight of *The Flame*, fought on Final Night at Ardoch, and leader of the elves. Her death cannot go unavenged, yet has for five long years. My Order would cast me out if I cannot be her reconciler."

Aeren placed her finger on Chitthra's lips. "Say no more. Tonight is not the time for decisions of this sort."

Chitthra's hand found Aeren's shoulder and she grinned. "What decisions should we make then, my lady?"

Aeren smiled. "Take the bed with me this night. I desire only to know you safe and hold you close."

Chitthra's grin widened. "Only?"

Aeren blushed, as deeply as Chitthra remembered. "Still you tempt me, and I understand now the reasons better. Yet tonight, only may we whisper thanks for your coming to my life again."

* * *

*A*eren reined her horse away from the crashing waves toward the small copse of wood, the only shelter seen. Wounds stung, and her legs scarcely held her in the saddle, bleeding as she was, and weak. The horse, she knew, was nearly at its end, for they had been running since the sun began to set, and it now lay heavy on the horizon.

Why in the name of *Jhad* are Drow here, on the coast, only a day's ride from Ardoch? And in numbers!

The arrow caught her horse's flank, and Aeren could only release the reins or be crushed as the animal fell. The stony ground came up hard against her side and her wind was lost, but she struggled through her cloak to stand and draw her sword.

If I die this day, let my death be a noble one. *Jhad* protect me or hold me in his arms as he wills. I am not afraid.

The first rider was too bold and Aeren's blow unhorsed him. Never did the chance to recover his wits come, as his head rolled down the slope and into the sand, trailing dark blood and a scream of surprise more than pain. The second rider was more wary, but the javelin, recovered quickly from the still-quivering body of Aeren's victim, pierced his chest fully, while the horse continued past her, and on.

Aeren's senses grew dark, her balance unsteady, and her sword hand weak. Her last vision was of the third rider, approaching with sword high, then descending. The blow drove her down, her blood bright in dimming sunlight, sword ringing against the stones as it fell from her hand. Then darkness.

70

Aeren rose shaking from the bed, held a hand to her breast, and prayed for calm upon herself. She paced, opened the shutters, and gazed beyond the palace to the temple in the distance.

Chitthra drew back the covers, walked quietly from the bed and stood behind her, hands gently massaging Aeren's trembling shoulders.

"Two years, and I thought the nightmares past. Three times now in the last moon I have had this dream, and I cannot know its reason."

Chitthra turned her gently. "Speak of it and I will listen with my heart."

Aeren motioned to the table and they sat. Chitthra poured tea from their late supper, still warm within the pot. She added honey and bade Aeren drink, then waited.

"It is death I see, my own, at the hands of Drow. And you know I mean no offense in saying." Aeren sipped, then continued. "Somewhere along the coast, as I hear sounds of the sea, perhaps a day's ride from Ardoch."

"Why Ardoch? A sign perhaps?"

Aeren shook her head. "I cannot know, but feel I must travel there for reasons still unknown. Yet I cannot leave the city."

Chitthra smiled. "It is in good hands. You have grown in many ways and show your mentor's touch of leadership. Should you take a respite, they will understand."

Aeren drank again, gazing beyond the window, contemplating. "Sheynon took *Annatar Yarhetha'an* to Ardoch, set it on the plain just beyond the crevice, nearly as a gatehouse. His thought was not only protection of a holy place, but…" Aeren's voice trailed as she gazed into her cup.

Chitthra touched Aeren's hand and squeezed it gently. "Say on. This must be faced, dream or vision, calling or warning. I will stand beside you in its learning."

Aeren only nodded, then spoke after a long moment. "Sheynon never has forgiven Coronis for their attempt upon Galandria's life those years ago. Tho' never said, I know he keeps Ardoch hostage against Coronis, the birthplace of *The Flame* now held away from them. That, and more. He has retreated into himself, only those most loyal allowed within the fortress. He seeks solitude and shies from the world. Truly, I despair for his spirit."

Chitthra refreshed their cups, thinking. "We will go together. My plans were next to travel to him and now there is a task. We will find the meaning of your visions, and speak with Sheynon of his manner." She raised Aeren's face to hers. "You will not stand alone in this endeavor."

* * *

Aeren met with her advisors in the morning, introducing Chitthra to them all, then gave instructions to be followed in her absence.

Celeste, wife of Thalion Lahai, and now leader of the Faith, sang blessings on their journey. General Torgensonn gave orders for horses and provisions to be readied, and an honor guard to escort them and beyond the city gates. Minister Arna offered maps and a letter of introduction, should it be necessary, and saw their purses filled with gold and silver.

Then out the gates they rode, one hundred soldiers as an escort, through the villages below the city's plain, and at the last, onto the road alone.

By midday Chitthra saw on Aeren's face a look of joy, thinking it was one she had not shown since coming to the city. It was a look as one starving, seeing a banquet laid before them.

Adventure, once again, was singing praises in Aeren Greywald's blood.

BOOK THREE
WITHIN THE FORTRESS

"Annatar Yarhetha'an.
'Great Gift of God', this is your castle's name?"

The Duchess of Stormguarde
Castle, to Sheynon Calidriil
in the North

Dennis Young

Lahai Castle…

The castle on the Silver River had changed many ways in the five years since defeat of Archane's army. Two new towers had been erected in the gatehouse, and the bridge, once a construct of wood alone, now was stone, with edifices on either shore of quarried rock and iron. Guardhouses east and west kept tally of crossings to either side, marking carefully those who passed and those departing.

In that time, the leadership began to change as well. Thalion Lahai, Patriarch of the Faith and leader of the Church of the *Rising Star* in the City-State of Truth, was seen less frequently within the castle halls or walking on the battlements. His son, Carmichael, nearly five and twenty years of age, was now Master of the Castle, aided, as his father for many years, by Omer, lifelong friend and confidant of the family.

Five years of peace had come, and though Thalion knew the happenings of Crysalon's stand against Archane, still he missed his liege, and wondered of the future.

"The Steward, Aeren…" Thalion paused his cup, sitting with Carmichael and Omer at the gatehouse battlements, watching summer sun glinting off the Silver River. He motioned to the parchment at his hand. "Celeste says she has ridden from the city at the side of a dark elf woman, this Chitthra, known to Aeren and only now having reappeared. Such talk suggests Archane was never found. Might this be the beginning once again of turmoil?"

Omer, more rotund than ever, and Carmichael, tall as his father and slender, grinned to each other. "You wish to ride beside them, yes?" Omer drained his tankard, nudged Carmichael, and grinned again. "Your father yet is unwilling to settle in his life. Once adventure finds its way into your blood, never will it leave."

Thalion chuckled. "Yet we sit in pleasant company and watch the river, having seen little more than a score of farmers crossing in a moon." He motioned to the bridge and soldiers in the distance. "Naught have we seen of dark elf soldiers, and our sorties to the Black Forest find little trace."

"You speak as tho' you wish a battle, Father," said Carmichael, sipping ale and nibbling at the plate before him. "Blessings must be counted, and vigilance maintained. Still, you leave for the city-state tomorrow, yes? We will see your journey is a quiet one."

"And in that time, your sisters beg a visit from you. My thought is, they should come herein and see your new home for themselves. Surely they will learn a bit of their older brother's work."

"Young women now," said Omer, "no more the girls I once sat upon my knee." He sighed and drank once more.

"Your lady has graced you with children, has she not?" asked Thalion, a twinkle in his eye. "A son and daughter growing well. Blessings, as said, should be counted. Peace is not to be taken lightly in this day."

A silence set upon them as they contemplated words and thoughts. "What reason?" Omer asked at the last. "What cause would Aeren have to leave the city-state?"

Thalion raised the parchment. "This Chitthra says Archane still lives, and another, Mors'ul'jyn, murderess of Galandria Telveperen. They seek to give warning to Sheynon."

Omer's face was stern. "They must be found, Thalion. If Archane lives, she cannot return to her people, stirring war once more."

"To say nothing of the danger to Sheynon's family," added Carmichael. He paused, then asked carefully, "What may we do to aid them?"

"For now, prayer, and a guiding hand from the *Rising Star*. More practically, I will speak with ministers of the city-state once returned. Five years of peace cannot be for nothing."

"May our blessings be accepted from our hearts," whispered Carmichael. He looked to Thalion. "Therefore, Father, will you join them? Still you are spry enough for an older man." He grinned.

Thalion laid his elbow on the table, flexing his fingers. "Test you this arm, boy? *Gil Estel* yet fits my grip well and will serve me."

They laughed together and raised their cups. Still, in his mind, Thalion knew the unspoken warning and wondered of it. Yet today was not for worry, but remembrance. Five years. So much had changed.

* * *

They walked the entryway within the gatehouse, to the western bridge tower and across the river, seeing fishermen on both banks, human and dark elf. None were seen together, and even after five years of living side by side, trust was something rare. But neither was there violence, and as Thalion walked beside his son and Omer to the eastern shore, they paused to watch, reflecting.

"Blood flowed deeply in this river," said Thalion, as he made a sign before himself and cast flowers into the water. "Blood of valiant humans defending our land and homes. Blood of dark elves bent on taking it away by orders of Archane." He looked north along the shore. "Now villagers sit side by side fighting over only fish."

"A trade worth having," replied Omer, kneeling and plucking grasses. "Two Drow villages have been deserted in the last six moons, the dark elves moving north. Scouts tell of counting no less than five hundred now in three villages, one nearly a town in size, and no soldiers seen." He rose and lowered his voce. "Tho' still we search."

"Father, I have ordered parties further north. We have spoken with dwarves of Malton Manor and ride beside them each moon. Our vigilance will not falter."

"Do not ride the same time every moon," replied Thalion. "Show no pattern in your sorties. Give them nothing with which to plan."

Omer shook his head. "Five years on, and yet we cannot trust."

Thalion nodded. "Too many years of hate and ill content. Too many years of threats of Archane coveting our land. Trust comes, but slowly. And now..."

"Will you seek Sheynon?" asked Carmichael. "Years it has been since you saw your cousin last."

Thalion pondered for quiet moments. "An idea, and a good one." He laughed. "But a long ride."

"Pause at the city-state," replied Omer. "Speak love into your lady's ear and hold your daughters once again."

"That I will do, my friend," said Thalion, smiling. "Surely, that I will do."

$$* * *$$

Three days across the land, and Thalion's column paused in assessment. They took time at graves dug in part by Thalion's own hands five years before, when five hundred of the emperor Crysalon's finest were slaughtered by Drow advancement into the plains. They spent time in villages, human, elf, and Drow, speaking of crops and weather, water rights and other daily matters. Of soldiers, none were seen in Drow villages, and Thalion nodded in acceptance at the last.

We see them now, Great Lord, having lived beside us twenty years. Little do I fear of them, for with the leaders of the land disappearing in only days, peace once more has come. How so? Are we victims of mad plans of only but a few, driven by their own fears? Those as Galandria Telveperen, leader of the elves, Crysalon himself ruling humans for many years... even Archane. What cause ignites desire to subjugate others? What courage is needed to raise the sword against the enemy? Is it true, that a single person can bring the world to ending?

Thalion rose from his devotions, given at dusk in a copse of wood as the Star rose in the heavens and the sky darkened with the setting sun.

"Five years," he said, as to himself, "now we learn Archane may yet live, and this Mors'ul'jyn still at large. Once more we gird our loins and sharpen swords. Once more blood will flow and darken the fields and plains." He shook his head and leaned gently against a young tree. "Is there an ending to it, or is the world caught deeply in a cycle? Only can I say that in my life, little have I seen but challenge rising, bringing chaos once again."

He gave his benediction, turned and walked back into the camp, wondering if the world might survive once more.

* * *

Annatar Yarhetha'an…

Sheynon Calidriil stood at the eastern battlements, looking to the darkening skies as sunset fell heavy on his shoulders. The chasm lay before the gatehouse, nearly ten elves wide and more than fifty deep, the rocky plain on which the monastery of Ardoch set, split nearly in two by its presence. With a killing field sweeping north and south, and the mithril-laced walls of *Annatar Yarhetha'an* all but impregnable, the ancient birthplace of *The Eternal Flame of Truth and Light* was safe against its enemies. Even those of the Faith itself, such as seen in the city of Coronis.

"There comes a time," Sheynon had said to Earion, on leaving Telveperen near four years before, "holy places must be protected, especially from those who would use them as a place from which to rally and bring evil to the world. If, in isolating Ardoch from those in Coronis who would use it for that purpose, I may keep them calm and agreeable, then I shall do so. Whatever names and curses they send my way, I will laughingly accept. Let them come, Cousin, and we will fill the chasm with their dead."

"You remind me of my brother." A light voice was heard, sounds of soft boots on stone breaking Sheynon's reverie, and he turned to see Ysilrod ascending the steps behind him. "Ah, you *are* my brother!"

A laugh, and Sheynon motioned Ysilrod to his side, clasped him closely, and smiled. "You should be with Caramir, should you not?" Sheynon ventured. "A father must greet his child coming into the world." His arm tightened around Ysilrod's slender shoulders.

"Too anxious you are, and not for moons, says the midwife."

The eve was warm, but still Sheynon felt his brother shudder. "You worry, yet she is strong. Blessings, Brother, and she will bring forth your child in health. I promise."

78

Ysilrod nodded silently, then motioned attendants set a tray of food and tea. "Word from Telveperen? How fares Earion in his duties?"

"None yet, tho' this moon's message is not due. Three days, perhaps four, and we will hear."

"Coronis? Eirioch tends the flock well therein? The Lady Jewelle and Leyland hold Conservatives by their collective throats, yes?" Ysilrod grinned tightly.

Sheynon gestured to the castle and the naked plain about. "Here it is done. Five years Coronis has been dormant, and I pray only do they bicker with each other."

Ysilrod was quiet for moments. "Something stirs. Too silent is the land, too long without word of evil's doings. Be vigilant, Sheynon, for it will come in unexpected ways."

"Prophecy? You are a Seer and a sorcerer?" He chuckled.

"I worry, Brother. Archane, Crysalon, this Mors'ul'jyn… all now gone. A blessing in surety, yet uncertainty remains."

Sheynon's face tightened. "I have done all I may to protect my children. Galandria's spirit speaks to me each night and tells me to be wary. Now you come with warning and I wonder of it."

The night grew deeper as *Mina* rose in the east and *Grand Selene*, half full, hung as a ruddy lantern in the sky.

Ysilrod brought a mug of tea to Sheynon's hand and they drank quietly. He nodded to the east and movement on the escarpment. "Riders, two. At night?" Ysilrod set away his cup and gestured before them. The air grew as a great lens, and detail showed of those approaching.

"Two females, one human, and… Drow?" Ysilrod's brow furrowed.

Sheynon studied the images and grinned widely. "I know those faces. Come, and I will make your introduction."

He hurried to the steps, descending quickly. Ysilrod followed, waiving guards to attend.

* * *

Ysilrod cast a bridge across the chasm and the riders crossed it quickly.

Sheynon ran through the gatehouse way as his brother called guards to follow, then readied himself, should enchantment be needed for protection. But Sheynon motioned the soldiers away and stood grinning as Aeren and Chitthra dismounted and approached. They bowed, then returned his smile, hugged each other that he was safe and in their sight.

"Too many years, my lord," said Aeren at the last. "My liege sends greetings and her admiration. She prays *Jhad* will watch over you and your children."

"All the gods are welcome here, and you know this," replied Sheynon. He turned to Chitthra. "Well met again, and welcome to *Annatar Yarhetha'an*. We will speak soon enough of your reasons, but for now…" He motioned attendants forward, and they held goblets of wine and water to the women, dusted cloaks, and offered scented bowls from which to wash their faces.

Sheynon motioned Ysilrod forward. "My brother Ysilrod, and I am sure you have heard tales of his derring-do." They shared a quiet laugh as Sheynon nodded to Aeren. "From the court of Audrey Vincent, Aeren Greywald, protégé and esquire, now Warden of the City-State of Truth." Sheynon looked her slender figure up and down. "Well done for such a whip of a girl, yes? Now the same age as Audrey when first come to Ardwel, by my count."

Aeren only blushed and smiled. "I pray my work is worthy of her name and for the good of all. By the teachings of so many, I have found purpose herein. My thanks."

Sheynon looked then to Chitthra. "Daeron smiles upon you, my lady. Where have you been so long? We worried for your safety."

Chitthra's dark eyes moved from Sheynon to Ysilrod's look of inquiry. She bowed to him. "Of the Brotherhood, and *Din'daeron'dae*, whom I follow. I understand you knew him in his mortal time."

Ysilrod stood aghast. "*Däe Quivië*? Daeron Foxxe, elf-brother to us both?" He shook his head as Sheynon laughed again. "Know you his wife, Tolemey, and their daughter Joi? I am…" He closed his mouth slowly and only shook his head, then bowed. "The honor is mine, dear ladies. Such wonders the world holds these days and now two of them stand before me." He bowed again.

"My lord, we bear news and thoughts needing of discussion urgently," said Aeren. "Regarding those of the past… missing now for many years."

Sheynon nodded knowingly. "First a meal and bath for both of you. Then we will hear your tales. I have waited years for your coming, and now you are here. But first, welcome to our House, and find your comfort. Sunset is best for parley as the evening cools."

* * *

They met atop the southwest tower, overlooking Ardoch as darkness came and stars winked into the sky one by one. *Selene* was a shadow descending slowly in the west, and *Mina* rose, silvery and bright. A pot of tea bubbled on a sideboard, as they nibbled greens and a meal of roasted beef, succulent and hot.

Chitthra told her tale of the Black Blade, and Ysilrod listened with intent, nodding as she spoke. He raised a hand for pause. "A place beyond our realm where time may pass in different manner." He looked away for moments. "For you, years have passed, yet I wonder... is it the same for all?"

The women traded looks, then glanced to Sheynon, and Ysilrod once again. "I do not understand," said Chitthra.

Aeren took her hand gently, shrugging.

"The blade was a trap, constructed by one of ability."

"By Mors'... by Re', Teresa Drakenmoore. Steffyn Foxxe said as much," said Sheynon.

"Then in doing so, surely her abilities and knowledge would allow her control of the artifact." Ysilrod rose and paced away, then turned. "She might herself return nearly the moment she was trapped within it. You, my lady, having no such control, might have remained for all eternity. Such ability requires the greatest of intellect and study."

"Intellect as your own?" asked Sheynon, troubled at the thought.

Ysilrod smiled wryly. "As in all learning, schools of thought and subject are considered disciplines. Necromancy is no specialty of mine."

Sheynon shuddered. "Necromancy! Study of the dead?"

"That, and things to deal with the other worlds beyond our own, and of course, what lies beyond the realm of passing from this place." Ysilrod motioned about himself. "To some, residing in those other places, we are but shadows, and hardly worth the bother. Yet others in our own world seek to know them, and thereby use their power."

"It seemed only moments," said Chitthra softly. "I was there with her, then found myself in a field, nearly naked, and the shards of the Black Blade scattered round me."

"You brought those shards, yes?"

Chitthra nodded. "For your study, and I pray you hold them away, lest she come for them. I cannot know the reasons for my release, however."

"A condition of the spell perhaps," replied Ysilrod, "should her ability not be enough within the enchantment. Five years to an elf or Drow is nothing in a life of centuries."

"And long enough, perhaps, for her to pass from memory in the land," added Sheynon. "Still... why would she seek escape so quickly?"

"You, my lord Sheynon, and your family." Aeren's voice was but a whisper. "Vengeance, yet something drew her attention from that cause. But what?"

"She was wounded when you and Steffyn found her, yes?" Sheynon motioned for tea to be poured around as attendants cleared the table.

Chitthra held her words until they were alone once more. "He would not allow me to end her life. Now she is free, and I stand shamed for it."

"Nonsense," said Sheynon. "Through no fault of yours, or any at this table, the mad woman may be free. Again, why so?"

Quiet descended, then Aeren spoke. "We found no trace of Archane's body. We know not if she lives or where. Yet five years the Drow have been silent in their absence and we hear tales of struggles in the hierarchy. Might we find a way to know? If dark elves bicker, Archane must be absent from her place. From my liege, never have they known another leader in all Ardwel's time."

"Archane's immortality is certain," said Ysilrod. "Twice she returned in my own sight, your liege and other dearest comrades bearing witness there in Shadow Mountain. Never doubt it, for her curse is real."

"To bear the pain of death, not once, but forever." Aeren shook her head, sighing. "Then return, knowing it may happen once again. Truly, madness must fill her mind. How many times in all the ages of her life has she died? And now we face her as a creature filled with vengeance for her death. Therefore, her reasons, coming to the city-state. She laid the blame for her dying at the feet of Crysalon, when it was Kaul and his mercenary band. Hawk struck the killing blow himself."

"And died in Raven's arms," replied Chitthra. She squeezed Aeren's hand as she saw a tear forming on her cheek.

"Hawk? Raven?" Ysilrod shook his head.

"Siblings, and a pair as never you have seen," said Sheynon. "Bodyguards of Kaul, my hireling, yet neither cared for him at all."

Chitthra barked a laugh. "Raven might have taken Kaul's head, but wished payment before doing so."

"You have met interesting persons in my absence, Brother," said Ysilrod, laughing as well.

"Continuing this thought," said Aeren, "Mors'ul'jyn escapes, yet then where? To Drakenmoore? It is but a ruin."

"Hidden places, deep within the earth, reachable only by her magic." Ysilrod shrugged. "Such would be a simple task for her."

Chitthra's face came up quickly. "Might she hold Archane?"

"My lady?" Sheynon looked to Aeren, then to Ysilrod. "How so? Was she seen in the city-state?"

"To my knowledge, no," replied Aeren, "yet chaos took the city on Archane's appearance. As Crysalon and I stood against her, nearly were the palace grounds destroyed."

"You fought at Crysalon's side against Archane?" Ysilrod shook his head in wonder. "My lady, amazement at your exploits grows with every word. I am more than impressed."

Aeren nodded sadly. "I would have given my life for his without question."

"His plan was set, and masterful," said Sheynon. "He drew her in to destroy her. Did he succeed?"

"Let us assume," said Ysilrod, pacing once again, "Archane survived. Let us also suppose upon this Mors'ul'jyn's finding of her in the aftermath. Where then?"

Chitthra shrugged. "As said, Drakenmoore."

Ysilrod nodded. "Beneath the ground for five years? How to hold Archane? A blindfold, a gag within her mouth, held naked and in chains?"

Chitthra smirked. "Archane was known for... unusual taste with concubines. Perhaps this was her choice." Her jest fell before them. "What then, my lords? A pact?"

"To return her to her place? Bold assurance would be needed," said Sheynon. "Safety must be confirmed, or Archane would have her on the sacrificial altar soonest."

Aeren raised a hand. "A third party, an arbiter. Someone with power enough or knowledge of the both to force cooperation."

Sheynon nodded slowly. "Yes. One known to both, perhaps not as an ally, but with strength enough to seal a bargain. Kaul."

"Your hireling? Surely not, Brother."

"He rules the city-state now, once Vichelli, now DragonFall. Mors'ul'jyn traveled with him, and owes a debt. Without him, she may never have recovered her hidings in Drakenmoore's caverns. Archane..."

"It is a beginning, my lord. Our thanks." Chitthra smiled to Ysilrod and took Aeren's hand once more.

"Shall we ride come morning? Or would a day from the saddle be a blessing?" Sheynon grinned, and the women nodded gratefully.

* * *

They took the road, and on the second day storms chased them in their travels. They camped beneath an overhang of rock, set their bedrolls in a shallow cave, and built a fire. Ysilrod cast flame, and as they watched the rain and ate their fill, Sheynon poured elven wine around.

"Kaul's city is the den of iniquity you might suppose. His reach is far into the southern plains, near the hills of Duerkas's dwarven clan. He treats not with elves or men, but finds dark elf farmers and dwarves willing to pay his taxes, selling wares in DragonFall." Sheynon paused as lightning flashed and thunder rumbled through the clouds. Slowly, as they sat in quiet, the rain abated, leaving the air fresh with forest scents.

"You have not been in his presence since Archane's forces were driven out?" asked Chitthra.

Sheynon shook his head, as did Aeren. "Nay," Sheynon answered, "and surely he has no wish for me to appear, thinking it a nightmare." They laughed around. "The land has changed, as each and all draw into themselves." He looked to Aeren. "No insult is intended, my lady. The council in the City-State of Truth has been a blessing with your calming hand."

"Learned from those in my presence now," replied Aeren. "There was a time I was but a foolish girl."

Chitthra touched her shoulder to Aeren's. "Days long past, and now we sit together once again."

Aeren nodded, a wistful look upon her face. She stood. "Pardons, prayer calls me."

They watched her walk into a copse and kneel beside a young tree. Ysilrod bid good eve and found his bedroll as Sheynon poured Chitthra's cup half-full again. They drank in silence as the forest round them calmed and *Mina* peeked between the clouds.

"She is special to you," he said. "You return and see her grown a woman now. Earion takes the task of watching in Telveperen as Aeren keeps the City-State of Truth apprised of elven issues by way of Drakkon as emissary. What think you of the changes all around?"

Chitthra sipped, contemplating. "Still my mind is struggling. I left a land in chaos and return to one well-ordered, or so it seems. A dream, perhaps, and will I wake and find myself yet within the Black Blade? Nearly am I afraid to sleep at night."

Sheynon nodded, thinking of his next words carefully. "She is more than a dear friend to you. She shares your bed."

Chitthra paused her cup and grinned. "We hold fast and keep each other warm, my lord. Nothing more."

"Yet…"

"It is her decision. Hawk was her lover, first and only. That we are close, yes, tho' still she is very young."

"More the reason." Now Sheynon grinned.

Chitthra shook her head, stifling a chuckle. "Would you have me then seduce her, as did he? Very well."

They laughed together for a moment, touched rims and drank again.

* * *

Aeren kept her counsel, yet prayer eluded her. *Too many thoughts, too many earthly feelings, and now we venture once again to find Kaul. Dare we trust him? We parted with words between us, and I cannot think he will consider our offer true. He will seek a way beyond it, should the chance arise.*

She laid her head gently to the tree and closed her eyes. *Dearest Jhad, give me sign. I have spent these years in company of those whose Faith is different, yet in many ways the same. Good people, all, and trusting, who knew my mentor in her day. Now I work beside them in her stead, and I could not ask for more. Why, then, is there so much angst within my heart?*

She glanced beyond her shoulder, to Sheynon and Chitthra talking quietly together. *An elf-lord who has fought Drow for nearly all his life. A dark elf woman of the greatest Brotherhood the elves have known, protectors of the Race, and she among them. Such changes! Such is the world moving to the light! They sit together sharing stories, as comrades in the struggle. And I am blessed to be a part!*

She rose, returning to the fire, sat, accepting a cup from Sheynon's hand. Her gaze touched his, then Chitthra's, and she noted the look of mischief in both their eyes. She raised an eyebrow of inquiry.

"Lord Sheynon wagers I might seduce you this night and know your pleasures." Chitthra showed a look of bold salaciousness.

Aeren's eyes widened as she paused the cup before her lips. She mulled the words for moments, drank, then nodded. "I will see that wager, my lady. And redoubled."

They laughed together, poured wine around, and laughed again.

* * *

The City-State of DragonFall…

The scroll hung from Kaul's meaty hand, proclaiming Calidriil and others ventured to his realm. Kaul motioned to the lackey who had brought the message from the gates.

"None appeared, My King, as it came upon the wind."

"The message delivered by itself? How then do we know it is not false?"

"My King, a whirlwind came, say the guards, and the parchment fell at their feet. I cannot say otherwise, as I was not present. Yet as you see, the seal was unbroken when delivered."

Kaul growled, motioned the lackey away, and rose, stretching out his bulk as the midday sun filled the throne room. *First Mors'ul'jyn and Archane, now the elf-lord whose bidding set me on this path. I must be careful in my words to him, else he will know his enemies have preceded his coming.*

He motioned the lackey to his side again. "On arrival, receive them well. Bring them to me in safety, with guards as necessary. They are… acquaintances from my early days in this land." He dismissed the servant, then called attendants to his side. "Bring my royal robes and armor. Be quick. See the throne room is suitable for guests."

Kaul paced away, anxious in his waiting. Guards in corners watched, they, themselves, as Kaul had been, mercenaries, yet now they stood as soldiers. Kaul knew it was through little of true loyalty, and only by the city-state's successes he held his place. *Perhaps I may gain notoriety in their eyes when they see the elf-lord in my presence. Who might attend with him? Family? The fop Earion, whom I almost killed, tho' bore no blame? Others?*

Attendants came again, trailing tailors and fitters behind them. They draped Kaul in his finery, armor polished to a glow, the *NorthWind* sword given him by Reena, now Mors'ul'jyn, and a scarlet cloak, heavy nearly as his breastplate. They placed a simple crown upon his hairy head, beaten gold with blood-red gems and sable onyx, then he sat as war boots of polished leather were fitted to his feet. At the last an artist stood before him, darkened his heavy lids with oils, drew a bit of color on his lips, and touched sweet waters to his face and hands.

I might have bathed, had I the time, he thought, chuckling, *but my concubines would have kept me in the waters far too long.*

At last he waved them all away, then sat, waiting for… what, he did not know. Therefore, he rose again and paced, wondering of his nervousness.

At last Kaul forced himself to sit, draped his cloak carelessly about the throne, and waited.

The doors parted, creaking slightly on their hinges. His seneschal entered, a woman who had been Kaul's first concubine and now his confidant. Following were guards, four figures close behind them, then more guards. More it looked as an execution than a visit from a dignitary.

The seneschal bowed and took her place beside the throne. The guards cleared away, standing close to either side.

The four came before Kaul and bowed. He growled, showing points of teeth. "Calidriil brings before me one who took my destiny away. Tell me why I should allow any here to leave alive."

Sheynon looked to Aeren, then to Chitthra, and once again to Kaul. "I am unaware of any disagreement between yourselves… Your Majesty."

Kaul rose and moved his bulk before Aeren, half a head taller and twice as wide as she. "This one. She held away the city promised, and nearly did we come to blows."

"That would be unwise, even here," said the slender elf at Sheynon's side.

Kaul looked his way, then to the elf-lord. "Who is this? Another cousin as Earion?"

"Ysilrod, my brother, and member of the Guild of Learned in Telveperen. A mage of… some ability." Sheynon held his face serious as he might.

Kaul huffed a breath, then turned his eyes to Aeren once again. She met his stare with strength. Chitthra stepped to her side, and Kaul nearly laughed. "So, all rally round the human woman?" He looked Aeren up and down. "At the least, womanhood as set upon your form, I see. No more the skinny girl."

He turned away, sat again and motioned to his seneschal. "Rohesia, and she will see to your comforts. What business have you?"

Sheynon looked to his charges, then spoke. "We would speak in privacy, should you allow it. Urgent news, and confidence is asked."

Kaul nodded, turning to Rohesia. "See the speaking chamber is prepared, then show them to the dining hall where they may wait." He glanced to their road-weary look. "See they are brushed of dust and fed. Then advise me when prepared."

Rohesia bowed, spoke quietly with attendants, then left without further word to Kaul, exiting aside with two guards. The attendants came and led Sheynon and the others beyond the throne room.

Kaul watched, thinking all the while. *Ill tidings, with the Drow woman and the skinny girl. Something stirs, and it will not be pleasant. I must choose words carefully in our parley.*

He took his leave to find his harem, knowing the eve in Sheynon's company would not be a cordial one.

* * *

They waited in the dining hall as servants tended and set a meal before them. Ysilrod poured wine and paced away, goblet in his hand, and soft footsteps sounding on the polished floor. Sheynon watched with care, sampling his meal, as Aeren and Chitthra spoke quietly together.

At last Sheynon rose and walked to his brother's side. "Angst fills your heart and I know the reasons. Years have passed, Brother, and the Purge no more. Should you speak of it, our lady friends would surely listen."

Ysilrod nodded wordlessly, then drank and blew a breath. They returned to the table, sitting as the women watched with care.

"Did the stains upon the throne room floor catch your careful eye?" asked Ysilrod. "Do you wonder of whose blood it was and how it came to pass?"

Chitthra looked to Sheynon as Aeren bowed her head. "I know of it," she said.

Ysilrod drank again. "My own blood, and spilled before the emperor of this city many years ago. We came with a purpose, done at the last, but not without its price." He poured his goblet full and looked away. "The Purge... you know of it?"

Chitthra nodded at the last. "Tales told only in whispers, and anger as a fire, driven by revenge. Yes, I know them well."

"Then you know it was Daeron Foxxe himself who slew the Forum Master of Vichelli during the Purge in single combat, took his very heart to the City-State of Truth, and held it before the emperor there. Yet not before my blood stained the marble floors." He looked to Aeren, pain upon his face and hers. "Not before the gracious lady Audrey Vincent was tortured in the dungeon. Not before..." His voice broke and he rose to walk away again.

"Lord Eledaur," said Sheynon, "and his madness, driven by the sword *Black Fire*. The duel between he and my brother, desecrated by our cousin Thalion Lahai, and the reconciliation following that near-breaking of our comradeship. Dark times, my ladies, darker than ever Ardwel has seen in many years. Ysilrod carries still those wounds, and thereafter, could not remain within the land. Only in these recent moons has he returned. And now we stand in the very city where it all began."

"I did not consider..." began Aeren, then signed herself.

Sheynon shook his head. "No matter, for neither did he nor I, yet here we sit. I pray this visit does not repeat the past."

Chitthra scoffed. "Surely Kaul would not think to harm us."

Aeren touched Chitthra's hand with hers. "I turned him away from the City-State of Truth. I held the prize he coveted so greatly from him, causing him to lose face before his followers. He may hold the lot of us as guilty."

"Would he take us prisoners for perceived digressions?" Chitthra nearly rose, yet Aeren begged pause and calm.

"The emperor of Vichelli himself did," replied Ysilrod, returning to the table. He sat in silence as they waited, casting looks of worry to each other. "As I do not know him, only may I say there is malevolence in his manner, but a touch of honor there as well."

"True," replied Aeren. "He might have crossed blades with me when last we met, yet held his hand. We shared a bond in our doings for Lord Sheynon, and he felt, if not responsibility, then at the least a mark of sympathy for Earion's wounding. He is not evil, only selfish and alone."

"We will not be held against our will in this city," said Ysilrod through clenched teeth. "I will protect us all by what ability I have."

Sheynon held a hand. "Care must be taken in our words. While we search for answers, he may anger quickly if we approach the truth."

Chitthra shook her head. "I do not understand."

"Consider," said Ysilrod, "he did not ask our reasons for appearing. Therefore, he knows of them already."

Aeren stared, aghast. "Dearest *Jhad*… the mad women arrived before us."

Ysilrod nodded. "And have offered, or will soon be offering, a pact. We know this now, and it must shape our message to him."

Chitthra chuckled. "My lord Sheynon, your brother's mind is sharpest I have seen." She raised her cup. "Let us plan therefore, not against Kaul, but against the evil where it seeks to hide."

Ysilrod touched his goblet to hers. "Bring him in, give him purpose in our venture, that he becomes the key to all. It will feed his ego and that, my ladies, is his weakness."

"I pray you are correct," said Aeren. "For if I know Kaul in the least, he may decide all of us, Mors'ul'jyn and Archane as well, are more trouble than we are worth."

* * *

Rohesia soon returned, and led them to a meeting hall much smaller than the throne room. Dust lay in corners, the table top showing signs of recent cleaning, and a stench of something dead hung within the air. Sheynon pointed to a rat's carcass in a niche, and Aeren only shook her head.

Servants set tea before them, a platter of withered greens, and meat appearing days old at best. "A message," said Sheynon quietly as they sat, "that he wishes we will not tarry in our words. He has seen us fed in the dining hall. All this simply says we are no longer welcome."

Ysilrod waved a hand before the table as the attendants took their exit. "Touch nothing, for I cannot vouch for safety."

"Is he so bold he would poison us?" Aeren drew her cloak about herself, for though it still was summer, the room was chill and dank.

Sheynon chuckled. "My thought is, this room is used rarely if at all. Surely Kaul prefers the throne room and its trappings."

"A place for murder, then," replied Chitthra. "Be on your guard, my friends. We may well need to fight our way beyond this place."

Kaul entered from a doorway at the side, and they stood as he approached. A gilded chair was set, and he took his place, then Sheynon and his charges sat again. Six guards entered, standing three aside, and Chitthra looked to Aeren, who shook her head and showed a frown.

"We ask privacy, Your Majesty," said Sheynon at the last, as guards stood with spears in hand and shields upon their arms. "Further, I would say this display is of intimidation. We come with urgent news regarding safety of the land."

Kaul shrugged. "Say your words. They are bound to silence."

Sheynon looked to Ysilrod and then the women and shook his head. "Therefore, we will depart. When prepared for dialogue, you may find us at my castle." He rose, as did the others.

Kaul held a hand and spoke quietly to one of the guards. After moments, they departed, and Sheynon sat once more. Chitthra and Aeren stayed standing for heartbeats, hard eyes on Kaul.

Ysilrod only watched, noting the door through which Kaul had come was heavy wood. He rounded the table slowly, touched a hand to the latch, then took his seat again. "Now we may parley," he said to Sheynon, "and without interruption."

Kaul showed a questioning eye, and Ysilrod only smiled.

Sheynon turned to Kaul once more. "The Drow woman you traveled with, known to you as Reena, and now Mors'ul'jyn… you have seen her in recent days, yes?"

The question caught them all off-guard, and Aeren glanced to Chitthra quickly.

Sheynon continued. "And Archane, the Dark Princess of the Drow, accompanied her. This we know, and would hear your thoughts upon it."

Kaul began to speak, then paused. "It is a private matter…"

Ysilrod scoffed. "Trust me, my lord, I have ability to tell a lie when spoken. I urge you tell the truth."

Kaul shifted in his chair. "Presuming your words are true, what of it? I rule herein, meet whom I wish, parley as desired. My business is my own and none of yours."

"Mors'ul'jyn is a murderess," said Sheynon tightly, "of Galandria Telveperen, my Joined, and mother of our children. Archane you know of well. Neither of these women are allies, true?"

"Kaul." Chitthra leaned across the table. "We were comrades once." Kaul coughed a laugh. "Tho' not seen for years, I may tell you, Mors'ul'jyn seeks Lord Sheynon and his children still, for events long past and none of their doing. We implore you, say what you know of them."

"I know nothing. I cannot tell you of their whereabouts."

"Yet you have seen them, yes?" Chitthra pressed her question.

Kaul exhaled sharply. "Days ago, perhaps half a moon. My wits were not about me at the time."

"Did they touch you?" asked Ysilrod. "Did you accept a gift or perhaps a kiss?"

Kaul shook his head. "Hair tied in ribbons. No, I did not partake of their pleasures, elf. I am not so simple."

The elf-mage nodded, breathing easier. "Perhaps you may allow me to inspect their gift."

"Why so?" asked Chitthra. Aeren shrugged, not understanding.

"A scry upon… His Majesty." Ysilrod nodded to Kaul. "We wish no harm upon him by these villains."

"What words did they have for you?" Sheynon's gaze met Kaul's, the Mongrel showing signs of worry now. "Recall my brother's warning regarding truth between us."

Kaul waved his hands aimlessly and shrugged. "They paused to reminisce. Reena… this Mors'ul'jyn to you… she and I have a past between us."

Ysilrod shook his head, and Kaul paled for but a heartbeat. He swallowed and continued. "Archane seeks her place again within the Drow. Mors'ul'jyn, perhaps beside her, and my thought was, power behind the Dark Princess. Still, after these years, the dark elves are formidable."

"What was their offer to you?" asked Aeren. "For I know you will do nothing without inducement."

Sheynon grimaced at her words, but knew them true.

They waited as Kaul locked eyes with Aeren. "You, false ally, know nothing of my way. You think yourself clever to hold the city-state from me, still I may have my due. Still, unfinished business lies between us."

"Enough of this," said Sheynon, looking Aeren in the eye, then once more to Kaul. "Tell us of their place. Drakenmoore, or do they seek *Ung'gu'wi's* depths?"

"I cannot say."

Ysilrod raised an eyebrow. "Cannot, or will not?"

Kaul snarled. "Threaten me not, elf. I have said what I know. They departed as they came, in a carriage. I thought best not to follow them."

"Wise," replied Chitthra. "Between the two of them, they might well have simply taken the city from you, had they wished. Provocation would have been a poor choice."

"You hold DragonFall," continued Sheynon, "therefore, what might their inducement be? You want not for treasure, hold power over vast farmland and other means of taxes to support your holdings." He waited for reply, yet Kaul held his peace. "Therefore, what might they offer?"

"There was no agreement, only talk."

"Very well," said Ysilrod suddenly. Sheynon looked to his brother, the women exchanging puzzled glances. "We thank you for your truthfulness. May we leave your city now?"

Kaul showed relief. "My guards will escort you to the city gates."

Ysilrod rose, as did the others. "Your hospitality is grand. We will speak again, I am certain. Perhaps my brother will discuss trade, should you wish it."

Sheynon held his tongue, knowing something stirred in his brother's mind. A glance aside to Chitthra, and she nodded, then took Aeren's hand and held it firmly.

Truth has been found, thought Sheynon, *and Ysilrod sees what we do not. Once on the road and safely from this place, he will speak of it. Until then, only do we seek escape before Kaul himself thinks of what has happened.*

They made their way beyond the meeting hall in silence.

* * *

Kaul railed. Between the elves, the Drow woman, and the skinny girl, they had all but drawn his plans from his very mouth. The memory of Stokar's shop, and the old half-elf's threat of knowing a lie if told, had set hard upon his mind throughout the meeting. And now, only was he saved by a bit of misdirection, and the elf-mage thinking he had won the knowledge wanted.

Kaul crossed quickly through the throne room and waved his guards away, turned into a darkened hallway leading to the harem. But there he paused, pressed a stone protruding slightly near the floor, and slipped into a sanctuary chamber. He had found the room only by accident, and furnished it as a secret hideaway. Another covert entrance led into the harem's deepest passage, and there, escape beyond the palace, should it be necessary.

This day, however, it was not. He entered quickly, and two female servants rose from the pillows in the corner. They stretched, bowed before him, and set about their tasks of seeing he was fed.

No word from Mors'ul'jyn or Archane. Ten days and I have heard nothing from them, no messenger, no secrets coming in the night, no "gifts" with meanings hidden. Have they set their plans in motion without my knowing? Dare I venture to Drakenmoore and attempt to dig them from beneath its ruins?

He sat as the servants brought a plate before him, filled with bread and meat and roasted corn. He ate slowly, hardly tasting of the meal, as the women hovered closely by. He glanced their way, knowing, should he wish it, they would disrobe and serve his lust or whatever his desire might be. Yet Kaul felt no lust. No desire. No need.

Five years, and how old I have become in that span of time. Surely it is only the missing of adventure, and the boredom of ruling a city I did not want. Dare I leave the city for a length of time? Who will rule in my stead, and might I return to find it held away? As did Aeren with the City-State of Truth. Damn her, and her righteousness! Damn them all, the gods and those who think they do their bidding.

The dark-haired servant poured wine before him, and as she did so, her light chemise drooped openly, showing tender flesh. Kaul grinned, drew her closer, and straddled her across his lap. She drew her gown away, breasts warm and firm cupped before his eyes. He laid his face between them, sighing, relishing the sensation of female skin and perfumed hair about his shoulders.

Soon. I will force Mors'ul'jyn to do my bidding. Archane... I will think of ways beyond her immortality. Rule of the Drow may become my way unto the city I desire. Yet for now...

He pushed away the thoughts and lost himself in the pleasures of his servant's offering.

* * *

93

In the depths of Drakenmoore…

Mors'ul'jyn watched as Archane paced before her. Days returned from Kaul's city-state, and having allowed the Dark Princess a respite from her prison, Mors'ul'jyn now pondered how best to proceed. She searched her mind for the vengeance sought those years ago against Calidriil, and found it missing from her thoughts.

Too much time away from the land, too much attention paid to Archane and how to deal with her. Years slipped through my fingers as I caught myself up in study, once more the student of the magics I held so closely in the past. Now what to do, with Archane, with Calidriil, with even Kaul. Do I truly wish to follow in this path and seek the rule of Drow through Archane? Dare I trust Kaul again, now that he wields power of his own?

"What say you?" Mors'ul'jyn spoke to pause Archane's incessant pacing. "What will you gift to Kaul for his aid, if anything?"

The Dark Princess turned a withering eye to Mors'ul'jyn. "I will not bed the brute, in certainty. I will leave that in your most capable hands."

Mors'ul'jyn did not rise to the insult, but only laughed. She poured wine and bade Archane to sit. They drank in quiet for a time, eyes locked, suspicious and contemplating in their look.

"Let us set aside our differences for the nonce. You seek to regain your stature. Therefore, if you have allies in the House of Iyllyeth, should I not know of them?"

Archane placed her cup before her. "You spent years as my servant. Surely you should know."

"Mor'i'jil, in certainty," replied Mors'ul'jyn, "tho' what if he no longer lives? Who, then?"

"If Mor'i'jil is dead, then likely those beneath him are as well, or have sworn fealty to another House. Only Hovenethra would be so bold as to attempt upon his life. If they should fail…"

Mors'ul'jyn nodded. "A purge, therefore, their leaders, the family, those closest in support. Yes, in these past years, blood has surely flowed freely in the caverns." She drank again. "Let us ponder consequences."

Archane shrugged. "If Mor'i'jil lives, I may return with little fanfare, tho' likely the Houses will press for answers and favors, should they align themselves with me. If he has not survived…"

"And therein comes Kaul's offer. An army not of Drow, seeking little besides gold, or perhaps the pleasures of what bounty they might take."

"Speak honestly. Do you believe Kaul will be satisfied with gold?" Archane poured wine and drank again.

"Dear lady, the power will rest in your hands alone." Mors'ul'jyn grinned wickedly. "And mine, as your consort, perhaps? Or shall I remain behind the curtain?"

"Never will you rule my people." Archane nearly hissed the words, though in her mind she wondered of the possibility.

"Let us, as said, put aside our disagreements. How best to proceed?"

Archane shrugged, an unladylike gesture. "First, gain Kaul's trust and agreement."

Mors'ul'jyn nodded. "What then? And how to confirm his bargain?"

"Take him to your bed. Pledge yourself in flesh and lust, giving to his desires. As you have spoken many times before, he was easily led by his maleness into whatever bidding you desired."

Mors'ul'jyn cast thoughts back, knowing in part the words were true. "Presuming I may garner such a promise, what then? What surreptitious thoughts might you have to find the happenings in *Ung'gu'wi*?"

"Likely there are Drow yet within the city-state, or better, farmers who once were soldiers, seeking a way back into the fold."

"A spy?" Mors'ul'jyn laughed again. "How bold! Intrigue and assassination, they go hand in hand, do they not?"

Archane paused until the room quieted again. "Then a better way, should you have it. I am listening."

"I propose a pledge, you and I, unto each other. No back-stabbing, no trickery, no lies, and no deceptions. Cooperation, between the two of us, unto this goal. Agreed?" Mors'ul'jyn raised her cup.

Archane raised hers as well, and they touched rims. "However..."

"Yes?"

"Should we be successful, what then? Once I rule again, what becomes of our... partnership?"

Mors'ul'jyn grinned fully now. "That, dear lady, is a question whose answer we may both find a surprising end."

* * *

The road beyond DragonFall...

Darkness halted their travels less than half a day beyond the walls of Kaul's city-state. Sheynon found a niche and set their camp, then built a fire as Chitthra and Aeren hunted for their meal. Shortly they returned, three rabbits and two squirrels in hand, and they roasted them in quiet, all contemplating Ysilrod's sudden leading their departure from the meeting.

At last, the elf-mage cast a spell about their camp, a wall of shimmering silence, that they could talk in private, should they have been shadowed unbeknownst.

"I would have known if we were followed," said Chitthra.

"And your judgement is accepted," replied Ysilrod, "yet to be certain, we are now free to speak our minds."

"Therefore, why did we leave so quickly?" asked Aeren. "I cannot reason in my mind your behavior."

Sheynon chuckled. "Trust my brother. More times than once I have seen his manner."

Quiet set upon them once again. Forest sounds soon filled the air and glowing eyes were seen beyond the campfire.

"My lord, speak if you will," said Aeren. "I grow weary of these games."

Ysilrod nodded. "To Kaul it is a game, and likely to the others it becomes one, with wits tested, plans made, contingencies projected, all casting lots to see who becomes the victor."

"Victor of what?" asked Chitthra. "Surely Archane desires her place again, and Mors'ul'jyn a chance to control her there. What else?"

"What is Kaul's desire?" Ysilrod looked round the fire. "Surely not their charms, for he has a harem. Gold? Perhaps to pay his mercenaries, thereby not drawing from his wealth. Land? If so, where? Drakenmoore's lands were overrun by settlers years ago, and *Ung'gu'wi* lies beneath the earth."

"Recall Kaul's brashness," said Chitthra. "Nearly did he attempt to seduce me in our first encounter."

Aeren laughed. "A sight to see, as you would lay him in his grave for such an insult."

"We made a pact therein, that we would guard each other's backs. With fortune, the time never came to do so."

"Always did he speak of kingship," added Aeren. "In the tavern, he boasted of it to any who would listen. And now he has it in his hands, yet still desires more."

"What is this regarding of a false alliance?" asked Ysilrod.

Aeren sighed. "Always was Kaul's eye upon the City-State of Truth, tho' how he thought to take it, I could never know. To him it was as a woman he could not possess, always wanted but never taken. He gave orders, explicit in their words, to hold the city against all enemies." She shrugged. "I deemed Kaul an enemy of the city, and when come to claim it, I held it away, with the city ministers beside me."

"You stood against him, with courage, as always, in your heart." Chitthra squeezed Aeren's hand and smiled.

"Say on, Brother," said Sheynon. "You have our interest piqued."

Ysilrod nodded to Aeren. "You show the way. Kaul desires power and the status it provides. It is my thought he seeks rule of the Drow."

Chitthra huffed a breath. "Archane would have his heart in her hand should he ever try."

"Not so." Aeren held a hand for pause. "If allied with Mors'ul'jyn, any goal becomes attainable."

Chitthra ruminated. "Mors'ul'jyn is, herself, insane. With lust for vengeance, lust for power, the thought of raising Drakenmoore from the ashes. Should she make a pact with Archane, surely it would only last long as it took the Dark Princess to regain her place."

"Power behind the throne?" asked Sheynon. "Archane was worshipped nearly as a goddess by her people. Should she return, alive and whole, will they not see this as a sign?"

Aeren nodded. "It would be thought a miracle, and those not falling into line would be cast out… or worse."

"Therefore," said Ysilrod, "Kaul seeks rule of the Drow. This came to me as a flash of insight, and I thought it best we leave before the thought was broached. Better Kaul thinks we have what was desired."

"Well thought, Brother." Sheynon smiled and poured cups around half-full. "What, then? We prepare as tho' we do not reason thusly, and in secret set our moves against him?"

"A fair question." Ysilrod sipped, pensive. "Let us think upon it. We may give him pause, or prepare an offer of our own, or simply remove him as a piece from the board of play."

Aeren paused her cup. "You think him dangerous as that, my lord?"

"My lady, I do, and not because he is so crafty, but his nature is as a beast. In Kaul's mind the world still is against him, and whatever he must do to survive, he will gladly pay the cost."

* * *

They bedded as the darkness deepened, stars bright above and *Mina* rising in the east. Ysilrod cast spells of protection, that they would not need a sentry in the night.

Chitthra knelt in meditation 'neath an oak tree, considering the day's events. *Should Ysilrod's musing be correct, the land lies in peril once again, this time from those known well in manner. Yet would Kaul risk loss of DragonFall to gain rule over the Drow? Dare I take this further, that Kaul, with the might of dark elf*

97

sorcerers and priests, would take war to the City-State of Truth itself? Why has Archane not attempted such? Because she knew it would cost her life if failed? Yet if she is in truth immortal, how would this play? Those knowing of it would not offer her as a sacrifice upon the altar, but one whose life would be lived in chains?

She raised her face to the sky above. "Dearest *Din'daeron'dae*, I pray this is the answer. I must speak with Sheynon and his brother come morning of my revelation!"

She calmed herself, gave benediction, and retreated to her bedroll in the niche. Sheynon slept closely to his brother in a copse away from the rock and outcrop, and as Chitthra drew deeper in her blankets, their quiet voices lulled her nearly into sleep.

A snap of twig brought her instantly awake. She turned as Aeren knelt beside her, face filled with angst Chitthra could nearly taste. She reached a hand beyond her blanket and Aeren rolled into her arms. Chitthra held her as she trembled, wondering of the cause. At last she drew away and looked into Aeren's eyes. "Tell me of your troubles and I will listen with my heart."

Aeren laid her head on Chitthra's shoulder. "I thought this done years ago, and I took the task of aiding in the city-state. You were gone, and I mourned you as a sister lost, but other feelings lay beneath those known. I knew not if you lived, or died in some happenstance I was not aware of." She slid her hand beneath the blanket, resting it on Chitthra's hip. "I knew only that I missed you dearly, and prayed for your safety every night."

Aeren rose up, tossed away her tunic, and slid beneath the covers. She took Chitthra's hand to her breast and held it there. "Touch me with your loving hands. Show the meaning of the offer you made years ago, and teach me of a woman's love."

Chitthra held her words, eyes locked with Aeren's, barely a hand's-width apart. She unlaced her tunic slowly, and Aeren helped her wriggle from it. They embraced, close and warm together, breast to breast, hands touching and exploring, sensations growing warm and real. They giggled nearly as little girls as they shucked their breeches from beneath the blanket, wrapped their legs about each other, and gently shared a breath.

Chitthra's hands roamed Aeren's curves, pressing hard against her slenderness.

Aeren's urgency grew, female flesh hot with desire, and they found a rhythm, bodies growing slick with sweat. Her ecstasy enfolded her, higher, higher, exploding nearly in the stars above.

Chitthra tensed, crushed herself once more to Aeren's body, panting out her pleasures, a scream of raw delight held within her throat.

In moments, they lay curled tightly in each other's arms, entwined, adored, satiated as not before.

At the last, and for long and tender heartbeats, they kissed.

BOOK FOUR
CROSSINGS

"You have heard the rumors of Vichelli,
and of Drow soldiers crossing at the Silver River, yes?
If so, why are you, a veteran of Coronis' liberation,
waiting in this tavern?"

Anon Gûl to Drakkon, at the
Green Dragon Inn in Jeseriam

The City-State of Truth...

Thalion's column rode through the villages below the city-state, noting markets brimming with summer bounty and merchants briskly doing business. Little mind was paid to soldiers weaving through the towns, other than a call by women round the taverns to join their company and share whatever then might come.

The priest spoke with the captain to release the column, as Thalion was certain he would not be attacked between the last village and the city gates only leagues away. Quickly, and with enthusiasm, Thalion's soldiers dispersed, only the captain and his bodyguard remaining.

As they topped the rise on which the great city rested, a trail of wagons beyond the walls was seen. Draped in colors bold, of red and blue and silver, Thalion's heart leapt, knowing well the livery. He spurred his horse to a gallop, and the captain's guard was hard-pressed to keep him in their sight.

Slowing near the largest of the wagons, Thalion dismounted, running up the hill, calling out a name. "Audrey! Audrey Vincent!"

From out the wagon came a presence; tall and fully-figured, dressed in breastplate and a flowing skirt of azure silk, she stood formidable as ever. Though her dark hair showed streaks of gray, and her freckled face the lines of leadership deep around her eyes, Thalion knew her simple beauty well.

He paused before her and bowed, deeply and with respect. She returned the gesture, then they embraced for the first time in far too many years.

"*Jhad* brings me to your company again, my lord... my dearest friend." She hugged him closely, and he nestled in her arms, tears leaking from his eyes in heartfelt remembrance. She wept quietly, and tears mingled, then held him away, kissed his cheek, and hugged him once again.

Never did Thalion want to let her go.

* * *

Thalion made introductions, and the captain bowed, awe showing in his face. The priest bade him take word to the palace, that Ardwel's own Champion had returned.

Attendants set a table, poured wine and stood away as Audrey and Thalion simply gazed into each other's eyes, memories between them nearly palpable.

"I… what, pray tell, brings you to Ardwel again, Excellency?" Thalion could barely force the words from his mouth, so happy he was in seeing her again.

Audrey smiled, offered him a seat, then sat herself and slowly ate. "Your pardon, we had only just arrived. I have not eaten this day, my excitement grew so much."

They partook in silence, neither wanting to disturb the magic felt between them.

"More than twenty years," said Thalion at the last. "And you appear at our doorstep, so to say." He smiled wistfully. "Too long, Excellency, and with realms to tend and children round, we both follow lives once only dreamt of."

"Your lady is well? Soon I hope to see Celeste again. And your children!" Audrey sipped and motioned to the rebuilt walls about the gateway. "Her letters told of Crysalon and Archane. And Aeren, standing at his side against the evil. My protégé, it seems, was brash as I."

Thalion only nodded. "Your teachings show in her glowing spirit. Now she holds the city dear, and with the ministers around her, learns the task of ruling. Some day she will rise to heights she still knows nothing of."

"And herein I return," replied Audrey. She waited for Thalion to speak, yet he held his peace. "As does the evil, Lord Priest. You know I cannot stand apart."

He nodded once more and blew a breath. "And all this time I thought perhaps this was but a cordial visit." They laughed quietly together, then silence came again.

"Tell me of it and spare no words. If we are to take up the sword once more, I must know it all."

Thalion shrugged. "Your squire left the city some days ago with a dark elf woman by name of Chitthra, a companion in the fight against Archane's armies. Celeste says they had the look of adventure in their eyes."

Audrey sighed. "Already she is entangled in the fight. Surely they seek counsel with the elves."

"So says Celeste, and yes, my thought is, Sheynon has made himself involved as well."

"Old friends and comrades, coming together one last time. How exciting!" Audrey grinned fully now, and Thalion caught the twinkle in her eye.

"You, my lady, are in need of our city's mead and close talk. My fear is, we may see more excitement than wished."

Audrey set her cup away. "If evil comes, we will stand against it as before. Until I leave this world, Thalion, I will hold fast in its protection. Ardwel is my second home, and I keep it dear."

Thalion thought for moments. "Aeren's letters. Therefore, you return."

"And dreams, Lord Priest, and *Jhad* whispering in my ear at night. Husband Higar said I spoke while sleeping near ten days. He bade me come, to find respite for my soul and tend my friends in need. Tho' yes, Aeren's letters said of deep concerns. Archane not seen for many years, the one known as Mors'ul'jyn likely gone. You and I know, as Aeren herself has learned, when the land is quiet, it means evil sets its plans again."

Thalion ate slowly from his meal, thinking all the while. "You feel we have not kept our vigilance?"

"The thought occurred," replied Audrey at the last. "We grow older, our children not understanding our deep apprehensions, having not lived those horrors. Still the old enemies remain, driven by agenda as before. Time is our true enemy, and if only we can set the righteous path, what choice have we in the end but fight?"

* * *

They met in the palace garden, Thalion having sent a messenger from the gates to Celeste herself, and Audrey embraced Thalion's wife and accepted bows from their daughters; Anne, the older, and *Lo'theril'lë, Bright Flower*, both young women now, no longer the little girls Thalion yet recalled them as. "Too many moons spent away in the castle, defending the eastern borders."

They joined hands around the table as the priest gave blessings on their bounty.

The daughters only watched Audrey closely, awed nearly into silence. At the last *Lo'theril'lë* raised a question. "My lady… Excellency… you have a family, yes?"

Audrey nodded, smiling. "Two sons, Thomas and Vincent, and a daughter younger than are you, her name Rebecca."

"Your realm is vast, says Mother." Anne offered fresh greens to Audrey as they talked. "Yet so much is sand, how do the people live?"

105

"Cities underground, and now dwarves teach of irrigation, to grow the oases further in the land. My son Thomas is learning of the way, and will teach it further to our soldiers."

"Underground cities, such as *Ung'gu'wi?*" *Lo'theril'lë* asked. The table was silent for a moment. "Your pardon, I did not intend discomfort on our meal."

Thalion took her hand. "No ill intent is taken. And yes, Her Excellency will tell you of the Gnome cities in the desert."

"RasTa'nurra is nearly large as this city-state itself," said Audrey, and *Lo'theril'lë's* eyes grew wide. "Gnome guards keep the city safe, as do those of this city-state at the gates. And dwarves keep the sands free of bandits."

"Dwarves?" Anne showed surprise. "In Ardwel they are solitary in the hills. The city trades with them for gold and other metals."

Audrey nodded, smiling. "Tarnak, a trusted friend, and dwarf-brothers from Ardwel and mountains in the north. Pacts were made between cities in the Kingdom of the Sun, and now they, as well, trade with dwarves."

"Your realm thrives, as does Ardwel," said Celeste, offering bread and honeyed butter. "Yet your visit is more than this."

Thalion and Audrey traded glances. "True, and I would speak with your ministers when prudent," replied the warrior-woman with much care.

"Might we ask?" Anne showed interest, and *Lo'theril'lë* listened closely.

Thalion nodded to Audrey. "They are learning of this city's rule and how the Church involves itself. Anne is an acolyte of the Order and *Lo'theril'lë* studies with the ministers. I see this as opportunity to show the world's working from your mind and how opinions differ."

"Very well. Our comradeship comes together once again." Audrey motioned to Thalion, then Celeste. "We three, the family Calidriil, Steffyn Foxxe, with others no longer in the world or gone from our presence, met the evil fairly, and with the grace of gods, yours, mine, and of the elves, fought for its demise. Thrice, my ladies, have we assembled. Now, once more."

"Aeren becomes a part, does she not?" asked *Lo'theril'lë*. "Minister Arna bade me learn at her side. Tho' still young, I see your teachings in her manner. Now we sit at table, and I know the wisdom of my parents, that they fought by your side. In honesty, I am awed."

Audrey blushed and bowed gently in her chair. "That aside, work comes to us once again. And tho' older, still we fight as necessary."

Thalion showed a toothy grin. "I have found the enthusiasm of youthfulness may be countered easily by age and cunning," he jested.

Audrey and Celeste grinned, raising cups to each other. "We seek the reasons for unrest," said the warrior-woman.

"There is unrest?" Anne looked to Thalion quickly. "Father, the land is now at peace, and has been so for years. Archane is gone, and we learn of Crysalon's sacrifice to rid the land of her."

Thalion motioned attendants to clear the table, then led them to a sitting room for privacy. They arranged themselves as wine and mead were poured, holding their peace until at last the door was closed. He leaned forward in his heavy leather chair, elbows on his knees, eyes stern upon his daughters. "Where did Archane go? This is the reason for our concerns, and as the land has calmed, still this question is unanswered."

"That and others," said Celeste.

Thalion nodded at the last. "This Mors'ul'jyn, murderess of Galandria Telveperen, pledging vengeance upon Calidriil for… things done in the past."

"Things as what, Father?" asked Anne.

Once more, glances were traded round by Audrey, Celeste, and Thalion.

"Great misunderstandings, having consequences for more years than you have been alive," said Celeste at the last.

"I do not understand," said *Lo'theril'lë*. "Yet I hear truth withheld before me. Why so?"

Thalion shook his head. "We hold truths that cannot be undone. Still, good has come of it, as you have said."

Silence filled the room, and Audrey bowed her head for quiet moments, then drank from her goblet.

"Let us set aside these differences and think upon this day." Celeste laid a hand to Anne's shoulder. "In time, we will speak of other things."

"Where is Archane, therefore?" asked *Lo'theril'lë*. "Minister Arna says no trace was found of her or Crysalon. Only Aeren, it seems, survived."

"Dear lady, we have no answers," said Audrey. "I am here to find the truth of it, and see the evil ended once again. If Archane lives, we know ways to deal with her."

Thalion thought for moments, then nodded. "Blessed steel. Yes, now I understand your coming."

"Only your weapon, *Gil Estel*," whispered Celeste. She raised her holy symbol from the chain around her neck and pressed it to her forehead.

"Father… no." Anne's eyes began to fill with tears.

"There is no other way, dear child," said Audrey. "The world must be rid of her forever."

Celeste held her daughter closely as she cried. *Lo'theril'lë* said nothing, fighting back tears of her own.

"May all the gods be with us once again," whispered Thalion, then held his younger daughter close.

* * *

The night was late as Thalion and Audrey walked the palace garden. *Mina* hung at zenith, full and bright nearly as a lantern. Fountains bubbled in the darkness and voices drifted from the temple singing benediction.

Little had they said since departing the palace doors. Celeste bade them speak plainly with each other as she calmed the daughters, worried now of their father's deep considerations.

"We know her manner, Thalion, and have seen her rise from death, not once, but twice. There is but one way to deal with a creature of this sort."

The priest nodded as they paced their way amongst the flowers and shrubbery, and the quiet of the night.

"I would not ask, but we have faced so much together." Audrey slowed her pace and turned to the priest.

"Had you *Calawen* still, it would not matter."

Audrey caught a breath. She knew E'dhel'wen, once the Spirit of the Sword *Calawen*, was somewhere in the land, though the bond they shared had quieted. *I cannot ask of her what she can no longer give, and I will not risk the life returned by her great lord for such a danger. No, this falls to us and family Calidrül, so deeply are they involved.*

"That time is passed," Audrey replied at last, eyes cast downward. "You and I, Sheynon and perhaps his brother. Yet where is Steffyn Foxxe, my lord? A sorcerer such as he is would give us advantage."

Thalion shook his head. "Excellency, he is gone."

"Please, only Audrey. We are in no presence but our own."

They took seats on a wooden bench and sat close by. He gazed into the night as Audrey waited patiently, whispering a prayer.

"Sheynon penned a letter on Galandria's death, sent by courier and telling of… Steffyn's complicity."

Audrey drew a breath and shook her head.

"Not as you think, but had he acted, Galandria yet would be alive. He thought to trap this Mors'ul'jyn, tho' she was more clever than was thought. He confessed to Sheynon and was forgiven, yet still he could no longer live in such a world."

"He is… dead?"

"None know, my lady, not even his wife Emildir. Nearly twenty years have passed since she saw him last. More than five since his admission to Sheynon of his guilt."

"Dearest *Jhad*… Sheynon said no words of this to me in his missives since. I am… saddened, Thalion, that his spirit carries such a burden I knew nothing of."

"That now is passed, and we must face the threat with all we have. Yet where shall we look for Archane if she lives? Truly, my mind has been on other matters."

Audrey laid a hand on his. "Together, Lord Priest, and we will go first to one who surely has the answers."

Thalion raised an eyebrow. "The elves?"

Audrey smiled.

* * *

Annatar Yarhetha'an…

Two days more upon the road and they returned to Sheynon's castle once again. They took up the task of plans against Archane and plans against Mors'ul'jyn, should she be found.

"Kaul seeks rule of the Drow, then to bring war upon the land and subjugation," said Chitthra as they stood at a table filled with maps and writings. "It came to me at prayer, and *Din'daeron'dae* leads my heart."

"Your words hold truth," replied Ysilrod, sitting at the side. "We have conspiracy between the three of them, I am certain."

Sheynon shook his head. "Archane desperate for return of her place and rule, Mors'ul'jyn seeking power behind the dark elf throne, and Kaul to displace them both."

Aeren raised her face and asked a simple question. "Which would be preferred?"

The room was quiet as glances passed between them all, then Sheynon began to chuckle. Laughter spread, and soon all were wiping tears of amusement from their eyes. Sheynon motioned to the doorway, and they took time in the garden, sitting in the sun.

"Your point is made, my lady, and very well," said Ysilrod at the last, still grinning. "Yet there is another task needing to be done."

Chitthra nodded understanding. "How to know, and when. We cannot wait until the Drow army sets upon the world."

"Might a scrying spell be set?" asked Sheynon.

Ysilrod shook his head. "Not within *Ung'gu'wi*, Brother, as my magics would be noticed. I will think upon the matter."

Attendants soon approached, handing Sheynon a message tied with golden ribbons. "From a herald, my lord, come this very morning," said one of their number.

Sheynon nodded, untied the ribbons, and read slowly to himself. His eyes widened, and a smile began to form. He looked to Ysilrod, the elf-mage tilting his head in query. "We are to receive guests once more, Brother. From the City-State of Truth."

Ysilrod grinned. "Cousin Thalion? How long has it been?"

Sheynon turned to Aeren. "And another, my lady, dear to you."

Nearly did Aeren leap from her seat. "My liege? Audrey Vincent is in the land again?" She turned and embraced Chitthra, then sat once more, weeping tears of joy.

* * *

Quickly Sheynon set an honor guard about the gatehouse as Ysilrod cast a bridge across the chasm. A column then was seen, riding on the rocky plain, two wagons following with livery of red and blue and silver.

Aeren had quickly donned her armor, slung her sword and waited, nervous as a kitten. Chitthra stood beside her, their hands entwined, as riders came before them.

Sheynon greeted Thalion, embracing the half-elf priest for the first time in many years. Ysilrod followed quickly, then Aeren knelt as Audrey dismounted from her steed.

The warrior-woman laid a hand on Aeren's shoulder. "Rise, dearest Aeren, and stand before me in your successes. You have become a light in Ardwel of your own accord."

They embraced, and Aeren bade Chitthra join her. "Excellency, Chitthra of the Brotherhood. More now than a friend, a companion close as ever I could ask for."

Chitthra bowed. "From *Din'daeron'dae's* teachings I greet you, Excellency. Your legend is bright in the Brotherhood of *Däe Quivïe*.

Audrey looked Chitthra in the eye and smiled. "All the gods show us miracles each day. Well met, my lady, and we will trade many stories, I am certain."

Chitthra bowed again as Ysilrod and Sheynon stood before Audrey. They bowed as well, then found themselves embraced in Audrey's arms.

110

"So many memories herein," said Sheynon quietly, his arm around Ysilrod's slender shoulders.

"Best of times and worst," replied Thalion, and they shared a simple laugh.

Sheynon passed orders down the way to see the escorts fed and sheltered. "First, for the both of you, rooms to clean and dress. Then we will find the garden once again and speak of things done and things yet to come."

"Legends stand before me," said Chitthra, and Aeren at her side nodded slowly. "Soon we will set the way to deal with what now threatens. My thought is, evil should be wary."

* * *

The night was late, Thalion and Audrey having retired to their beds, fatigued from the long ride across the plains to *Annatar Yarhetha'an.* Ysilrod retreated to his workshop, bidding Sheynon a good eve, as the castle lord took solitude in the garden once again.

Chitthra left the bed, kissing Aeren lightly upon the cheek, then smiled, their hands entwining for a moment. The dark elf woman donned an evening robe and took her exit, asked Sheynon's whereabouts of the nightly guard, then found her way softly through the castle.

She stepped into the garden and came to Sheynon's side. "My lord, I would ask a moment of your time."

Sheynon turned, then motioned to a chair close by, and Chitthra took her seat.

"Wine or mead, my lady? Perhaps a brandy to aid your sleeping." The elf-lord smiled, awaiting Chitthra's questions.

"I would speak to you of honor needing to be done."

Sheynon nodded. "Insults given by Kaul to your beloved. Yes, I understand."

"An issue Aeren will address, should come the time. I speak of this Mors'ul'jyn and her crimes against your family."

Sheynon looked away, moonlight playing on his face. "We will deal with her as plans progress and opportunity arises. Five years I have waited. Another year will not matter."

Chitthra held her words for moments as an attendant set a glass of scented brandy at her side, bowed and took her exit. "I speak of an oath, given to my Brotherhood and myself, protection of your family from the evils of Mors'ul'jyn. In that, I have failed, and only now can I become Galandria's reconciler."

111

Sheynon showed a grim look of face. "You may stand in line, my lady, for I claim first chance. She was my wife, mother of our children, and leader of the elves. Her death brought more heartache than you will ever know."

Chitthra nodded. "That place now is yours, as my opportunity was taken from me. I speak of one known well to you, who held my hand against my very will. Your elf-brother, Steffyn Foxxe."

Sheynon swallowed hard and shook his head. "What is this you speak of?"

"On capturing Mors'ul'jyn, I set myself to end her life." Chitthra's words hung in the night as Sheynon motioned her to continue. "Steffyn Foxxe held my ability away, then sent us both into oblivion for eternity. I was to guard her there, the Black Blade itself a prison."

Chitthra sipped from her glass and blew a breath. "A task I accepted on my failure, for my oath as *Däe Quivïe* was broken. My life was forfeit, not once, but twice. And while I relinquish to you the dealing with Mors'ul'jyn, I cannot stand apart from the duty now before me in dealing with Steffyn Foxxe."

"You cannot seriously consider —"

"My lord, it does not matter if I live or die. Steffyn Foxxe, one dear to you as companion and friend for many years, is complicit in the death of Galandria Telveperen as Mors'ul'jyn herself. The power was his to stop it. He did not, and for reasons of his own, which I have heard. But no matter.

"I am honor-bound to speak as I have done. The choice now is yours how to proceed. If it be your wish, I will leave this night, and never will you see me from this day forward."

Sheynon said nothing as she waited in the darkness. At last he waved a hand. "You are dearest to the protégé of a legend in this land. Never would I drive you from her for any reason. I beg you think upon this, and as matters come before us one by one, we will find a way between us."

"I have considered, and I cannot stand apart. When time comes, my lord, if Foxxe is found, I will do as I must for honor's sake." Chitthra rose and bowed, then disappeared through the doorway to the castle.

For many moments Sheynon did not move and barely breathed, wondering how this new revelation now would play.

* * *

Chitthra slid her lithe form between the blankets, turned her back to Aeren, and quietly wept into the pillows. She had done as honor there required, given notice of intentions, and now awaited destiny. Might Sheynon yet cast her out? It was her thought he would do no such thing, hoping against all hope he might convince her of the fallacy within her plan.

Sheynon is honorable if nothing else. Never would he send agents as assassins. Yet he, himself, was once a thief, skilled in covert means. Must I watch my back? I cannot involve Aeren in this doing, for it is not her place. And should she know of it, she would insist to guard my life with hers. What have I done, other than set matters worse than they were before?

She rose and walked to the window ledge, opened the shutters, and gazed away to the ruins of Ardoch in the distance. *So much history therein, and now Sheynon holds it hostage against Coronis in truth. Tho' numbed as all the land by Galandria's death, still Old City thinks itself the leader of the elves. Only hearty spirits keep the evil there at bay, Knights of the Flame, Eirioch, Jewelle Chandler, and Leyland Ashling. A bold stroke, to stand before the holy ground of Ardoch, that Conservatives in Coronis would see him lead by deeds and hold them to their vows.*

A sound from the bed, and Chitthra turned to Aeren, standing quiet behind her. They embraced, softly kissed, and stood together, *Mina's* silvery light shining on their faces.

"I dreamed again," said Aeren, "of blood to come, tho' not of mine. I fear we have woken a sleeping giant, and must be vigilant."

Chitthra raised her face to Aeren's. "My lady, there is a thing I must do, as I am bound by honor of my Brotherhood. It is not a thing you may enter into, for I will not put your life or soul at risk."

Aeren looked Chitthra in the eye. "You seek Steffyn Foxxe. Still, I cannot think him guilty of any crime."

"He is guilty for not preventing of a crime he had the power to avert, and chose not to do so. Sheynon knows, as Steffyn begged forgiveness and was granted such. Thalion knows, as he is cousin to Calidriil and of the family. Your liege knows, as Thalion himself would have imparted it, and they band together once again, not only to face the evil of Archane, but the evil allowed to continue by Steffyn Foxxe."

"He is not evil, Chitthra. Misguided, confused, perhaps driven mad by his own inaction. Tho' not evil."

"I love you." Chitthra's eyes filled with tears.

Aeren caught her breath. "Never have I heard such words from dark elf lips."

"Yet I say it now, and to you wholly and completely, for there may not be another time. Whatever follows, do not think ill of me, should I do what must be done or die because of it." Chitthra took Aeren in her arms with tenderness and held her as the light of *Mina* filled the room. "Nothing comes that would not have done so, regardless our involvement, notwithstanding Archane's living. This is honor speaking in my heart, and I must follow."

"Yet now we stand in strength, giving pause to darkness as it gathers."

"Together, Dearest."

"Together," whispered Aeren. "Undefeated."

* * *

The depths of Ung'gu'wi…

Mor'i'jil drew the blankets tighter as his concubine curled herself about his body, giving warmth. Always did he awaken cold, even with her close and tightly held. Age, he knew, set upon him every day, yet still his mind was sharp, if worried.

Again, the dreams come just before I wake, he thought. *Again, I shiver as tho' death seeks to drag me into darkness and freeze the very bones within me.*

The concubine whispered devotions into his aged ears, took his maleness in her hands, aroused him, then drew him in and warmed him with her movements. He let her take him to near-ecstasy, then she would slow, and begin again until her warmth had fully woken him. Only then would she complete her task, her womanhood drinking every drop of essence from him as he clung to her, heart thundering in his ears, and gasped his pleasure into her fragrant hair.

He would drift away once more, then wake and find himself alone, blankets tossed aside and muscles cooling slowly. It then was time for him to rise.

He waited as his servants bathed him, fed him, and poured morning wine into his cup. All the while he thought upon another day without Archane, and wondered how much longer he could keep the Race from collapsing of its own selfish notions.

At last he donned his vestments, as this was a day of sacrifice to come, and while acolytes gathered in the waiting chamber, a servant brought a missive tied with cording the color of the sea.

From Hovenethra. Mor'i'jil grimaced and unlaced the message, read it quickly and looked the messenger in the eye. She cringed, and he raised a hand in pause. "Your heart is not in peril. Wait beyond the door and I will pen a reply."

The woman bowed and exited quickly as she could. Mor'i'jil chuckled grimly. *Too many of these messengers have been victim of their duties. I will not succumb to the other Houses' wrath upon those who have no part.*

He waved away the servant dusting his shoes and made way to the waiting throng of priests beyond his chamber.

* * *

M or'i'jil called the *Burzn'kraes,* the *Black Web,* to the council chamber, waited wrapped in wool as they gathered in the Circle. The Dark Priestess Alystin came before him, bowed, and took her place at his left side. Others, too, the priests Molva'yas and Narlros, and the youngest of them Xa'lyyth, a priestess known to have been a favorite of Archane. All gave reverence to Mor'i'jil and sat, arrayed about a warming fire and delicacies at their sides on simple tables, as mute and deaf servants waited round the room.

Mor'i'jil led chanting prayers, small sacrifices tossed into the fire, and as the room warmed and filled with the scent of burning animal flesh, they raised cups of wine tinged with the sacrificial blood. Then drank, awaiting Mor'i'jil's first words.

He raised the message sent. "Hovenethra claims right of Household, demanding conclave be called. Five years Archane has been lost to us, and the Race suffers for it. They seek not only leadership, but hint at conspiracy and guilt."

Molva'yas shrugged his shoulders 'neath a blanket. "This is nothing not seen in past times, done when a year had passed, then three, as I recall. Now five, and it is the same." He chuckled. "Is the wording unalike, or perhaps the message is a copy?"

The others did not share the jest as Mor'i'jil looked hard upon him.

"What say our searchers, Dark Lord?" asked Xa'lyyth. "Is there yet no sign since the Seers' words more than a moon ago?"

The priest Narlros gave the woman a withering look. "How might there be, if five years of searching has yielded nothing?"

"We may hold hope and offer sacrifice on the Dark Moon again," replied Xa'lyyth. "My own concubine has offered."

"The Seer giving of those words was sacrificed." Mor'i'jil grimaced, recalling the old woman's wails as he had cut away her heart and held it before her dying eyes. "False prophesy and suggestion of occurrence brought angst among those knowing of it. Their crèche now will be more careful of their duties."

115

"What harm is there in calling conclave?" asked Alystin. "It was done before, and no one died of it."

"Other rumblings," said Molva'yas, and Mor'i'jil raised an eyebrow. "Dark Lord, this very night I was approached by acolytes of Karachitthra asking favors."

"Of what sort?" Mor'i'jil shivered beneath his blanket, and a concubine slipped her naked slenderness beneath the wool and held him closely. "Why did you not come earlier with this?"

Molva'yas nodded apology. "Dark Lord, so many rumors, so much of dissention in the Race, how to know what is the truth? Should we follow every utterance, we might search forever."

"Therefore, would we do so," replied Alystin before Mor'i'jil could speak. "Archane must be found or the Race will fall to war within itself."

They traded glances round, then looked beyond their shoulders to the brace of guards. "All here would be sought by assassins," said Xa'lyyth softly. "Or as sacrifice."

"Only as we search do the Houses stand together. If no trace is found soon, we cannot hold them back." Narlros sipped from a goblet, then drank a healthy draught.

Molva'yas raised a hand. "Should rumors persist..." He looked to Mor'i'jil, then the others, one by one.

Alystin slowly nodded. "Sign, perhaps? A clue or article found far afield? Hope, to keep focus as we gather strength?"

"We have strength," said Mor'i'jil, the concubine still holding him closely by. "Warinethra stands with us, Modennethra will do as necessary against Hovenethra with... inducements. Karachitthra has no ability, save concubines and pleasures." He glanced to the woman in his blanket, who smiled at his words. "And always will deception return unwanted wrath. No, we stand with truth. Still we search, and pray to *Iyllyeth* for guidance."

"What then?" Alystin drew her cloak tighter. "How to hold the Race in our hands while searching. Five years we have spoken thus."

Xa'lyyth pondered. "Keep vigil, see those with questions share tasks, and are shown to be needed." She nodded to Mor'i'jil. "I will take this message to Hovenethra, should you command it, Dark Lord."

Mor'i'jil considered, knowing the young priestess sought his favor, yet could not discredit her within the Circle. At last he nodded. "Do so, yet we will show respect. Dark Priestess Alystin will stand beside you in this duty. Take word, and see Hovenethra understands their place."

* * *

116

It came to Mor'i'jil as he drifted in his sleep, his concubine gently snoring in her slumber at his side. The Lancer Captain's sorties into the land, with his soldiers dressed as merchants making way about the city-states, had found no trace of Archane. Yet on her disappearance, the City-State of Truth, humankind's ruling place, was filled with stories of a battle in the palace garden. Only had the *Black Web* concluded this was Archane's struggle against the demi-god called Crysalon, ruling humans with a fist of iron and laws unchallenged. Tales said of Crysalon's disappearance in that battle, and no trace of his assailant. Once more, the *Black Web*, with prayers and Seer's confirmation, accepted it was Archane who had vanished there as well.

Yet...

Supposing someone else had come?

Supposing Archane's body was taken from the gardens as they turned into a conflagration of unholy fire, chaos reigning in the city.

Supposing Archane had been found, wounded, spirited away, and held a prisoner. All for five long years.

Who might have this power and ability, a place none in the world could find, away from searchers and from soldiers? Away from Seer's visions? Away from prayers and sacrifices?

Great power would be essential. The power of a god? Perhaps. Had this Crysalon taken Archane's body where none mortal might ever find her? A possibility, yet Mor'i'jil, in his near-slumber, could not accept it.

Reflect on mortals with the ability.

Reflect on those who knew Archane for who and what she was.

Reflect on those who would be an enemy and seek advantage.

He woke, shaking with revelation. He knelt away in prayer, seeking solace, and giving thanks too many times to count for *Iyllyeth's* guidance.

He called his servants, sat and penned a missive with trembling hands. He sealed it, wrapped it in dark ribbons as he summoned a messenger. "To the Lancer Captain of the Household Guard. Be quick! Bring him to me on this night."

The servant bowed, ran from the room, as others poured wine and waited quiet for orders before their lord. The concubine rose, came to his place and knelt before him, cupped her breasts and licked her lips sensuously.

Mor'i'jil sighed and nodded to the pillows. "Return to your slumber. Should need arise, you may give your pleasures to the Lancer Captain once reply is come."

The concubine smiled graciously and bowed, laid upon the bed and teased the Dark Priest's eyes with intimate fingers upon herself, smiling all the while.

* * *

The priestess Alystin, with Xa'lyyth and guards arrayed, met with Hovenethra's clergy in the depths of the Black Forest, the silvery moon high in the sky and the orb called *Selene* by humans rising in the east. Lualyrr the priestess, and Ry'lld, a younger male, stood apart, twenty Hovenethra soldiers alert and close.

Alystin bowed before them. "*Iyllyeth's* blessings on your House, and we give thanks for your time and consideration."

The Hovenethra clergy nodded, yet did not reply.

Alystin continued after glances to the younger Xa'lyyth. "Word comes from Mor'i'jil, Archane's minister and Dark Lord of *Iyllyeth*. His message is a simple one. We continue to scour the land in search of the Dark Princess. Aid is needed, and from all the great Houses of the Race, that her place may be found wherever she may be."

"Archane is gone," replied Lualyrr, before Alystin could continue. "We search no more. It is time new leadership was chosen, and Hovenethra claims right of conclave for that purpose. Should Mor'i'jil or others of your House desire to lead, let them lay claim before all the council."

"Mor'i'jil does not disagree." Xa'lyyth waved a hand, dismissing threats implied. "Yet we would ask, as you say Archane is gone, what proof is offered? No trace found, no artifacts, no body, no remains. Say your reasons, for should she yet live and return, those taking power may rue the day."

"Such impudence from the young is expected." Lualyrr chuckled. "Give your pleasures to Mor'i'jil and I am certain you will find a place in his entourage. Little more do you have to offer."

"Insults bear no fruit," replied Xa'lyyth, head high. "Reply to my mentor Alystin's words, should you have such. Else keep silent and learn decorum."

A tense quiet settled, and at the last Lualyrr bowed to Alystin. "Very well. Again, conclave is right of all Houses, and we ask it. On the dark of the silver moon, ten days hence, the Council of the All will be called. With Mor'i'jil or without, with the House of Iyllyeth and regardless your attendance, leaders will confer and decide the way forward for the Race. Should Archane return in *Iyllyeth's* grace, matters will be decided then."

Xa'lyyth looked to Alystin as the older priestess mulled the words, then spoke. "Formal request from all Houses is needed. We will send messengers for such."

Lualyrr shook her head. "We have heard. All claim the right."

"Yet we have not, and without confirmation, there will be no conclave. Always has it been done thusly."

Lualyrr began to speak as Ry'lld laid a hand upon her arm. "As said, and we accept. Forgive, the Dark Lady Lualyrr only wishes best for all of Drow. Too long we have suffered the missing of Archane."

Alystin again looked to Xa'lyyth, and they bowed together to the Hovenethra clergy.

"Until conclave, may *Iyllyeth* look with favor on your House." Alystin's voice held little of inflection, yet Lualyrr took no offense.

"And yours." The Hovenethra party took leave quickly, the trees and bushes moving aside without sound.

"Dark Priestess, I sense enmity."

Alystin nearly laughed. "Their hate is strong. Centuries they have lusted for the leadership of Drow, and with Archane's disappearance, began to move soon after."

"Yet they have no allies. Hovenethra's legacy is one of deceit and treachery against the House of Iyllyeth. They cannot succeed against the whole of the Race."

"One would think not, yet Mor'i'jil, for all his loyalty, is ancient. And as Hovenethra is known as you say, I cannot discount assassins in our midst."

Xa'lyyth held her peace for moments. "We will search, therefore."

Alystin shrugged as they turned and soldiers gathered round. "Seek the Lancer Captain, as he is loyal. Speak forthrightly and say what you have heard. Should you desire a place higher in the *Black Web*, keep your wits and serve the House. And should Archane return, you will be well-placed to serve her."

* * *

Conclave was called. In the deepest chambers of *Ung'gu'wi*, barred from any not of priest or priestess rank, they gathered. The Great Houses of the Drow, centuries of leadership and animosity held in check by Archane's force of will, all came in attendance.

And now, only holding them from each other's throats and blood running in the corridors, Mor'i'jil, Dark Lord of *Iyllyeth* and confidant of

Archane more than five hundred years, watched as the entourages set themselves in council.

From Hovenethra came Ba'tula, the matriarch known for many years, with Lualyrr and the younger Ry'lld, whose calm had held the clandestine meeting in the forest from becoming worsened.

Warinethra's clergy had sent Dris'i'nil and her mates, the priests Durdyn and Xundus, brothers by their former leader, now gone to *Iyllyeth's* favor.

Karachitthra's priestess Ki'zran, staunch ally of Mor'i'jil's stewardship and lover long ago, entered in full regal dress, followed by two younger males, Belaern and Jeggred, and a female acolyte Mor'i'jil did not know of. He frowned, knowing enticements would be offered in cloistered parley, should opportunity arise.

As others settled round the Circle, Gurin and Lael'lae, Head and Second of Modennethra entered, guards about and a sorcerer at their side. Sharp looks were exchanged with the Hovenethra clergy, and Mor'i'jil gave an earnest prayer the conclave would not end in blood. Too many years, he knew, too many deaths lay between those two great Houses for reconciliation.

Servants made way quietly to and from, trays of delicacies from the kitchens, and scent of wine filled the chamber as cups were poured. Acolytes from each House stood in silence, or chanted prayers, or sang quietly their songs of exultation as Mor'i'jil observed. Alystin sat at his left, the priest Molva'yas his right, and Xa'lyyth closely with the others of his sect. He glanced her way, a slender leg, bare and glistening, showed from a slit within her robe. She caught his eye, opened the slit further, nearly to her naked hip, and smiled demurely. Mor'i'jil only sighed and shook his head.

A roasted loin was placed within the Circle, servants tending, and the Dark Lord watched as glances made their way about the room. The House of Iyllyeth, as leader, must show its wealth, and Mor'i'jil knew many moons had passed since the other Houses had seen the power of Archane's rule.

Time passed, and as the leaders ate and spoke among themselves, and thoughts of matters turned, Alystin lifted up a silver bell, ringing it. Talk quieted, and all eyes looked upon her place.

"Conclave is called, and here, by grace of *Iyllyeth*, the Great Houses of the Race sit in counsel. Herein advice is sought, herein wisdom is asked and offered. Speak minds and hearts, but know violence and threats are not accepted. Only of the Race do we discuss, the way forward from this day, for the good of all." She glanced to Ba'tula. "Hovenethra speaks as prime, therefore, Dark Priestess, time is yours as needed." Alystin bowed and sat, the bell now placed before her on the low table.

Ba'tula nodded recognition, sipped from her goblet, and quietly cleared her throat. "Archane is gone, likely dead, and the Race without a leader." She looked to Mor'i'jil, who made no gesture. "Conclave has been called to decide how best to proceed. A council, perhaps? Likely this would be the first and best decision, for too much turmoil is in *Ung'gu'wi* for any single spirit to take the reins."

"We have no proof of Archane's demise," said Priestess Gurin of Modennethra. "Your words conceal nothing of your desire for power. Too long has Hovenethra thought themselves more worthy than the Dark Princess."

"Little matters if Archane is not here." Ki'zran's voice was weak, yet she raised a hand for quiet as she spoke. "Tho' Dark Priest Mor'i'jil in his efforts has been earnest, there is a time for decision to be done. None in this room is worthy of Archane's footsteps in which to follow."

"Proof!" cried Dris'i'nil, Matriarch of Warinethra. "None found, therefore nothing certain. Perhaps she wanders in the land, her mind stripped of memory, no longer sane. Yet stories of mad Drow women have not been heard! Archane lives, and I know this in my heart."

"Perhaps we should examine it closely, then," replied Ba'tula, and the room was filled with angry whispers.

"No threats." Alystin raised the bell, but did not ring it. "First warning to Hovenethra."

"You say council." Durdyn held a hand to Ba'tula as his brother Xundus nodded at his side. "Say on, for this, for all, would be fairest and most worthy. Who, then? Elders, leaders only, or those of less position? Who, then, would lead the army? Shall the Lancer Captains be admitted? And what of sorcerers?"

Voices once again made way around, questions hovering in the air. Mor'i'jil motioned quiet, and the room stilled slowly.

"To be decided," said Ba'tula at the last. "Elders at the first, then others as chosen for their worthiness."

"Ideas with merit," said Mor'i'jil at the last. All the faces in the room turned to him. "Yet there are revelations to be made before any such event. I have had a vision."

The room was still for many moments, then Ba'tula spoke once more. "Convenience is your friend, Dark Priest. Only now, or did this come to you as you ravaged your concubine in the night?"

Chuckles were heard from Hovenethra's gathering, yet Mor'i'jil did not rise to the insult. "As we speak, I have sent an envoy into the land called Ardwel, seeking one of familiarity.

"Consider… Archane fought the demi-god in the City-State of Truth, destroying him forever. Yet she, herself, was never found, not seen for all these years. Was she, with him, obliterated? This has been our postulation, has it not? Yet there is another answer."

"Too many sorties have found nothing, Dark Priest, tho' we have searched everywhere we may." Alystin spoke softly beside Mor'i'jil, and the old priest nodded.

"Not all places, only those we find accessible."

Ba'tula shrugged and waved a hand. "Secret lairs, hidden enclaves, realms beyond our own. Yes, we have considered, and must I remind yourself, these suppositions were dismissed. As I recall, you sacrificed a Seer who offered false visions of Archane. Shall you be next?"

More rumblings made way around the room, and guards began to shift in nervousness. Mor'i'jil held a hand. "There is one in the land with power and knowledge, and I have known her well. Do you recall the concubine Reena, who traveled Ardwel at my side?"

Ba'tula shook her head as Lualyrr spoke into her ear. She shook her head again, then turned to Mor'i'jil. "What of this, for I know nothing."

Mor'i'jil nodded. "As thought, therefore, we will set a privy council and discuss. For the nonce, I will confirm, I have seen a vision of Archane alive and in the clutches of one whose very spirit is no longer. Yet the body lives, and as I sit before this conclave, I so swear, you will find her to be more formidable than any we have ever known."

* * *

The soldiers led away, and in only moments Mor'i'jil considered this could be his salient time. With others of the Houses confined to the conclave chamber, and heads of Houses now following his guards, he could slay them all, leaving the House of Iyllyeth the only one with leaders, and seize control of the Race, undisputed and unchallenged.

Yet never did Archane take such actions, and only with her tolerance has the Race not succumbed to war within itself. I must be vigilant and show humility in my stewardship! Five years I have succeeded, and only now do matters come to this; that a chance may be in our hands to find the Dark Princess alive! Calm, old fool! Seek their aid and give them what honor you can afford!

The chamber door opened before them, and Mor'i'jil ushered the heads of Households into a smaller room. Set nearly as a prayer chamber, servants stoked the small hearth quickly as a fountain bubbled in the corner. A tiny table was laden with delicacies and drink, and symbols of *Iyllyeth's* greatness hung on every wall. Pillowed places were laid about in the center of the chamber, and Mor'i'jil offered seats. Servants took exit quietly, then the soldiers followed, and in moments the most senior of all the dark elf Houses sat in company around.

Mor'i'jil spoke quietly in grave tones. "What we say herein is confidence, only for our ears. Once in your own domains, you may share the knowledge with those trusted most, tho' I caution you, keep close all you hear. The fewer who hold this, the better chance we have to find Archane alive."

Ba'tula passed a glance to Mor'i'jil, then Dris'i'nil and Gurin, Ki'zran of Karachitthra meeting her eyes with strength. "Say of this Reena, for only rumors have been heard."

All faces turned to Mor'i'jil as he drew a breath. "A favored concubine of Archane, she accompanied Ma'chen'der and myself to the human place called Drakenmoore years ago."

"The ruins?" Dris'i'nil coughed a laugh. "Nothing there has been found by many searchers. As you will recall, it was of the earliest considered."

"True, tho' searched only by soldiers with servants sent to dig. Nothing found was of value to our knowing."

"Who is she?" demanded Ba'tula. "Share your words or let us depart and seek a leader of the Race."

"The true leader of our people is Archane, and she lives. Reena holds her captive."

Once more, glances passed about.

"Dark Priest, you have this knowledge?" Gurin shook her head. "How may a concubine hold Archane in any way?"

"She is no longer Reena. By my own eyes, I watched as the human wizard Teresa Drakenmoore stripped away Reena's very spirit and implanted her own essence. Her 'soul', as it is said in human words, akin to the spirit we possess. Reena, once a simple concubine and pleasure servant, now is the wizard-woman Re', as humans call her. And known as an enemy of Drow."

Silence came as Mor'i'jil waited for their words.

"Absurdity!" Ba'tula sneered and waved a hand. "Such sorcery does not exist."

"It does," replied Dris'i'nil. "Warinethra has studied, tho' such power is unique. It is necromancy, that which lies beyond this life and world. Few have ability to control it."

"And this… woman Drakenmoore?" Gurin's tongue struggled with the human name.

Dris'i'nil nodded. "She is known to our Guild of Knowledge, perhaps more powerful than any in the land, save the Vermillion Mage himself."

"He has not been seen for many years," replied Gurin.

"Elf-sorcerers take leave, never seen again," replied Dris'i'nil. "Twice it has happened in our House. They seek solitude, escaping the world of mortal distractions. In time, thirst for knowledge consumes them."

Ba'tula waved a hand once more. "Enough. So say you, yet proof? And should this creature Reena hold such power, how to find her? How to bargain with her? What could she desire to free Archane? Why should she do so?"

The old female Drow showed a sour look, met Mor'i'jil's eyes boldly, and continued. "I will acknowledge, and only in the confidence herein, you, Dark Lord, have done credible service to the Race these years. So has Hovenethra held its hand, that blood not fill our corridors and chambers. Yet now we hear of visions, stories, and bold assumptions. How to prove? How to find the truth of it? How to hold the Race from false hope and anticipation, should these things be found untrue?" She showed a wicked grin. "Is your heart prepared for the sacrificial dagger, should you be shown a liar?"

"Take great care," said Gurin, warning in her voice. "Lest your own heart be prepared for such a venture."

"Dark Lady Ba'tula's query is one of merit," said Mor'i'jil. "Such venture awaits all our hearts, should the Race fall to war within itself. What choice have we in this time? Choose a council to lead the Race, as she has said? Therefore, it sits here now. Choose one to lead? Who, then, and how to do so without disagreement?" He shook his head, and bowed slightly to Ba'tula, who only frowned. "Continue with hope, and a possibility where none existed. Presume Archane is prisoner to Reena, or whatever name she now carries. I have sent an envoy to one known of Reena in her time spent in *Ung'gu'wi*. Soon we shall have answer and until then, I beg patience. Return to your domains. Give prayers to *Iyllyeth* that soon Archane will be found. If she is not, my heart awaits your judgement."

* * *

124

Conclave soon was announced at end, and as leaders and entourages made way from the council chamber, Mor'i'jil thought of bathing and of sleep. *For always do I feel soiled once from their company, so much selfishness and hatred. Never did Archane think in such a manner, and always was the image of Iyllyeth in her mind and heart. This is why she never claimed the title of Dark Queen, as always did she think it the province of Iyllyeth alone. Praise be now we have a clue, and may find her yet alive!*

Guards watched closely as the soldiers of each House found exit, servants trailing, and grumblings heard as clergy followed leaders, muttering 'neath their breath.

As the chamber emptied, Mor'i'jil spoke with the steward of his servants. "See all is cleaned with care and no poison instruments left behind. Scour for items dropped or hidden, that scrying objects might be studied by our sorcerers. Then place scented candles on the tables and in sconces. Take the stench of ill feelings from this place."

The steward bowed and hurried out, shouting orders to the servants. Mor'i'jil called his acolytes and guards, then slowly made his way through dim corridors and passages, up stairways causing his ancient joints to protest, and at last, arriving in his private chambers.

Servants filled the bathing vessel with waters clean and new, scattered sweet-smelling powders on the surface, then aided Mor'i'jil to undress. He lowered himself into the waters carefully, attendants washing him with gentleness, cleaning dust and dirt from his near-white hair. They doused him with the waters, laughing as he sputtered, wiped his face and bade him stand, that they might dry him.

Soft and gently they rubbed him dry, wrapped him in a heavy robe and led him to the bed. There they curled about him, warming him with closeness, and one of the younger females tended to his needs with the pleasures of her sensuous mouth. His ecstasy rose quickly as she took him to his climax, then raised her head, smiling coyly, and swallowed as he grinned. Only could he collapse in the afterglow and drift away, wondering if this were the most gentle of assassinations.

Then he slept, three concubines close and warm, and at the last, they covered him with fur and kisses, doused the candles, and closed the door behind them.

* * *

Ba'tula led the Hovenethra entourage through the passageways and into her private meeting chambers. There, she imparted the tales from Mor'i'jil and his plans, asking of her clergy for guidance in their future doings.

"Dark Lady, how can we believe such stories? Surely Mor'i'jil is seeking time for other plans to be laid." Lualyrr sat as servants combed her hair and brushed dust from her vestments, then offered wine. She waved them away, intent on Ba'tula's scowling face.

"And if true?" asked Ry'lld. "What then, should Archane be found? Tho' nothing done by our great House might be construed as treason, still we have spoken boldly."

"Always has Hovenethra spoken boldly," replied Ba'tula, "and never will we cease. Still, as Lualyrr's words have merit, the old priest's story has a ring of truth. I know of this Reena, and on return from the human place, she had changed. Where before she was subservient to Archane, and would have offered her heart at any moment, never was this seen again in her manner. She was... withdrawn, sullen even, rarely speaking. Yet I cannot believe the necromancy said of."

"Warinethra confirmed, Dark Lady?" asked Ry'lld, and Ba'tula nodded. "Then we must consider it a possibility, if only slight."

"Should Archane be found, what then?" asked Lualyrr.

Ba'tula pursed her lips. "We maintain our place. We have ventured conclave and debate, and had this wild allegation not arisen, a council would be formed. There we would be equal to all and subservient to none. Now Mor'i'jil plays his gambit well, and the other Houses meet as we, I am certain."

Mage apprentices entered bowing, asking forgiveness for their late arrival. They placed rocks within the Circle's center, incanted words, and the stones began to glow, giving blessed warmth. All held their hands from their cloaks and felt the glow upon their flesh. The apprentices bowed once more, exiting quickly.

More servants entered, with light meals and spirits in decanters, the fragrance strong and dark. Ba'tula took a crystal glass and sipped, contemplating.

"What of this envoy?" Lualyrr picked at berries on a spit.

Ry'lld spoke before his cup. "What of it? One known to this Reena in her time, after returning from Drakenmoore, yes? How might we know?"

Ba'tula raised her head. "Who, indeed? Years she spent as Archane's body-slave. Yet..." She turned her head aside in thought. Quiet came upon them as they waited in the Circle.

"Find those who knew her," said Ba'tula at the last. "Servants, concubines, acolytes or others. Seek knowledge of this Reena and any knowing of her once returned. Soldiers, perhaps, who took pleasure with her or guarded her as Archane tended other things. There must be many! Find them! Only through their knowledge can we find this Reena, or whatever name she carries now, before the House of Iyllyeth does so!"

"And if successful then, Dark Lady?" Lualyrr gave a nervous glance to Ry'lld.

"We shall have much to bargain with. If she proves worthless, or protests, kill her! Remove her from Mor'i'jil's plans, in one manner or the other!"

Dennis Young

BOOK FIVE
PLANS AFRESH

*"Too much quiet in the land
has given evil time to make its plans once more."*

Audrey Vincent to Thalion Lahai
before battling The Shadow Horde
in the Kingdom of the Sun

Dennis Young

In the chambers of Ung'gu'wi…

Steffyn Foxxe, if nothing else, was known as a clever and resourceful elf, to say little of his sorcerer's abilities. And in that cleverness lay intelligence with few equals in the land of Ardwel, and guile to keep him safe, not only from those known as enemies, but others who might become so. Therefore, knowing his dearest elf-brother Sheynon might enlist Ysilrod's abilities to find him and keep him from harm — harm, herein, being a term relative — he chose his place of hiding with great care.

He did not hide in the open land, where Ysilrod's spells would find him with little trouble. He did not choose to venture into the realm of "other places", those beyond the world of mortals, where magic was a common thing. Rather, his reasoning was to go where least expected, where even those pursuing him would not venture.

And since he had established for himself a disguise drawn only from his mind, he chose the lair of the enemy in which to sequester. Deep below the Black Forest, posing as a dark elf sorcerer with no attachments, few loyalties, and even fewer of acquaintance, his time passed in solitude. The sorcerer Mend'rys became his doppelgänger, wild and with an attitude few Drow exhibited, living in seclusion, deep within a chamber never finished in the many ages of *Ung'gu'wi's* existence.

Appearances were kept, but only as were necessary. Disguised as a dark elf male, more than once advances from concubines and those seeking to gain favor were fended off.

Many times, he thought to surrender to whatever might have come, and return to Ardwel. To his home. His wife. His friends. A life abandoned, fear and guilt and deep despair pushed away, to keep him from the madness dwelling in his spirit.

Five years went slowly by. In time, he found it best to take a female servant, though seldom took her pleasures as a concubine. Steffyn marveled at her subservience, and wondered if the instruments of pleasure had become a coin within the realm of Drow. If nothing else, somehow Steffyn kept his humor and would laugh, for if not, there were times with certainty, surely would he cry.

* * *

Her name was Jyslin, and the sorcerer Mend'rys chose her as servant, though hardly was she that when first they met. Jyslin was a beggar, young and with a withered arm, somehow not become a victim of infanticide, common in the great Houses when a child imperfect had been born. Mend'rys took her in, fed and clothed her, and when sequestered in his chambers, gave her the illusion of a body whole and perfect. Jyslin wept and offered herself however he might want her, and so Steffyn Foxxe, in the guise of a dark elf sorcerer, became her master.

Jyslin soon became a source of information, gathered from guards and others undesirable as she had been when found. Steffyn's intellect sifted through the rumors, innuendoes, and bits of fact, and he soon began to understand how fragile dark elf society was, with Archane gone so many years.

It seemed, in the beginning, to be a way beyond the chaos Steffyn assumed had taken Ardwel, and though pangs of guilt found him in his sleep and other times most inopportune, his curiosity was great, and at the last he began to wonder, if he, himself, might find a way to lead the Drow. Not into warring against Ardwel; not in domination of lands beyond, or other thoughts of conquest. But in benign existence, of knowledge, pursuit of the greatest secrets in the world, and perhaps, someday, how to save the magic from disappearing altogether.

Here he was, among the very people who had brought magic to its zenith, and when the dark elves had come into this place and time, they kept it close and guarded.

How might he do this? How to bring the light to those living in darkness for, some said, ten thousand years? How to gain the trust of those as Mor'i'jil, Archane's minister... and not end as a sacrifice beneath those aged hands.

I must know more. And with Jyslin now accepted as one known in certain places, perhaps knowledge might be gleaned. Patience is not a virtue with me, and I must think how best to find the answers.

And it was through her surreptitious searches, Jyslin came upon evidence that could not be denied; a soldier, enamored by her simple charm and wit, had revealed Archane yet lived, or so had said when sharing wine with her. He begged Jyslin to say nothing of it, and at the last, claimed to have told it only to impress her. Jyslin, herself cleverer than any guard might think, promised thusly, then hurried to Mend'rys's chambers to impart the news. Mend'rys, being the magnanimous of sorts, gave her wine and bread, then pondered in his study of this revelation.

And from where did this come, so lately in the game? Five years! And now she is found alive? Does Sheynon know? Do others of the quarreling comradeship, Chitthra, Aeren, Kaul, Drakkon... Where are they now?

132

I have secluded myself from Ardwel far too long, thinking other things more important. And they were, yet for reasons only selfish. Here magic flourishes! Here there is no thought of the ending of it, as it is kept afresh and new!

Yet the Guild of Learned in Telveperen holds it all away, thinking themselves wise in doing so. What has it cost them? What has it cost the Elven Race? Sorcerers murdered, others victims of Mors'ul'jyn's madness. The Guild now weaker than it was, Galandria Telveperen dead of vengeance misdirected. My own crimes against those I loved, and thought less of than my own concerns...

He bit back bitter tears, stifling a mournful sigh, that Jyslin might hear. He poured wine and drank it all, then poured again, contemplating.

Rumors of a stranger seen in the City-State of Truth the day of Crysalon's disappearance. A dark elf woman, never seen again, riding to the ruin of the palace grounds, and leaving then with a bundle cross the saddle. If true, the Black Blade was not the prison I had thought, for once within, Re' in the guise of Mors'ul'jyn surely found escape. And with her, likely Chitthra, bound by honor to avenge the death of Galandria. Irony! That one of the Brotherhood, now following in the footsteps of my own son, seeks my blood!

* * *

Steffyn set his plans in motion. With confirmation of Archane alive from an acolyte, when Jyslin took him to a darkened corridor and pleasured him completely, Steffyn knew the die was cast, and likely with it, his fate. Still, absolution was the only way he might survive, for he knew with certainty, Chitthra would hold responsibility on his head. For in her mind, he had held the blade that killed Galandria Telveperen, surely as did Mors'ul'jyn.

He sat with Jyslin and spoke his way, then watched as tears fell on the table there before him. "What shall I do, Master? Where might I go that my withered arm will not send me to a beggar's life again?"

Steffyn ruminated, for the girl was truthful in her words, and he knew she would not survive returning to her former life. "You have no family, yes?"

"Only you, Master, as you took me in. I am faithful evermore and not ungrateful. Yet I beg you, take me with you. My life is yours to hold."

Steffyn thought again. Seen not as himself, but as Mend'rys, who of course, was unknown beyond *Ung'gu'wi*, might be advantage. As a dark elf, he could journey in the land unnoticed and unsuspected, gathering word and rumor as he might. And Jyslin had proven many times of her way with gaining evidence, and she, as well, never had been beyond the dark elf lairs.

133

At the last, Steffyn nodded. "Gather your belongings and prepare. We leave at the changing of the guard, into the Black Forest. Be assured, we will not return. Are you accepting of that fate? We will travel where dark elves are, at times, unwelcome."

"You are a great sorcerer and will protect us," Jyslin replied. She smiled and bowed to him. "My life is yours forever. What you need, should it be in my humble ability, I will provide."

She took his hands and kissed them, then knelt away at the tiny fountain, giving prayers.

Prayers to Iyllyeth and Mother Darkness. How have I done this? How have I hidden away these years, in the house of the enemy? Where has my conscience gone, that I would do these things?

Still I am Joined with Emildir, yet her life has changed, I know. What have I done, Great Yarhetha'an, that I took matters in my hands and destroyed so much good within the world? How could I fail in such miserable fashion?

He poured wine again and drank, wondering how much longer he might live.

* * *

The City-State of DragonFall…

The messenger once more stood before the throne, offering a missive. Kaul drained the tankard in his hand and waved at the parchment. "Read it to me. The day has been long, and I seek company in the harem."

The messenger bowed, broke the blackened seal and perused the words, then looked to Kaul. "My King, it is written in a hand I do not know."

Kaul growled, snatched away the message and examined it. He paled. "Call my minister of antiquities, at once. Bring him to me now!"

The messenger bowed again. "Sire, it is near the mid of night…" Her voice trailed at Kaul's scowl. "Yes, My King, at once."

Kaul rose to pace, guards in every corner and every entrance watching closely as he muttered to himself. In time, the messenger appeared once more, the minister in tow and dressed yet in his night clothes. He bowed perfunctorily as Kaul thrust the parchment to his waiting hands.

"This is Drow rune-writing, is it not? Read it to me, word by word."

The minister's eyes followed the runes, and his lips moved quietly as he read to himself. "My King, it is a request for parley this very night. At the zenith of the moon called *Mina*, an emissary will wait at the city gates. One alone, with words only for your ears."

134

Kaul sat. *More visitors, more enticements, and all searching for the same thing, Archane. Likely from one of the Houses, or possibly Mor'i'jil himself. How to make a bargain of this, for Drow will have no answers but what they desire.*

"How soon?"

"My King, very soon," replied the minister. "I suggest we go now."

"Bring my armor," said Kaul to his guard captain, now standing at his side. "We will see what this emissary in the darkness has to say."

* * *

The figure was but a brightened shadow, with *Mina* high in the sky and full. Kaul stood with fifty guards behind him as he faced… whatever this specter was, for certainly it was not a man. A head shorter than was he, vaguely human in its shape, there was nothing Kaul could see within what seemed to be a gently flowing robe and cloak, drifting in the nighttime breeze.

The figure bowed, but otherwise did not step forward. At the last Kaul spoke. "You asked parley, therefore, proceed. I am Kaul, master of this city. Say your purpose, for I have matters waiting."

Again, the figure bowed. "The Dark Princess, you have seen her?" The voice was as nothing Kaul had ever heard, a hissing whisper, and his guards shifted nervously about him.

"Who asks? Why should I answer to naught but a shade, from where and whom I do not know? I treat only with those of this world, no others. Be gone if you are not mortal. I have no use for parlor tricks."

The figure bowed once more. "Dark Princess…"

Kaul growled and drew his *NorthWind* sword, advancing. Twenty guards followed, encircling the thing, spear points gleaming in the moonlight. "Leave my lands or treat with respect. I answer to no apparition." Kaul raised his sword, and the figure vanished. He grunted, turned about, and began to walk his way back to the gates.

"My King, look…" The guard's words trailed, and Kaul turned once more.

Something came from the darkness, floating in the air it seemed. Two figures grew to nearly man-size and paused before him. Once more guards raised their spears, as one of the figures held a hand.

"We come in peace," said a female voice within a darkened hood. "That which preceded us was to test your patience."

"Test it no further," snarled Kaul, raising his sword once more. "My rule is law in this city. Say your purpose or be gone. I will hear no more."

The figures drew back hoods, revealing dark elf faces, one young and fresh of face, the other older, though Kaul could not tell Drow by their age. They bowed. "I am the Priestess Alystin, and this Xa'lyyth, my counterpart. We come at behest of Dark Lord Mor'i'jil, with whom you are acquaintanced."

Kaul scoffed. "I know of him, yet he is no friend. He ordered my death, as I am certain he has told you. Have you come to claim my heart?" Again, Kaul raised his *NorthWind* sword. "Look around you. Regardless your abilities, you cannot slay us all."

"As said, peace. And an offer."

"Your apparition spoke of a 'dark princess'."

Alystin bowed. "Archane, ruler of the Drow, right hand to *Iyllyeth* her own self when mortal."

Glances made way around the guards' line. Kaul chuckled. "Yes, Archane, who ordered Mor'i'jil to take me as a sacrifice. What of her?"

"We seek her whereabouts," said Xa'lyyth, her voice a croon.

Kaul watched the rise and fall of her breasts 'neath a silky, near-transparent robe, and showed a salacious grin. "You tempt me with dark flesh? You are desperate, yes?" He laughed. "Very well, into the harem with you! I will sample your pleasures at my convenience."

"Dark Lord Mor'i'jil requests your presence for a parley," said Alystin, as Xa'lyyth drew her cloak about herself.

"Bring the old man here and we shall see." Again, Kaul laughed. "Tell me, how did he escape the city when my army took it?" He spat upon the ground as laughter made its way around the guards. "Surely I should have cut his throat when tempted."

Alystin's face grew grim. "We ask indulgence, and I am bound to find a way between us."

Kaul strode to Alystin, guards following. He waved them back, paused an arms-length before the dark elf woman, and laid his sword across her shoulder. "What is your offer? The girl's pleasures? Yours, or perhaps both at once? I need not for gold, and have a harem. I command an army and hold a great city, greater than *Ung'gu'wi*." He glanced without interest at Xa'lyyth. "What might Drow offer I would find of value?"

Alystin's face rose to his, her eyes as rubies in the night. "Alliance. Perhaps power as you have not known. Perhaps a way to find your true desires in this land."

Kaul kept her gaze for moments, the sword edge laying close beside her slender neck. "I have heard those promises from others and been betrayed. What ransom shall I hold? Your life, or that of the girl? Mor'i'jil become my prisoner again?" He shook his head. "I trust few in this world, and dark elves are not among them."

"Allow us to meet your needs, and all will profit."

Again, Kaul chuckled. "You seek Archane? Might you know she died years ago, and only now you search? Your timeliness is suspect."

"We have word," whispered Alystin. "She lives, so says Mor'i'jil, tho' as you say... years ago."

They know! thought Kaul. *Sorcery perhaps, or scrying in the land? Or words heard in a tavern? Archane and Mors'ul'jyn would not venture to such a place. Surely by magic, this is how they found her.*

Kaul's mind sat in turmoil. "Should I give my knowing, what then? How to hold Mor'i'jil to this bargain?"

Xa'lyyth kept her eyes averted as Alystin replied. "You seek a queen, perhaps? One stands before you, willing, young and fertile."

Kaul shook his head. "I have more children than I might ever want."

"My pleasures are great, my lord," said Xa'lyyth softly. "Alliance is key, and we become allies in the struggle. As your queen, I become the way between us."

Kaul ran his eyes over both women. "How do we seal this agreement? Who will offer first that promised?"

Xa'lyyth gave a nervous glance to Alystin. "I shall. Lead me to your harem and I will pleasure you however you desire."

Kaul's blade lifted from Alystin's shoulder, and he placed it then on Xa'lyyth's. "Let us see your pledge. Here. Now. We will consecrate the earth before my city with your offer."

Xa'lyyth began to speak, then paused. She dropped away her cloak, unlaced her robe and let it fall. Kaul's hand found her shoulders, then drifted on her body. Her skin was dark and smooth, breasts firm and high, and she nearly cringed beneath his touch. She knelt and spread her cloak upon the ground, then laid herself upon it, and held her hands to him.

Alystin looked quickly away, then drew a shuddering breath, and knelt beside the trembling girl. "*Iyllyeth grant you courage, for your offering is for the good of all,*" she said in Drow.

Kaul laughed, tossed off his breastplate and drew his breeches down, took his knees between her legs, and fondled her again. Xa'lyyth gasped as he found her warmth, then held tears away as he moved within her, harder, faster, building to crescendo. He grunted out his climax as she bit her lip and nearly cried, shame and harsh reality crashing down upon her spirit.

137

The guards drew closer in a circle, watching, laughing, crude words and gestures round. At last Kaul rose, breathing heavily, dressed himself and took Xa'lyyth by her wrists. He dragged her to her feet, tossed her into Alystin's arms. "Tell your Lord Mor'i'jil I will parley with him alone and not with lackeys. Bring him to me or leave my lands forever. Kaul Morg'ash bows to no one ever more."

Alystin's eyes blazed in the moonlight, Xa'lyyth sobbing on her shoulder. They turned, walked twenty paces distant, and disappeared, dust swirling in their exit.

The cry of soldiers round was nearly deafening.

* * *

Kaul walked his way back into the city, climbed into his carriage, and rode in silence to the palace. He had only now given insult to a priestess of the House of Iyllyeth, likely one who would deliver news to Mor'i'jil before the night was done.

He grinned lewdly, Xa'lyyth's whimpers yet in his mind's ear, and the struggles of her slender body 'neath his own.

I am a king! I treat with none who are not equal in my eyes! I brought this land to its very knees, leading my army into combat! And they call us ruffians and outlaws! We killed Archane! We fought the Drow within this very city, and should I have chosen, Mor'i'jil's life would have ended 'neath my blade! And they dare send apparitions to test my temper! Who laughs now?

Rohesia met him at the palace gates, escorted him into the royal edifice and led him to the throne room where a table waited. Kaul sat and was served, wine poured, and his plate filled before him. He drank, then motioned Rohesia to a chair beside himself.

"Your thoughts? The world, it seems, seeks my aid in finding of Archane. How to bring this to advantage and not die because of it?"

Rohesia motioned to Kaul's goblet, and a servant filled it once again. She took her own and slowly drank. "My King, your strength is in your boldness. First, the dark elves have not the power to take your city. Secondly, assassins, while a threat, cannot enter if the gates are barred."

Kaul huffed a breath. "Then you know little of their sorcery. They might send a brace of soldiers to my bedchamber and slay me as I sleep."

"You have given insult to their House, My King, and piqued their ire, but my question now becomes, what sort of intellect is this Mor'i'jil? Will he see your doing as one of strength or a challenge to his holdings?"

Kaul mused, frowning, and picked slowly at his meal. "I held him hostage, killed a priestess in his sight, and spoke insults to his face. Now he sends messengers beneath my notice, and knows my manner. Comely faces and warm woman-flesh are a weakness to me." He leered Rohesia's way, remembering her in his bed, many years ago. "He might well have dangled her before me himself, to see if I would rise to the bait."

Rohesia grinned, knowing his look well. "As you took me, My King? Might you want to do so once again, for remembrance? Still I serve in whatever way you need."

They shared a quiet laugh, then touched goblets and drank together. Silence settled then, and Kaul blew a breath of resignation. "I need Archane's ear, but have no way to gain it. The Reena girl, now this Mors'ul'jyn, controls her as none have ever done. Little doubt is in my mind Mors'ul'jyn sees Archane as the way to power she would wish to hold."

"Mors'ul'jyn is a danger to the whole of the land, My King. She covets power for personal gain and stature. Chaos is her end, for she is likely mad with vengeance-fever."

Kaul nodded slowly. "Therefore, how to win her confidence and find a way beyond her plans? I must think upon this, but for now, naught but sleep is in my plan."

Rohesia rose and took his hand boldly to her waist. Kaul stood, moving his hands upward, resting them upon her ample breasts. She leaned into him with breath upon his neck. "Might I offer company this night? Warm hands to soothe your flesh, warm lips to give you pleasure."

Kaul chuckled once again as they walked hand in hand beyond the throne room.

Surely, it was good to be the king.

* * *

It came to Kaul as dawn's light peeked between the shutters. The way to Archane lay through Mors'ul'jyn, that he was assured of. Yet she, herself, sought what Kaul might want, the rule of Drow, and thereby the land. Why so? He knew she was an enemy of elves, Calidriil in certainty, for crimes against her family years past. But Mors'ul'jyn's mind lay unbalanced, and in truth, she might seek to burn the land before her, thinking the whole of it against the family Drakenmoore and all it had been.

Therefore…

How to gain her trust, to find a way to Archane? Or should he think the opposite, Archane to work beside him, opposing Mors'ul'jyn? What might he offer to either, not both? If he could find control of one, the other, then, would be more vulnerable.

Kaul held power, the power of DragonFall and all within it; soldiers at his call, farmers and merchants paying tribute, a treasury full to nearly-bursting with gold and silver.

Archane cared not for wealth, but power. Mors'ul'jyn might then be more the interested. As his queen? Would she bind herself, as humans said, in marriage to him? Warm his bed… again? Bear his children? Thereby standing with more power than Archane herself? Then what of the Dark Princess?

Sorcery once done might be done again. Would Mors'ul'jyn consider it? Become Archane as she had become the girl Reena? Take her body, then her place as leader of the Drow?

He turned to Rohesia, laying quiet at his side. There had been a time Kaul thought her worthy, and still, she was that, and loyal completely. How might she react, to see Mors'ul'jyn in the place she held, thought of perhaps by right?

Too complicated for so early in the day, he thought, grinning to himself. He rolled aside and Rohesia came to him, warm and welcome. He drifted once again in sleep. Once woke, he would consider. *For now, take time in welcome arms. Others might be less so.*

* * *

Ung'gu'wi…

Alystin paced before the hearth as Mor'i'jil waited for her angst to calm. Thrice now she had sat, poured wine, then rose to pace again, muttering, railing, cursing as she did so. Servants stood away, passing looks between their number, wondering what would come of this disgrace.

"He took her there, in the dust upon the road, defiled a priestess of *Iyllyeth*, then banished us with laughter! I want his heart in my hand, on the rising of the Dark Moon!" She spun, stalked to the table at which Mor'i'jil sat listening, and pounded fists upon it. "Do you hear me? His heart!"

The Dark Lord poured her goblet full again and motioned to the chair. "Your anger is surely just, but still, your manner was your own downfall."

Alystin's eyes pierced him to his spirit.

Mor'i'jil held a hand for calm. "What was expected? You knew him to be a mongrel, naught but a soldier in House Modennethra. He held

140

our council captive in the city, beheaded a priestess there before the lot of us, and would have slain me should he have had the time."

Alystin kept his gaze as she drained her goblet. "Then we march, burn his city to the ground, and take all Ardwel for our own."

He shook his head slowly. "We have not the army, for between the decimation of the North Legions at the castle on the Sliver River, and losses in the city against the men and elves, little now remains. A thousand, perhaps twice that, should we send servants as fodder before the soldiers. Warinethra holds away their sorcerers, saying there is little glory in dying for no purpose."

"No purpose!" Alystin slammed her goblet on the table. "Archane alive, and they say no purpose?"

"Still, where, Dark Lady? Should she be captive of the wizard-woman Re' in the guise of Reena, how shall we find her? Warinethra has searched, scryed, sent their sorcerers to all points in this land and those beyond. They find nothing. Yet we know, somewhere, somehow, she is alive, and must wait for her next appearance."

Alystin was silent for long moments. "What of…"

Mor'i'jil raised a pale eyebrow.

"Legend says she had a lover, human, and of great power in the Black Arts." Her voice was but a whisper, as though blasphemy was spoken.

"Venic. Yes, I, too, have heard the tales, but this was before Drow came into this land."

Alystin gestured broadly. "Might he have followed? There is one in this world who is much alike the stories."

Mor'i'jil slowly shook his head. "You speak of the Vermillion Mage, Veniculis, yes? He is known to be an agent of elves and men. And even so, where, again, should we search? Years it has been since his seeing."

Alystin was quiet as she sipped once more. "We seem to have found an impasse. Kaul will not bargain other than with yourself. Archane seen only once, and that yet unconfirmed." She looked Mor'i'jil hard in the eye. "And your suppositions, Dark Lord, are all left to us. Perhaps truly she is gone. Perhaps a council would be best for now, to set the way until Archane returns. Or does not."

"This is your wish? To raise the other Houses to our stature? No longer the House of Iyllyeth supreme, only one of many?"

She shrugged. "What is left? If you will not treat with this Mongrel, how then to proceed for the Race?"

Mor'i'jil considered, then nodded. "A point taken. Therefore, I will go before Kaul and pledge agreement. And perhaps even garner apology for his sullying your priestess."

* * *

Five years Mor'i'jil had lived with the absence of Archane, searching for the truth of her disappearance. He pondered his approach, then recalled Archane's entrance into the City-State of Truth. Stories had been told by human soldiers there surviving, heard by dark elf infiltrators in taverns round the city. Nearly had she destroyed half the city, the palace and its garden left in shambles, and from there, he had surmised, she disappeared. Somehow, Re' in the body of the concubine Reena, had known of the battle nearly as it happened, found Archane, and spirited her away.

Mor'i'jil knew his preparations to meet this Mongrel must be thorough. Kaul's arrogance must be taken down and shown as naught but bluster.

The Dark Lord ruminated as he sat alone, his private chambers empty but for himself and a favored concubine, asleep within the bed.

Kaul will assert his dominance in whatever way he might. Yet if confronted with power greater than his own, how might he react? With fear? Doubtful, tho' violence is certainly not beyond his way. Capitulation? Again unlikely, for he will not submit except to save his life. Therefore, a greater threat. Should he not agree, might I have the power to force his hand?

Mor'i'jil rose and stretched the stiffness from his limbs. His concubine stirred and rolled to face him, tossed back the blanket and cupped her breasts, then smiled. Mor'i'jil rolled his eyes and shook his head. "Return to your crèche and bathe. Your duty here is done for now."

She rose, bowed quickly, then departed.

He called a servant at the door. "Send for the Lancer Captain, and the Mistress of the Sorcerer's Guild at once. Say they are to attend me in the meeting chambers. Attend them well therein. Then enter and aid my dressing for an urgent meeting."

Power, thought Mor'i'jil, *is what Kaul will submit to. I will show him that, and convince him dark elves will not be trifled with again. He held me hostage in the city, nearly taking of my life, and there is little doubt our anger now is justified with his treatment of Alystin's acolyte. We will see how this mongrel king might react when confronted with his fate on the altar, a dagger in my hand.*

* * *

Plans were laid and soldiers gathered. Six mages were to accompany the troupe, and twice that of assassins. The planning of the timing was complex; find way into the palace beyond the city gates, beyond even those of the royal grounds. Bar the way for city soldiers to gain entry, once the palace was secured. Slay what guards were found and take hostages as necessary.

Mor'i'jil cautioned the Lancer Captain, that his soldiers were not to take the pleasures of the harem, once found and locked away. All were to be kept alive… and unspoiled by his troops.

Assassins and the sorcerers were to find the way into Kaul's chambers, kill guards if there were any, and capture concubines and servants. Kaul was to be taken alive, and this was for the sorcerers to be certain of. Dead, he was of no use, but alive, he would bargain, once knowing his city might be lost.

This was a point of consideration for Mor'i'jil. Show Kaul how easily he had been captured. Prove true power and ability, yet show him mercy in his living. Offer a bargain he could not refuse, that of his life. For if Mor'i'jil was proven there correct, the only life of value to Kaul was his own.

* * *

The City-State of DragonFall…

Mina was descending in the west, and *Grand Selene* not yet risen, when the first of Mor'i'jil's sorcerers appeared at the gates of DragonFall. The guards there fell into a sleep, then dark elf soldiers entered and took their places, as the unconscious forms were dragged into the gatehouse.

More mages soon appeared at the palace gates, and the scene repeated, then assassins moved toward the palace proper, dark and silent.

Through the doors and darkened hallways, up the stairs where the master's chambers likely were. A sorcerer walked boldly to the double oaken doors in the corridor, and as guards drew weapons and shouted challenge, assassins in the shadows took them down.

The doors then were opened slowly, and in silence the assassins rushed in, leapt upon the bed, and pulled forth Kaul in his nakedness, and a human woman clad in only a chemise, both shouting oaths and curses.

Kaul woke quickly, drew a dagger from beneath the pillow, and drove it into an assassin's stomach. Another fell to his teeth and claws before the others took him to the floor, and the struggling mass of flesh writhed around the room.

At the last, they dragged him to his feet, bloody, beaten, but still gnashing at a hand straying close. The sorcerer approached and waved a hand before Kaul's face. The Mongrel's jaw clamped shut, yet his struggles there continued. The sorcerer waved again, incanted words none in the room might know, and Kaul screamed as his arms were drawn to either side. Fire erupted in his shoulders, joints aflame with pain, and he tumbled to the floor, whimpering in his agony.

Guards circled round as one held the woman in a corner. Kaul rolled to his back, panting out his fury, eyes wild and jaw yet tense with anger. In time, he rose to his knees, and they dragged him to a chair, bound him with the blankets from the bed, and stood round with weapons drawn.

The door opened once again. Kaul raised his bloody face as Dark Lord Mor'i'jil came into the room.

* * *

Until sunlight touched the gardens beyond the master's chamber's windows, Mor'i'jil sat before Kaul, saying nothing. He only watched with a gentle smile of satisfaction as the blood about Kaul's head and face ceased its dripping and dried upon his skin. The woman, her name Rohesia, sat bound in the farthest corner, her silence assured by the sorcerer who placed a cantrip on her lips.

As servants entered for their daily duties, they were taken by the dark elf guards and led to separate chambers. The Lancer Captain soon reported the palace securely in their hands, gates guarded by his soldiers, and entries to the city closed and barred. Only then did Mor'i'jil address Kaul and tell him of his coming.

"We might have done this any time within the years gone by." The Dark Lord motioned to the guards arrayed. "With less than three hundred, I have taken back the city from your hands. We hold your harem hostage, your offspring, your concubine." He nodded to Rohesia. "My soldiers hold away your army, such as it is, by locking doors with magic and shuttering the windows. All not dead are trapped within their barracks. We have sent forth heralds in the streets, announcing all business will remain closed this day due to…" He chuckled. "A holiday proclaimed by 'Our Great King'. Therefore, it is only you and I, and what agreement we may reach."

Kaul said nothing, only spat dried blood onto the floor, then showed teeth to Mor'i'jil in a deadly grin. The Dark Lord shrugged, rose and walked away. He poured wine from a bottle on the table, then drank slowly, waiting for Kaul's senses to accept the words as given.

"You seek apology for defiling of your priestess?" Kaul rasped at last. "Regrettably, her pleasures were not as great as hoped. Words against her mentor or yourself? I think not, old man."

Mor'i'jil took his chair again before the battered face. "These are not important in this time, tho' be assured, I will have them should I deem it necessary. Questions of more importance lay between us, answers ungiven to those who came in civility and were met with insult. Therefore, I reasoned to show only what you would understand." He motioned again to the soldiers. "Power, and the use of it to take back what Drow wrested from the humans. This city was not won by your hand, is was gifted to you by those whose blood took it from us. You know nothing of righteous combat, only killing those helpless in your sight."

Kaul chuckled. "My army killed your Dark Princess! I held her dripping head, burned her body, looted wagons of her heirlooms. You say I know nothing of the fight? I should have killed you when the chance was mine."

Mor'i'jil looked Kaul in the eye for a silent moment. "Yes. And in certainty, you should have. Now your life is in my hand. Soon enough, your heart may be as well."

For only the time it took for Mor'i'jil to blink, he saw true fear in the face of Kaul. He grinned. "Yes, this you are afraid of, and rightly so. Therefore, let us parley."

Still, Kaul would not admit defeat. "What is your offer, and what do you seek? My knowledge is not without a price."

"My lord Kaul, I have what it is you would want… your city and your life. What will you offer to gain them back?"

Kaul turned away, breathing hard, sweat trickling down his temple.

Mor'i'jil spoke softly. "Archane… you have seen her?"

At the last, Kaul nodded.

"When and where? And more than once?"

Kaul shook his head. "Once only, a moon or more ago. I do not know their whereabouts."

Mor'i'jil raised an ancient eyebrow. "You said of 'they'. Who besides Archane?"

Kaul met Mor'i'jil's stare with his own. "The concubine Reena. Now called Mors'ul'jyn by her choice."

Mor'i'jil closed his eyes and bowed his head, giving thanks to *Iyllyeth* for her guidance and granting courage. "She lives," he said with reverent quietness.

145

"Yes, again, old man," growled Kaul. "So the tales were true of her living forever. She dies, but then returns. And I would give her a thousand deaths, should I be able."

"Take care, Great King," replied the Dark Lord in a mocking voice, "or perhaps I shall grant you the same. I might hang you on a dungeon wall and cut your body into pieces. There you would see your own flesh before you with each cut. Shall we begin with your maleness you covet so greatly?" He showed a wicked grin, then rose to walk away, pausing at the table to drink once more. "You know who this Mors'ul'jyn truly is, and the power she holds? Power enough to capture and enslave one as Archane? How to break the Dark Princess from her grasp?"

Kaul only glowered and shook his head.

Mor'i'jil returned to his seat again, facing Kaul, a breath away. "When are they to return for your parley? What inducement have they offered?"

"We made no agreement, only talk. I know not if they will return."

"Yet what did they want of you?"

Kaul shrugged once more. "Soldiers, wanting nothing but of payment."

"Gold?" Mor'i'jil chuckled. "Or other forms?" He pondered for a moment. "Surely they reside in Drakenmoore, beneath the ruins where they cannot be reached by mortal means." He glanced to Kaul. "You took her there, yes? How many levels down into those ruins, where Ma'chen'der met his fate?"

"I…" Kaul paused in thought. "Seven, as I recall, tho' I am not certain."

"Archane will need your army, yes." Again, Mor'i'jil held Kaul's gaze, then he nodded. "We will wait, therefore. In time, the Dark Princess will return to find agreement."

Kaul's eyes narrowed. "Wait where, old man? This is my city."

Mor'i'jil grinned. "No, Great King… it now is ours. Pray we do not keep it once Archane is back safely with her people."

* * *

The Depths of Drakenmoore…

"We depart." Mors'ul'jyn swept into the central chamber, a cloak of colors draped about her shoulders. Archane watched from her reading stand, unsure of what the words had meant. She had been granted freedom from her prison, once she and Mors'ul'jyn pledged to each other for common cause. Now dressed in robes more suited to herself, and being tended by unseen servants of her captor, she had begun to study Drakenmoore, and the land about it.

"To where, and for what reason? Were you not awaiting a missive from Kaul regarding our parley? I have wondered how he might inform you."

"Kaul waits with other… guests." Mors'ul'jyn grinned knowingly. "Surely you do not think he would send a messenger. I left a way to know the time was right."

Archane stood, brushed her robe, then closed the book. "And what is our offer for his soldiers? You know my thoughts on this, and I will not become his pleasure toy."

"Your virtue is not at risk." Mors'ul'jyn's tone was one of mocking, and Archane's ruby eyes flashed in anger. "My offer will be made when proper."

Archane considered. "You said others. Who, and what part will they play in this… agreement?"

"You will see, dear lady, and be amazed how plans come together. This day will be a dawning of alliance as Ardwel has never known."

* * *

The City-State of DragonFall…

The sorcerer Mend'rys, with Jyslin attending, walked quickly through the gateway into Kaul's city, unseen by the doubling of guards he saw there, which told him matters had changed greatly since the warning in *Ung'gu'wi*. Here was known the source of whatever in the land might be wanted by those wishing to remain unknown to authorities, or those of lawful bent. Steffyn, as Mend'rys, had spent his time before retreating to the Black Forest, deep within the thieves' quarters, in an abandoned shed hidden by a growth of shrubs so dense it could not be seen from streets. Only if one followed through a passageway between shops nearly collapsing on themselves could it be found. That, and Steffyn's own magics, which kept away the unwanted or suspicious.

They wandered through the merchants at the edges of the market, smells of dust and animals and roasting meat filling the air about them. Twice they paused as handlers led beasts of unknown species past, and Jyslin huddled close to Mend'rys, more in wonder than in fright.

They purchased a meal of something-on-a-stick, washed it down with watered ale and wine, watched a juggler in a sideshow and a bawdy play of women whose armor fell away when captured by a burly man.

147

In time, they drifted to a shop away from crowds, slipped through its doors and out the back, then down a muddy alleyway. At last they came to an overgrowth of brush Jyslin at the first refused to walk within. Mend'rys grinned, waved his hands, and the thicket parted there before him. Her eyes grew wide, and they entered the dilapidated shack beyond.

Within, Jyslin marveled. Here was no filth and grime, but a suite to rival the finest inn. Three rooms, one with beds, a hearth with stew smelling freshly stirred, and a sitting room with books and tomes and scrolls in shelves finished as a library. Aside stood a door, a sigil there upon it, and Mend'rys led her there, pointing to the inscription.

"Never enter. Never. Within is my workshop, guarded by something not of this world. Only I may enter, as others will not return once there."

Jyslin bowed. "Master, never would I disobey. Tell me how to serve you in this..." her words drifted. "In this place of dreams. Is this the home you speak of in your sleep?"

Mend'rys swallowed, paling as he did so. "You have heard me talk of another home?"

She drew closer and lay her head upon his shoulder. "You only ask my pleasures when worried or afraid. And yes, some nights as we lay together, you mumble words I do not know the meaning of. Yet still, I know you came from beyond *Ung'gu'wi*, and loneliness lies in your heart."

Mend'rys stepped away, drew a breath, then another, turned and smiled weakly to the girl. "In ways, you are correct, but regardless, we now are here and have work before us.

"I will ask of you to use your wiles in this place, tho' I know it will take time to grow accustomed. The people we will deal with are not dark elves, but for the most part humans. They can be more cruel than you may imagine, yet also, in many ways, more willing to cooperate for simple things."

He drew a small pouch from his cloak and tossed it to her. She opened it and once more her eyes widened in amazement. "More silver than ever I have seen!"

Mend'rys chuckled. "Less than a hundred pieces, yet it will buy the information needed, and we will begin on the morrow. For tonight, rest and a meal, then to your studies once again."

He approached and held a hand to her, and she took it. "You have learned much of simple cantrips and spells these years. Perhaps I will teach you of true magic in the coming days."

* * *

Three days they spent about the city, and twice each day Mend'rys and Jyslin ventured to the palace gates, noting the changing of the guard. They spent time and silver at the taverns, listening for talk of Kaul, his manner, and how the city fared in his grasp. Times were, Jyslin asked Mend'rys of this, and when once more in their hideaway, he would speak in quiet tones.

"I know of this man from past times, the ruler of DragonFall, tho' have not met him face to face. However, there are those of my acquaintance who know him well, and from them I discern his way. I search for one known to him years ago, now a different person in reality. I cannot know if ever he will see her again, but in my mind, this is my only chance with any certainty to find her."

"A woman from his past?" Jyslin grinned. "What would her reasons be? That he is a king now, with power and position? What might she offer, as he has a harem and wants not for pleasures? Or is there more, Master, that you will not say of?"

Mend'rys paced to the hearth, cast a cantrip, and the fire sprang to life. He looked into the flames as they crackled in the darkened room, wondering how best to proceed.

He sat once more with Jyslin and continued. "I seek her for crimes against dear friends long ago. Once I held her life in my hands and did not take it. For that, I, too, am hunted. Therefore, if my only chance of mercy is to become her ending, I must do it. I do not wish to die, yet know even that may not save me, come the time."

"Master, I would give my life for yours if chance arose."

Mend'rys sighed and touched her cheek. "Never would I ask such of you. You are a sweet spirit, more than any I have found in all these years."

She took his hand and kissed it, glanced to the bedroom door and smiled. "I would please you this night, should you wish it."

Mend'rys sighed again. "Your simple touch and company please me every day. Yet closeness would be welcome this night, if you are willing."

He rose and led her to the bed. They laid together closely, only touching gently without disrobing. Mend'rys drifted half-asleep, wondering how he had strayed so far from the life once known and given thanks for.

A tear trickled down his cheek as he contemplated now, that never could he return to what had been before.

* * *

All the knowledge held in the mind of the sorcerer Mend'rys, was, of course, that of Steffyn Foxxe. And as days passed by, and Jyslin returned with bits of news and information, Mend'rys began to understand what had transpired throughout the years.

Little doubt there was Archane lived, and Mors'ul'jyn as well. Too many guards, retainers, and servants of the palace recounted tales of two dark elf women at the gates parleying with "the mighty king", the Mongrel Kaul himself.

And as they appeared together, Mend'rys reasoned accord had been accepted by the women, and now they worked to bring Kaul into the fold. For what, Mend'rys could only guess, but an army seemed to be the best of reasons.

Rains came, and for two days Mend'rys and Jyslin stayed within the hideaway, as city streets turned to flows of mud and water. In his workshop and his solitude, Steffyn dropped away the look of Drow, and gazed upon himself in the mirror as he truly was; a slender elf, pale of skin and dark of eyes, disheveled hair, and worry lines about his brow.

He glanced at the door, thinking of the lie he had told Jyslin to keep her from his sanctuary, sat with a cup of tea in hand, and thought once more of his wife, Emildir.

Never would I have thought of leaving her and Barad Anna, yet once returned from Audrey's Kingdom of the Sun, I knew the Drow were the fundamental enemy of Ardwel. Now, I cannot turn away, and must see this venture to the end. May Yarhetha'an forgive my transgressions as I seek to end the tyranny of Archane and Mors'ul'jyn in this land.

A small bell on the table softly rang. Steffyn stood quickly, assumed the look of Mend'rys once again, and looked into the mirror. He waved a hand before it, drew golden dust and scattered it before himself. Images grew within the glass, swirling in their forming, and he saw, not female Drow, but the palace gates, where he had left a scrying sigil.

There within the mirror was a scene that gave him pause. Dark elf soldiers entering the palace, and a dark-clad ancient Drow with retainers at his side. Guards fell before them, and in only moments, the Drow disappeared beyond the great oaken doors.

Rebellion? Surely not, with Drow entering the palace. Therefore invasion, and Kaul's life at stake. Might I intervene? If so, who do I face? Is this Mor'i'jil himself, come to reclaim the city in Archane's name? Why so? What purpose would this serve with Archane yet missing?

150

Archane here, then gone. Might Mor'i'jil know of her appearance, and therefore, return? Or if only knowing she was here, has he come to wait? Regardless, he is here, for in the end, Kaul becomes the center of it all.

He gathered scrolls, a bag of scented stones, and tossed on a heavy cloak. Out the door and back into the hideaway, he found Jyslin at the table reading. "Come. We have visitors and I wish you to aid me in their knowing." She rose and bowed, donned her cloak and stood beside him as he waved her close. Then he incanted words, and as Jyslin squealed and clutched his arm, they disappeared, dust and wind blowing parchments from the table.

* * *

Mors'ul'jyn and Archane did not take the carriage to Kaul's city; rather, by magic they appeared within the palace grounds, met there by dark elf guards to Archane's great surprise. The soldiers approached slowly, and took to their knees in praise. Archane stood silent, then walked among them, touching each upon the shoulder, whispering words in Drow tongue Mors'ul'jyn could not understand.

After moments, the great oaken doors of the palace opened, and Mor'i'jil, with guards and clergy, descended the steps as in a trance. They bowed or knelt, all with tears rolling down their cheeks, and at the last a chant of exaltation was heard among the priesthood.

Mors'ul'jyn stood away, watching carefully as guards rose to gather round Archane, keeping her from sight.

The ancient dark elf approached and nodded curtly. "I recall you from your time in *Ung'gu'wi*. It seems fate brings us together once again."

"Dark Lord Mor'i'jil," Mors'ul'jyn replied, recognition in her voice. "I bring you a miracle, in the flesh once more, and an offer." She glanced to the soldiers gathered round Archane. "We have accord, she and I. I will hold you to that bargain as well."

Mor'i'jil tilted his head slightly, as though considering. "Yet now she is here and protected by her loyal guard, as you see. How might this accord be kept if you cannot enforce it?"

Mors'ul'jyn raised her face to his. "You have no power in the land, and the other Houses will scream trickery when Archane returns to claim her place. Even now they plot against you."

The old dark elf priest shook his head. "Your words have truth, yet what of it? Dealings of the Drow have little to do with you now." His voice dropped to a dangerous whisper. "Leave while you may, and carry on your life as chosen."

Mors'ul'jyn's eyes met his, and they took each other's measure for a long and terrible moment. "May I say adieu to the Dark Princess? I would ask her word of our… agreement."

Mor'i'jil looked beyond his shoulder and motioned to the guards, then turned back to her again. "Very well."

* * *

Mend'rys and Jyslin appeared in an alleyway, near the palace gates, but unseen by passers-by. He held her as she shook, kissed her forehead and motioned to the street. They emerged from the dimness and made way unhurried to the iron portcullis, now barring entrance.

Mend'rys turned to the girl, still trembling, and held her hands in his. "You will see dark elves in number, and I must know if one I think is here. It is important you speak truthfully."

She looked into his eyes, her voice yet absent, grinned weakly, and then took a breath to calm herself.

They made way to the portcullis, guards about and watching carefully. Mend'rys made a shushing gesture to Jyslin and she nodded, then gently waved a hand before himself. Guards turned away, seemingly indifferent. Slowly the portcullis lifted, and they slipped beneath it quickly.

They found a place within the shrubs and trees around the reflecting pool, and watched the crowd of dark elf soldiers at the steps. Mend'rys recognized Mors'ul'jyn and cursed beneath his breath, then quieted as Jyslin looked to him in query.

They waited in their silence, as the brace of guards parted, and an older male stepped forth, walking slowly to Mors'ul'jyn, Mend'rys nodded to his place.

"Mor'i'jil," whispered Jyslin, "minister of Archane and trusted confidant for longer than I have been alive. It was he who returned with Reena, the concubine. Tales say of her changing in their journey to a human place."

Mend'rys looked to the girl. "Drakenmoore?"

Jyslin thought. "Yes, Master, as I recall that is the name."

Mend'rys nodded to himself. *Fool dark elves, thinking they could rule Drakenmoore… and NorthWind! Surely that was their reason!*

Jyslin's hand tightened fiercely on his arm as the Dark Princess stepped from the clergy circle. "Archane is alive!" She threw her hand across her mouth as she nearly shouted out the words. Guards turned, drawing weapons, and Mend'rys's heart leapt nearly to his throat.

152

No! Not once again! All three here, and I might end it all in one gesture, one incantation! Yet now…

He rose, began an incantation, yet Mors'ul'jyn was quicker. She threw her heavy cloak about Archane, wrapped Mor'i'jil within it too fast for his ancient limbs to stop her. She shouted out a spell Mend'rys knew the meaning of, then the trio disappeared, sending dust into the air.

The guards paused, then advanced again upon Mend'rys and Jyslin. He gestured, a wall of unseen force cast against the soldiers. Down they went, losing weapons in the process, then rose and fought to find their way beyond what they could not see.

Mend'rys called the wind, then dragged Jyslin from the bushes, ran for the portcullis once again, where more guards stood with weapons brandished. He shouted words of magic, and the ironworks simply fell to dust. He tossed scented stones from his bag at the soldiers' feet, and they burst into crimson flame. The guards screamed, dropped their weapons, and ran for the watering troughs to douse the fires, as Mend'rys and Jyslin hurried beyond the shattered gates.

Down they ran once more into the alley and across another street, as alarms sounded in the central tower of the city. Mend'rys knew their time was gone, and he shouldered his way through a door into a storage room.

He wrapped Jyslin in his arms, closed his eyes and begged his temper calm. All the while she shook with fear, then he clasped her closer, wondering of the feelings in his spirit. He shoved it all away, met her dark eyes again, and gave a smile of resignation. "Fate has brought us here together. It will keep us thusly. Hold fast."

He drew a breath, called the Craft once again, and they disappeared, shutters rattling in their exit.

BOOK SIX
TIMES COME

*"There comes a time
when the enemy of my enemy
becomes an ally."*

Wolfe'ik Cal'id'reil to Sar'a'don
on the Steppes of Marillion

PART ONE
CHANGE OF FORTUNE

Beneath the Depths of Drakenmoore...

Mors'ul'jyn tumbled to the floor, bruising knees and elbows, as Archane and Mor'i'jil landed nearly atop her. She struggled from the cloak still wrapped about them, stood and called a cantrip. Chairs slid from the corners of the room and in only heartbeats, the Dark Princess and her minister sat within them, bound by silver threads.

Archane's eyes were as a fire, Mor'i'jil's yet clearing as he came to understand what had happened. He looked about the chamber, to Archane, then to Mors'ul'jyn standing before them, cradling her injured arm.

Archane's gaze locked with Mor'i'jil's. "Say nothing. We are once more in her sanctuary."

Mors'ul'jyn paced to the table, poured wine and drank it all, cast her eyes to the hearth, and the fire roared its warmth into the room. She stood before it, contemplating how her plans and schemes had nearly come to violent ending.

She returned to stand before Archane once again. "Yes, we are returned to a place of safety. Nearly did the three of us die in the courtyard of Kaul's city-state." She laughed scornfully. "Irony, that we would meet our ending where bargains only dreamed of were dashed in the midst of treachery between us. And by another!"

"I do not... understand," said Mor'i'jil, looking once more to Archane.

"The other who approached." Mors'ul'jyn laughed again. "You saw nothing? Surely, tho', you felt magic in the air."

Archane looked thoughtfully away and nodded. "Two figures, a dark elf male and a girl, yet I knew them not."

"The spell he thought to cast!" Mors'ul'jyn turned away once more, nearly trembling in her steps. She spun, facing them again. "An assassin from a rival House? A renegade, perhaps from Modennethra? I must think upon this! Tho' never seen, there was a taste of... remembrance in his doing."

Archane shook her head. "None from *Ung'gu'wi* that I know of, not of our House or others." She speared Mor'i'jil with her heated gaze.

157

"What has transpired in my absence? Have you let the other Houses insinuate themselves into our leadership?"

"Dark Princess, no! Conclave was called, demanded by Hovenethra, yet the House of Iyllyeth rules! I have kept your memory alive within the Race, and only came on revelation through a vision! Never would I dishonor you in such a way!"

Mor'i'jil's voice nearly was a pleading whine, and Mors'ul'jyn caught it all. "You reasoned Kaul was the key, yes? Astute of you, and my complements. Tensions in *Ung'gu'wi* must be balanced on a dagger point... a sacrificial dagger point. Surely your own heart must be sought by Hovenethra and others." She smirked. "This was your only chance, Dark Lord Mor'i'jil. Should you return with empty hands, your life would be forfeit for crimes against the Race. Irony, once again."

Mor'i'jil shrugged. "And now? Plans on either side lay broken, and the Houses soon will set war upon each other. How to stop dark elves from committing genocide upon themselves?"

Mors'ul'jyn huffed a breath. "It was my plan, to keep them from doing so, with Kaul's forces! In your rush to be of service and show power to the other Houses, you dashed those plans as so many eggs upon the ground. Now..."

She walked away, anger nearly at her limit, then turned. "Why should I care? I have no love for your kind, tho' I wear the look." She glanced to Archane again. "Your Dark Princess held me prisoner to her whim, and I to her for five years past. Slowly, the scales are balanced. Now I have you both, and we may watch as all the Houses decimate each other. Who will remain? What will be left of Drow, if anything at all? How many years might assassins roam the chambers, as leaders and those who think to lead are murdered?"

She rubbed her aching arm again. "How many hearts, Dark Princess? And should you return, might yours be first?"

Archane said nothing, looked away with disgust, then slowly faced Mors'ul'jyn again. "What then? Do you hold us five years more as *Ung'gu'wi* crumbles and our numbers dwindle to nearly nothing? What of this sorcerer you say there may be knowing of? How to find victory when naught but chaos stands to reign?"

Mors'ul'jyn shook her head. "I have no answers for the nonce, only questions, as do you. Therefore..."

The silver threads about Archane and Mor'i'jil fell away, and they massaged their tingling arms and legs. "Take rest and sustenance." Mors'ul'jyn motioned to the table, now filled with food and drink. "You know not where we are, therefore cannot escape. You have little power within these chambers, and regardless, should I be harmed, still you would be entombed. Think upon our quandary and take note. The fates have put us here, and only by agreement will we all survive."

* * *

Mors'ul'jyn left them alone, retiring through a door on the wall opposite the hearth. Archane and Mor'i'jil took time to search the room, finding no other entryways. Even the hearth had no chimney, yet was a construct of magic, giving heat and light, but without smoke, and never burning out. A pot of stew bubbled at the side, and the table had been left with carafes of wine and water there upon it. Two settees had appeared, fine wool blankets and pillows looking fresh and clean.

Yet there was no way without, no secret doors, only a room of stone decorated as a castle, with rugs and trappings on the wall, furniture with the Arms of Drakenmoore carved upon them, and a suit of *NorthWind* armor in the corner. Archane knew this was a scrying thing, and cautioned Mor'i'jil.

"It moves, and my thought is, may fight if necessary. Power, Dark Lord, and we see it in our surroundings. The wizard-woman Re' held ability as few within this land."

She looked with meaning into his ancient eyes, as they sat at table, whispering in the quiet. "A match for any in *Ung'gu'wi*, yes? Perhaps even my own self."

Mor'i'jil spoke carefully. "Yours is power of *Iyllyeth*, and *Mother Darkness*. Surely this… mortal cannot stand against you."

Archane cast a gaze into her goblet. "You spoke of Conclave and Hovenethra's demands. Yet you appeared in the usurper's city with soldiers and assassins. How so?"

"As said, a vision came to me, and I reasoned the Mongrel at the center of it all."

Archane shook her head. "There is more, I am certain. Why would you think him involved at all? He was a guard and a deserter. It was he who aided her escape from *Ung'gu'wi* and set this all in motion." She raised her face in understanding. "Ah, yes… she led him by his maleness into treason against the Race."

"That and more, Dark Princess. Surely power was offered, not only gold."

159

Archane thought for moments. "She said as much in those years of my imprisonment, tho' hardly did I listen. Five years of life she stole away. How may I reclaim it?"

"Yet you are immortal…"

Archane slowly stood and loomed above him. "Think you I am here without suffering? I died, Dark Lord, in agony, and nearly so again, had Mors'ul'jyn not found me! Therefore, irony, that I would be rescued by one who stole the body of a traitor. Then nearly rescued once more by yourself, a flaw in her own plans. Then your own designs spoiled at the last by intervention of a stranger!" She chuckled with a dryness in her voice. "Fates, as she said, have kept us in each other's company."

Mor'i'jil looked away, then to Archane again. "There is more, Dark Princess. All are intertwined, more than you have learned. All the land searches for this Mors'ul'jyn as the murderess of Galandria Telveperen, leader of the elves."

Archane sat again. "What is this, and when?"

"Years ago, not long before your righteous fight against Crysalon, and Mors'ul'jyn's finding of you. In only days, the leaders of all the land were taken. Crysalon. Telveperen. Yourself. Five years the land has set stunned to inaction. Five years I have kept *Ung'gu'wi* whole and without war." His voice rose slightly, and his shoulders shook. "Five years, Dark Princess, I have worried every day you would not return. And then, on Conclave, worried that you might."

Archane's fiery gaze pierced him to his spirit. "You think yourself a better leader? Is this your true wish, that I had not been found?"

She took him by the throat, his ancient hands tightening about her wrist, but he did not struggle as he might. "Had that been my true plan, never would I have come to the Mongrel's city. I would have left you to his base desires and whims. And hers."

He pulled away and Archane sat, shocked to silence. "Kaul wanted power," he continued. "That of the Drow. Whatever he might do to hold it, he would do. Surely his thought was through Mors'ul'jyn."

He rose and hobbled to the hearth, his back to Archane, struggling with his breath. At last he turned to the table once again, and knelt before her. "No night has come and gone I did not wish you there to lead! Tho' in truth, your disappearance made us stronger, forced us to think more for ourselves, and know war among our own kind was not the answer. Should you return now, Hovenethra will challenge, of that I am certain. Yet if done carefully, and with spoils in your hand, none would raise a voice against you.

160

"Kaul is the key, Dark Princess, and his city those very spoils! The city taken from us by the elves and humans, given then to the Mongrel for his aid. For his killing of you in your former incarnation! Take back the city, this was my thought, as we awaited your return."

Archane laid a hand at last upon his head as his tears fell on the stones. "Worthy work, Dark Lord, and I will grant you solace for it. Yet what now? We are prisoners, are we not? Not only ourselves, but her as well."

She shrugged. "And her words were true. Only as we agree might we survive. We retreat a step, therefore, and reconsider. Tho' little time, we must proceed with care and patience. Praise *Iyllyeth*, that we have now the two of us. And if the land, as you say, searches for Mors'ul'jyn for crimes against the elves, should we escape, we have a token with which to bargain."

* * *

Mors'ul'jyn rose from her bed. Sleep would not come, though fatigue lay heavy on her soul and body. Still her arm ached, and now her back and shoulder. She pushed the pain away and glanced to the mirror in the corner, seeing the image of Archane and Mor'i'jil talking softly at the table in the larger chamber.

Secrets between them, still, they are at my mercy, and will do nothing to threaten their own safety. Yet will the dark elves fall to war upon themselves, with both Archane and Mor'i'jil absent? Surely there are no others in the House of Iyllyeth with strength or allies to hold the Race together. What will remain, or will the warrens and chambers of Ung'gu'wi stink of death forevermore? How will it play, and should I even care?

She thought to interrupt them, but to what purpose? She scoffed within her mind. Nothing they might do would change their circumstance, which now was more tenuous in many ways, yet also held more possibilities.

What would the House of Iyllyeth do for return of Archane and her minister? How, once more, to hold them to a bargain, for as I have seen, should advantage come into their hands, they will not honor any word. Therefore...

She thought once more of Kaul, likely dead by now, or fighting for his life with the dark elf soldiers in his city. Might she make a pact with the City-State of Truth, to deliver the leaders of the Drow to them for... safekeeping? She chuckled.

Holding Archane and Mor'i'jil gives time into my hands. Time to renew my vengeance on Calidriil and the elves, and even then, the city-state for its alliance with them.

161

Yet as she searched her soul, she could not find the fire once burning. The death of Galandria Telveperen, and her blood running on Mors'ul'jyn's hands, had calmed the fever for these years. It was though the heart of Elvenkind had died, and she knew, to this very day, Sheynon Calidriil carried that bitter agony of his wife's death within his spirit. Agony Mors'ul'jyn wanted him to have, and prayed he held it as a dagger in his own heart until the day he died. And there upon, she wished him a long, long life in which to suffer.

Where then is my purpose in this world? Raise Drakenmoore again? The House is gone, NorthWind as well, naught but a tumble of stones into the ground. Rule the Drow? How so? Even should I take the body of Archane, as I did of Reena, Mor'i'jil would know. And little might I do without his guidance in the manner of the Houses. Others, too, would soon realize it was not Archane before them, and my soul would surely not be immortal as is her spirit. Something else. Something… unexpected.

She glanced to the bookcase on the wall opposite the door. Behind it lay a hidden entrance into what once had been her workshop, yet now held only a trap for those prying in her sanctuary. Something there had been bargained with a daemon, to lie in wait for those foolish enough to think themselves more clever than was she. A thing not of this world, evil, base, and hungry. Always hungry.

Her true realm of magic, where none had been since… Draxa's disappearance? Had it been so many years? That place could be entered only as the sanctuary in which they now resided, through the power of spells, known only to Mors'ul'jyn. Constructed by what then was the greatest wizard triad in humankind, she was the only one in certainty remaining.

For I was ancient when Reena's body became my own, and surely Draxa now is dead. Zakara Thelena I slew myself, for transgressions against the Family. Others? Only Veniculis might approach my power, and he has not been seen for years.

She thought to brew a sleeping draught, yet paused, something picking at her mind with the thought of other mages in the world. She sat again upon her bed, laid back and closed her eyes, clearing clutter from her consciousness. Drifting, she saw faces, felt the touch of other powers she had been in the presence of, for if nothing else, the wizard-woman Re' knew the taste and feel of abilities held by those of the Craft.

The dark elves in the courtyard of the city-state. Yes, that whiff of essence, she knew it, yet had not recognized the face.

Years before… many years. Draxa still alive. Thelena freshly dead. Diatus and the Cave of Bells. Eric the Crimson, her betrothed, naught but a lout and drunkard. *Kingmaker.* Calidriil, and the clergy of the *Rising Star*, damn them all!

Her eyes opened then in revelation. *Steffyn Foxxe!*

* * *

The City-State of DragonFall...

The fighting had been fierce, and had Kaul's bodyguard not freed him from his bonds soon as the dark elf Mor'i'jil exited the palace, likely his blood, not that of Drow, would have stained the marble floors.

The Mongrel stood amidst the carnage, his *NorthWind* sword dripping, eyes yet seeking enemies. Ten of his bodyguard had died, another dozen wounded, but the dark elf soldiers in the palace grounds had all been killed, and the tolling of alarm bells in the city's central tower could still be heard upon the wind. Kaul knew the barracks of the army would empty on the sounding of those bells, as his plans for such had been laid many years before.

Enemies at the city gates would be engaged. Assassins roaming the palace still would be found and put to agonizing death. Any found hiding in the harem would be beheaded there, as a warning to those females, particularly of dark elf Race, that treason would be dealt with swiftly.

Mors'ul'jyn was rightly as said in our first meeting. I have grown soft, ill-advised, and lax in training. No more. This day is an awakening, and Kaul Morg'ash will return as the beast he was before.

He ordered any living of the dark elves brought before him. Six were dragged from hiding, two others moaning as they lay wounded. Those he dispatched quickly before the others, taking heads cleanly with his *NorthWind* blade. He looked the others over carefully, seeking a leader there among them. He paused at the third figure on his knees.

"Lancer Captain?" Kaul laughed. "You were cowardly as the rest, hiding in the stable. Where is the dark elf courage I have heard so much of?"

He took the head of the Drow soldier on the left, and it bounced between the Lancer Captain's knees. Eyes wide and lips moving as in search of words that never would be said, blood flowed from the severed neck. The Lancer Captain said nothing, only glared at Kaul in hatred.

"Shall I take another? And another? And yours the last?" Kaul laid his blade across the Lancer Captain's shoulder, the blood-splattered edge against his flesh. "Your Dark Princess is gone where none may find her, your minister as well. Poor planning and over-confidence by Mor'i'jil that your soldiers were a match for my city guard."

Kaul knelt on his haunches, eye to eye with the dark elf leader. He spoke in Drow, though slowly, as it had been many years since his using of the tongue. "You ask yourself, what does this brute want?" He shrugged. "Nothing, as our quarry goes to ground. What then is left? Valor?" Kaul spat. "I will not ask that you beg, for I know the better. I say only this; take word and your worthless life. Tell the Drow Kaul Morg'ash never again will be trifled with or used. And with your leaders gone, live in fear of my coming to claim *Ung'gu'wi* as my own."

He rose, took another head, then another. At last the Drow left alive screamed as one, and shook in abject fear Kaul could smell, as a hunter smells the prey.

* * *

Kaul lounged in the bath, three concubines beside him, washing, stroking, tending to his every need. Night had fallen, and with it the quieting of the tower bells, as his captain of the city guard reported all was well.

Kaul was not so certain, and ordered gates barred and guards doubled, then sent assassins of his own within the palace, to search for any of the dark elves who might still live. Two were found, and Kaul killed them both himself. Not with weapons or by execution, but with his teeth and claws, not used for many years. The taste of flesh, with blood spraying in his face, running down his chin, and the ragged sounds of dark elf throats torn out, brought back memories long forgotten.

Now he brooded as his harem sat about the bath, minstrels playing softly in a corner, and two concubines trying to arouse his interest. He chuckled, rose in the bath to give them better purchase, then splashed water o'er them both. At once a water battle then erupted, and the chamber drenched from side to side and floor to ceiling, as the musicians ran to save their instruments.

Kaul's instrument was tended with much more care than theirs.

* * *

He called Rohesia to his throne room at high sun on the day that followed. Her wounds were light, and he had ordered her be tended in whatever manner she had wished the night before. She begged only a simple bath with a single male attendant, but the word in Kaul's ears come early morn was, she had rung every drop of essence from his body.

Now she stood before him dressed in simple finery, and he watched her with a careful eye. "I have a task for you, one needing of a woman's delicacy." He waved a hand at her inquiring look. "Not of pleasures offered, but a better manner than my own."

He rose, and they walked to a sitting lounge, servants hovering close, food and wine set before them as they watched in silence. At last they were alone, and Kaul poured her goblet full. "This city, for all I have done in my time here, no longer is secure. We have seen in these past days what may happen."

He drank slowly as she listened without comment. "Archane and her minister Mor'i'jil are now in the clutches of Mors'ul'jyn. This bodes ill for all. DragonFall, the land at large, and even the Drow. Once word is given to those waiting in *Ung'gu'wi*, likely the dark elves will fall upon each other, fighting for control of a dying Race."

He motioned to the meal before them, and they ate in quiet. "Therefore," he continued, refilling her goblet and then his own, "it is time treachery and lies are set aside. For only when they are useful should they be tools, for whatever purpose."

Rohesia raised an eyebrow. "My King, you are clever —"

He raised a hand. "More so than many think, yet I cannot face this threat alone, for the good of the city. You will become my emissary to those once allied, and with hope, will become so again." He let go a heavy breath. "I have given far too many insults to offer of that alliance. You, as my voice, will speak the truth to them, for they would not believe me should I swear upon whatever holy book thrust before me."

Rohesia gave him a wry look and nearly smiled. "It would burn likely on your touch."

Kaul chuckled and they touched rims, then drank. "You will travel with an honor guard, to the elves. Calidriil, to whom I was once a hireling."

Rohesia's eyes widened.

"Yes, and tho' I earned my gold by blood and battle, still, had he not chosen me, all this," he waved his hand at the throne room about, "might have never come to pass. I say this to you in confidence, for you have been close for many years, and earned my trust."

"My King, never would I betray that trust, I swear."

Kaul nodded. "And this is why you are chosen. Take three waiting ladies as you need, and I will see the guard detail set ready. Prepare to leave two days hence. Tho' it vexes me to ask for aid, I know it must be done. If nothing else, elves are honorable and will fulfil a pact. Humans, only those of religious bent would I consider. Seek Sheynon Calidriil, speak truth into his ear. Tell him Kaul Morg'ash seeks his aid, and will give him what was asked for when last visiting my city."

* * *

Somewhere in the Mists of Magic…

Mend'rys knelt, searching for his calm, hard in finding. Jyslin lay beside him, retching, moaning, tears pouring from her eyes, until she quieted in exhaustion.

He stood at last, knees weak, and cast his gaze about, knowing their situation grim. His incantation had been a spell set before, should predicament arise, a single word to take him to a place not traveled by sorcerers of good decision.

Close by stood… something, vaguely of elven shape, two arms, two legs, a single head, but otherwise… different. Mend'rys glanced to Jyslin lying on the hardpacked earth, devoid of reason in her eyes. He raised his gaze to the thing before him and spoke. "We mean no harm and will leave quickly as we may. My companion is yet unable to withstand another transit. Therefore, we will only wait."

The thing sniffed the air. "Female? Then I will claim my due for your intrusion."

"No!" Mend'rys held a hand, more calmly than he truly felt. "She is under my protection. Stand away."

A second creature appeared from the mists around, larger than the first. Both appeared as red-skinned horrors, nude and most certainly male. Mend'rys was not convinced he could defeat them both, should challenge come.

The second grinned. "We will have our way, or you will not survive. Give her to us and perhaps she will recover. If not…" The creature shrugged heavy shoulders.

Mend'rys knew his power here was limited. In this place, where never would he have taken another living thing, he relied on guile and wit, not the Arts. He tucked a hand into his pouch, feeling three stones still there, then paused. "Where is the master of this place?"

The creatures looked to each other.

Mend'rys continued. "I will speak only with the one who rules, no other. If you decline, then you show cowardice. You would lose face to he who rules, and any pleasures taken would not be yours, but his. Stand aside or call him. Allow us leave and none will know."

The first creature coughed a laugh. "You speak well for a dark elf."

Mend'rys glanced to Jyslin, yet unmoving. He spoke again, more quietly. "This is but a shade. I am known to the one here ruling. We have dealt in past times with success for both."

The second creature sneered. "Then show your true form or you will not leave alive."

"That I will not do, yet I shall say my name. Dare you hear it?"

Again, the creatures traded glances.

"Names carry power. Is yours so great?"

Mend'rys nodded. "Shall I speak it?"

The creatures backed away a pace. "Stay silent. We will grant you leave, this time. Do not intrude again." They disappeared into the roiling mists once more.

Mend'rys let go a breath, sagged to his knees, and lifted Jyslin into his arms. Her eyes focused slowly on his face, and she raised a shaking hand. "Master?"

* * *

The City-State of DragonFall…

He took them to the sanctuary shack, thinking time had passed enough to make it safe. He carried Jyslin to the bed, laid her down with a warm compress upon her forehead, then set the hearth aflame. He sat beside her for a while, contemplating his actions, understanding what had been seen in the palace courtyard was naught but plans falling into ruin, for Mor'i'jil and Mors'ul'jyn alike.

How did the priest know of Mors'ul'jyn's coming with Archane? Likely he did not. Yet did Mors'ul'jyn know of his arrival? More the possibility there was for that occurrence than the other, surely. Yet Mor'i'jil reasoned Kaul at the center of whatever plans were being made, for his forces, if no other.

Mend'rys thought back, of *Ung'gu'wi* and rumors there of dark elf soldiers, battles fought, and outcomes won or lost. He shook his head; too little time had been spent in search of military matters, yet Jyslin, once woken, may have known.

Jyslin. Too deeply now was she involved to abandon her. More times than he could count, he had crossed the line of what humans called infidelity with the girl. Intimacy with one not Joined to, when Joined with another. Elves, as Steffyn Foxxe had known, were more pragmatic, and those who chose relationships with looser boundaries not uncommon.

167

Yet Steffyn was not among them, and only in the guise of Mend'rys had he lain with Jyslin.

Only when torment, pain, and guilt were near to overwhelming him.

Only when his lust had risen to a breaking point.

Only when his thoughts turned to his wife, Emildir…

Only afterward would his tears fall in knowing his transgression.

He rose and made his way into his workshop. There, at last, he could drop away the look of Mend'rys, sag into a chair, and curse how it all had come to pass.

But future times were clouded, and his intellect must wake and find an answer. Where could he go for aid? Whom might he turn to?

The Guild at Telveperen? They, too, had suffered losses at Mors'ul'jyn's hand. And surely Steffyn's guilt had been spoken of in darkened corridors.

The Drow? None he could trust, for none were known.

Ysilrod, Sheynon's brother? No.

Veniculis himself? Not seen for years, the Vermillion Mage returning to nothing but a legend.

He raised a trembling hand. The effort to keep the image as Mend'rys had taxed him to his limit. He knew, in time, it would fail him, and Jyslin see the truth. And more, what power it took might be that needed to save his life. Or hers. Where would the nightmare end?

Should he return to Sheynon, ask forgiveness once again, and huddle in the walls of *Annatar Yarhetha'an*?

Surely Chitthra yet sought his blood.

Surely in time she would find him.

She was *Däe Quivië*, as had been Steffyn's own son Daeron, avengers of the elven Race. No tenets Steffyn knew of in the Brotherhood prevented elves to be thought as enemies. Especially those whose hands were covered in the blood of Galandria Telveperen, however allegorically.

Should he surrender to that fate, allow her vengeance on him to be consummated?

What would she think, a follower of his own son, should Steffyn appear and offer her his life?

Yet answers never come. Time continues, and with it, my existence. Where did it go, the life I had, so sweet? When did I choose to leave it all behind and embark upon this… venture?

That Steffyn knew, surely as he knew anything in this day.

Audrey Vincent.

The Kingdom of the Sun.

168

The Shadow Horde.

And behind the Horde, Archane.

* * *

Annatar Yarhetha'an…

Chitthra had decided. Nearly half a moon had passed since her declaration to Sheynon, and on arrival of Thalion and Audrey, the fortress had been filled with merriment and laughter, and tales of the comrades' past. And in that time, Chitthra's darkened manner grew and she withdrew, seeking solace in prayer and meditation, knowing only she was delaying what was necessary. She must find Steffyn Foxxe, for honor could be set aside no longer, and though knowing it could mean her death, she was bound by vows to carry out her mission.

Aeren, always close and warm beside her, listened every night, as Chitthra poured her heart out, tears running down her ebon cheeks. Aeren then would hold her close, and together they would share the grief, that it would be lessened.

Never did Aeren speak to sway her. Never did she chide Chitthra for her task. Only did she pledge her own life to stand beside the dark elf woman, that should death come to claim her, they would face it side by side, and as Aeren said, undefeated.

The bond, therefore, was strengthened. Chitthra, too, did not speak again of Aeren's safety, or bar her from a duty sworn. Eyes meeting through tears and laughter, through concerns growing in their minds, their hearts were intertwined, and never would they let each other go.

Love, it seemed, had settled deeply in the hearts of Chitthra of *Däe Quivïe* and Aeren Greywald.

* * *

Early morn, and Sheynon was called to the eastern battlements. He quickly dressed, called attendants for his armor to be taken to the gatehouse, and bid Ysilrod be wakened. Down the steps and through the courtyard, he paused only long enough for a weapon to be handed to him before following his guards up and to the lookout. There, he saw approaching from the east a column, with banners of the City-State of DragonFall. Sheynon could but wonder what chaos this might bring.

"The brute sends us gifts," said Ysilrod, standing now at Sheynon's shoulder. He waved before them, and the air lensed greatly, then showed the column closely in detail. "Led by a woman, likely his minister Rohesia." Ysilrod waved again, then nodded. "Yes, I recall her in the palace." He chuckled. "Kaul will not grovel before you, therefore he sends a woman in his stead. He has assumed you will be more willing to offer parley with a pleasant face."

Sheynon shook his head slowly. "Ill portents, Brother. If Kaul offers parley, it is only that his bargaining position has worsened. Yet by sending an entourage as this, he plays the game and keeps his face. In many ways, he is not so much the brute we think, and when necessary, can be clever."

"Wiles, Sheynon, as an animal. I could send him away in a heartbeat if he became a danger."

"He is no danger in his city. Yet surely something happened for such a thing as this. Never has Kaul in these years sent an emissary. We see uncommon action by one who simply will not yield, even in his own betterment."

Sounds from the stairway, as Thalion and Audrey appeared. They took places at the elves' sides, marveling at Ysilrod's magics.

Thalion nodded. "From Kaul. At last we may hear the truth of it."

"This is the Mongrel spoken of?" asked Audrey. "Yet he, himself, does not come." She motioned to the scene, soldiers marching calmly, the woman at the lead.

"Kaul once was my hireling," replied Sheynon. "This is to remind me of his doings, that his gold was earned, and we now are equals. Soon enough we will learn what has brought him to this circumstance."

* * *

Sheynon called for mounts and led his soldiers to the chasm. The column from DragonFall paused on the eastern side, the woman dismounting and walking to the edge. She glanced into the darkness at her feet, then raised her face to Sheynon. "I am Rohesia of DragonFall. I come at the behest of my king, His Majesty Kaul Morg'ash, with a matter regarding safety of the land."

Sheynon and Ysilrod exchanged surreptitious glances. "She speaks well for the concubine of a brute," whispered the mage.

Behind him Audrey cleared her throat. "My ears hear well, elf-friend. Manners, if you please."

Sheynon took a step forward, nodding in acknowledgement. "What business is this you bring? We recall you in the city, and to my knowing, your king provided answers as we sought. Have you further news to offer?"

Rohesia glanced beyond her shoulder, then back. "I would speak with you in private, my lord. I will enter without guards, if you so wish."

"Bring them in if you choose," said Ysilrod into Sheynon's ear. "I will set alarms about and cantrips they cannot penetrate, should they have mischief in their minds."

Sheynon shook his head. "Cast a bridge and bring them forth. There is no malice in this meeting, and my thought is, Kaul is in need. Let us see what stirs as we spend time with friends from past adventures."

Ysilrod worked his Craft, and the entourage gasped as the bridge appeared across the chasm. Though it took some time with the horses, at last the column was across, and Rohesia stood before the elves.

She bowed. "Our thanks for your receiving us. Please, urgent matters are at hand. May we find a quiet place for parley?"

Sheynon turned to attendants who had followed. "Set a table at the gatehouse for our guests, that they may rest and take refreshment. Then matters will be discussed."

Rohesia's eyes drifted to the figures at the side, coming at the last to rest on Audrey. "I am honored to see such a Champion once more in Ardwel. I was very young when last I saw you, as you left the City-State of Truth to fight in Coronis." She bowed.

Audrey nodded. "Your memory is true, for some years have passed since then."

Rohesia's eyes returned to Sheynon. "Kaul sends greetings and a request. Matters worsen in the city and the land. Of that, likely you are aware, but there are words that must be spoken."

Sheynon glanced to the preparations at the gatehouse. "First a formal greeting, then parley. We offer welcome to emissaries of the City-State of DragonFall."

Thalion and Audrey looked to each other, suppressing smiles.

* * *

By the mid of day, and as Rohesia's manner calmed with wine and a hearty meal, they spoke as the sun rose and shone upon the fortress. Chitthra and Aeren had joined the table, sitting aside quietly and listening.

Time to time, the woman's eyes drifted to the gatehouse walls. Looking as though stars were shot within the stones, the ramparts glistening as with a scattering of diamonds.

"Mithril," said Sheynon, "and mined more than a thousand years ago in a land so far away, you cannot reach it in a lifetime."

171

Rohesia only nodded, looking upward to the battlements. "Tho' Kaul's city is most grand, this place is magic, I can see. Surely the gods must smile upon it."

"They do," replied Audrey, "and Lord Sheynon is its keeper for all Elvenkind. No other is worthy as is he." She placed her hand on Thalion's at the mention of "Kaul's city", as the priest's fingers tightened.

Sheynon motioned Rohesia to continue. "Say on of these events. Dark elves came, took Kaul and his palace prisoner, then what followed? More soldiers?"

Rohesia drank quietly for a moment. "An ancient dark elf, Mor'i'jil his name, minister to Archane. They knew each other, my king and him, and the animosity between them flowed as a river. Hate, my lord, is not strong enough a word. He came to reclaim the city for the Drow, and said only had it been given to Kaul for safe-keeping, nothing else."

"True in part," said Thalion from his chair aside. "Kaul's duty was done, and with honor. Therefore, he has been allowed to hold the city in this time."

Sheynon caught the blush of color in Rohesia's cheeks, and knew it was a touch of anger. "Kaul did duty for the elves. His place is earned for the nonce."

Rohesia drank again, then nodded.

"Continue, if you will," said Ysilrod.

"Mor'i'jil said to Kaul he would wait for Archane's return, however long it might take. He held us in the palace, bound as prisoners in Kaul's own House. Then, he was called away, beyond the doors. What transpired I did not see, but was told of by soldiers there."

Sheynon glanced to Audrey, who nodded slightly. "We are certain your words are true," he said.

The woman drew a breath. "I was told this Mors'ul'jyn and Archane returned, and in those tense moments, nearly did the city fall. Yet another was said to appear, and the trio vanished into the air. The dark elf women and the old priest, gone. Then the other vanished as well, in pursuit or simply to escape, I do not know."

"This other… elf, perhaps?" Ysilrod leaned forward, intent.

"Drow, said the soldiers, accompanied by a dark elf girl. This one took the palace gates down on their escape, turning them to dust."

Sheynon passed a glance to Ysilrod. "Then all disappeared? Might they have worked in concert?"

"My lord, I cannot say. Yet the soldiers' words were, Mors'ul'jyn threw her cloak about Mor'i'jil and Archane on sight of the new arrivals.

172

If true, it would seem whatever might have happened between the three of them was intruded there upon."

Once more Sheynon's eyes met Ysilrod's and held there for a moment. He turned his gaze to Rohesia once again. "Further news? How fares Kaul and the city now?"

The woman stared into her goblet before answering. "His rage was great. He held their captain in chains with other soldiers, then killed three of them while bound. The rest he set free with a warning to their cavern homes in the Black Forest." Sheynon motioned an attendant to refill her cup, and Rohesia drank again. "Never had I seen his anger in this manner. Yet he calmed in time, and bade me bring the news."

"And now?"

Rohesia raised her face. "My king begs your attendance for advice. He asks for the city and the land. I only pray my words have been worthy."

Sheynon blew a breath, looking to his compatriots. Audrey closed her eyes and nodded to him once again. "That they are, and you have done well. We will confer and make decision how best to deal. Your soldiers may set camp beside the walls, and you, my lady, I will have attendants show to a room and bath, should you choose."

"My waiting ladies will attend," said Audrey, and Rohesia smiled.

* * *

They met at the mid of night, Sheynon, his brother, Thalion and Audrey, in a tower away from the greathouse and the evening castle duties. Though summer, the night held a chill, and the flames in the fireplace welcome.

Audrey had shed her finery, dressed simply as in bygone days, and Sheynon noted her plain appearance still did not dim the depth of her charisma, always held. Thalion sat in quiet, his hand passing o'er his cup before he drank. The elf-lord thought again of Kannan and her mannerisms, and how that glowing life, in his humble notion, had been given for a purpose ill of thought.

Ysilrod stood at the window, shutters open and the nighttime air brisk and fresh. He spoke quietly to himself, and Sheynon wondered if a cantrip was in place, for safety of them all.

"Her words were true, my lord," said Audrey to Sheynon's unspoken question. "Our choice now is how best to reconcile with Kaul."

Sheynon gave her a look, noting the absence of Chitthra and Aeren. "Your esquire?"

The warrior-woman shook her head. "Later, and in private. For the nonce, let us speak of the coming circumstance."

"Excellency, this is truly not your fight," replied Thalion.

Audrey showed a gentle smile. "In this company, titles are unnecessary. And tho' I do not know this man, or Mors'ul'jyn herself, I know Archane, and Galandria Telveperen was a mentor. I come at behest of my great lord *Jhad* to stand beside my friends and offer what I may."

Thalion chuckled. "We are not the brash adventurers once we were."

"Yet we are here, and all that stands before the evil, my friend." Audrey offered her hand, and he took it gently. "Can we say we are not ready? What brings us together one last time, if not the struggle?"

Thalion did not answer, nor did Sheynon. There were no words to say in reply to Audrey's pledge.

"Let us contemplate the future," said Ysilrod, turning from the window. "Mor'i'jil reasoned Kaul to be the center of it all, as did we, yet acted with decisiveness."

"You say we should have taken Kaul our prisoner?" Sheynon grinned.

"I might have left a scrying sigil, or remained in hiding. Still…" Ysilrod paced away as the others waited. "Let us assume Mors'ul'jyn has captured Mor'i'jil with Archane. Kaul allows word to be taken to *Ung'gu'wi* of this occurrence. What then of the Drow?"

"Five years and what has been done within that time?" asked Thalion. "If the dark elf Houses make war upon each other, it weakens them as a Race, and our land does not suffer."

"Agreed, yet what is Mors'ul'jyn's need? How does she gain from this with Archane and her minister in hand?"

"A move of desperation," said Audrey after a quiet moment. "This… other… forced her hand."

"Once more, agreed, my lady." Ysilrod paced away again, then back. "Mors'ul'jyn arrived with Archane, expecting parley. Yet why? Surely, if she knew Mor'i'jil in the city, she would surmise he would not arrive unprotected. Therefore, disagreement, yes? And she, then near losing of her advantage, once more showed her mind yet is sharp. When the other dark elf appeared…"

Thalion nodded. "Again, as said by Her Excellency, a desperate move. One which may bring down the Drow threat to Ardwel."

"*Jhad* be praised," whispered Audrey, and signed herself.

"Yet who is this other? And why appear at this very moment, with the highest of the high in dark elf priesthood and Mors'ul'jyn herself there as well…" Ysilrod fell silent, thinking.

"And our part?" Thalion raised his hands. "I see no reason for involvement in this time."

"Something stirs in Kaul's mind, however," replied Sheynon. "To send an emissary speaks of desperation in his dealings. I would know his reasons."

Audrey smiled. "A ride across the land?"

Thalion could but shake his head and grin.

* * *

The gatehouse battlements were quiet before the new day's dawn, and Sheynon found Audrey there alone. He approached with a mug of tea and offered it. "Good morrow, Excellency. You said we would speak of Aeren when in private."

Audrey sipped and sighed, then nodded gently. "They both have gone, yet I begged them stay. Sheynon, know little of what happened between yourself and Steffyn. Tho' forgiven, still his heart is broken, I am certain, and never will he recover."

Sheynon looked away. "He did what he thought best for reasons of his own. I cannot hold him guilty for what happened."

Audrey drew closer. "Nonetheless, he carries guilt, and Chitthra knows the truth of it. Eternity, Sheynon, he was willing to sacrifice her to watch over Mors'ul'jyn. Surely one as Steffyn should have known a mind as that of Teresa Drakenmoore would find a way from a prison she herself had conjured. For only once, Steffyn did not use his reason, but his heart, and thereby it cost the land, and yourself and family, dearly."

She held him close, and he returned the embrace gently. "None in our comradeship understands the reasons. Ysilrod himself may have a notion, yet Steffyn always was a troubled mind." She held him away. "What will you do? Chitthra swears her vengeance upon him and my own esquire rides to protect her back."

He drew apart and shrugged. "She spoke to me of honor. The horror of it all, a dark elf woman following the son of Steffyn Foxxe, now becoming the avenger of my wife against the father of the one she holds as holy!"

For an instant, anger crossed Sheynon's countenance, and Audrey paused before it. "Therefore, your choice?"

175

He raised his arms as in surrender. "What choice have I? I fight against an elf-brother or the woman seeking his very blood. Irony, that I would fall between them!" Sheynon barked a chuckle and turned away again.

"Kaul's offer... is the importance more therein, or this?"

"The safety of the land is paramount, my lady, and you know this."

Audrey nodded. "Then let us tend this duty and give prayers Chitthra's heart will change. We both stand to lose in this vengeance venture, Sheynon. I do not wish to hear of Aeren's death trapped within a feud of bitter blood."

"Nor I. She is a sweet soul, and your teachings a blessing on her life." Sheynon paused and drew near. "You are aware... she and Chitthra have become lovers, yes?"

Audrey showed a smile. "And I wish them only happiness. Perhaps together, hearts entwined, calmer feelings will prevail."

* * *

PART TWO
ASIDE, TOGETHER

Along the way to DragonFall...

They set a camp well off the road, beneath a rocky overhang beside a stream. Aeren hunted for their dinner as Chitthra took time in meditation, decisions heavy in her mind and sadness in her heart. *Tho' Sheynon stayed his anger, will it be always so? Should I find Steffyn Foxxe, will I have courage to do what must be done? He is a sorcerer, and if in danger, as already I have seen, will not hold his hand against me.*

Aeren returned forthwith, three rabbits in her hand and a knot of greens plucked from the shore. She prepared the rabbits for a spit and set them out to roast, as Chitthra boiled water for the greens in an old tin pot. Both women said little as they ate, then drew blankets up as darkness filled the forest.

Aeren sat and faced Chitthra in the growing night. "Your heart is troubled, filled with dread. Speak, and I will listen."

Chitthra thought in quiet before she answered. "We face a fearful task. And I hold no knowing if my courage may falter, not because I lack ability, but because of who Steffyn Foxxe is. Elf-brother to Ysilrod and Sheynon, how may I find it in my heart to take vengeance on such a troubled spirit?"

Aeren nodded solemnly. "None but you can decide, and perhaps a better way will come, that blood is not spilled by any. Have you weighed the possibility of your own death at his hand?"

Chitthra's eyes cast downward and she nodded at the last. "Yet as I, perhaps he will see his own ending in my eyes. Pursued by one following *Din'daeron'dae*, his own son, may bring the solace he truly seeks."

Her gaze rose to Aeren's. "Five years I was gone from this world, and would have been there forever had his plan not failed. His callousness was such he would sacrifice me to oblivion with Mors'ul'jyn, and tho' my honor lost when he denied my revenge upon her, still I would be there.

"And he would be free, Aeren, no one to avenge Galandria, even Sheynon offering forgiveness. Only Steffyn's conscience, and a life of torment." She sighed. "I ask myself each day, is this not enough? Must I seek vengeance on one who has borne so much?"

Aeren laid her hand to Chitthra's. "Therefore, I stand beside you. Whatever comes of this, it will be righteous. Vengeance, or forgiveness by your own heart upon him, the choice will be yours only. I will accept your doing, and to my mind, he will as well. He may bloody both of us in battle, or kneel with tears before you. Still, we will triumph, together."

Chitthra showed a warm smile. "You speak as your mentor, now I have met her. I see her teachings in your manner."

Aeren smiled in return. "You honor me."

"I love you."

Aeren's smile broadened. "So you have said. And my love is yours." She motioned to the bed roll. "A night of rest, then on the road at dawn. Two days to Kaul's city, then our search begins."

"Still you feel this... other may lead us to Steffyn, and yet is in the city?"

Aeren shrugged. "It is a poor beginning, but perhaps Kaul will speak with us. Surely his confidence is shaken, with his sending Rohesia to Sheynon's court. The Mongrel may yet hold a bit of honor, and help us find an answer."

* * *

They arrived in the late of day, passed through the gates with much harassment by the guards, then made way to the inner city. They found an inn, took separate rooms for privacy, and met later in the bath. At last they ventured to the common room and partook of a meal neither had prepared as in the three days before.

Chitthra refilled their tankards with cool light ale and broke their final loaf. Both women sat, weary from the road and saying little.

"Shall we seek an audience this night?" Aeren looked about the crowded room, noting soldiers, ruffians, and merchants all minding business of their own. "We might leave a message for Kaul's reading on the morrow."

Chitthra sipped as she pondered. "We seek magic in this city, of which there is little. My thought is, dark elves would be the ones who know."

"The bazaar at morning, then, before crowds gather?"

Chitthra nodded. "I trust you brought inducement enough for greedy hands."

"Ten days, no more. In truth, we are in need of Kaul's knowing, and sooner met, the sooner we may follow whatever trail is laid before us."

"A dark elf male, accompanied by a younger female. This becomes our only clue."

Aeren glanced about the room once more. "Shall we line them up and inquire their whereabouts on the given day?"

Chitthra chuckled. "Always are you finding ways, Dearest, regardless our predicament."

They ate their fill and Chitthra poured the pitcher empty into their cups. The common room grew full to bursting, three gaming tables along the wall, cards and dice played in the center, and a pair of figures hunched about a table in the corner. Aeren's eyes took in the room again.

"Your liege was not happiest on our leaving Sheynon's hospitality." Chitthra watched above her tankard rim.

"But understood, as events move quickly, and her blessing of confidence upon our venture was surely welcome." Aeren showed a wry grin. "Further from Sheynon and the elves, we may more freely move as needed."

"Rohesia likely will return within two days with Sheynon's answer. We must have Kaul's ear before that time."

Aeren nodded, thinking once again. "Therefore, a message this night to the palace gates. Yet I beg you, look to the table in the corner. Two figures, backs to the room itself, as hiding."

Chitthra glanced quickly to her side. One larger than the other, both with hooded cloaks drawn close. She raised an eyebrow to Aeren, who nodded, then rose, moving toward the corner table.

* * *

Mend'rys had taken Jyslin beyond the sanctuary, for both needed respite from the silence. The girl had complained of thirst for drink and the taste of food not cooked by their own hands. Therefore, as the eve grew late and long, they had taken a table at a nearby inn and sat, backs to the crowd, to pass the time.

Mend'rys kept eyes from the merchants round, and when soldiers entered, both he and Jyslin huddled deeper in their cloaks. He could not be certain of their privacy, and more than once considered an illusion of an empty table.

"Master, I thank you for this evening." Jyslin lifted her goblet of dark wine in salute, and drank it dry. She huddled closer, her hand upon Mend'rys's leg. "Might we return to our refuge, where I will give you pleasure to show my gratitude?"

Mend'rys sipped and shook his head. "For now, enjoy the time away. Might you wish a game of chance at the tables? Ten silver pieces are yours should your luck be interested."

179

Jyslin laid her head upon his shoulder. "Will you join me? Together we may have a bit of fun. I want only to spend the time together."

Mend'rys considered. The room was crowded, food and drink served about, and laughter in the air, only merchants, farmers, and dealers seen in number. He nodded at the last. "Let us try our skill. Still, if we should double our purse, then we will end the eve. Too much of luck draws unwanted attention from those watching." He nodded to a trio with the look of thieves closely following the dicing table fortunes.

They rose, and Mend'rys turned to face two figures slowly wending way through the crowd, coming to their table.

Chitthra! And Aeren at her side, here in the city! Near-panic clutched his heart, then he sat, shaking, though knew they did not recognize him as Drow. Still, the haze of fear and death nearly caused his swooning.

"Master?" Jyslin knelt at his side, then rose to face the women, now standing closely by. She scowled. "Stay away! My master is ill, can you not see? Let us pass and I will take him to a healer."

Chitthra nearly smiled at the girl's wily pluck. "No harm intended, and we would only inquire of information." She motioned to the chair beside Mend'rys. "Please, sit and tend your master. I will fetch brandy for him." She cast a glance to Aeren as she turned to the bar.

Aeren sat, watching the dark elves before her, not knowing exactly what to do. She offered a kerchief to the male, and he accepted it with shaking hands, then dabbed his sweating forehead.

"You are brave, and thoughtful for your master," she said to Jyslin. "I am Aeren Greywald of the City-State of Truth; my companion, Chitthra. Say your names, that I may know them."

Jyslin began to speak, then paused, looking to Mend'rys. He nodded, his voice still absent. "Jyslin, my lady, and my master, Mend'rys. He keeps me well, and I him."

"You tend your master with dedication, and he will reward you. Pray tell, might you know of dealings at the palace some days ago? A ruckus there, and rumors of magic."

Chitthra returned, set a brandy before Mend'rys, and took her chair beside Jyslin. "We seek a friend, perhaps injured in the struggle at the palace. We will pay well for information."

"How..." Mend'rys sipped the brandy and cleared his throat. "How do you come to know of us, of this occurrence? Before we share our secrets, speak of your involvement."

Aeren traded looks with Chitthra, who nodded. "There are two in this land of great power, and they now become three. All dark elves, two

180

female and a male. Five years Ardwel has been at peace, and now danger rears its head again in their presence. We seek to pause that happening."

"We know nothing," said Jyslin.

Mend'rys raised a hand. "Say your allegiance, for I know the City-State of Truth still holds DragonFall in their administration. The king herein thinks otherwise."

"We know of him," replied Chitthra. "And yes, we understand the politics involved. This matters not to us, only safety of the land."

"Need you a healer?" asked Aeren, as Mend'rys's hands yet shook.

"An old affliction. Soon it will pass. My thanks for the brandy." He raised the glass and drank.

Chitthra nodded to Jyslin. "Your... servant tends you well."

"She is my ward, not servant. She was an orphan when I found her."

Aeren watched the gentleness between Mend'rys and the girl. Jyslin's hands had not left his arm since they had come to the table, and her eyes were filled with more than simple gratitude.

"Might we know your thoughts upon the palace rumors?" Chitthra motioned for fresh goblets of elven wine around and waited as the serving wench set them at the table.

Mend'rys drew a breath after a long draught from his wine glass. "Little, other than as you say, rumor. Those I have spoken to tell of fighting there, and strange happenings."

"Strange as magic?" asked Aeren.

Mend'rys shrugged. "How may one know, in this city? There is little of the Craft known or seen."

"You speak of it as 'the Craft', words said by those familiar with it."

Mend'rys cursed himself, for such a slip of the tongue. He began to speak, then Jyslin interrupted. "I know the word, for I was in *Ung'gu'wi* before my master found me. Many times it was said in my hearing, and I told him of it."

Aeren looked to Chitthra once again, nearly smiling at the cleverness of the girl. "Very well, we will accept this. Still, tell us more. We must find these folk and learn their purpose."

"Little more," replied Mend'rys, "and stories dwindle. If such power was seen, none speak of it. Perhaps the king has issued warning."

Chitthra blew a breath. "Still, these three... you know of them?"

"As you say, rumors of power. Nothing more."

"How might you have found us?" Jyslin's question tumbled before them, and Chitthra spoke quickly as Aeren paused.

"Word that dark elves were seen therein, one male and a younger female. We took a chance you might be the ones we seek."

The table was quiet as they drank their wine and the clamor of the room rose even louder. Mend'rys set away his goblet. "We have said our words, now depart. We thank you for your attentions."

He rose and Jyslin followed. Aeren and Chitthra paused for a moment, then the dark elf woman tossed two silver coins onto the table. "Follow, tho' quietly. Let us see where they will lead."

Out the door, and seeing the pair turn into an alleyway, they walked quickly to the corner. Entering the darkened lane between the inn and a bakery, they saw it empty, though dust swirled in the gentle evening, and a sharp stench, as following a lightning strike, assailed their faces.

"Magic, I would wager." Aeren shrugged. "What now, Dearest?"

"The male was terrified at our presence, as tho' we were known to him, but unexpected. No reason I can say, for I do not know his face. Or the girl."

"More there is between them than of a father type to her."

Chitthra nodded. "Her eyes were filled with undying love. She would have fought us then and there as a mother cat protecting kittens." She chuckled. "I was captivated by her brashness."

Aeren laid an arm on Chitthra's shoulder. "Let us think upon this as we make way to the palace. Still we must deliver our message to the king and beg our audience."

* * *

They formed again within the sanctuary. Mend'rys caught Jyslin as she swooned and laid her on the settee, then stumbled to a chair. He sat and shook so badly his form of dark elf nearly faded. He rose, went to his knees, and crawled his way to the workshop door, clawed his way to standing, and fell through. He moaned in terror and in anguish as he set the latch, then laid down and let the feelings have their way with him.

Heart nearly frozen in his chest, images flashed through his mind so quickly, hardly could he tell one from the other.

Sheynon's torment all these years as I try to justify my doing.

Jyslin, and pleasures so delicious, can I ever hold another?

Emildir... my wife, and now abandoned.

Mors'ul'jyn, her head in Chitthra's hands, and I would not let her take true vengeance because... because I am a fool.

He choked out a laugh, one of desperation and near-madness. The illusion of Drow had faded. He held a pale and trembling hand before his clouded eyes, scarcely recognizing it as his. He ran fingers through his matted hair, felt ribs through his tunic and knew he was nearly dead of fear and angst.

Too tired and worn to even eat, and where do I find the strength to take pleasure with Jyslin when she comes to me? Why do I continue this path, when I know its ending? Where, oh where, has Steffyn Foxxe, the elven mage, now gone? Dead? Forgotten? Taken over by this... form I use to hide within? Is that the truth of it, that I hide in sight, disguised as the enemy of elves, to keep myself apart? Dearest Yarhetha'an, what have I become?

He slowly calmed, rolled to his knees and looked about the workshop. No changes there were seen, and once more he wondered how long before thieves or cutthroats found his little hideaway.

A sound from beyond the door, and he focused power once again to bring the form of Mend'rys into being. He tossed away his cloak, opened the door, and saw Jyslin shaking on the bed. He knelt, held her in his arms, and rocked her gently as she wept.

"Master..."

He kissed her forehead. "Rest, for we are safe. Your wit and charm helped save us, and I am forever grateful you are well."

She clung to him, ran a hand beneath his tunic to touch his skin. "You are real. I am real. When you take us to the other place, I fear I will lose myself forever. And you."

His own hand rested on her bare leg and he chuckled. "You as well are real."

He lay beside her, holding close her trembling body. Breath to breath and touching, no words were said, only feelings there between them. Gentle, blessed sleep came at last, and as the world beyond the sanctuary continued, quiet lay once more upon their minds and hearts.

* * *

Mend'rys woke to the smells of stew and soft steps across the floor. He turned from the bed to see Jyslin setting bowls upon the table and pouring tea into the goblets. She was dressed in a fresh and simple tunic, beautiful, and smiled to him as he stood.

"Midday finds you sleeping yet," she jested. She knelt before him, washed his face with a warming cloth, kissed him gently and helped him from his heavy robes. Mend'rys only stood in silence as she set a bathing bowl before him, washed his body as a servant, and dried him. Her eyes caught his as she touched him with intimate fingers, then smiled once more, draping a clean tunic o'er his head.

She offered a chair at the table and he sat, sleep still in his mind, and slowly stirred the stew within his bowl. He tasted, then smiled. Her face brightened in reply.

"I had dreams," he said at last, sipping from his cup. "The women at the inn… were they known to you?"

Jyslin paused her meal. "Master, no, never had I seen them before last night. Yet the human said she was of the City-State of Truth. The dark woman, Chitthra, I know nothing of."

"Nor I," he replied, knowing it was a lie. "They asked of the ruckus at the palace, therefore likely they are aware of who was there. They may ask Kaul's ear in the matter."

"The king? Why would he grant two unknown women audience?"

Because he knows them as comrades from the past! Surely this is the answer! They seek the whereabouts of Mors'ul'jyn, and if any in this city know, it is Kaul! He shuddered. "Perhaps they offer themselves to his harem for the information." He shrugged and gave a nervous chuckle. "Surely, we should find the matter for ourselves."

"But why do they search, Master? What business have they with those you fight against?" Jyslin took a bite, chewed and thought. "Are they allies to Archane? Master, I am torn! Archane led us a thousand years. Her leaving brought only uncertainty and fear. What is their purpose? Why would a human woman seek Archane if not to bring her demise?"

Mend'rys marveled at the girl's perception. "I do not think they seek Archane to end her life. As you say, Archane's wisdom kept the great Houses from falling on each other for more years than can be counted."

"And Mor'i'jil, Master, in Archane's stead. He kept alive her memory, endless parleys with the Houses…"

Mend'rys's mind wandered through his years within *Ung'gu'wi*. *Yet little attention did I pay to politics and maneuverings. Jyslin, however, becomes my eyes into that time.*

"What then?" he asked. "Your thoughts on why these women would seek Archane."

Jyslin stared into her bowl. "Little can I say, as I am not wise to the world as you." She thought, then raised her face. "Yet if they do not seek Archane for evil purpose, might they become our allies?"

Mend'rys paused his cup. Truly, the girl was brilliant in her mind!

* * *

Mend'rys lay with Jyslin in his arms. Her skin was warm against his own, and he drifted in the afterglow of her many pleasures once again. Nearly did he chuckle; the girl was insatiable! With youth and vigor never-ending, and a touch as fire itself, he knew her offerings to be the key to his sanity these many years.

Sanity. A life of quiet solitude and study. Deepest secrets of Drow magic at his fingertips. Watching, listening for mentions of Mors'ul'jyn in *Ung'gu'wi*. Yet when did it all become a way of life?

His purpose had been a simple one in the beginning: trace the mad woman Re' in Reena's body, and by rumors of Archane's whereabouts, find this Mors'ul'jyn and end her life.

As he should have done when first encountered.

As he should have bade Chitthra do when they found Mors'ul'jyn in the forest.

To keep all that followed then from happening.

Havoc in the Guild of Learned, two mages dead there by Mors'ul'jyn, and the wounding of the ancient Loriniel.

And the murder of Galandria Telveperen. Steffyn Foxxe's hands were covered in her blood, surely as were Mors'ul'jyn's.

Forgiveness by Sheynon, and Steffyn's flight.

Ung'gu'wi.

The finding of Jyslin.

The offer of her maidenhood.

The pleasures there of accepting it.

Forsaking of Emildir, and his infidelity.

Vows to *Yarhetha'an* shattered on the cold, hardpacked chamber floors of the Drow.

What now had he become?

He turned from Jyslin as tears tracked down his cheeks. She roused and wrapped her arms around him, her breasts against his back.

He took her in his arms, and she spread herself beneath him once again. He found her warmth with desperation, a fire burning in his spirit, and took them both to ecstasy with a cry. Passion, pleasures, sensations of her lithe and supple body as she drank from him every drop of essence. Crescendo. Then release. The long and gentle fall to reality again.

They lay together, bedclothes askew and sharing breath, hearts pounding only a finger-width's apart. She sighed and wrapped herself about him even tighter.

* * *

185

Two days, and no reply from Kaul's palace. Chitthra and Aeren had plied the taverns, seeking any rumor of dark elves in the royal gardens. Only twice were soldiers found who had been there, and though drink and silver loosened tongues, more they wanted from the women. A confrontation in a darkened room turned nearly to violent, as Aeren's sword was drawn in anger for the first time in many years. Chitthra's talents, too, were tested, and at the last the constabulary called. Too late they arrived, as all had escaped, laughing in the darkness as they scattered through the crowds.

In Aeren's room, Chitthra tended a sword cut on the human woman's shoulder, the blade having found its way beneath the pauldron.

"Luck more than skill," said Aeren, wincing as Chitthra sewed the wound with thread from a mending kit carried in her pack.

"This is what we face, Dearest. Men, dark or light, seek pleasure from a woman much as silver. Little will we learn otherwise."

"I am no harlot." Aeren paused at her own words, once said to Hawk, the first and only male lover in her life. A tear dropped to the floor, and she turned away.

Chitthra laid a gentle hand to Aeren's cheek. "Only may I say my sorrow for your loss, yet the gentleness he showed you is a blessing. Many men would not have treated your innocence with such tenderness."

Aeren laid her head on Chitthra's shoulder, raised her face and kissed her warmly. "Little of success is in our hands. How may we find the Dark Princess and Mors'ul'jyn if we become the coin? I cannot, Chitthra, nor would you, I am certain. Still no reply from Kaul, and in truth, he may choose not to answer."

The dark elf woman packed away her kit, thinking. She poured wine, offered a cup to Aeren, and they sat aside in quiet. "The sorcerer and the girl. Still they are our only possibility, yet how to find them?"

"Might they return? Surely, we piqued their interest with our queries. The girl was sharpest, the male, tho' ill, listening. Yet who they are, still I cannot know."

"Kaul has knowledge of Mors'ul'jyn's whereabouts. My thought is, this pair tracks them, yet why? Ill fortune in *Ung'gu'wî*? Assassins from another House?" Chitthra chuckled. "Poor luck at the dicing tables?"

They laughed together for a moment, embraced and touched cup rims, then slowly drank.

"Might we ask an apothecary? One seeming ill as the male might search for cure."

186

Chitthra rose, walking to the window, a hand held for silence as she thought. She faced the open window, smells and sounds of the evening drifting into the room. "I know the reason, surely as we love each other. *Din'daeron'dae* shows the truth of it."

"Dearest?"

Chitthra turned, her face a grim visage. Aeren rose and took her in her arms. "Fear not, I am here."

Chitthra nestled into her embrace. "We are given sign. No, I shall not say my knowing, for I cannot endanger you." She drew slowly away as Aeren shook her head. Chitthra laid a gentle finger to Aeren's lips. "Trust, I beg you. For if right, our search has ended. If not, you may be my own avenger. Yet for now, I must keep this secret for safety of us both. In time I will reveal it, but if we find these two again, we offer aid."

"I... do not understand, and beg you hold no secrets."

"I must. I love you. Your life lies before you as a tapestry yet in the loom. I have this task, one of honor I must complete. Whatever befalls me beyond that is the will of gods, not mortals. Bear witness, as we hold each other dearly. Chitthra of *Däe Quiviё* shall not fail in her duty."

* * *

They loved each other through the night, passions warm and real spent across the bed, and as Aeren slept, Chitthra stood away in a corner of the room. She donned her fiery ki, not worn for many years, knelt and offered thoughts and prayers.

Five years I have lost, and in that time, peace came to Ardwel as the leaders vanished. Now we stir the ashes of what some would call victory, rekindling the fire. Why so? Because vigilance must be maintained, and should we pay no mind, surely evil will have its way. Therefore...

She rose, wiped a hand across the grimy mirror, and gazed at her countenance.

Feelings deeper than any I have ever had, for Aeren, for my task, for those of this land who yet will stand against the darkness. Guide me, Din'daeron'dae, show the path of truth, that I may bring honor to my task. The spirit of Galandria Telveperen must be avenged, or my life forfeit in its trying.

The sun rose, peeking through the shutters as she sat at the table, contemplating. She glanced to Aeren sleeping still, and smiled gently, recalling words said not so long ago.

Undefeated...

* * *

Mend'rys sat in his workshop and considered. As Steffyn Foxxe, he was aware of Chitthra's mission. And as time had passed, began to understand his only hope of reconciliation, not to mention saving of his life, lay in dealing with Mors'ul'jyn himself.

Archane, to Steffyn, no longer was a threat. Should she return to *Ung'gu'wi* and her leadership, surely it would be tens of years perhaps, before the Drow would rise again. Archane's hands would be filled with the hearts of those daring to usurp power in her absence, and the purge of the dark elf Houses long and bloody.

Since Mor'i'jil, as well, lay in the clutches of Mors'ul'jyn, this all but promised war beneath the Black Forest, and a struggle for the leadership of Drow.

And longer with Archane and her minister absent from Ung'gu'wi, deeper will their society burrow into politics and assassinations. What elves and humans could not do, the absence of Archane will do instead. Drow may not survive as a Race, and to my mind, that would likely be the end of magic in the land. How to save it, while insuring safety of all Ardwel?

He chuckled. "One crisis before the next. Therefore, do I care Archane and Mor'i'jil are beyond my reach? How to deal with Mors'ul'jyn and keep Ardwel safe? Yet as her attention is held by them, and whatever plans she may have for leading of the Drow herself, time passes, and with it, growing matters for the dark elves."

His mind returned to Chitthra and Aeren, now surely contemplating who he truly was. Might they suspect disguise, Steffyn Foxxe hiding as a dark elf mage? Aeren, likely not, yet Chitthra…

She is clever, and in my desperation, showed her I hid in the guise of Anon Gûl, as we sought Mors'ul'jyn then. To her, something may be amiss, and should chance and decision lead us in the path together, I must be wary. My life will surely end should she suspect.

He rose, set his wards and protections once again, exited the workshop and sealed the door behind him. Jyslin stood from the table as he turned, and greeted him with a kiss. "May I serve your morning meal, Master? You have not eaten since the night before."

Mend'rys thought to say he no longer was her master, yet paused. *The ruse must be kept, for should we work with others, this would be the best way for us to be thought.*

"Only if you will join me," he replied, smiling.

They sat together, eating quietly, then Jyslin posed a question. "Have you given thought to my asking?"

Mend'rys knew her meaning. "To work with the women met would require discretion. Never could they be allowed within our sanctuary. This place is ours alone, no others."

Jyslin stirred her porridge, thinking. "Your wisdom is understood, Master. Still, if they seek the same as you, would they not be helpful? Yet do we trust a human?"

Mend'rys paused his answer, thinking of the implications. At the last, he nodded. "Your words have merit. Yet you saw her manner, her concern for me as I lay barely breathing. She gave her name and allegiance with no fear of knowing. This speaks manners of the court, and confidence in ability. This Chitthra, dark elf tho' she may be, is more than her appearance, to my thinking."

"Of what sort? Assassin from *Ung'gu'wi?*" Jyslin set down her spoon in worry.

Assassin! Mend'rys shook beneath his robes and nearly swooned again.

Jyslin came to his side and held him. "Master! Are you ill again? Please, Master, tell me what is wrong!"

Mend'rys leaned his head to the softness of her breasts and trembled. He let her hold him, breathing in the scent of her own worry, and slowly calmed. She kissed his forehead, then his cheek, and held him closely once again. "Never would I let harm come to you, Master. You have saved my life many times, and my honor as well. Truly do I care for you as my savior."

Mend'rys nodded weakly. *And here is the truth of it. We venture on or fade away, together.*

He lifted his gaze to hers and drew slowly away. "A passing concern, and your touch always is a blessing." He straightened as she sat once more, and continued. "Perhaps if we return to the tavern and speak further. Agreement may be reached, yet safety for ourselves is paramount."

* * *

The entourage from *Annatar Yarhetha'an* made way through the gates of DragonFall with little fanfare, and rode on to the palace entryway in the early morn. There they found the new portcullis and workers there about, with fifty guards halting them for searches. Rohesia waved them all away and led the column into the courtyard, called servants round to tend the horses, then ordered food and wine be set before Sheynon and his charges.

"I will advise the king of our arrival. Once prepared, he will receive you in his throne room."

"A request," said Thalion, as Ysilrod came to his side. "Might we meet here, in the courtyard, beneath the sun and pleasant day? Surely the king would enjoy the freshness of the air on his waking."

Rohesia considered. "I will ask. Perhaps the garden behind the palace will be acceptable." She bowed and retreated up the steps, disappearing through the heavy oaken doors.

"Our thanks, Cousin," said Ysilrod softly. "Seeing the stains of our encounter those years ago put my spirit to the flame our last calling. There is no need to subject the Lady Audrey to such memories."

Thalion only nodded, then turned to Audrey as she dismounted. "A long ride, Excellency, and you bore it well. As days of old, yes?" He grinned fully as Audrey showed a weary smile.

"And older, as my backside recalls all too well those days." She looked about the palace grounds, noting overgrowth and little tending of the gardens. "This Kaul prefers a more natural look to his royal setting, yes?"

Sheynon came to her side and pointed to the reflecting pool. "And there I would not bathe or swim for pleasure. Surely there are creatures making homes of the murky waters."

They waited patiently as the sun rose, warming the day around them. Servants set a table and pillowed chairs about, a wheeled brazier with a pot of stew and greens from gardens somewhere not in sight. Fresh juices were offered with wine and ale, and Sheynon traded glances with Audrey, who gave a look of quiet approval.

"Kaul, or Rohesia's doing?" asked Ysilrod, and Sheynon only laughed.

They took time, as the ride had begun before the sun was risen, to take the day with Kaul, if necessary. Discussions on the road had ranged, from thoughts on simple requests to those of more importance.

Ysilrod sipped juice and nodded with approval. "Kaul... the king is not one to ask a boon lightly, nor will he bow to demands. Yet in the end, his need is great, but we must see he saves face before his subjects and appears the master."

"No man is my master," said Audrey tightly, then looked away. "Forgive me, this place holds bitter memories and feelings. Friend Thalion, I beg your indulgence, that you speak for me. I cannot hold my tongue, I fear."

Ysilrod drew close to Audrey. "We recall," he nodded to Thalion, "of the time. Strength, my lady, and we are here only for a parley."

190

"No harm will come," said Thalion softly, "this man's measure has been taken by my cousins, and they know him well." He motioned to Ysilrod. "And we have the greatest mage in Ardwel at our side."

Audrey nodded briefly, then blew a breath. "*Jhad* protect us all from whatever mischief may be planned. It has been many years since I have done this."

"The *Rising Star* sits at my side," intoned Thalion reverently, "and never would harm come to us again within the city of his coming."

They drew about each other. "All the gods," said Sheynon, and nods were exchanged in silence.

The palace doors above the stairway opened. Six guards in livery red and black took places at the entrance, then six more, followed by two trumpeters. The noise they blew set the elves' ears ringing. Thalion and Audrey only looked to each other, suppressing grins.

Rohesia stepped onto the threshold. "His most royal kingness, Kaul, greets the visitors from the realms of elves and men." Her words were said with no hint of derision or mirth.

Kaul emerged, dressed more simply than they might have thought. Dark breeches, a plain tunic of his livery colors, sword strapped firmly to his hip, and a simple golden crown with two gems, onyx and a ruby side by side.

"A message," said Ysilrod, and Sheynon nodded.

"My lords?" Audrey drew closer to hear their words as Thalion stood at Sheynon's side.

"No regal trappings, no presumption of position, save his crown. Subtlety, my lady, saying this parley shall be more honest than the last."

Sheynon leaned to Audrey. "His sword is *NorthWind*, said to be given as a gift from Re' before she became Mors'ul'jyn, yet in the body of Reena."

Audrey shook her head.

"Re' took the name, becoming... what she now is."

"You know the sword?"

Sheynon nodded. "I have seen the forge-mark."

Audrey cast her eyes on Kaul, understanding Sheynon's warning.

Kaul descended the stairway, followed by Rohesia and four guards. He approached the elves, who nodded greeting, as his eyes swept to Thalion and Audrey waiting quietly.

"You bring others. Good. We have much to discuss this day." His eyes noted the rainbow sash of office across Thalion's chest, then moved to Audrey, who met his gaze unflinching.

191

"I did not expect a matron to join our parley."

Thalion bristled yet Sheynon held a hand. "Speak with respect, Kaul. You are in the presence of Ardwel's own Champion."

Light dawned in Kaul's face, and he laughed. "Champion! A granddame she is!" He wiped his eyes and nodded to Audrey. "I am no courtier, therefore my wit is raw. So, Audrey Vincent comes to DragonFall. What think you of our city?"

Audrey chose her words with care. "Once it was beautiful. Then it became a vile place of horrors born of the Purge." She looked around, locked eyes with Rohesia for a moment, then continued. "Now it seems reflecting of your manner... great king."

A hint of anger crossed Kaul's face for but an instant, then he laughed again. "Well said! I will not deny your words, for yes, my city is a place where anything, or anyone, may have a price! Might you wish to try your skill at the gambling houses?"

"Dicing and parlor tricks are not my forte, I thank you." Audrey motioned to the weapon at his hip and touched her own sword hilt. "However, should you need instruction of swordplay, my hand is ready."

Barely could Thalion keep a smile from his face. The elves had no such compulsion. Sheynon and his brother laughed aloud, then dropped their smiles at looks from the guards. Yet still they chuckled beneath their breath and turned their heads from Kaul.

The king ignored them both. His eyes were locked with Audrey's. "Might I interest you in marriage, dear lady? Always have I sought a woman my equal in combat."

Thalion raised his face, a scowl upon it. "Her Excellency is Baroness of the Eastern Marches, appointed by the Duke of Stormguarde Castle in the north. She is married with three children, and her husband, her mentor-in-arms. With all respect, we ask your tongue stay civil."

Audrey held her hand for pause. "Great king, my offer was sincere. I know of your weapon and would gladly aid you in its wielding."

"We do not come for sport," said Sheynon, at last his face sobering. "We come at behest of your invitation. Pray tell, how may we aid DragonFall and its king?"

Slowly Kaul's face calmed and he looked to the elves again. "You have refreshed yourselves? Then follow me."

He turned, and the guards fell in behind them, up the steps and through the hallways. Yet he did not lead them to the throne room, to their relief, but through corridors to the garden behind the palace. There they saw a sitting area of pillowed seats and flowers. Rohesia offered places, then drink as they preferred.

Kaul sat in a simple chair with pillows sewn as his livery, accepted a heavy tankard, and drank a draught. He nodded to himself as the others waited, then spoke quietly. "I will tell you of it all. Doubtless, this Mors'ul'jyn is mad, and the land must find a way beyond her plans."

* * *

They spoke as the sun sank in the west and shadows crossed the garden.

Of Mor'i'jil's coming to the city.

Of his taking Kaul and Rohesia hostage, and his threats of harsh reprisal.

Of Archane and Mors'ul'jyn's arrival, and the betrayal there, though admitted he did not see it of himself.

"Why would I lie?" He waved his hand in aggravation. "I have no allegiance to dark elves, nor this woman, whom I knew only as Reena."

"No lies are heard," replied Audrey calmly, and Kaul nodded at the last.

"And then they vanished, yes?" asked Ysilrod. "Rohesia spoke of others. They disappeared as well?"

Kaul looked to the woman, who spoke slowly. "Mors'ul'jyn took Archane and Mor'i'jil. The others followed."

Ysilrod thought for moments. "No trace of any left behind? This was ten days ago?"

Kaul nodded. "We have searched the city with no sign. We ask your thoughts."

Sheynon looked to Ysilrod, knowing well the meaning of the word from Kaul. "We would offer more, should you wish it. My brother is a mage of some ability, and Priest Thalion and Her Excellency stand in good stead with their gods. Between the Craft and blessings, perhaps we may find the answers needed... together."

Kaul looked once more to Rohesia, then back to Sheynon. A servant refilled his cup and he drank again. "I accept your offer."

* * *

Beneath the Depths of Drakenmoore...

I am certain it is he. Mors'ul'jyn paced her chamber, questions spinning in her mind. *Tho' why would he track us, other than for Archane? Is he aware of what happened in Telveperen? Has Sheynon sent him as an*

193

avenger of his wife? Or is his only interest the Dark Princess and her minister? I must think on this.

She looked once more into the scrying mirror, seeing Archane and Mor'i'jil curled upon their beds, and slowly calmed. *Still they are at my mercy. Yet what to do with them at last? I cannot hold them here forever. Tho' nearly have I done so with Archane. A plan. I must have a plan for safety of us all, or surely I will die.*

She lay abed again, at last drifting into restless sleep, visions of fire and death and bloody hearts held in bloody hands running through her mind. When she woke, her robes were drenched in nervous sweat. She disrobed, and unseen servants bathed her as she once more deliberated how to stay alive.

Thoughts tumbled, and as she considered, clarity arose.

She donned a simple robe and cloak, for the chamber yet was chill. She looked again into the mirror, seeing Archane and Mor'i'jil at table, speaking quietly. She passed through the doorway and they rose.

"It occurs to me, while safety for all is a consideration, there is another way." Mors'ul'jyn raised a hand, and a bolt of silvered lightning leapt across the room, striking Mor'i'jil fully in the chest. Archane screamed as the old dark elf's body scattered into ashes through the room. Nothing there was left of the Dark Lord but dust in the air and a stench of burning flesh.

"Foul murderess!" Archane screamed again, running at Mors'ul'jyn, arms outstretched, and fingers clawed. Something unseen lifted her and dropped her to the bed, then pinned here there. Struggle as she might, she could not break free or even speak.

Mors'ul'jyn looked down upon her, face hard and eyes as slits. "Time comes for desperate measures. Only one way may I stay alive, and that is as other than I am known. Yet I will offer compromise. You will be returned to your place of power, but only on my say. I will stand as your new minister and none will know the fate of Mor'i'jil, save our words, sworn to each other." She grinned tightly. "It is that, Dark Princess, or I shall become you, as I did with Reena. Choice is yours. Decide wisely, for the death I give to you is for eternity."

BOOK SEVEN
FEET TO FIRE

"Your name is Reena, I recall.
I have seen you in the temple,
and more than once you attended
sacrifices in the forest."

Archane, on her first meeting
of the concubine Reena

The depths of Ung'gu'wi…

The Dark Priestess Alystin knelt in prayer alone in a private chamber, away from the din and worry of her acolytes. There she might give focus to the needs of House Iyllyeth, and how fortunes hung in the balance for the Race.

Should Mor'i'jil claim success, and the city once more in the hands of Drow, Archane's return will bring turmoil, regardless any welcome shown. Tho' even one as cunning as Ba'tula must understand, more is needed than word of law. Love, devotion, and subservience to the memory of Iyllyeth and Mother Darkness must be sincere. Sincerity sorely lacking in Ba'tula's heart.

She rose, then called her coven, and together they stood round, chanting in the formal tongue of ancient scripture. On it went, as the symbols on the walls glowed crimson with the power. At last their gathering quieted, exchanged touches, words of praise, and nods and bows of respect and duty. At the last, only Alystin and Xa'lyyth remained within the room. They gave a final prayer together, then made way to the bathing place.

"Mor'i'jil is gone now near ten days," said Xa'lyyth as she disrobed. Servants aided her to enter the warm springs and bathed her gently as she waited for Alystin's reply.

The older priestess slipped into the water. "Questions are, should he return with empty hands, what then? I cautioned him regarding his proclamation of sending envoys, only to result in your being disgraced by the brute Kaul."

Xa'lyyth bowed her head. "Dark Lady, my shame is great. Still I pray for absolution, yet cannot feel my sin is lifted."

"You have no sin, and only did as necessary. Truth be told, fortune and the grace of *Iyllyeth* kept us alive in his presence." She shuddered, though the water warm and soothing. "I will attend with you this night, and your worry will be lifted."

Xa'lyyth nodded thanks. "Still, Dark Lord Mor'i'jil knows this mongrel's measure and will take it. Surely success will be his, and the city ours once more."

Alystin nodded absently, thinking. "He thought to wait for Archane. In time, she must return, for a pact was needed by this Reena, or whatever name she holds now."

A servant entered, breathless, and bowed deeply. "Dark Priestess, word comes from the city. Messengers speak of the Lancer Captain returning, and bloodied fairly."

Alystin called for attendants to bring their robes. "See him to a meeting chamber quickly, and tend his wounds. We will join soon as we may."

The servant bowed again and retreated as they drew themselves from the water, then stood quietly as they were dried by attendants. Alystin looked to her acolyte. "Ill news comes."

"Dark Lady, I concur. Still, we must be prudent. Mor'i'jil will prevail and Archane found alive."

Alystin looked away. "I pray your words are truth. If not..."

* * *

They entered, and the Lancer Captain stood, favoring his right leg. Alystin motioned him to a chair, then ordered a healer to the room, then faced him once more and nodded him to speak.

"Dark Lady, Lord Mor'i'jil is gone!"

Alystin traded looks of horror with Xa'lyyth. "Gone... where?"

"To wherever Archane has gone! The woman, the one Dark Lord Mor'i'jil called Reena, took them both away by magic. Others came, and this Reena woman threw her cloak about them, disappearing, then soldiers from the palace —"

"Stop." Alystin held her hand, and the Lancer Captain ceased his words, collapsing in the chair, wincing. The healer entered, tended to him as Alystin took Xa'lyyth by the arm and led her to a corner. The women stood silent, eyes locked, words unsaid, both afraid to speak their thoughts.

"Dark Lady, Archane lives, says the Lancer Captain," Xa'lyyth whispered at the last.

Alystin nodded, looking past her shoulder as the healer did her work. "Yet now both are taken, and this confirms Mor'i'jil's own fears, that she has been a prisoner. What now?"

"Seek the truth of it, for surely there is more."

"That we will do, tho' not yet. I wish to hear it all from his own lips."

They faced the Lancer Captain once again as the healer bowed and exited. Alystin motioned to Xa'lyyth and the younger priestess raised a healing draught to his lips, then soothed his face with a practiced hand.

Alystin took a chair and gazed into his eyes. "Take time and tell your story. Spare no words, for we need to know it all."

The Lancer Captain nodded and spoke more calmly. "The Dark Lord took the city back with only three hundred soldiers, captured the brute

198

Kaul and his minister, then taunted them with death. His plan was to wait for Archane to reappear, should she be alive."

"This is known. Archane appeared, yes? With this Reena-woman?"

"Dark Lady, she did, and spoke with Mor'i'jil away from the Reena-woman, so I was told."

"Told? You did not see this with your own eyes?"

The Lancer Captain shook his head. "I was left to guard the prisoners as Mor'i'jil went to the courtyard. My soldiers, my second-in-command, saw it all and advised me. Tho' now they are dead."

Xa'lyyth looked to Alystin and nodded.

"Continue," said the older priestess.

"Others came soon after, a dark elf male and a girl barely of age. It was then the Reena-woman took Archane and Mor'i'jil away."

Alystin considered implications, her mind awhirl. "What of these others? Where now are they?"

"Escaped, Dark Lady, yet to where, I know not. Then…" He bowed his head. Xa'lyyth's hand caressed his cheek, and he continued. "City soldiers came, too many for us to fight. We were bound before the brute, and he took three heads of those unable to defend themselves. Dishonor to our Race, and to soldiers willing to die for *Iyllyeth*, yet this was murder. I offer my heart as payment."

Alystin thought for moments. In times as these, she was more militant than even Mor'i'jil, but here, these soldiers held no blame. *Their duty was to live to bring the news, and in that, they should not be held guilty.*

She shook her head. "Unnecessary, as you were bound as well. I will offer a chance for your revenge, should the possibility arise. Say nothing of this to anyone, and advise your soldiers the same. You are to heal yourself soonest. *Iyllyeth's* blessings on you. Return to your chambers and take rest."

The Lancer Captain stood, bowed formally, and took his leave. Xa'lyyth looked to Alystin, questions in her eyes.

"Call the Black Web, yet say only we have urgent matters to discuss. This cannot become known to the other Houses, else blood will flow."

"Hovenethra," said Xa'lyyth, and Alystin nodded gravely.

* * *

They gathered in the chamber where Mor'i'jil held privy council, when Conclave had been called. Alystin with Xa'lyyth at her side, the priests Molva'yas and Narlros, and priestess Vrammyr sat as servants scurried in their duties, setting sacrificial animals upon the stones before them, hearts of which were tossed into the ceremonial fires. As before, they drank of the blood dripped into their wine, and chanted prayers to *Iyllyeth*, though all the while, Alystin and Xa'lyyth traded worried glances. With formalities complete, the servants took their exit, leaving the Black Web to their concerns.

"There is news," Alystin began, when silence stretched too long. "Word comes, Archane lives, seen by soldiers of the House. By their own eyes and ears, they confirm the Dark Princess is alive."

Molva'yas rocked himself and began to weep. Narlros chanted prayers, and they held each other dearly. Xa'lyyth, too, showed tears upon her cheeks, yet Alystin knew the reasons why. Vrammyr showed little in her face.

Molva'yas bowed deeply. "Dark Lady, wondrous news! Praise *Mother Darkness* for her delivery! Praise *Iyllyeth* for her grace upon Archane!" Nearly did both priests leap to their feet in joy, yet Alystin held a hand for pause before them.

"More there is to tell, and with each miracle comes a price. Dark Lord Mor'i'jil's words of the Reena-concubine were true, and now she holds both captive, Archane and Mor'i'jil."

Narlros's chants faded quickly. He looked to Alystin, disbelief upon his face, then turned to Xa'lyyth, who only bowed her head. "This you know as truth, Dark Lady?" He drew back as Alystin's eyes flashed anger. "Forgive, I only ask to clarify. Archane lives, we now know, but... where?"

Alystin's calm nearly broke, and she took a breath. "None know, tho' we presume to wherever Archane was held before. Those of the city may hold the knowledge, but my thought is, this Mongrel Kaul has no more knowing than do we." She looked to Xa'lyyth, who sat speechless still.

"Yet the city. Might we send an envoy once again?" asked Molva'yas.

"They would die," said Xa'lyyth, snarling out the words. "Kaul is naught but a brute, a defiler of all holy. The Lancer Captain told us of his manner. I, myself —" Her voice broke and she paused, then drank wine and blew a breath. "An army would be needed now, as surely he has barred the gates."

"The matter is," said Alystin, and all eyes returned to her, "this cannot be said in presence of the other Houses. Should they find Mor'i'jil missing now, they will press for... advantage."

"They will come with weapons drawn," said Vrammyr nearly in a whisper. "They will kill us all, by the sword or by the sacrifice, it matters not. The House of Iyllyeth will be no more."

200

"Then we must silence every tongue that knows," replied Xa'lyyth, looking to Alystin.

At last the older priestess nodded. "The Lancer Captain, his guards and soldiers, whatever servants followed to the city. How many, I do not know the count, but surely too many for us to be certain of."

"Then... what?" Narlros drank from his goblet, drained it, then poured it full once more. "Dark Lady, we must prepare defenses, perhaps even cordon passages from other Houses. Otherwise, we will be outnumbered by far too many."

"Not so," said Xa'lyyth.

Narlros waved a hand. "You are not schooled enough to know, regardless Mor'i'jil's insistence you are more than a concubine to him."

"Say no more." Alystin raised the silver bell before her. "Xa'lyyth has borne more than any male ever shall. Say apology, or leave this council."

Narlros glanced to Molva'yas, who only shrugged. He bowed to Alystin, then Xa'lyyth. "Apology is hereby given. My concern is great. Please say your thoughts and I will listen."

Xa'lyyth drew from her goblet once more, thinking. "Only Hovenethra threatens. Modennethra carries great hatred for Ba'tula's House and will not oppose our own. Karachitthra once was a staunch ally of the Dark Queen herself, and remains loyal. Warinethra always has sought the favor of Archane, and even still, their sorcerers are best of all. The House of Iyllyeth will not fall, for Hovenethra, while strong, is not stronger than the Race."

Alystin nearly smiled at the younger priestess's oration. Few knew the depth of Xa'lyyth's study of Drow history, and how she kept Mor'i'jil apprised of rumors concerning other Houses. Whether in his bed or in his privy chambers, Xa'lyyth's loyalty to Mor'i'jil was unquestioned. As was Alystin's own.

"Therefore," Narlros began, "we have no fear of the sacrificial dagger wielded so well by Dark Priestess Ba'tula? Care you to test this proclamation?"

"*Iyllyeth's* mercy shows the way," replied Xa'lyyth. "If we cannot silence every voice knowing of this tragedy, we must use it to solidify the Race."

"Archane's disappearance nearly fractured our people," replied Molva'yas. "With both gone, how will this stand to our advantage?"

Xa'lyyth raised her chin, replying, "Should Hovenethra wish war, four Houses will oppose them. Should Hovenethra wish peace, there is no change. They will press again for Conclave, as we search once more for Archane, and now Mor'i'jil as well."

"I see no advantage." Narlros drank once more, then looked to Alystin. "How to proceed? Where now to search? I have no answers."

"Desperate times, Dark Lord. Desperate measures now must be called upon." Alystin considered. "Do not the humans and elves search for this murderess, this Reena with the essence of Teresa Drakenmoore within her?"

Narlros began to speak, then closed his mouth. He shrugged and shook his head. "Surely, this is madness."

"Agreed," replied Alystin. "Yet what choice have we?"

* * *

The rumors soon began to swell. A messenger brought news to Ry'lld, who took it then to Lualyrr, and they fretted in the dankness of a corridor aside.

"Ba'tula will want war," said Lualyrr, hands nervous as she paced. "With Archane and Mor'i'jil gone, the Black Web is weak, as only Alystin remains with power."

The young priest Ry'lld watched in silence, then raised a question. "Might we approach in Ba'tula's stead, to know the way? Then go to her, asking patience?"

"Ba'tula's patience is at end. Years, centuries she has waited as Iyllyeth's House gained tribute from all, Hovenethra forced to nothing but a servant. Hold word from her and your heart will beat its last within her hand."

Ry'lld shuddered, closed his eyes and whispered prayers, then raised his face once more. "What then? Corridors filled with blood? Should Ba'tula choose sacrifice of Alystin or others, and Archane return, Hovenethra will not survive. All will find themselves upon the altar… you and I among them."

Lualyrr nodded, face filled with worry. "We must gain Ba'tula's favor to parley with Alystin. We may say as equals, we would understand concerns within their House better than would she. Still, Ba'tula may take this as a sign, that time is now for Hovenethra to rise and take the leadership."

"Dark Lady, I fear now as never I have before. Ba'tula is greatest of Hovenethra, and led with strength for near three hundred years. Yet her thirst for power at times clouds her judgement. To this time, we have aided her to find ways other than of violence. Now…" Once more Ry'lld bowed his head in silence.

"We must convince her of our sincerity, as done before. We must be her voice to those who have lost their own." Lualyrr laid a hand on Ry'lld's shoulder. "Give homage to *Iyllyeth*, and we will face Ba'tula together. We go now."

* * *

They asked audience with the Matriarch of Hovenethra in a private chamber, and there spoke word of Mor'i'jil's disappearance. Ba'tula listened carefully, head tilted in thought as Lualyrr laid the words before her.

"Confirmed, yes, and by whom? Soldiers only? Even Kaul, this Mongrel, not seeing with his eyes these happenings? Servants?"

Lualyrr bowed deeply. "Dark Lady, we know few details, but offer service of ourselves. We beg, let us venture to the House of Iyllyeth and confer with Alystin. There we may speak with those claiming to have witnessed the events. Proof, as you say, is needed before decisions can be made."

The older priestess sat quietly, her jaw working nervously as she considered. "Why would they lie? What advantage if this tale untrue? A trap to force Hovenethra's hand, encourage us to march against their House, and thereby be shown traitors to agreements? Yet agreements were made with Mor'i'jil, yes? Therefore, agreements may be set aside."

Ry'lld glanced to Lualyrr before replying. "Dark Lady, your assessment may be correct, yet if Mor'i'jil offered agreements in Archane's stead, therefore agreements should be honored. It is with the House of Iyllyeth these bonds are made, as in ancient times."

Ba'tula's eyes met his. "You hold our hand from righteous taking of the leadership? Are you Iyllyeth or are you Hovenethra? Shall we examine your heart for confirmation?"

Ry'lld stood tall as he might. "Dark Lady, my heart is yours in service or in sacrifice, and you know this. We ask only time. A day, perhaps two at most, and we will find the truth of it."

Ba'tula kept her gaze with his, then looked once more to Lualyrr. "Two days, no more. Bring proof, a soldier willing to submit to my interrogation, if possible. Otherwise, sworn parchment from Alystin with her seal and that of the House. We will have evidence, therefore, of lies, should it come to that, to prove to all the Houses. Time has come for Hovenethra to challenge with more than words. Next shall be the cleansing, with blood of soldiers and the hearts of the Black Web in my very hands."

* * *

Lualyrr and Ry'lld were dismissed, and once gone, Ba'tula called her Lancer Captains to conference. They gathered, ten in all, crowded in the meeting chamber, as the matriarch told the tales and set forth her plans for war, should it become necessary.

"We will cleanse the way with valor, Dark Lady," said her most senior of the group. "Too long we have waited to place Hovenethra at the pinnacle of the Race. Too many centuries Archane has drawn tribute from the other Houses as losses against the elves and humans mounted. She is unworthy."

Ba'tula nodded absently, thinking. "Whatever is done must be swift. We cannot allow time for such as Modennethra and the others to rally. Yours will be only to face Archane's soldiers, secure strategic passages, and keep other Houses away." She eyed them, five males, five females, all veterans of battle, eyes coming to rest once more upon the senior-most. "We will strike only on my command, no others. You understand, yes?"

The Lancer Captain bowed. "Dark Lady, your orders will be carried out unquestioned. It is only our desire to fight and die for the glory of *Iyllyeth* and the House of Hovenethra."

"Keep losses at a minimum, yet show no quarter to Archane's soldiers. No prisoners."

Again, the Lancer Captain bowed.

Ba'tula dismissed them all, then called her servants to set a meal and bring her writing table and pen. The chamber filled with the aroma of fresh meat and wine, and the rustling of parchments smoothed upon a penning board. Ba'tula thought as she slowly ate, how matters now were coming to a dagger point after all these years.

Years of Archane's missing, Mor'i'jil delaying one year after another, until at last we forced Conclave upon the Race. Then more delays, and now he, himself, is gone. Fool! But a cunning fool, and one whose work was worthy for a time. Now Hovenethra will take its rightful place, and should Archane and Mor'i'jil return, they will answer for their insolence. Hovenethra will wait no more!

She scratched out a message, sealed it with a drop of blood and her signet ring, then tied it with black ribbons. She called a messenger, who bowed and knelt before her as she spoke. "This is to be delivered to the Guild of Assassins immediately. Only to their Guildmaster, no other's hands. Have you the courage for it?"

204

The messenger, a woman, rose, accepted the parchment, and bowed again. "Dark Lady, I will give my life, should it be necessary. I will return with a reply, should you wish it."

Ba'tula nodded. "Tell those you encounter at the guild I said you are not to be harmed or pleasures taken of. You are under my protection, for this is of the Race, not only the House. Return with their reply, and quickly. Go now."

A third bow, and the messenger was gone, leaving the matriarch alone. She nibbled at her plate, still thinking, wondering what would happen, should her plans not come to fruition. In her heart, she knew there was but one answer.

* * *

The City-State of DragonFall…

Two days they waited with false patience, for Kaul to answer questions of the whereabouts of Mors'ul'jyn and Archane. Two days, and at the last they met in the guest house, to speak their way forward, should there be one.

"Kaul does not know," said Ysilrod, pacing about the room, eyes on the tapestries and trimmings, mind spinning with questions of his own.

"What then, friends?" Audrey sat with Thalion closely, goblets untouched between them, as they watched him pace.

Sheynon drew from his cup and shook his head. "We must presume somewhere in the depths of Drakenmoore's ruins is her hideaway. There was her power, and there is no other possibility I can imagine."

"I have not been in Drakenmoore," said Ysilrod, "therefore I cannot take us there with expediency."

Thalion shrugged. "My father was there with Kaanan." He looked to Sheynon. "You, my lord, tread those steps as well."

Sheynon nodded. "With Remo and Steffyn Foxxe. A cadre we were then, yet foolish to set in motion things we could not know or understand. *Kingmaker*, Eric's court… the Purge." He drank again, then fell silent.

"Speak of your powers, if you will," Audrey said to Ysilrod. "If within the lands, might you know her place? If descended into the dungeon, and she there, would you know her? We must break this impasse and find a way."

"Maps, plans of the castle and the depths below, have they survived?" Sheynon thought for moments. "Only one we know may aid us, that

Steffyn Foxxe himself. Yet Kaul, too, has been there, yes? In the Forge, he said, and from there she sent him by magic to Jeseriam."

"And likely, her lair cannot be reached by digging," reminded Ysilrod.

"Yet why not, Brother? Should we know it's place, are there not powers to move the very earth?"

"The power of gods," whispered Audrey.

"My brother speaks truth." Ysilrod poured himself a goblet and drank, then resumed his pacing. "If known, the lair is a true thing, of this world, not another. Yet how would she breathe beneath the ground, what would she eat, how to keep clean as time passes?"

"Her power is yet a mystery," said Thalion. "My father spoke of a young and vibrant woman, immodest but feigning modesty, drawing few questions of her true ability."

Sheynon shook his head once more. "She was one of three who created *NorthWind*. What sort of power therein was needed?"

"What of Kaul?" asked Audrey. "What does this venture gain him? Naught but revenge?"

"To him, a worthy goal," replied Sheynon. "My thought is, he will provide soldiers for whatever work is needed."

"Yet our goal? What is it we would wish?"

Sheynon looked to Ysilrod, then to Thalion, as they pondered Audrey's question. "My lady, the time may have passed that we seek to hold Archane guilty of crimes against Ardwel. Her armies were defeated, here and at Thalion's own castle. Likely the Drow are teetering near war within themselves, and should word of her recapture reach the ears of rival Houses, it soon may come to pass. It is Mors'ul'jyn we seek, for what she has done. With that, I would be satisfied with Archane's release to her own people."

Audrey sat speechless for long moments, then looked to Ysilrod, who only shrugged. Her eyes met Thalion's again.

"Excellency, what would you have us do? Near twenty years since you have been in Ardwel, and five years past have seen peace as we have never known. Did Crysalon, in his divinity, know what his disappearance would bring? The loss of Lady Galandria, while horrific in its doing, has calmed even Coronis's quest for power. Archane's people are surely stunned as we. The land now is calm and war unknown." He glanced to Sheynon. "Elves are united as not before. If gods move, as we often say, in ways we cannot understand, might this be a time as such?"

Audrey raised her cup and slowly drank, then set it on the table once again. "As always, words of my comrades are filled with merit, and I hear them well. I cannot say our path, therefore."

"Find Steffyn Foxxe," said Ysilrod. "Only he may aid us in our doing."

* * *

They met again at sunrise in the garden, tended well by servants, fed to break the night's fast, and offered drink as they would wish. At last Kaul and Rohesia came to them, and the Mongrel spilled all he knew.

Of escape from *Ung'gu'wi* with the concubine known as Reena.

Of learning who she truly was and the sorcery she held.

Of Reena's fate, her spirit cast away, and the soul of Teresa Drakenmoore taking of her body.

Of their flight across the land, and descending into the ruins of Drakenmoore.

Of *NorthWind* Forge, found cold and dead, yet power still within.

Of waking at the inn, and all the followed; Chitthra, Aeren, Drakkon the elf, the maiming of Earion, and the revealing of the Black Blade's purpose.

"The rest is known to you," said Kaul, drawing deeply from his cup. Rohesia took his hand and kissed it gently.

Thalion glanced to Audrey, Sheynon traded looks with Ysilrod, as a thousand questions lay unanswered still.

"You were in the Forge, yes?" Ysilrod rose to pace while listening.

"I lay exhausted in a ruined foyer as she searched, then woke in a room, the *Whispering Banshee,* as I recall." He chuckled, drank once more, then motioned a servant to refill his cup. "Yet there was a way beneath, and even now it may be followed."

Ysilrod mused as Sheynon spoke. "Therefore, we go, Brother? Clues you seek, to Mors'ul'jyn's whereabouts, still there?"

Ysilrod turned to Thalion and Audrey. "What say you? Once more to adventure, a mad woman as our quarry?" He nodded to Sheynon. "We follow where my brother tread those years ago, setting all this into motion."

"Not by his hand," said Thalion, and Sheynon looked away. "Tho' I know the reasons, even in this day I question deeds and purpose."

"Yet Kaanan," replied Audrey softly. "The *Rising Star* was raised to heights never known."

"And the Purge nearly wiped my kin and kindred from the land," said Sheynon tightly. "Things done for reasons, yes, but suffering by many who had no part."

Kaul shook his head, listening closely. "You still fight battles lost, and for what reason? Archane is real. Mors'ul'jyn is real. The old dark elf Mor'i'jil sought to take this city once again for himself. Cease this prattle and find a way beyond what lies before us!"

Audrey looked hard upon him. "When your hand has fought the battles we have known, then you may speak against our worries… great king."

"We offer no offense," said Thalion, a hand held before them. "We reminisce only as the feelings come again while in this city. Much has passed this way, and all of us have bled to right those wrongs."

Kaul rose. "I have said my peace. When your plan is ready, I will listen." He turned, and guards fell in about him, then he disappeared into the palace. Rohesia stood and bowed. "I will calm his manner." Then she was gone.

Silence fell, and the morning light lay quiet about them, thoughts their own and feelings deep within their hearts.

Sheynon looked to his brother. "As said, to Drakenmoore?"

Ysilrod nodded slowly, eyes focused inward. "Yet we will not dig. There may be a way."

* * *

The tavern once more was crowded, as it had been the night before, and two nights before as well. Chitthra sat with Aeren at the corner table, watching for Mend'rys and Jyslin to appear. They had sparred early in the day to keep their fighting trim, taken to the bath, then wandered shops in the merchantry, whiling time and saying little of their search.

Now Chitthra sipped ale and watched the doorway, eyes intent and a frown upon her face.

"Speak, Dearest, for I worry of your silence." Aeren laid a hand on Chitthra's forearm and forced a smile.

"Rumors say Sheynon and his entourage arrived and met with Kaul. Therefore, our thought of his assistance is likely dashed, and we wait for strangers with whom to cast our lot." Chitthra drank again. "I worry our search is all but over."

"Have faith," whispered Aeren, "and look to the door."

208

Mend'rys and Jyslin entered, faces deep within their hoods and eyes searching round. Aeren began to rise, yet Chitthra held her arm. "Let them approach, should they wish to. If not, we will follow on their leaving."

Aeren showed a crooked grin. "Little did that gain us before."

"We will be swifter now." Chitthra raised her face as the dark elves came to their table.

Jyslin bowed. "We wish parley. My master seeks your wisdom."

Chitthra traded glances with Aeren, then nodded to the girl. "Sit and refresh yourselves." She poured tankards round as Aeren offered the remnants of her supper. "Say your concerns and we will answer as we may."

Aeren's eyes caught the look of Mend'rys' trembling hands beneath his cloak.

"Is your health yet a concern?" asked Chitthra to Mend'rys.

He shrugged. "We fled moons ago and still watch beyond our shoulders. The reach of Archane is long, tho' she still is absent *Ung'gu'wi*. There, they worry of her whereabouts."

Chitthra sipped. "Yet there are tales she was seen here, at the palace. Might you confirm?"

Jyslin's hand tightened on the arm of Mend'rys as he shook. "There is a price for our words," he said.

Aeren huffed a breath, sitting back. "No tricks, no pleasures offered, no secret rendezvous. We speak here in plain and simple terms. We seek those of great power who have done harm unto the land."

"Archane has not harmed this land, she tends her people well," replied Jyslin, affronted.

"Our meeting is fortuitous," said Chitthra, seeking to calm rising tempers at the table. "As said before, politics are not our interest, only those opposing peace."

"Enough." Aeren met the eyes of Mend'rys. "Say your price or this meeting ends."

Still Mend'rys trembled in his cloak as Aeren held his gaze. "A pledge of safety, for myself and my ward, honor-bound. Nothing else."

Chitthra held her peace, knowing well the meaning of his words.

"And no harm to Archane," said Jyslin.

Aeren glanced once more to Chitthra. "Unless in our own defense."

"Master…"

"Accepted," said Mend'rys, and Jyslin dropped her eyes away.

Aeren nodded. "Say your knowing, and spare no words."

Mend'rys drew from his cup before beginning. "Archane's minister came to the city a moon ago."

"Mor'i'jil. Yes, we know of him," said Chitthra.

"Intent was to reclaim the city for the Drow, hold it until Archane and this Mors'ul'jyn arrived."

"He knew of their arrival, or only supposed upon it?" Aeren sipped to moisten her tongue, and forced herself to calm.

"Unknown," replied Mend'rys, "yet little does it matter. Mors'ul'jyn took them both away to wherever her sanctuary might now be."

"And her place?" asked Chitthra.

"Also unknown, yet clues were left, of which I study."

"And you know this because…"

"You were the other, yes?" Aeren's eyes bore into those of Mend'rys until he looked away. "Why would one as Mors'ul'jyn wish to escape from your own self? Have you the power to confront her?"

"Show respect," said Jyslin, warning in her voice.

Aeren's gaze shifted to the girl, then back to Mend'rys. "Answer, my lord, as we have a pact."

A sudden tremble caused him to pale, and Jyslin once again placed a hand upon his arm. "Patience, I beg you, as my master yet is ill."

"Ill of what, is my question?" Aeren sat back, waiting.

At last Mend'rys nodded. "We were there, yes, but too late to intervene."

"For what purpose?" Chitthra now leaned across the table. "Your role in this perplexes me, and I cannot think of reasons."

"And I will not reveal them in this time, tho' later, should it become necessary."

"You void our agreement, therefore," said Aeren, shaking her head.

"Not so, for we agreed only to say what we know of the happenings in the courtyard. Beyond that, reasons of our own for being there are not of your concern."

"They become our concern if we are endangered," replied Chitthra. "And little time would there be to explain, in the midst of confrontation, with the likes of Mors'ul'jyn and Archane."

Mend'rys shrugged. "Therefore, you know their power and will be wary of such a time." He looked to Aeren. "Your business with Mors'ul'jyn is likely known, as you are of the City-State of Truth. My question is, what does a dark elf mercenary seek, other than to claim a bounty?"

Chitthra raised her chin. "I am no bounty hunter, and as you have said, reasons are our own. Yet know I seek to end her, should I be able."

A silence settled at the table, then Mend'rys raised his cup. "Therefore, to our hunting. Three days, and we will meet once more. By then, I will know if my searching has borne fruit."

* * *

The depths of Ung'gu'wi...

Ry'lld and Lualyrr trod passages again between House Hovenethra and the grand entry chamber of *Ung'gu'wi*, where paths diverged, leading to all the great Houses of the Drow. Many tunnels led away, not only to the chambers of the Houses, but stores and workshops and council rooms, prayer fountains and passages to the surface. Nearly for a league they had walked, and once entering the pathway to the House of Iyllyeth, were paused by guards at a smaller room aside.

"No further," said a soldier, bowing slightly, "the way is shut until clearance given for your entry."

Ry'lld's eyes flashed anger, yet Lualyrr laid a hand upon his shoulder. "Pray tell, by whose authority are we detained? We travel at behest of Dark Lady Ba'tula, Matriarch of Hovenethra. We are known to all within the ruling caste of Iyllyeth. We ask escort, if it must be, to parley with Dark Lord Mor'i'jil."

Lualyrr's words had the effect she hoped, as the soldier paused before his reply. "The Dark Lord is beyond the House on missions of great importance. Dark Lady Alystin sits in rule."

"Then take us to her, as time flees before us. We ask in *Iyllyeth's* name."

Again, the soldier paused, then retreated, speaking to another. Both returned to Lualyrr and Ry'lld. The second was the Lancer Captain of the Passage Guard, and he nodded recognition. "As said, you may wait within a chamber set aside. We will see you are refreshed after your journey. Dark Lady Alystin will be advised of your arrival."

Lualyrr and Ry'lld traded knowing glances. "As you say," she replied, "then lead on and we will wait."

The chamber was small but well appointed, as though set for such occurrence. Again, the clergy of Hovenethra looked to each other, then sat, sipping wine as the Lancer Captain closed the door behind him.

"They are no fools," said Ry'lld softly, and Lualyrr nodded without reply.

"Regardless Mor'i'jil's whereabouts, Alystin anticipates Ba'tula's every move. My thought is we will be allowed no further, and Alystin or her proxy will come before us here."

"I saw no less than a score of soldiers," replied Ry'lld. "And where there is one score, likely are there more. Every passage will be fortified."

"What then?" Lualyrr set her goblet down, considering. "What of the other Houses? They will prepare, yes?"

Ry'lld paused his cup in thought. "And Alystin has likely sent a message in that manner. Ba'tula misjudges the House of Iyllyeth once more."

"Hold that tongue!"

Ry'lld nearly cowered as Lualyrr turned away, pacing to a tiny fountain in the corner, water playing music on the rocks within.

Ry'lld dropped his eyes away, yet did not quiet. "Dark Lady, you know it true. Whether Archane, or Mor'i'jil, or now Alystin, always is the House of Iyllyeth a thought ahead of Ba'tula. Little does she think of the Race, only her desire to hold the power."

Lualyrr paced slowly to the younger priest, malice in her eyes. "Should the matriarch know these thoughts, she will have your heart out. Dare you to speak such words as we seek parley to avoid blood between the Houses?"

"Ba'tula desires that blood, I fear. At times, I wonder if she seeks her death in favor of it. Martyrdom for all time within the Race, a dagger between the Houses, and animosity her legacy."

Lualyrr's eyes grew wider and she backed away, returning to the fountain. As Ry'lld sat and drank, she knelt, then rose once more, returned, and sat before him. "How can you serve Hovenethra with such feelings? It is by Ba'tula's grace we are granted time."

"My love for Hovenethra is great, Dark Lady, but my dedication to the Race yet stronger. Blood is not the answer, tho' Ba'tula is convinced. In your heart, surely you understand Hovenethra would stand alone against the House of Iyllyeth, should it come to war."

"Therefore, we cannot fail. Two days given, and half the first is gone. Are you yet Hovenethra, or do you set aside allegiance?"

Ry'lld raised his face. "I am Hovenethra, yet will see the Race as whole, regardless the time or cost."

Lualyrr nodded at the last. "These words are ours, I pledge. And I say, your point is made and taken. Therefore, let us find a way to keep all the hearts about us beating."

The door opened slowly, and Alystin entered with Xa'lyyth at her side. Servants followed, setting a meal upon the table and a crystal pitcher of sparkling wine.

Lualyrr and Ry'lld rose and bowed, Alystin and Xa'lyyth returning the honorific after the servants' exit. Alystin waved a hand and they sat again as Xa'lyyth poured wine before them all.

"You come unbidden," said Alystin at the last. "Are we to receive harsh words again from Hovenethra? Complaint of our leadership? Demand for Conclave?"

Lualyrr's dark features flushed and she drank to quell her growing anger.

"None of this, Dark Lady," replied Ry'lld before his counterpart could speak. "We ask clarity of rumors heard. We wish only truth between our Houses."

"Truth of what?" asked Xa'lyyth. "Conclave was called, decisions made, and Dark Lord Mor'i'jil laid a plan before the Council a moon ago. What now is asked?"

"His state, concern for his safety, as we hear he is beyond *Ung'gu'wi*," replied Lualyrr. "As said, rumors swirl and apprehension grows. Can you say the truth of it?"

"Mor'i'jil treats with those of Ardwel to learn of the Dark Princess." Xa'lyyth's voice was wary.

"Say your knowledge," said Lualyrr, "or we will leave knowing events are amiss."

Alystin sat, eyes locked with those of Lualyrr, then she sipped wine and nodded. "Word comes... Archane is alive, seen by Mor'i'jil's own eyes."

"These are his words? You have heard them from his own voice?"

"From trusted mouths," replied Alystin. "Mor'i'jil continues his mediation for Archane's return to her people."

"With whom? This Reena-woman, the essence of a human within her body? This creature Mor'i'jil says now holds the Dark Princess captive? How so? One of such power as Archane held by a concubine?"

"This is old debate," replied Xa'lyyth. "Word comes lately, and we prepare for Archane's return."

"Rumors say of otherwise." Ry'lld's words were nearly whispered as the room drifted to silence.

"Rumors are but that," replied Xa'lyyth. "And well you know, these are dangerous times for all. Have patience and be rewarded."

"Tell us where he is, that we may take word to Ba'tula's ear. We come only seeking truth," said Ry'lld.

"We must have all of it," hissed Lualyrr. "Hovenethra waits no longer. Should Mor'i'jil not return, what then?"

Xa'lyyth's eyes narrowed. "What have these rumors said, and from whose lips? Do you give credence to false words to set us at each other's throats? Who might benefit from such a thing?"

Silence came as Ry'lld and Lualyrr traded glances.

"That Mor'i'jil is captured by this... female. And Archane as well, again." Lualyrr drank, hands shaking.

"Believe what you will," said Alystin at the last.

"It is not what we believe, but thoughts running in the mind of Ba'tula." Lualyrr showed a wicked grin. "Dare you wager your hearts upon those thoughts?"

"Threats have no power here," replied Xa'lyyth. "Should we decide, your bodies would not be found."

"Enough." Alystin held a hand. "Take these words to your Lady. The House of Iyllyeth yet rules and always shall. Archane's return or not, Hovenethra's accusations, regardless of what grain of truth they hold, will not stand against the whole of the Race. If war is your intent, Hovenethra will not survive. Should Dark Lady Ba'tula wish martyrdom, I will provide it to her with my own hands, and with gladness."

Lualyrr stood, nearly shaking in her robes. "We leave this place and never will return. The Matriarch of Hovenethra will hold your heart within her hand before a moon is crossed."

"Before that," replied Alystin, her voice a harsh and bitter whisper, "she will be dead."

Ry'lld followed an incensed Lualyrr out the door.

* * *

Word was passed down the ranks in the House of Iyllyeth; no more would Hovenethra or their agents be allowed beyond the grand entry chamber. Messengers made way through the other corridors, to Warinethra and Karachitthra, to Modennethra asking the Guild of Sorcerers be well-informed. Two days, then the passages to the House of Iyllyeth were closed to all but trusted allies. Two days, and the Lancer Captains set soldiers beyond the entryway, barricades and a palisade of timbers carried from the Black Forest above *Ung'gu'wi*. A century of crossbows marked the emplacements, and another kept the watch in other corridors. Stores were locked away, weapons oiled, and armor donned, as songs to the grace of *Iyllyeth* were heard throughout the ranks.

From Warinethra came Cak'koths, leader of the Guild of Sorcerers, and for a day he met with Alystin and Xa'lyyth behind doors guarded by a dozen soldiers. Then came Dris'i'nil, accompanied once again by Durdyn and Xundus, her mates. Then Ki'zran of Karachitthra, and Hovenethra's mortal enemies Gurin and Lael'lae of Modennethra. All the Race, it seemed, save Hovenethra's House itself, came at the call of Alystin, now leading in the absence of Dark Lord Mor'i'jil. And though questions rose, and rumors still were heard, a cold resolve began to form, that Hovenethra's insolence must, at the last, be ended.

* * *

"They have barred the way!" Ba'tula paced as Lualyrr and Ry'lld knelt before her, both with marks of punishment upon their flesh and soldiers at their backs. They were naked, stripped of vestments and symbols of the House, tears running down their faces, mingling with blood.

Ba'tula stalked before them, a ceremonial dagger in her hand. They cringed, for more than once they had seen that very dagger pierce the flesh of a sacrifice upon the altar.

"You promised word and returned with only threats! Now only war is left as you fail your purpose!"

"Dark Lady—"

"Silence! Spare your excuses and your platitudes. In less than a day, the House of Iyllyeth prepares! You are nothing!"

"Words were said, and yes, while cryptic, I know they tell us rumors said are true!" shouted Lualyrr. "Mor'i'jil is gone, as is Archane once more. No other explanation can there be!"

"Proof! You promised proof!"

"Alystin spoke truth," replied Ry'lld softly. A cut above his eye ran rivulets of blood down his face, dripping to his chest.

"And you know this how?" Ba'tula loomed above him, her dagger at his cheek.

"Her words, the 'grain of truth' as spoken. It was her way to deny the rumors yet say the truth of things. I believe this in my heart."

"Then let us closely examine it for confirmation." Ba'tula nodded, and two guards picked up the priest, carried him to the altar, and laid him harshly on the cold obsidian. Two more joined them, and they held him tightly as Ba'tula pressed her dagger point against his chest.

Ry'lld shook and cried and struggled as Ba'tula watched his face. Then he calmed, looked her in the eyes with deep conviction, and drew a breath. "Should it be your wish, my heart is yours, as pledged to *Iylhyeth* on my confirmation. Yet know this, Dark Lady; none will think the better of you for dispensing anger on one who only lived to serve this House."

He glanced to the dagger and the spot of dark blood beneath its point. "Do as you will. I go to *Mother Darkness* knowing I have done my all."

Rage and indignation crossed the face of Ba'tula. Never did Ry'lld's eyes leave hers, even as she pressed the dagger deeper. Lualyrr softly sobbed, still knelt before the other guards. At the last, Ba'tula drew the blade away and motioned the soldiers to raise the priest before her.

"Your courage is great, yet know this. War comes, and if we face this alone, it is our destiny. The House of Hovenethra never has shied from duty or from confrontation."

She glanced to Lualyrr, who rose, ran to Ry'lld, and held him dearly. "I give you one more attempt to break this impasse. Tell Alystin your very lives are offered to her blade in sacrifice, should she wish it. For if you return again in failure, your hearts will be sought by my own hand!"

* * *

Beneath the Depths of Drakenmoore…

Archane lay abed, not kept by Mors'ul'jyn's spells, but her own lethargy. Mor'i'jil was gone, and with him, her greatest ally in the quest to regain her power over the Houses of the Drow. Likely, too, her only chance for freedom.

Had it been the plan in Mors'ul'jyn's mind these many years, simply hidden where Archane could not draw it out, or but a flash of brilliance by her adversary? More likely the latter, for Archane was certain Mors'ul'jyn had no thought Mor'i'jil would be in the city-state awaiting their arrival.

And therefore, only circumstance and ill fortune transpired as we saw it. Yet why, then, kill Mor'i'jil? Certainly, to remove the danger of us planning our escape, or overpowering Mors'ul'jyn and making her our prisoner. In truth, she is as much a prisoner as I, however. Therefore, to further plans against the Houses. Her threat, to use my body as that of Reena…

Archane pushed aside the growing horror of true death, not knowing if the sorcery allowing her to rise would remain, should Mors'ul'jyn decide to carry out her words.

216

She rose, walked to the table and sat, poured a goblet half-full and drank. Her mind yet refusing to believe what had transpired, only could she wonder what now would come, and if she ever would be free.

She carved a slice of beef, still fresh, and forced herself to eat. She laid the eating dagger on the table, chewed without tasting what was in her mouth, then paused. Her eyes found the dagger once again. The blade was sharp, she knew, twice a finger's length, the point keen and bright. She dared not touch it as thoughts began to form. Cold, desperate, deadly thoughts, never had before. Thoughts only those mad or willing to accept defeat might have. Not herself, the Dark Princess, leader of the Drow.

Dearest Iyllyeth, what are these judgements now running through my mind?

She stood and paced, slowly though, for she knew Mors'ul'jyn scryed upon her and would notice any change. She knelt before the hearth in prayer, face drawn and without feeling.

The sorcery. Venic. All two thousand years ago and more. Where did he go, disappearing in that time, never seen by Archane again? Never offering his touch… his affection… his love, something dark elves had little use for, yet had found a place in her life with him. Did he yet live? Surely not, though Venic was a master of the Craft.

How may I do such a thing? Would the sorcery then hold, or would I die forever? What are my chances to be free? With Mor'i'jil, it might have been, but Mors'ul'jyn saw the danger there. What choice have I? To be free, yes, but to die forever to find its solace? Do I even have the courage?

She sat at table once again, carved the loin and slid the dagger beside the plate. She drank once more, eyes closed, lips trembling against the goblet rim, tears stinging in her eyes.

She set away the cup, took up the dagger and slid it 'neath her sleeve. Pacing slowly to the hearth once more, she knelt, back to the room, and drew the dagger out. She touched the tip between her breasts, beneath the bone, upward toward her heart. Her hands shook, tears streamed down, and she drew what in her mind she knew might be her final breath.

Iyllyeth forgive me, and Mother Darkness, take me in your arms.

She shoved the dagger deep beneath her ribcage crying out in pain, collapsing on the floor. She wrenched away the blade and screamed again, her blood pouring on the stones.

At the last, she beheld it pooling there beneath her. She smiled and closed her eyes, letting the darkness flow about, and welcomed it.

Dennis Young

BOOK EIGHT
DAUGHTERS OF DARKNESS

"Hear us, Mother Darkness, for your Children ask a boon.
Give us sign, show the path taken by our foes.
We ask only as your glory may be served,
with blood of enemies and sacrifice
upon your altar in the Blood Moon time.
Show to us your power,
that we may praise your name!"

Iy'lly'eth at prayer in the
Other place and Time

In the depths of Ung'gu'wi...

Dark Mistress Ba'tula did not wait for Lualyrr and Ry'lld to make their way again unto the House of Iyllyeth. Once certain they were beyond Hovenethra's corridors, she ordered her Lancer Captains forward, then retreated to the prayer chambers with her entourage. Little did she care if the younger priest and priestess were killed or captured, for now her only thought was the seizure of power while both Archane and Mor'i'jil were gone. And in doing so, prepare those ruling now the House of Iyllyeth for sacrifice, that Ba'tula not be thought a murderess, but only wishing strength for *Mother Darkness* with her offerings.

The Black Web would be her first, Alystin and Xa'lyyth, then the sniveling priests Molva'yas and Narlros, both little better than pleasure toys for true believers. Rumors for many years said Archane had used them both to gain favor with the lower priesthood, keeping satisfied both male and female with base gratifications. Ba'tula scoffed. Pleasures of the body held no interest for her now, only the thought of warm and bloody hearts within her hands. Hearts of Alystin and Xa'lyyth, of Molva'yas and Narlros, and any others who would oppose her quest for leadership.

She did not grin. She did not smile. Rather, she faced her task with a grim determination learned, with irony, from Archane her own self.

And should events proceed as planned, and Archane return, her heart might also beat its last in Ba'tula's hands.

* * *

The great river running underground called *Z'hr'henn Charnag*, the *Flowing Deep*, fed by lakes and mountain streams to the north and east, set the eastern borders of *Ung'gu'wi*, far below the Black Forest. There Alystin had sequestered a company of soldiers, that Hovenethra would not seek the river as a way into the House of Iyllyeth. And as Lualyrr and Ry'lld had fled, Ba'tula's final words to stop the war both knew now the matriarch of Hovenethra sought, they took the river's way, thinking it the safest.

They huddled in a crevice as the waters glided past, hearing soldiers marching as they fell in step upon the hardpacked earth.

"Dare we show ourselves?" Lualyrr peeked beyond their shelter as a dozen guards passed by.

"Shed whatever sigils might declare your allegiance to our House," said Ry'lld, and they removed their amulets. The priest then buried them beneath a rock.

"What now? Surely their Lancer Captain may know our faces." Lualyrr shivered in the dank hideaway, more of fear than cold.

Ry'lld held her close. "You stood beside me as I lay on the altar, Ba'tula's dagger keen upon my skin. For that, I thank you." He drew her in his arms and she responded, huddled close, and pressed her cheek to his. "Here we must show courage once again," he continued. "Should we live beyond this day, we will find answers against Ba'tula."

"How can she not care for our survival, or that of the House? Is she mad? Is her mind so filled with hate against Archane she no longer cares for a thousand years of history?"

Ry'lld could not answer, for truly, he did not know. He only shrugged, then motioned as the last of soldiers passed beyond the niche. They emerged in quiet, looked to the column as it disappeared beyond a bend, then faced upstream and began to walk… into the waiting silence of the rear guard.

"Hold or face death!"

Ry'lld paused with Lualyrr behind him, raised empty hands and nodded her to do the same. Three soldiers clad in heavy leather armor approached, two with weapons drawn and the third with torch in hand. A fourth came from behind, the mark of many battles on his face. He grinned at Lualyrr, disheveled as she was, base lust within his eyes.

"A prize," was all he said, as he held her face with his hand, then turned her round. The others watched, nodding in agreement.

One with a sword raised it to Ry'lld's belly and pressed the point against him. "Your allegiance? Quickly, as we have duty and cannot tarry."

"We… I…," Ry'lld licked dry lips, looking at Lualyrr with deep concern as the soldiers continued to appraise her.

"We seek Dark Lady Alystin, that war may be avoided." Lualyrr spoke with a confidence she did not feel, stepped away from the hands straining to touch her with impudence, and stood at Ry'lld's side. "We beg you, take us to her quickly. The House of Hovenethra writhes in the grasp of a woman mad with power."

The scar-faced soldier frowned, closing once again on Lualyrr, ran his fingers through her hair, then dropped them to her shoulder. "There is a price for such a request." He looked her hard in the eye.

Lualyrr took his hand away and placed it on her breast. "Alystin first, then pleasures."

The soldier scoffed. "I think not." He nodded to the one holding his sword at Ry'lld, and the guard thrust. Ry'lld screamed as his dark blood gushed, then Lualyrr tore herself away from heavy grasping hands.

Then all was chaos. Two soldiers tore away her vestments, pushed her chemise above her hips, raised her in their arms, and spread her before the scar-faced guard. He dropped his breeches quickly, Lualyrr screaming, clawing at the roguish hands upon her body. He grunted as he found her warmth, thrusting hard within her as the others laughed, hungry eyes drinking in her violation.

Ry'lld lay gasping, bleeding, yet conscious still. He panted out a prayer of dark fire, and the soldiers watching were caught within it. They screamed, dropped Lualyrr to the cavern floor, then rolled into the water. The scar-faced soldier fell, swung his sword at Ry'lld while lying prone, missing badly.

Lualyrr's boot came down upon his neck, and she drove a castoff dagger into his heart, crying oaths into his face. She drew it out, drove it in again, and then again, only ceasing when Ry'lld called her name.

"Ry'lld!" She turned to him and rolled him to his back, blood covering his robes, her hands, the ground about. She pressed upon his wound, called a healing prayer, then held him as he shook. Long moments passed as he trembled, his body forcing itself whole once more in far too little time.

They lay there for a while, three scorched bodies drifting in the current, as the scar-faced soldier's blood leaked its last into the earth. Lualyrr kissed Ry'lld deeply, held him to her breast, and shed tears as he clung to her with all his strength.

Never had he raised a hand, let alone cast a prayer, against another Drow, and now his spirit cried revulsion. *Outcast! Alystin will seek my heart, and Ba'tula as well! None will claim us for fear of retribution.* He took what solace he might for long moments, nestled in Lualyrr's embrace.

"We cannot remain in *Ung'gu'wi*," he whispered at the last.

She nodded wordlessly and held him tighter. "I know."

* * *

Within the caverns of the Drow, along the banks of the river *Z'hr'henn Charnag*, were crossings, centuries ago decreed as not held by any House. And at three of those crossings were ascending stairways, known only to the highest clergy, hidden in caverns set so deep within the rocks and seldom used, nearly were they forgotten in the passing years. Only once, and heard by Ry'lld when those speaking did not know his presence, did he learn of them, then sought to find a way beyond the caverns, should time ever come in need.

Lualyrr's vestments had been shredded by the soldiers, and as they cast the body of the scar-faced guard into the river, they buried what they could not salvage. Therefore, the priestess garbed herself in a grimy tunic, ill-fitting breeches, and a leather thong to hold them. Ry'lld's blood-covered robes they washed in the river's waters, then hung them on a rock to dry. He shivered in the cold, thoughts roiling in his mind of the blade cutting through his gut, pain exploding in his body, and the helplessness felt as he lay bleeding.

They took refuge in the niche as before, and when other soldiers came, backed their way deeper in the darkness. Breath held and eyes clenched hard in fear, they waited as a column passed, then dared a glance beyond their hideaway.

"They have gone," whispered Ry'lld, but Lualyrr held him back, waiting as the river rolled before them. Only when silent moments passed did she nod, and quietly they emerged.

They took stock of what they had; a worn pack holding cheese and bread and little else, two daggers and a castoff sword now worn on Ry'lld's back. They filled a waterskin from the river, drank their need, then filled it once again. Ry'lld donned his robes, still damp, and they took the shoreline south. Torches, ever-burning, lit their way, and shadows played upon the earthen walls as they walked in silence for a while.

"How far?"

Ry'lld shrugged at Lualyrr's question. "A day, perhaps, tho' how will we know?" He nodded ahead. "I have searched this passage and likely it is not patrolled. With the soldiers encountered and now avoided, we may be safe."

Lualyrr shuddered and he drew her close. They paused, embracing, and she buried her face in his still-damp vestments. "My thanks," she whispered, and clung to him for many moments, then drew away and touched her forehead to his in warm affection. "We would have died, and our bodies cast into the river, had you not..."

He pressed a finger gently to her lips. "Once free and in the forest, we will speak. There are villages round, lying to the east and filled with Drow, set there by Archane in years long past. There we will find refuge, and a better life."

She blinked, and then again. "You would have me? As your mate for all our lives?"

He grinned and drew her close once more. "If nothing else, a companion trusted and admired."

Again, Lualyrr held him close, wrapped him in her arms and whispered in his ear. Her hand drifted 'neath his robes, found his maleness and roused him well, then led him to a darkened corner. He sat, and she straddled him, drew him deep into her warmth, and he gasped, for she was wet with desire. She took him to the edge of ecstasy, held him there, held him there, then drove him o'er the edge. He cried, raking fingers on her hips, nearly drawing blood from her ebon flesh. She smiled teasingly, satisfaction on her face, not only of the pleasures, but repaying him, knowing males thought well of fleshy tributes. He sank away in deep release and drifted into sleep.

She leaned herself upon him, kissed him again, and thanked *Iyllyeth* and *Mother Darkness* for his courage in the fight.

He laid upon the altar, and nearly did he dare Ba'tula to take his heart. He bled his life onto the ground, yet saved me in his wounding. Yes, here is a male I might find worthy of trust, for no matter his own pain, he finds a way beyond it.

She kissed him once again, then curled beside him, knowing now there was time enough to seek a way beyond the cavern.

* * *

In the Black Forest…

They emerged in daylight, the sun nearly blinding them as clouds drifted across the sky, and Ry'lld led Lualyrr back to the stairway, where they waited until dusk.

They coupled once again, finding release in the closeness, and Ry'lld wondered if ever he could be satisfied with another female, so tender was her touch.

Lualyrr, for her part, grinned to herself, for always had she been fond of males endowed as Ry'lld, and gave a mischievous thanks to *Iyllyeth* for her fortune. Then she curled within his arms and slept as the sun lowered in the west.

* * *

The village was not large, and they entered it to looks of curiosity, apprehension, and children running for the thatch-roofed cottages about. Ten dark elves approached, two with weapons and others watching closely, and Ry'lld feared they had made a terrible mistake.

"Strangers from below are not welcome," said one, a shortsword in his hand, though he did not raise it.

"We are… refugees," replied Ry'lld, as Lualyrr pressed closely by. "We bring news and warning. We beg only that you listen and give us shelter for a day."

The villagers passed a look around. Two shrugged, three others nodded without words, the rest simply dispersing, walking away with words between them. The leader motioned to a hut aside. "There, and I will hear your tale."

He sheathed his sword and motioned them to follow, set them at a table beyond the hut and poured ale as they nodded thanks.

Ry'lld raised the cup, the ale a balm upon his tongue, as Lualyrr sipped quietly, nervous in her look. He touched her hand and spoke. "Dark times below, Master…"

"Vorn," replied the villager, "and you are not the first to say so. News precedes you by a moon or more." He cast a look to the others as they sat. "Shonn, Ga'bra, and Nybae, all came with word Archane was gone." He motioned to the women at the table. "Concubines of the Great Houses, seeking a way beyond the coming war."

"War?" Ry'lld's voice was wary, and he glanced to Lualyrr.

Vorn laughed. "Surely you have heard, else why would you be here? You want no part, yes?"

Ry'lld had no answer, only a thousand questions forming in his mind. "Rumors, perhaps, nothing more."

"I know your face," said Ga'bra. "Do not presume to untruths or we will send you back."

Lualyrr laid a hand on Ry'lld's arm. "Say no falsehoods."

The priest nodded, then spoke again. "Your words are true. Archane is gone five years and more, Mor'i'jil missing, say the rumors. The Houses set to war upon each other for control, but in truth of fact, only Hovenethra seeks it. The rest will oppose them, allied with the House of Iyllyeth, or stand apart." He glanced once more to Lualyrr. "We were… cast out for failure to reconcile with the leadership of Iyllyeth's House."

"You were of Ba'tula's inner circle?" Vorn leaned his elbows on the table, now intent.

"Second Caste," said Lualyrr, "dispensable, if necessary, to Dark Lady Ba'tula's thought."

"Therefore, you sought escape." Vorn sat back, nodding.

Ry'lld only cast his eyes away, as did Lualyrr. Quiet moments passed, then he looked once more to Vorn. "In time, they will come for the villages, should Ba'tula be victorious."

Vorn shrugged. "The villages feed *Ung'gu'wi*, do they not?"

226

"She will seek to starve the other Houses," replied Lualyrr. "Her mind is fixed only upon power, and she cares not about the Race."

"Yet you said Hovenethra stands alone."

"For now." Ry'lld shuddered. "Should all others give pause and wait, Ba'tula will decimate her own House to end Archane's rule."

"Leaving nothing," said Ga'bra. "Can she be so foolish?"

Lualyrr only nodded. "In desperate times, desperate measures are called upon."

"What then for the villages?" asked Vorn, worry showing on his face.

"Seal the stairways from the forest. Keep Ba'tula's hand from your fields and hunting grounds."

Vorn looked to the women at the table, all in contemplation. "You have earned your day of shelter and a meal." He motioned to their ragged look. "And we will provide clothing suitable for the forest and lands beyond." He chuckled once again. "It is my thought, you will not be returning to *Ung'gu'wi* in this lifetime."

* * *

The night was deep as Ry'lld and Lualyrr lay together in a tent apart. Warm flesh and whispered words had filled their night once fed and clothed, as prayers were given to the *Blood Moon*, and a quiet word with Vorn again.

Sated and content, they drifted in each other's arms, the nighttime forest sounds strange to their ears and keeping them from sleep.

"What now?" Lualyrr nestled closer, giving silent thanks for their deliverance.

"Might we find a place within this village, or perhaps another?"

Lualyrr rose to her knees, a frown showing in the crimson moonlight. "Tho' we escaped our deaths, still we have purpose to our people. Somehow, some way, we must find Archane and return her to *Ung'gu'wi*. Only she can bring calm to the Great Houses."

Ry'lld sat. "She would seek Ba'tula's heart, and you know this. Then purge Hovenethra to cleanse those loyal to the Dark Mistress." He glanced her way. "Should we have stayed, our hearts would become as counted."

"Still, we are not discharged of our duty."

Ry'lld shrugged at the last. "I have no thought of where to find Archane."

"Then we retrace Alystin's steps. The city of the Mongrel Kaul, and seek their help."

The priest barked a laugh. "What coin will we engage them with? Your pleasures? A life as body servants or concubines at his call?"

Lualyrr drew closer. "*Iyllyeth* will show a way. *Mother Darkness* will protect us, as she has done now. We must find Archane, if for no other reason than giving thanks for our lives yet spared."

Ry'lld was silent for many moments. "We have pledged to each other in this time, shared danger never contemplated and grown closer." He sighed. "When the soldiers came…"

Lualyrr touched a finger to his lips, as done before. "You saved my life, and for that I am indebted."

He shook his head. "No. Decisions made were together, and you owe me nothing. We stand side by side, and in that, *Iyllyeth* smiles upon our devotion. What is done is for her glory."

Lualyrr bowed her head. "As said, therefore, the choice is mine. I give what I choose, and ask only you consider it as so." She gave him a wink. "Tho' with gladness do I say, you satiate me as no others."

Ry'lld grinned to himself, yet outwardly only nodded with reluctance. "Very well. We will leave come morning, yet…"

Lualyrr raised an eyebrow.

"I do not know the way."

She smiled and held him to her breast.

* * *

In the depths of Ung'gu'wi…

Beneath the villages and forest, beneath the moons and sky and stars watching with disinterest, blood began to flow in *Ung'gu'wi's* passages. Alystin, no general, bade her Lancer Captains keep the memory of Archane and Mor'i'jil within their minds, and songs to *Mother Darkness* were heard throughout the House of Iyllyeth.

Ba'tula sought to press the battle, find a weakness, and break through quickly, before any thought Archane might yet return. Though Alystin's soldiers held their ground, knowing defense within the caverns was less costly than a bold and bloody charge.

Three days they battled in the great joining cavern, three days of dark elves making war against each other, never seen in this time and place, and seldom even in the ancient past.

Each day was called a truce, that wounded and the dead might be recovered, else disease would kill the lot of them below the ground. Each day processions walked the way beyond *Ung'gu'wi's* darkness, pyres lit, and chanting heard throughout the forest high above.

228

Then once more they would descend, weapons sharp and arrows nocked, to battle in the caverns. Yet only the two Great Houses, of Iyllyeth and Hovenethra, fought, as others stood apart. Karachitthra sent only spies, or scouts who ventured no further than the central chamber. Warinethra held away their sorcerers, for, as they said, should the Dark Arts come in play, the whole of *Ung'gu'wi* would be shattered. Yet of those who did not fight, it was Modennethra who Alystin had depended so much upon, and as they were the sworn enemy of Ba'tula and Hovenethra, she could not understand. Therefore, she called the Black Web into council, that reasons might be found.

* * *

They stood together once again, meeting in a tiny chamber hidden far beyond those used in ceremony. Here was the most secret of the House, nearly as a niche within a niche, safe from prying eyes or swords seeking blood, where clandestine words might be spoken without reprisal. Here was Archane's last bastion, set centuries ago, should times come where truth must be spoken, and hearts sought otherwise were safe.

So tightly were the walls, nearly did the clergy touch, and this was set to purpose. In other times, Archane and Mor'i'jil would there be present, yet now there were only five, the Black Web left leaderless. Yet even in attrition, Archane's plan was kept alive. So long as one remained, the Black Web would lead the House of Iyllyeth, and therefore, all the Race.

"Speak your minds," said Alystin. Her eyes met those around, the priests Molva'yas and Narlros, and priestess Xa'lyyth standing close. Vrammyr, for her part, stayed by the door.

"The Lancer Captains say of losses on both sides," said Narlros, seeming nervous in his words. "Yet Hovenethra has no success to be spoken of. Therefore, our soldiers keep the fight apart from the House."

"So long as fighting is with weapons only, little do we have to fear." Molva'yas gave a sign before himself.

"You think as much?" Alystin shook her head. "Still if losses mount, there will be a time of no return. If Hovenethra, it will end their efforts. If ours, we will suffer death at Ba'tula's hand."

"Warinethra offers no aid of sorcerers," said Xa'lyyth softly. "We dare not use prayers for ill against our own, else draw wrath from the other Houses." She looked to Alystin and sighed. "Time, Dark Lady, yet on whose side does it give allegiance?"

"The impasse must be broken," said Molva'yas. "If not Warinethra, then Modennethra surely will oppose Ba'tula's efforts."

"Why would they?" Alystin shrugged. "Should our House fall, they then would feel justified in fighting Hovenethra. If Hovenethra falls, might they think our weakened state would give them benefit?"

Narlros's eyes widened, horror on his face. "You suggest Modennethra would seek leadership over us? Dark Lady, surely this is folly!"

"Nay, for in all the centuries, Modennethra never has been loyal completely to any but their own." Alystin glanced round once again, eyes meeting hers reluctantly. "It is a possibility, one we must prepare for. Therefore, our soldiers fight only as they must, and hold the line against Ba'tula."

"I will go to Warinethra, should you command," said Xa'lyyth. "I would beg them send sorcerers, if only as a threat."

Alystin thought for moments, as Narlros and Molva'yas traded surreptitious looks.

"I will go beside her," said Narlros. "Two perhaps may present offerings more so than one."

Alystin and Xa'lyyth touched hands, and at the last, the older priestess nodded. "Do honor unto the House of Iyllyeth." She looked with knowing into Xa'lyyth's eyes. "Offer that which is asked, whatever it may be."

They departed without ceremony, Alystin's eyes on Vaymmyr as she followed. "See she is watched," she said quietly to Molva'yas. "Something stirs within that devious and disaffected mind."

* * *

The City-State of DragonFall...

Rohesia met with the Companions once again, pledging one hundred soldiers and ten score laborers for the trek to Drakenmoore. They departed in the early morning to cheers and tankards raised by the mercenary guards, Kaul himself standing at the pinnacle of the city gatehouse tower, resplendent in red and sable trappings.

Ysilrod and Sheynon kept smiles of innocence upon their faces, as Thalion and Audrey rode behind them, passing looks of humor barely repressed. In all, it took nearly to the mid of morning before the caravan was beyond the city and villages around, and only when the leading party was well on the road did the Companions speak among themselves.

"I cannot fault his offer of this entourage," said Sheynon, "yet will we need them all in time?"

230

"Fewer mouths to feed within the city," replied Audrey, looking o'er her shoulder at the trailing column. "And opportunity to show his power to the land about. My thought is, little as Kaul considered how to grow influence in Ardwel's heartland, he begins to learn." She nodded to Rohesia at the fore. "Her manner finds his eyes and ears, that courtliness may be learned. A king he may be, but of a city little more than a den of thieves."

"Invitation has been extended through the years," said Thalion. "Each summer's conclave of the land seeks the mood of Ardwel and its peoples. Elves and humans, dwarves and even of the dark elf villages, none are barred, yet Kaul declines attendance."

"Yet older as he grows, in time change must come, and his children petition for his seat," replied Sheynon.

Audrey looked to Thalion, revelation on her face. "How old? Surely his eldest child must be no older than a handful of years."

Sheynon nodded as the column settled into a trot at a call from Rohesia at the fore. "And another dozen before matters become interesting for an aging Kaul." He drew his mount closer to Thalion. "Speak Cousin. What thoughts stir in the City-State of Truth? Aeren and the ministers yet lead, tho' is consideration given to a monarch? Five years have passed since Crysalon's… disappearance."

Thalion was thoughtful as they rode through wood and plain rich in the greening of late summer. Rain throughout the season had turned lazy creeks and streams into small rivers, needing care in crossing.

"In this time, no cause has come, nor is the Church unhappy with the current state. The council meets twice each moon, clergy, ministers, and city guildsmen." He looked to Audrey, listening closely. "As said before, even in the darkest times there is sunlight breaking through the clouds. With Crysalon and Archane gone from the world, peace found a way into the land."

Audrey nodded solemnly, then showed a smile of understanding to the half-elf priest. "*Jhad* provides," she said softly.

Sheynon looked away, tears of memory stinging at his eyes. Ysilrod spurred his horse closer and took his brother's arm. "She lives in your heart, always and forever, Brother. Never will she leave you or be forgotten by her people."

Sheynon snarled a bitter oath, snapped his reins, and moved from the column into a copse.

"Our pardon, dearest friend," said Audrey, now beside the elf-mage. "I will tend his heart." With that, she rode aside, following Sheynon's path.

* * *

Sheynon dismounted and knelt beneath a young oak tree. Tears spilled before he could even stop them from descending, and he sobbed quietly into his hands.

Why do I have these thoughts again, after five tormented years of setting them aside? Is it only that once more I am in the company of comrades dear, not seen for many years? Galandria, help me understand! How I miss you! How our children still question workings of the world and how evil comes to break our hearts. Why you, of all? Why not my own self, that your love and leadership survive? Yarhetha'an help me! Save me from dark thoughts once more finding way into my mind!

He turned at the sound of boots on deadfall as Audrey walked slowly from her mount, then knelt at his side. He fell into her arms, wept into her armored shoulder, and clung hard as he might. He shook with rage and anger, letting go his feelings for the first time in many years. Audrey only held him dearly, stroked his hair and whispered words in Elvish, that he would know his grief was shared.

In time, his tears subsided, though she would not let him go. Still they embraced, comrades brought together once again, elf and human, bound by feelings deep and real, lives shared and dangers met together, more times than could be counted easily.

He drew away at last and she wiped his face with a kerchief, then smiled sadly at his look. "Dearest Sheynon, all the gods smile on your spirit every day. You are the light to elves and humans as myself, courage deep glowing as the sun. Never doubt your destiny as time rides upon your shoulder."

"More than twenty years since we have been in each other's presence." Sheynon sniffed and wiped his eyes with a tunic sleeve. "As done before, you open up my heart and show the world to me as it truly is. And therefore, I must face it, as you say." He motioned to the caravan passing in the distance. "The world is never done of us, is it, my lady? Why, in the name of all the gods, will it not let us rest, to seek solace needed desperately?"

Audrey touched his chest, then hers. "Solace is here, elf-friend, in our hearts, soul to spirit, love to love, and never will we part. We are kindred, now and in whatever lies beyond this mortal life. Always will we be

232

together. You, Ysilrod, Thalion, my own self. We are bound by needs of the world. Give thanks we are together once again."

Sheynon looked away, then met her crystal eyes once more. "I cannot think of anyplace I would rather be."

Audrey smiled, and embraced him once again.

* * *

Drakenmoore…

"Should we find the forge intact, I may seek her hideaway." Ysilrod stood at the shattered ruin of Drakenmoore's front gates. Only after clearing forest overgrowth two days had the workers found the castle entrance.

The Companions stood watching round, Sheynon with eyes lost in times below, Thalion and Audrey wondering of the dangers they might face, trading glances as they held their peace. Kaul had not come, though given maps made "to my knowledge, yet it was many years ago I tread those darkened corridors". The king, it seemed, wanted no part, and contended yet with nightmares of his own, remembered from that time.

Yet now, rain had set upon them, tents hastily erected in the deluge, and quickly earth turned into mud, and work halted in the storm.

Thalion's attendants brewed tea as he and Audrey waited quietly in his pavilion, Sheynon and his brother conferring in a tent away. The priest passed his hand above his cup, whispered prayers, then drank, meeting Audrey's eyes. "Your family is well? Higar tends the castle and children as the baroness rides again into adventure?" His toothy grin brought a smile to Audrey's face, remembering such times and danger.

"I fear for Sheynon's heart," she said at the last. "Five years he has led the elves of Ardwel, kept his family safe, and been tasked by responsibility to his people. He has grown so much, now even as a diplomat with the city-states, Coronis, the dwarves…" She sipped tea as her voice faded and her eyes sought memory again. "Now…"

"And now we bring him face to face, perhaps, with the one who perpetrated all this." Thalion waved his hand gently. "Thoughts again of vengeance, you say? Of betrayal by an elf-brother, never envisioned? The lives of elves are long, as well you know, Excellency. At some time, perhaps a hundred years from now when both of us are gone, his ire would rise. Is it not best we are here beside him in that time? Comrades all, trusted with each other's lives, never fearing danger in our presence?"

"Yet not only this Mors'ul'jyn, but Archane."

Thalion shook his head. "As said before, Archane will seek nothing of ourselves. Should we free her from Mors'ul'jyn, honor binds her with a debt."

Audrey's eyes were hard upon the priest. "Never would I think of honor in Archane's manner, and you know this."

Thalion was silent as he drank once more. "She surely has changed in many ways, Audrey. Five years a prisoner, her people likely now at war against themselves, Houses squabbling for advantage, blood flowing in the depths. Archane will have more concerns in her mind than us."

The attendant refreshed their cups and set a meal before them. Audrey gave it little notice, drinking once again, as Thalion watched.

"How do I reconcile, Thalion? How can I stand apart from evil's surrogate?"

"Faith," he replied.

Audrey nodded at the last. For the nonce, what else could she do?

Thalion gazed away, sharing Audrey's deep concern, knowing there was truth within her questions. Still, with the land at peace and Archane's manner known, he swore, should the Dark Princess seek opportunity against Ardwel again, she would die forever 'neath *Gil Estel's* keen edge.

* * *

Two days it rained, and on the third, workers sought entrance once again into the castle. Another day of effort brought little change, and at the last Rohesia met the Companions in a copse, speaking the way forward. "The entry marked by His Majesty is impassable. Five years of weather and shifting earth have shut the way." She pointed to the map upon the table. "Here lies the entrance leading to the greathouse, and workers now proceed in their recovery. Sunrise on the morrow will confirm if it is safe."

Audrey shook her head. "The map was drawn with a different entrance?"

Rohesia smiled. "Years ago, hucksters from Jeseriam made an attraction of the castle. They found a way below, perhaps three levels, but never into the greathouse. In time, the way was closed, and we find it still as such." She met their eyes, one by one. "The king's workmen and soldiers take risk, that the way found is not compromised by faulty structure... or other things."

"What other things, my lady?" asked Thalion.

"Tales, my lord. Two workers from Jeseriam speak of haunting sounds and spirits in the night. One says a companion died of fright when they sought a way from below into the greathouse."

Sheynon traded glances with Ysilrod. "The prophesy of Drakenmoore. Likely this is what caused the downfall of the House and all within it. Prepare yourselves, my friends, for we will see not only death, but sadness."

"Spirits of the dead," whispered Audrey.

"Speak of this prophesy, if you will, Brother," said Ysilrod.

Sheynon gathered them closer in the waning sunlight. "Re's minister Diatus, in the Cave of Bells, met during our adventure in the quest for *Kingmaker*. The foreshadowing of the ending of the House, and what would follow. Once the last of Drakenmoore had passed, the castle and all around it would succumb, perhaps all the world. Set by the wizard triad of Re', Zakara Thelena, and Draxa, before they fell to argument and murder." He caught Thalion's eye, and the priest nodded. "Still... Re's soul is no longer here, for she fled to the body of Reena, yes? Then who?"

"Reena herself," said Thalion, after a moment. "Trapped when the castle fell in upon itself, seeking release... perhaps vengeance of her own."

Ysilrod scoffed. "Reena was but a concubine, tho' enough surely to frighten away those curious or seeking treasure."

"If so," said Audrey, "might we give her peace? Find a way to release her spirit to the afterlife?"

Thalion showed a warming smile. "The Lady Audrey always seeks a way to aid those in pain." He gave a slight bow to her.

"How to proceed, my lords, my lady?" asked Rohesia. "I cannot promise the courage of our workers. The soldiers will follow orders, true, but even they..."

"There will be no need," said Sheynon, after looking round to his companions. "See the castle doors are secure and safe, but send no one in. We will take the vanguard." He chuckled. "Tho' it has been many years, we have faced much worse than the spirit of a concubine."

* * *

The doors were opened at the last, and the stench of old death wafted from the castle entrance. Workers sealed the doors again, gagging as they sought fresh air, and nervous soldiers standing watch traded glances round. The evening passed without further entry or discussion, and after morning prayers upon the sunrise, the Companions readied to enter what was now thought as the tomb of Drakenmoore.

Thalion led, Sheynon following with enchanted torches giving light without flame or heat. Ysilrod had studied in the night, and read spells of protection over the assembly before they entered. Audrey, *Mír'rë Cala'wyne* in hand, guarded at the rear.

Through the great doors and into the entryway, they held their breath against the reek as Ysilrod cleared the air with cantrips. Beyond the vestibule, passing by corridors aside, and into the ruined great hall, little did they see but cracked and crumbled walls, tapestries turned by time and damp into little more than heaps of rotted cloth, and remains of servants having died as they sought escape. Mold upon the walls crept from the torchlight as Thalion drew *Gil Estel*, and holy brilliance melted it all away, as rats skittered from the chamber.

"I cannot fathom the fear in their hearts in that time," said Audrey. She glanced around, seeing naught but ruin. She looked to Sheynon, the elf lord lost in memory once again.

He shuddered. "Here we met Re' and pledged ourselves to the task of *Kingmaker's* recovery. We could not know the cost as years fell away."

Thalion laid a hand gently upon his shoulder. "A cost borne by all the land, my cousin. Even in Kaanan's Sacrifice, your people were persecuted for events not of their doing."

"That injustice was at the last avenged," said Ysilrod, an edge within his voice. Audrey turned his way and nodded grimly. Thalion, too, acknowledged understanding.

"Daeron," said Sheynon. "He fought the emperor of Vichelli, returned his heart to the City-State of Truth."

Thalion chuckled, and even Audrey showed a grin. "Nearly did our emperor and empress faint away upon their thrones when I presented that artifact. I wondered then if I might spend my life in chains."

Ysilrod now drew closer. "A day I wish you might have seen, Brother. The end of the Purge, and all the evil with it."

Quiet descended for moments as they stood together. A rush of air caught Ysilrod's attention, and he turned quickly, the globe within his staff *Ringil* glowing brightly. "Something comes."

They raised their swords and stood back to back, awaiting what might appear. Sheynon held his torches aloft, moving them from side to side, seeking motion in the darkness.

"There is a presence," whispered Ysilrod, and he raised *Ringil* higher. In the farthest corner, something drifted in the air, yet they could not see a shape, only a void within the light cast by the staff.

"We mean no harm to you," said Thalion, sheathing *Gil Estel*. He nodded to Audrey, and she followed suit, sliding *Mír'rë Cala'wyne* into her scabbard. Sheynon covered the enchanted torches with his cloak, leaving only *Ringil* to light the ruined chamber.

They waited, yet no sound or voice came forth. The room grew chill, more so than before, and they felt a growing malevolence all around.

"It cannot harm us," said Ysilrod. "Yet there is great anger there within. My thought is, this is the spirit of the concubine Reena, trapped when the House fell in upon itself."

"How is that possible?" asked Audrey. "Surely a soul or spirit cannot be caged by mortal things."

"The magic, my lady. It permeates this place, Drakenmoore nearly a construct of the Craft itself. The dungeon, *NorthWind*, the wizard triad... Nowhere else in Ardwel, save the Vaults of Time in Telveperen, was there a seat of such power." Ysilrod nodded to the wafting shadow. "Since the fall, she has been trapped, as were those mortal. Yet she survived."

"Might she lead us to... the ones we seek?" asked Sheynon.

Ysilrod shook his head. "Doubtful, tho' perhaps we may attempt to speak and find a way."

Thalion showed a wry grin. "My command of Drow is not the best."

Ysilrod grinned in return. "Yet mine is, Cousin."

"Is this wise?" Audrey whispered into Ysilrod's ear. "You say this presence cannot harm us, yet we stand here rooted, unmoving."

"Fascinated," replied Sheynon, smiling now himself. "Never have I met a spirit such as this."

Audrey nodded. "Speak then, Lord Mage," she said to Ysilrod, "and give us sign."

The elf-mage stepped before the others and faced the corner. "As said, we mean no harm to you. We search for others living in the depths below."

The Companions traded looks, as strange it was to hear Ysilrod's own voice saying dark elf words.

There are no others living!

Ysilrod staggered back and Sheynon caught him before he fell. Audrey touched the hilt of her sword, but Thalion motioned caution. Sheynon lifted his brother gently to his feet. Ysilrod leaned upon his staff, then raised his head, nodding. "As said, great anger. And yes, we may communicate." He drew a ragged breath.

"We heard nothing," said Thalion, Sheynon and Audrey nodding in agreement.

"She spoke into my mind, there were no words, no sound. There is no physicality to create such, and only in the spirit level may she speak."

"Is it Reena, or another?" asked Sheynon. "And if Reena, how might she aid us?"

"She said there are no living, yet my phrasing may have been in error." Ysilrod raised his staff once more, the apparition yet in the corner, and spoke. "We seek the one called Archane, leader of the Drow."

They waited, and at the last Audrey asked, "Why ask of her and not… the one perpetrating this evil upon Reena her own self?"

"As said, my lady, anger. Let us attempt distraction, for where we find Archane, surely we will find our quarry."

"Excellency, there is much here to be discovered," said Thalion. "Trust our comrade, as he knows our need."

She is fled!

Ysilrod gasped, and then once more. Sheynon aided him again. "Brother?"

"Archane is gone, should I understand the meaning."

All there exchanged glances, one to the other, then back again.

Sheynon's face grew hard. "Gone… where?"

Ysilrod motioned to the corner, where the shadow no longer could be seen. "My thought is, Reena does not know. And if Archane is free, likely she would not say."

They waited in the silence, yet nothing came to challenge them but their own thoughts and imaginations. At the last, Thalion spoke to break the rising tension. "We must find the way below, otherwise we have no purpose. No specter should keep us from our duty."

"I recall the way," said Sheynon, and he led them down a hallway choked with debris and carcasses of the dead. Once more Ysilrod used his cantrips to clear the air, else they would have succumbed to the stench of age and death.

* * *

They marched, it seemed, more than a day, down flights of broken stairs and landings with so little room they must pass one by one beyond them. Through halls and corridors deep and dark as any cavern, rats in numbers they simply could not count, and other things they could not even name which fled the light, they moved downward in quiet determination. All the while Thalion led them tirelessly, *Gil Estel* blazing in his hand, Sheynon at his shoulder, and Ysilrod behind. Audrey once more followed, *Mír'rë Cala'wyne* shining as a firebrand.

Three flights down, pausing to make their way through debris and fallen stonework, more remains of the dead, and not always human. Twice they were forced to find another way, and twice more Ysilrod used his powers to pass beyond rubble that kept them from continuing. All the while, they spoke quietly of their thoughts, how Kaul and Reena-cum-Teresa Drakenmoore, had been this way before.

"Only the two of them," said Audrey, shaking her head. "Ill-provisioned, no mage to aid their passage, for in that time Reena... Mors'ul'jyn was devoid of powers."

Sheynon looked to her beyond his shoulder. "You know this? How so?"

Audrey smiled. "Rohesia spoke of it. Kaul still is plagued by nightmares, not only of who Mors'ul'jyn is, but as well, perhaps the single time within his life he feared to die."

She slowed, and they paused about her. "Think, my friends. Entombed here, as so many we have stepped carefully around in our own passage. Never found, never mourned, endings but a mystery to loved ones." She bowed her head in reverence. "May we meet our ends with eyes wide open, facing whatever comes."

"May our blessings be accepted from our hearts," said Thalion softly. He drew his holy symbol from his pouch and pressed it to his forehead.

Sheynon clutched Ysilrod's shoulder tightly. "Our duty is to find the truth, as always it has been."

Thalion motioned to the stairs beyond the doorway they had just opened. "Therefore, we continue downward."

"How far?" asked Ysilrod.

"Seven levels, and this is but the third," replied Sheynon.

"One more, then we take rest." Thalion raised *Gil Estel*, still glowing. "Onward, friends, for we are close. My great lord tells me."

* * *

The City-State of DragonFall...

Three days Aeren and Chitthra waited for Mend'rys to return to the tavern with words of wisdom. And as they sat at the corner table, empty plates and a pitcher there before them, Aeren spoke of what was found as she had wandered near the palace.

"Two days ago, my liege and the others left, an entourage of soldiers and workers trailing. Word says Drakenmoore was their destination, and surely they are nearly there. They seek as we, and now are days ahead."

"With a mage of great power," replied Chitthra, sipping dark ale and wondering of their way. "Danger for all, should Ysilrod, Mors'ul'jyn, and Archane clash. The south of Ardwel may not survive."

"What will you do, Dearest, should they bring Mors'ul'jyn to justice? Might that be enough to keep your hand from Steffyn Foxxe, should we encounter him?"

Chitthra stared into her tankard, unsure how to answer. "What matters now is Mend'rys and his findings. My thought is, we will follow to Drakenmoore and join the fight."

Movement at the entryway caught their eyes, and they watched as Mend'rys and Jyslin came to their table and took chairs. "I have word," said Mend'rys, and Chitthra traded glances with Aeren, saying nothing.

Jyslin motioned to a server for a fresh pitcher and two tankards. Mend'rys waited as they were served, then drank after Jyslin poured before him. "You know the tale of this Mors'ul'jyn you seek, yes? Therefore, you must know her place of power."

Aeren nodded reluctantly. "There is but one place, as her true identity is known. This is all you have determined?"

Mend'rys drank again. "The king has sent a working party ahead, led by notables of the land."

"This, too, is known," said Chitthra.

"Then why involve yourselves?" he asked. "It has become a matter of the king and ruling parties, not mercenaries."

"We are no mercenaries, as said before," replied Aeren, holding back her anger. "As agreed, our reasons are our own, and now we know little more than before. Your wisdom seems not as great as hoped."

"Regardless, our pact must be honored, and you are bound to cause no harm to us. I have done what I may."

With that, Mend'rys and Jyslin rose and bowed, then walked quickly through the evening crowd and beyond the door.

Chitthra seethed, and Aeren laid a hand upon her arm.

"We have been played as fools, given nothing, for a promise of no reprisal," said Aeren. "My liege would not be pleased."

"Tho' not for the reasons you may think, Dearest. I know his true name and nature."

Aeren began to speak, then held her words, thinking it a matter of dark elves before Chitthra's departing of *Ung'gu'wi*. "Then to

240

Drakenmoore, and rejoining those whose nature better suits us. This city is no place for honest folk."

"I now find myself in not one, but two dilemmas, both of honor given." Chitthra poured her tankard full and drained it. "I will not be taken for a fool again."

"You are no fool, but one who's heart is seeking answers for things yet to be explained." Aeren rose, offering her hand. "A night of rest, then on the morning we will depart. Prayers tonight will calm us both. Let us hope we are not too late to aid the cause of righteousness."

Chitthra did not reply, only stared at the doorway where Mend'rys and Jyslin had taken exit. She slowly stood, unblinking, and moved through the crowd, nearly as a silent shadow.

Aeren followed, knowing well the look on Chitthra's face, and gave a prayer beneath her breath that blood would not be soon to follow.

* * *

Mend'rys led Jyslin around a corner, then down a darkened alleyway and through a back door, locking it as they paused. He shook once more, took a knee, and Jyslin held him as he trembled.

"Master, you were brilliant! Now we are safe from whatever they may have had in mind." She cradled him, stroked his hair and spoke words of true devotion into his ear. Slowly he began to calm, and drew away.

"Time has come for us to leave this city. Too dangerous it has become, and too well-known are our faces in that tavern." He leaned against her once again, and she kissed his forehead. "My thought is, they will ride to Drakenmoore and join the king's mission. We will follow, tho' not closely. There is danger, and I must be party to it."

"But why, Master? Can we not escape and live our lives together?"

Together! Mend'rys nearly swooned, thoughts of Emildir and a life abandoned, surely never to be found again. He clung once more to Jyslin, tears burning in his eyes, yet little could he do but hold them back.

Jyslin laid him down, curled beneath his arm and held him tight. He rolled atop her, lifted up her tunic, and she drew him quickly in. He took her hard upon the wooden floor, angst-driven in his urgency. She wrapped herself around him, and they lost themselves in the pleasures once again.

Mend'rys only wondered when, not if, the last time of such a blessing would come to them.

* * *

241

In the Depths of Drakenmoore…

The bell above her bed had wakened her, and Mors'ul'jyn sat, mind filled with fog and remnants of another nightmare. She rasped out a single word and the bell ceased ringing. Though she had set it as an alarm, still she could not make her body rise. She glanced to the table across the room, the wine bottle empty and goblet laying on its side.

I lose myself in drink, then wonder why I cannot wake. She stroked her temples, head throbbing with discomfort, and whispered a cantrip to ease the pain. Her head snapped up with clarity at last. She rose, tossed a cloak over her shoulders, and bolted for the door to Archane's chamber.

The scene presented was of horror. Before the hearth lay the Dark Princess, a pool of blood beneath her. Shocked to silence, Mors'ul'jyn's heart thundered in her ears before she rushed to the prone figure lying limp and pale and sticky with blood across her chest. A crusted dagger hung loosely from one hand.

Mors'ul'jyn raised Archane and chanted out a prayer. She laid her hand on Archane's forehead, then to the wound, desperate words and gestures having no effect. She howled in rage and madness, dropped away the body, and beat bloody fists upon the floor. She screamed, rose and ran about the room, knocking away chairs and standing lanterns, anything within her reach. She tore at tapestries upon the walls, turned and ran to Archane's body and raised it once again, chanting dark magic into her face.

"Speak, damn you! Speak, and tell me where you have gone! I will find you! I will bring you back! Never will you escape me, and now I know I must take your body for mine alone! No longer can I trust you!"

Mors'ul'jyn seethed, madness nearly overwhelming any sense within her mind. She caught herself as she found the dagger in her own hand, and looked upon the dead face once again. *Might I use her body, regardless her death? Might my own essence bring her back to life again?*

She pondered as her breathing calmed, yet at the last, dropped away the dagger and lay the body down. "No, for little more would I be than walking dead. I cannot know, if even I could force the magic into success. No… I must find her, whole and alive, or death will stalk me here."

She sat, drew her legs up closely, and wrapped her arms around them. She rocked herself, filled with angst and fright. *What now? Where has she gone? Where will she go?*

The thought ticked at her mind, and she pondered. *Kaul once more? Doubtful, for he promised nothing, and likely will not treat with her. Ung'gu'wi? Yes, but how so? It will take days at the very least, then…*

Mors'ul'jyn nodded to herself. "I must find her before she descends into whatever there awaits, war or none, to save myself from those now searching. Tho' there are many ways to descend into the caverns, likely she will choose the one nearest the House of Iyllyeth, and therefore safety. I must prepare..."

Mors'ul'jyn glanced to the body on the floor, her mind beginning once again to race. It was only after long moments of contemplation she realized the warning bell within her chamber was ringing once again.

* * *

Somewhere in the Mists of Time...

Archane woke. A cold haze drifted on her bare skin, and she shivered. She lay on... she was not certain, for it was not grass of the forest or a stone chamber she was within. Her eyes searched, side to side, and she slowly rose to sitting, looking round.

She touched between her breasts, the flesh yet tender, thinking of the dagger and the sharp sting of steel within her heart. The hot flash of pain, and blood covering her hands, all returned in a tumult, and she trembled once again. The mist clung to her form, droplets running down her sides and cheeks, and she wrapped her arms about herself.

This is not what was expected.

Yet she was free at last from Mors'ul'jyn, and she whispered prayers to *Iyllyeth* as tears flowed, her sobs nearly rising to a scream of victory.

Free! Free!!!

Five long, exhausting, wasted years! Drow society crumbling into chaos without her leadership, the great Houses nearly at each other's throats, as Mor'i'jil...

She caught her breath, and her face grew hard, eyes as slits, and nostrils flaring. Mor'i'jil, her minister for near three hundred years, gone, nay, murdered by Mors'ul'jyn!

She rose, noting what light there was seemed to come from everywhere. She cast no shadow, heard no sounds; only the mist, parting as she strode slowly forward, was all she saw.

Is this Iyllyeth's own realm? Did the taking of my own life break the curse at last, and I have truly died?

She paused, certain she had seen movement to the side. Though alone and unarmed, she turned, walking to the place the image had been seen. "Show yourself," she commanded, her voice stronger than she felt. *Still, should I be dead, surely nothing in this place can harm me further.*

243

She held the thought in her mind as the fog before her stirred. Slowly, a figure came in view, garbed in crimson, with a half-familiar smile upon his face. He was human, nearly as she could see, for his full white beard hid his features well.

Even as she stood naked, afraid perhaps for the first time in more than two thousand years, she would not yield. "Who are you?"

The figure stood before her, regal in his trappings, and memories of old began to form within her mind.

He spoke, his voice rich and deep and beckoning to her very spirit. "Do I look so different after all these years? These centuries, in truth?"

Archane's jaw dropped in near-horror and recognition. "Venic? *Venic!?*"

BOOK NINE
FIRE AND BLOOD

"Praise the Darkness for its worthy Handmaiden, Archane!"

Dark Priest Mor'i'jil

In the Depths of Ung'gu'wi…

Near ten days of fighting in the central chamber, and no headway had been made by Hovenethra's soldiers. Little could they do, as the House of Iyllyeth had shown more than a match for whatever courage Ba'tula's companies could muster.

The matriarch remained sequestered, hidden by the inner clergy and twenty loyal guards, offering prayers to *Iyllyeth* for a swift, successful outcome. Yet no sooner would reports from her Lancer Captains be delivered than once more she would retreat, leaving them with mumbled words of encouragement and little else. Her clergy soon began to worry that time was not an ally, as now the Dark Mistress had chosen the way of war, little could they do but pray themselves.

In time, both great Houses called their soldiers back, holding corridors aside the central chamber, only scouts and healers ministering to the wounded seen beyond the battle lines. It was, and by necessity, an agreement not spoken of, but accepted just the same, for the Lancer Captains, all veterans of conflicts beyond *Ung'gu'wi*, knew an impasse when it was seen.

As matters paused, the other Houses watched with interest. Modennethra, it seemed, was content to hold their forces in abeyance unless threatened.

Karachitthra, privy to rumor and innuendo of Mor'i'jil's absence, sent only missives, imploring the Houses to refrain from violence, all the while bolstering its remaining troops. For Karachitthra had lost far more soldiers than the others to humans at the Silver River battles. Castle Lahai, as the humans named it, had been a killing ground for near a thousand dark elf troops that fateful day, and more than half were Karachitthra.

Warinethra, however, became the unknown player, and it was Alystin's thought to bring them to her bidding. Yet even then, from her teachings by Mor'i'jil and the Dark Princess, she knew little could be asked of the greatest sorcerers in the land without recompense, full and as demanded.

* * *

The way to Warinethra was fraught with dangers, not only from soldiers of Hovenethra, but protections set by the House itself, that others may not enter without knowledge of the ruling Circle. And as noted many times by Mor'i'jil, to say nothing of Archane, Warinethra excelled in study and mastery of the Dark Arts as no other in the Race.

Therefore, an emissary met with Warinethra's minister, that Xa'lyyth and Narlros were known well and sent by Dark Priestess Alystin, ruling now in Mor'i'jil's absence. Two days it took for arrangement to be made, as the priest and priestess of House Iyllyeth waited in a chamber tended by servants neither could see or hear. Therefore, their words to each other were always guarded, as never could they be certain they were alone.

Cak'koths, a male priest of Warinethra's Circle, soon appeared, with two females dressed in robes of midnight blue. Xa'lyyth knew, from Alystin's stern warning, these were highest of the high in the Guild of Sorcerers in the House of Warinethra.

Xa'lyyth and Narlros bowed deeply before the trio, who only nodded in return before Xa'lyyth spoke. "Dark Priestess Alystin sends prayers and greetings to your House and *Iyllyeth's* blessings on Dark Mistress Driznill. The House of Iyllyeth seeks a boon of Warinethra."

Cak'koths only motioned her to continue.

Xa'lyyth nodded to Narlros, who bowed once more. "Our request is a simple one. That Warinethra offer aid to the House of Iyllyeth in the… struggle underway with Hovenethra."

"You wish the Dark Arts at your shoulder, yes?" Cak'koths showed little interest in his face, other than to catch the eye of Xa'lyyth. The priestess showed no response, knowing his intention.

Narlros smiled gently. "Only insomuch as words, Dark Lord. We seek peace again within *Ung'gu'wi*, that this… insurgency not spread to other Houses."

"A ruse," said one of the female mages, and she chuckled 'neath her hood.

"A warning," replied Xa'lyyth. "Already too many soldiers have gone to *Iyllyeth's* own hands, and we fear dark reprisal on the clergy."

"Assassins." Cak'koths nodded knowingly. "It is a concern as well of Warinethra."

Xa'lyyth gave a silent prayer, that *Iyllyeth* was watching. "We give thanks for your wisdom, Dark Lord. Driznill has chosen her speaker well." She smiled, warmly as she might.

"Your offer?" Cak'koths faced Narlros squarely as the mages watched Xa'lyyth.

"The House of Iyllyeth is prepared to be generous," replied Narlros. "What might we offer for your pledge?"

"A moment." Cak'koths motioned the mages, and the trio took their exit. Narlros looked to Xa'lyyth, her hands trembling beneath her robe.

He gave a reassuring nod and closed his eyes, then signed a blessing above her head. She slowly calmed, but still her face was drawn with worry.

The Warinethra entourage returned, the chamber door creaking on its hinges. Once more Narlros and Xa'lyyth bowed.

"We offer compromise," said Cak'koths after pausing for a moment. "Warinethra will prepare a missive to Dark Mistress Ba'tula, urging caution in her ventures."

Narlros raised a question. "And our House would be privy to this message, yes? Its words, and more importantly, its meaning? Surely this is not too much to ask."

"With all regard, and yes, we would ask your assistance on the phrasing."

Xa'lyyth held her peace and only prayed. Narlros mused, then spoke at last. "And for this worthy service, what does the House of Warinethra require of us?"

"Nothing. Our House has no desire to see *Ung'gu'wi* burn."

Narlros and Xa'lyyth bowed more deeply, then the priest spoke in gratitude. "We are in your debt, Dark Lord. Praises will be sung to *Iyllyeth* for such a gift."

"Very well." The door opened, and the mages exited quietly. Cak'koths turned before leaving. "Prepare your words, if you will, and I will see them set to parchment in our scriptorium."

"I will do so with haste," replied Narlros. He bowed once more and Cak'koths departed.

Xa'lyyth looked about, seeing no one else within the room, yet knowing in her heart they were not alone. "What shall we say, Dark Lord?"

"It is not what, but in what voice," replied Narlros. "And in my mind, there is more here planned than a warning."

Xa'lyyth shook her head, not understanding.

Narlros glanced to the door, his voice dropping to a whisper. "For now, let us set our minds to the task. We will speak again when returned to Dark Mistress Alystin. Surely she will seek answers from our doing."

* * *

They were escorted to the central chamber by Warinethra's soldiers, met there by a contingent from House Iyllyeth, and hastened beyond into corridors known to be friendly. Twice they ran from crossbow bolts fired from cover, and two guards went down with wounds. Alystin's orders were no fire was to be returned, and in silence the party found safety as jeers were heard from Hovenethra's soldiers.

Back into the passages they knew so well, servants met them with others of the Outer Circle. Taken to separate chambers, both were ordered there to disrobe fully, and their vestments burned. A priest explained to Narlros, once his temper had been tamed, Dark Priestess Alystin had ordered such, that hidden scrying spells or things exchanged by touch would hear nothing, once returned. At last Narlros understood. Alystin had learned well at the side of Mor'i'jil, trusting none beyond the House of Iyllyeth.

Once more in company they were sequestered, a table set before them and dark wine poured in crystal goblets by Alystin's own servants. Xa'lyyth glanced to Narlros, wondering if this was a final meal, and once their words imparted, they, as the garments worn, would become expendable.

Narlros smiled in reassurance. "A token for our successes." He raised the goblet to his lips, then paused as Alystin entered with two acolytes at her side. He rose, as did Xa'lyyth, and they bowed to her as one.

"Sit and partake. Speak your words of Warinethra's parley." Alystin drank, then picked from the platter there before them, eating slowly. Narlros knew it was to insure both he and Xa'lyyth there was no danger in the offering.

"Dark Lady, they will pen a missive from their scribes, words given them by Priestess Xa'lyyth and myself, tho' signed and sealed by Warinethra. A warning, they spoke of, to Hovenethra, that hostilities must cease. They have no wish for the Great Houses to spill blood of the Race."

Alystin set down her goblet. "And when will this missive be delivered, and by whose hand? Have you the words set down for my perusal?"

Narlros fumbled in his pouch, drew forth a crumpled parchment, and passed it to a waiting servant's hand.

"Burn it, now," said Alystin softly. The servant bowed and tossed it into the hearth.

Narlros shook his head and began to speak. Alystin held her hand as she watched the parchment burn with a greenish flame. The priest closed his mouth and sat back, chagrined.

"They surmised we would burn your garments, yet thought the words written by your hand would be a worthy place to put a scrying message."

Narlros paled, sweat showing on his brow. "Dark Lady, I beg forgiveness!"

Alystin showed a hard look. "Worry not, for this was not your duty to anticipate. Words with our mage guild spoke caution, and therefore we were prepared."

"Dark Lady, *Iyllyeth* blesses you with wisdom," whispered Xa'lyyth. She bowed her head and mumbled a prayer.

"Speak of this missive and how it was to be delivered," said Alystin.

Narlros drank a draught, then a servant dabbed his brow with a scented cloth. "As said, a warning, that should hostilities continue, Warinethra will enter the fray and bring their Dark Arts to bear. I urged caution in their words, that they not be harsh."

"Dark Priest Narlros said to me he kept your mind at heart when penning his words," said Xa'lyyth. "Words with strength, but tempered."

Alystin nodded absently, then motioned to a servant. A silver plate with folded parchment was held before Narlros. The priest raised an eyebrow and looked to Alystin.

"Peruse the missive, Dark Lord, and say your mind." Alystin drank again as Narlros read the message.

"Dark Lady, these are my very words!" The priest looked in horror to Xa'lyyth and passed the parchment to her hand. The priestess only shook her head.

"Delivered on my waking," said Alystin. "It seems we have another party in the fracas. One now threatening our House as well as Hovenethra."

"Yet... why?" Narlros motioned a servant to refill his goblet.

"As said, to cease the fighting. Does this not say if we obey, Warinethra rules the Race?"

They sat in silence, pondering the circumstances now turning round. Narlros and Xa'lyyth once more traded looks. "Might this explain," began the priest, "why our soldiers did not engage Hovenethra's guards when we were attacked? That you show compliance with Warinethra's... warning?"

"In part, and yes, we seek no anger from their House. More there is at play than this." Alystin motioned to the parchment yet in Narlros's hand.

"What will you do?" asked Narlros carefully, after a quiet pause.

"For the nonce, only return a word of honest thanks for their concern. Plans are in motion regardless of this missive." Alystin sipped, thinking. "Beyond that... there is other news to share. Word comes from a village in the forest of Hovenethra exiles."

"Exiles from their House?" asked Xa'lyyth.

251

"Two of your acquaintance, Lualyrr and Ry'lld, of Ba'tula's ruling circle."

Narlros and Xa'lyyth sat in shock, saying nothing.

"Word says they seek escape from Ba'tula's madness. As this will have little bearing on our plans, it is unimportant. However, it shows not all is in agreement in Hovenethra."

Narlros shrugged. "Where will they go?"

"Unknown, yet my thought is, they search for Archane. Perhaps they warrant our attention. Offer prayers this night and prepare yourselves for a trip beyond *Ung'gu'wi*, should it be necessary."

* * *

Beyond the Black Forest...

Ry'lld and Lualyrr stayed another day within the village, then trekked their way west and through the forest. Three days more and they came to an encampment of dark elves; not a village, but more a campsite, though felt ill at ease and stayed for little time.

Another day and the forest began to thin, yet still they knew the Silver River lay leagues beyond, and settled for the night. At last their eyes had adjusted to the daylight, and they traveled further with every day, then rested as the sun began to set.

"Will we ever see *Ung'gu'wi* again?" Lualyrr sat, her back against a tree, knees drawn up and chin resting on them. Her eyes showed tears, and Ry'lld drew closer.

"Should we be there now, our fate surely would be sealed. Our choice made, we now are here, and as you have said, duty calls."

Lualyrr sniffed, wiped her eyes with a sleeve, and let go a sigh. "Therefore, we proceed beyond the wilderness. Fill our packs with fruits, spend time to jerk meat and find clean water." She chuckled. "As when Drow first came to this land, and surely they fought to survive as we do now."

Ry'lld set a fire going and skinned three squirrels as he pondered. "Perhaps ten days to find this city of the Mongrel Kaul. Surely there are villages beyond the forest and roads to travel, farms where we may garner help."

"Humans," replied Lualyrr, shuddering. "Or elves, and neither will welcome us."

"Then a prayer or two may aid us." Ry'lld set down his dagger and faced her. "We took this task, as you reminded me, and now proceed to

252

find Archane. Let us presume we are successful. What then? How do two clergy of Hovenethra convince the Dark Princess of our sincerity?"

Lualyrr thought for moments. "And what of Mor'i'jil? Tales tell of his militancy and dedication to Archane. Might he seek our hearts as sacrifice for their deliverance?"

Ry'lld grimaced at the thought and hurried his words forward. "Both missing, both presumed to be captive... I know not how we may succeed." He held his peace, then motioned to the west. "Still, all ways lead to Kaul, for even should he offer nothing, we will be safer there than here."

Lualyrr eyed him closely. "And then? Should we find Archane and live beyond it, what becomes of us? We cannot return to *Ung'gu'wi*, as the farmer Vorn has said. Return to his village, or another? Live in Kaul's city amongst humans who might seek our deaths because we are Drow? What have we done, that we betray our own House and leaders?"

The priest turned away, Lualyrr's words cutting deeply, though he knew the reasons. At the last, he looked her way once more. "We will doubt ourselves into inaction should this continue, and we cannot allow it. What we have done is done, and we now face our destiny as it is." He held his hand to her. "Together we may succeed, apart, it is most unlikely. I would face this with you at my side. And I cannot think our pleasant nights mean nothing to you."

Her shoulders slumped, and she nodded. "I only worry... it is daunting, what we face. And yes, I will stand beside you in our venture." She took his hand warmly and with courage. "*Iyllyeth* watches to see our manner. Let us not disappoint her in our doing."

* * *

The City-State of DragonFall...

Chitthra paused Aeren with a silent hand as she peered around a shop corner. The turning lock heard in the distance was bright into her ears, and as she crept closer to the door, sounds within told her Mend'rys's attentions were not upon those who might have followed.

She motioned to the door and then her foot, nodded to Aeren's sword and backed away a pace. She closed her eyes, drew deeply of her breath, and leapt. Her foot struck the door just below the latch and splintered the heavy wood away with a crack. She leapt again, and her boot shattered the latching into flinders, and the door flew open, revealing Mend'rys and Jyslin sleeping on the floor.

253

Jyslin screamed as Mend'rys rolled quickly to his feet. The girl gathered up herself and ran to a darkened corner, tunic trailing and bare ebon legs flashing in the lantern-light.

Chitthra gave Mend'rys no opportunity, took him down with a sweeping foot, rolled aside and leapt again, delivering a cuffing blow as she passed above him.

Jyslin screamed again and rushed Chitthra with a dagger in her hand. Aeren caught her, took her to the floor and twisted away the blade. The girl fought as a dervish, but Aeren's wiry arms and legs were far too strong, and she pinned Jyslin in her grasp.

Mend'rys rose shakily and began a chant. Chitthra, once again, gave him no time for reprisal, and spun quickly. Once, twice, thrice she kicked about his head and shoulders, and he fell heavily to the wooden floor, unmoving.

A change began, and in only heartbeats, where there had been a cloaked and hooded Drow male, lay a pale and unkempt elf in gaudy, dirty robes, gold stars and moons upon a purple field.

Jyslin and Aeren, yet struggling away, gasped as one and paused their fight. Mend'rys came slowly to his hands and knees, and Chitthra stood in a warrior's stance close by, breathing hard.

Once more, the dark elf girl let go a scream, yet this was of anguish and betrayal, though even still, anger tinged her wailing.

Chitthra raised Steffyn by his hooded collar, clamped his head between her thighs, and tensed herself to twist and break his neck.

"Chitthra, no!" Aeren fell to her knees, Jyslin's fingers clawing at her arms. "Do not kill him, I beg you! We will find a way!" Aeren's eyes met Chitthra's, pleading for mercy upon the elf.

"Behold," said Chitthra, calming at the last, wiping her brow and nodding. "We see now the truth. Steffyn Foxxe returns to the land, facing the justice due." She eased her legs and Steffyn slid to the floor with a groan.

Aeren's eyes were wide, yet Jyslin's were filled with only deep betrayal. Steffyn slowly raised himself to his knees and Chitthra turned his way. He held a hand, blood running from his nose, cheeks flushed and bruised, and nearly did he swoon as Aeren watched in abject fascination.

Jyslin twisted once again in Aeren's grasp. "No! *No!!* I love you! I gave to you my body, untouched and unknown! I gave you admiration, obedience unquestioned, pleasures offered gladly! Now you show yourself to be an elf?!"

"Steffyn Foxxe, grand mage of Elvenkind, and reluctant member of the Guild of Learned at Telveperen." Chitthra relaxed her stance, yet kept eyes upon the wavering figure knelt before her. "Wed unto Emildir, a bounty hunter and tracker of those beyond the law." She glanced to Jyslin, tears now streaming down the girl's dirty face. "I am sorry for his deception played upon you, yet know his crimes against his kindred are deep and hurtful."

"How… how did you come to know this?" Aeren's voice was but a whisper as she clung even tighter now to Jyslin, as in protection.

Chitthra gave a wry and ragged chuckle. "I hazarded a guess. No, that is not the truth of it." She glanced to Steffyn, still stunned and barely listening, it seemed. "Anon Gûl, do you recall her, in Jeseriam? She was in actuality, Steffyn Foxxe, and once my mind thought clearly, I knew it could only be. What reason would a dark elf seek Mors'ul'jyn, other than to end her mortal time? Who but one of her acquaintance would even know her?"

Aeren stroked Jyslin's hair as the girl cried into her shoulder. "You took a fearful chance, Dearest, one that yet may cause the death of all of us."

Chitthra shook her head. "Not so, for now we may proceed with truth between us." She glanced to Steffyn, then to Jyslin, who turned her head to listen closely. "We hold now the strength to face Mors'ul'jyn together. Steffyn Foxxe is not a power in this land to trifle with, for I have faced him in the Circle."

Aeren only blinked and shook her head, not understanding.

Jyslin wrenched herself from Aeren's grasp, screamed again and ran at Steffyn, a killing rage within her eyes. He caught her in his arms, tossed her aside and raised himself with harsh discomfort. Chitthra took a stance, prepared to resume hostilities if needed.

Aeren leapt, taking Jyslin to the floor. "No! You are innocent as —" *As I myself in all of this!* Aeren swallowed, breathed a prayer, and continued. "We will deal with him in his true form! I beg you, do not force harm upon yourself! He is a master of the Craft!"

"Think you I do not know this?" Jyslin struggled mightily, but Aeren was too strong. The human woman caught movement at the side as Steffyn rose.

Chitthra spun, but Steffyn tossed a stone between her feet, another before Aeren and the girl. The stones exploded, a flash of fire and sparks driving them away and back as he staggered, wiping blood from his face and forehead. Chitthra rolled from the flames and tried to rise, but could see nothing for the smoke.

"Take care of her," came Steffyn's voice within the haze. "Truly I love her, but I must let her go to save myself."

With that, he vanished, and the room fell silent as the smoke began to clear.

"Master!" Jyslin rolled from Aeren's grasp, ran to the swirl of wind and dust where Steffyn Foxxe had stood, and collapsed, rage echoing in the air, and tears upon the dirty floor beneath her.

* * *

They gathered there in darkness, saying nothing, thoughts private in their minds, yet each knew the other's feelings as their own, at the least in part. Aeren had held Jyslin tightly as she cried, while Chitthra searched the shop, finding no one there and the front door latched and bolted.

"At the tavern, is my guess," said Aeren. Chitthra sat beside her, eyes intent upon the dark elf girl. She offered a hand, but Jyslin shied away.

"I am sorry for your loss," Chitthra said at last, "yet know it was necessary to bring forth the truth. Steffyn Foxxe has much to answer for in this world."

"His name is Mend'rys," snarled Jyslin.

Aeren's eyes once more pled with Chitthra, to hold her anger for the nonce. "She has lost her world," she whispered, "and now becomes our responsibility. Speak softly if you will."

Chitthra looked away, then nodded briefly. "Tell us of him, that we may aid you. And if he loves you as said, have faith he will return."

They waited for the girl to calm, holding patience they had little time for, wondering when the shop owner would return to find his door shattered and the store room disarrayed. Jyslin drew from Aeren's arms and wiped her reddened face. "I will show you to our lair, that we may wait, therefore."

She began to rise, but Aeren held her arm gently. "No tricks, young one. We will deal as we must and want no harm to come to you."

Jyslin nodded listlessly and they exited the shop. Chitthra closed the door and pressed the latch into the catch, that it would show little as possible the damage done.

They made way through the evening, *Mina* showing through clouds above, half full and bright, crowds thinning in the late-night air redolent with drifting smells of cooking meat, horses at the hitching posts, and dusty cloaks flapping in the breeze. Rain had fallen briefly as they battled in the shop, and mud pulled at their boots in the darkened alleyways.

It took some time, and as they pressed through brush and grasses tall as their shoulders, Aeren looked to Chitthra, then drew her sword quietly as she could. "Hold, Jyslin." The girl turned, seeing Aeren's blade gleaming in the moonlight, and gasped. "For our protection only," Aeren said. "Show us the door and I will enter first."

"Another corner, then the shack beyond the overgrowth." Jyslin turned and led them on again.

They came to the doorway, and Chitthra motioned the girl aside, took her place beside the door, and nodded to Aeren. She tripped the latch and Aeren rushed in, not knowing what to expect. What she saw, however, had not been in her mind.

"Greatest *Jhad*!" Aeren motioned Chitthra in with Jyslin, then stood beside the door. What had been expected as a hovel was more a well-appointed cottage of three rooms. They stood in the open doorway until Jyslin closed it and wandered to the table. Aeren followed her to a small bed chamber, the covers yet unmade, as though someone had only risen. Jyslin looked to the bed, then turned away.

Chitthra perused the sitting room, an open book upon the nightstand. She did not touch it, knowing well how sorcerers used traps and magics to protect belongings. A closed door with a sigil drew her attention.

"No!" Jyslin shouted from across the room. "The Master's chambers, and I was warned never to enter, as a daemon guards it."

"Well thought," replied Chitthra, and backed slowly from the door. She motioned to the hearth, a pot of stew simmering and tea upon the table. "Sit and eat. We have need to know your story, that we may continue in our venture."

Aeren sheathed her sword and set bowls upon the table as Jyslin brought them from the cupboard. They ladled out the stew, sat and ate in silence as Jyslin stared into her bowl. "He took me in near five years ago, as we dwelt in the depths of *Ung'gu'wi*." She raised her withered arm. "None would have me, as they thought me infirm and weak. Master gave me the look of one well-formed."

Chitthra glanced the girl's way. In truth, her face now appeared more plain, hair with less luster and her skin older than before. *Magic, and none may blame Steffyn for setting her look to be appealing, as she likely was his eyes and ears within the dark elf enclaves.*

"You served him well," said Aeren, then grimaced at her own words, knowing the meaning likely taken.

257

Jyslin's anger did not rise. "I loved him, and still do. I would die for the Master, for he gave me everything. I thought…"

Aeren replied softly, "You wanted to be his… mate, his wife, as humans say. To bear him children and a family, something Drow know… differently than we."

A tear dropped to the table and Jyslin nodded. "Now I find he is elf, wed to another, and I am but a concubine, something to be used for pleasure only." She set aside her bowl and laid her head within her arms upon the table, sobbing.

"Whatever he was as Steffyn Foxxe is likely gone," said Chitthra gently as she might. "As Mend'rys, his love was yours without doubt. He said it with his own voice."

Jyslin raised her tear-filled face. "And now? What becomes of me? When the magic fades herein, what will I do? Where might I go? I cannot return to *Ung'gu'wi.*"

"Remain here as you will." Aeren took Jyslin's hand. "We have a task and will not submit you to its dangers, as this is the safest place for you. Should he return, you will be here waiting."

"And should he not return?"

Aeren sighed. "Then we shall, and help you build a life. I have… friends in the City-State of Truth who would welcome you."

"My thought is," said Chitthra, "he had in mind this place would be a sanctuary for yourself, should times turn against him."

Jyslin nodded at the last. "Truly, I have nowhere else to go." She looked to Aeren's eyes. "I will wait, yet only for a moon. Beyond that, I cannot say what I will do."

"We will return before that time." Aeren said, and Chitthra nodded. "For now, we have much to do and little time." She dropped a pouch of coins onto the table. "This will pay your way in our absence. Once returned, we will make decisions on our path."

Jyslin laid her head down once more and sighed. Aeren kissed her hair and said a quiet blessing over her, then motioned to the door.

The latch clicked softly in their leaving.

* * *

They made way back to the inn and their rooms, packed belongings quickly, and stood together in the darkness, candles doused and only scattered moonlight peeking through the shutters.

"Do you hate me?" Chitthra stood apart from Aeren, not knowing what to say.

Aeren shook her head and took Chitthra to her breast. The dark elf woman trembled, quietly shedding tears.

"I love you," Aeren whispered. "Tho' your wisdom failed in stunning fashion, I must say."

"I have made matters only worse." Chitthra dug her hands into Aeren's shoulders.

Aeren gave a wry chuckle. "And not for the first time, Dearest. Surely, you must learn to hold your Drow temper with more strength."

"I will make amends." Chitthra wiped her eyes. "Still I knew truth had to be brought into the light. I could not allow Steffyn Foxxe to escape again."

"Yet he has, and now we hold something dear to him." Aeren thought for moments, then shook her head. "Nay, we cannot use Jyslin to draw him out. Still our way is Drakenmoore and friends. Surely our strength will aid their cause."

Chitthra drew away, washed her face, then turned. "On my honor, I will think more before acting, should times as this arise again."

"They will arise, Dearest, therefore, make no promises you cannot keep. Rather I would see your prowess in its duty than have you question safety for yourself."

"Or you." Chitthra gave a wan smile at the last, kissed Aeren's cheek and hefted up her pack. "Let us leave this place, returning only when our task complete. One more duty added to our ledger, and once done, recompense will be given in full term."

* * *

Somewhere in the Mists of Magic…

Steffyn stumbled, fell, rose and fell again. He lay in the cool and formless mists, aching head to foot, his mind numb with pain. He thought his shoulder broken, or at least bruised to disuse, and his nose was swollen and disjointed.

Many years it has been since I was beaten as Chitthra has done, and the irony of her being Däe Quivie is simply too much to believe. Surely, tho', I deserve every ache my body holds.

He tried to rise again, yet found no strength to do so. He drifted in and out of consciousness as the mists soothed his aching body, and wondered if he might die where he lay.

Something raised him to his feet, though he did not stand, but drifted in the mist. Two creatures of the realm held him up and a third faced him squarely, a reddish, grinning face before him. Likely the same seen when he and Jyslin had escaped the courtyard in DragonFall, when Mors'ul'jyn had escaped with Archane and Mor'i'jil in tow.

"You were warned not to return."

Steffyn wiped his nose, dried blood on his cheeks scraping against his hand. "I had no choice, as my life was in danger."

"This is no sanctuary," replied the creature, nearly laughing. It closed on Steffyn, an arm's-length away. "Give us the female and you may live beyond this."

Steffyn shook his head, then paused as the scene spun within his mind. He drew a breath and grimaced as the creature on his left twisted his injured shoulder, grinning.

"She is gone, no longer in my care." *Abandoned, as I have abandoned everything I once held dear!*

"Then you will bear her pain." The creature slid a long claw beneath Steffyn's torn tunic, into his belly perhaps a finger's-depth. The elf gasped and thrashed weakly as blood trickled from his nose once more. Another claw stabbed into his chest, nearly to his heart, and the creature's fetid breath blew across Steffyn's face.

The creature grinned and thrust more deeply, and Steffyn nearly retched. He swooned, and they dropped him in a heap as a voice boomed all around.

"Leave him."

The trio drew away, fading in the haze. A presence gathered; though in his delirium, Steffyn could feel no one else about. Still, he lay face down, once more the cooling mist a balm upon his torture. He opened one swollen eye, searching for a source of the command. A shadow fell across his body, and Steffyn's mind faded slowly away. His last thought was that death had finally come, and he wondered if he should welcome it.

* * *

Steffyn's crusty, swollen eyes pried themselves awake. The mists yet were all around, though he felt no malevolence within.

Still I live, he thought, and would have chuckled had his chest not been alive with fire. His tunic torn and tattered, blood dried upon it everywhere, he wondered if he had bled his last, and perhaps this was a god's jest upon him.

He rolled aside, groaning as every bruise and cut warned him to move slowly, for however long he had been away from consciousness, he had yet to heal. He thought to cast a cantrip, but his mind was clear enough only to accept he could not focus more than on the present moment.

He breathed, and then again, held a hand against the wound upon his chest and tried to rise, yet found no strength to do so.

Therefore, I will sit here until I find my wits or starve, and I cannot tell which will happen first.

He coughed, then looked about. *Someone… or something keeps me safe for now. But whom or what?*

Power seemed to gather in the mists. *"You have strayed far from the righteous, Lord Mage."*

A voice, female, and somehow with a hint of familiarity. Steffyn rolled his head side to side, trying to remember.

"Once none in the mortal world could have led you down the path you chose yourself."

Steffyn licked dry lips, coughed again and spoke. "Is that not why free will is sacred to the elves? That we may make our own mistakes and suffer for them, blaming no one else?" His voice was but a rasp, deep and throaty, dry as deadfall in the forest.

"You have tested that proclamation to its limits, have you not? You seek to right old errors, yet are reluctant to do what must be done. Is it fear that holds you back, or something other?"

Steffyn said nothing, knowing the answer to the question. And in knowing it, knew the entity surrounding him held the answer. He thought to change the subject.

"Why am I still alive, is more my query? If punishment is your goal, you might have left me to the creatures bent on torture. Had Jyslin accompanied me again, they would have ravaged her for pleasures before likely killing her for sport. Therefore, tell me, why am I yet alive?"

"Perhaps mercy is shown."

Steffyn coughed a laugh, grimacing as he did so. His chest exploded once again with pain, and he nearly swooned, but caught himself. Panting, he straightened and drew a breath. "You seek something of me, else I would not be alive. You seek balance, therefore I know who you are and why I live."

A pause came about him, and he knew he had scored a minor victory. *How it might proceed is another matter, yet one step before the next,* he thought.

"Always is your intellect among the very finest," came the voice again, tinged with a bit of humor in its recognition. *"The question now becomes, have you the courage, or will you falter once again?"*

261

Steffyn looked away, though the mist was everywhere and nothing else met his gaze. "You know my reasons."

"I know the excuses in your mind. You set aside everything held dear to you, and I ask you now, was the heartache caused worth it, in truth?"

"The land has been at peace for years."

"Through no doings of your own."

Steffyn shook his head, though carefully. "Had events not transpired as they did, who can say? Crysalon and Archane both gone, elf and Drow and humankind stunned to looking inward, saving what they may. Is this not the balance Crysalon decreed was paramount to the *Rising Star*?"

"Was all this worth the life of Galandria Telveperen?"

Sadness, deep remorse, and a touch of anger washed over Steffyn, and he set his mind firm as he might. "Yes! *Yarhetha'an* take me if I am wrong, but yes! In the struggle, some may die that others then may live! Galandria knew this! It was her destiny, therefore!"

"And your destiny is what, then? Still the mad woman Mors'ul'jyn is alive. Still the danger posed to Family Calidriil is real."

He snorted. "Others seek to deal with her, without the questions and reluctance I carry. Let them be her ending."

"Again, you step aside your obligations."

Steffyn nearly snarled. "Then take me! I will not destroy such a mind as Teresa Drakenmoore! I cannot! I will not!"

"Perhaps you should face your trials at the hands of those who loved you."

Steffyn bowed his head, nodding acquiescence. "Already I have done that, and you know this."

"You may fail to act, yet you will be a part. In this, you cannot stand away as before."

Steffyn nodded once again. "I understand and accept. Should I die at the hands of those I cherish, it will be as written."

A pause, and the power gathered once again. *"Perhaps a choice is needed to be laid before you. One thought impossible to afford."*

"You cannot force my mind to change. More than five years I have fought with this, given up my life, and sought escape. Nothing you may do will change that, regardless the power you wield. Again, free will."

"Very well. Shall we test your resolve?"

The sight faded once again from Steffyn's eyes as the answer came to him. *Surely, I should have known…*

Kaanan.

* * *

On the Plains of Ardwel…

Steffyn's mind slowly cleared, and he came to know he was in a copse of wood. The air was clean and fresh, as after a late summer rain, and he rose gingerly to look about. A stream ran north to south, two deer drinking at a bank nearby, and sunlight rising in the east.

I know this place.

Quickly as his wounds would let him, Steffyn ventured west beyond the wood. The hills of southern Ardwel met his sight, and he called a spell for a magic spyglass to appear.

Nothing happened.

He paused, knowing his mind now was clear of sorcery, likely wiped away by *Kaanan* in their meetings in the mists.

He glanced away, a road in the distance topping a rise and scattered trees about it, perhaps a hundred paces distant. He sat, taking stock of his wounds and his belongings. A small tome of spells lay hidden in an inner pocket, a dagger in his boot, and a pouch of coins dangled from his belt.

He touched his injured shoulder, stiff and bruised heavily, though unbroken. *Likely I will not be lifting much beyond a tankard*, he thought, with a dry chuckle. Other than cuts and minor hurts, and the wounding from the daemon, his body was intact, and he knew Chitthra had attacked to disable him and not to kill. *Else I would not be having this conversation with myself, nor met Kaanan in the mists.*

Kaanan. Why would she come to me? Goddess of the Rising Star, the patron of soldiers in the City-State of Truth… and companion in her mortal time of Sheynon, Shiva, and myself.

Steffyn picked absently at the grasses round. "Her prevue is one of Order, balance in the world, neither Good nor Evil holding sway. Why then does she grace me with her presence, however harsh and pointed?" His voice was dry and raw within his ears, and he made way to the stream, to drink and wash away the crusted blood upon his face.

Why not to Thalion, or even Aeren, now warden of the City-State of Truth? He paused with his hands in the cooling waters. "Perhaps she has." He nodded knowingly.

He removed his boots, then lowered his aching feet within the stream. "If she comes, Order must be at risk again. Five years the land has been at peace. Crysalon, gone in that time, surely must be safe, otherwise, imbalance would be present. Archane captured, the Drow turned inward, else Chaos would raise its head once more. Five years Mors'ul'jyn has tasked herself with keeping Archane as her prisoner. Therefore, Evil paused."

263

A fish nibbled at his toes, and Steffyn jerked his foot from the water, laughing. He donned his boots again, plucked low-hanging apples from a nearby tree and sat streamside, eating slowly, thoughts drifting to Jyslin and his escape. He blew a ragged breath and shoved the memories aside.

Steffyn paused mid-bite with a flash of inspiration. "Should Archane somehow escape, surely she would seek her way back to *Ung'gu'wi* and regain her place. That of itself would not cause imbalance, for likely they are at war or nearly so. And years might pass before her dominance once more was asserted. However..."

Steffyn trembled with the sudden understanding. "It would mean Mors'ul'jyn may focus her own self to other mischief. Such as Sheynon's family once again. Therefore, Kaanan coming to the world."

His tome rested at his side, and he threw the apple cores in frustration, wincing at the effort. He raised the slim volume to his eyes and slowly began to focus, then sounds from the road reached his ears. He rose, stepped behind a tree, and squinted in the growing daylight.

Six figures riding to the south, toward where Steffyn knew his tower, *Barad Anna*, lay. A standard drifted in the breeze, deep blue with a golden quarter moon and a single star above it. His standard. His heart skipped a beat as he recognized the leading pair. A stocky, dark-haired half-elf woman, streaks of grey showing in her hair, and a slender fair-haired elven maiden dressed in leather armor. They were laughing as they made way without hurry, and Steffyn's eyes filled with tears.

Emildir and E'dhel'wen. My wife, and a dear companion from the Kingdom of the Sun. Dearest Yarhetha'an, what have I sacrificed for five years out of fear?

He turned away, knowing if his will was weak, he would run to them begging forgiveness for his sins. As the party disappeared beyond the rise, Steffyn sat once more, and cried his heart's sadness into the forest bed.

At the last he calmed and began to think once more. His staff and other items still were in the City-State of DragonFall, and he knew return was necessary. How to avoid Jyslin, to say nothing of Aeren and Chitthra, would be a challenge.

He raised the tome once more, turned a page and began to read again. Slowly and with focus he had not felt in many moons, a plan began to form within his mind.

* * *

In the Warrens of Hovenethra...

Ba'tula sat with Aysa'lil and Kreothren in a private chamber, as the priest Dhuunyl entered, late upon the summoning. The matriarch gave him a warning look and he bowed, then took his place between the others.

"Dark Priestess, my apologies —" Ba'tula's hand paused his words, and she nodded Aysa'lil to speak.

"Word from our Lancer Captains says Narlros and Xa'lyyth were seen within the central chamber two days past, seeking way to Warinethra." The priestess raised a scroll with broken seal. "This missive arrived a day beyond their seeing, warning Hovenethra of grim reprisal should our soldiers continue against Archane's forces."

"I cannot think they would send sorcerers against us, and they have little of soldiers to be considered." Kreothren, the priest youngest of them all, hurried on as Ba'tula glared his way. "Only do I mean Hovenethra's strength would hold them away, and this is but a pretense."

"Shall we send you then to confirm it?" Aysa'lil's headdress tinkled in the dimness as she shook her head. "Warinethra is not known for speaking falsehoods, and I would caution against strong reply."

"The question being," said Ba'tula, sipping from a golden goblet, "are other Houses warned as we, or is this a ploy arranged by Alystin?"

"If clergy from the House of Iyllyeth met with Warinethra only a day before the missive..." Dhuunyl mused. "Either an agreement, or the most curious of coincidences."

"Therefore, our righteous claim to leadership is paused, Dark Lady?" Aysa'lil huffed a breath. "Does Hovenethra cringe from the word of sorcerers and charlatans?"

Ba'tula stared away for long moments. "If they have sent warning to all Houses, I will accept this as a plea for patience. Yet if only Hovenethra has been warned, stern issue must be taken."

"How many sorcerers of worth does their House have, Dark Lady? Unknown, yes? And ours, perhaps a score?" Kreothren showed a worried look. "Dare we take a chance?"

"We must know the truth of their demands," replied Aysa'lil. "Else we do nothing out of fear."

Ba'tula looked the council in the eyes, one by one. "Prepare a parley, decide which two of you will venture to Warinethra. Take whatever offerings you think necessary. Find the truth and return quickly, that we may continue our advance. The Race withers with the absence of a true leader, and now is the time for Hovenethra's ascendance to that place."

* * *

Somewhere in the Mists of Time…

Archane did not move, nor did she speak again for many moments. Only did she stare at the man before her; undoubtedly it was Venic, now aged, though not decrepit.

He stood apart, a smile showing from within his beard, and spoke once more to quell her angst. "You are beautiful as always, filled with fire and questions. So very, very beautiful."

Archane still could not speak, as she held her breath and massaged the place the dagger had pierced her heart. A tear wended down her cheek, and then another. She swallowed, calmed her breathing as best she might, and lifted her chin with what courage she could muster. "Am I dead at last forever? Is this *Iyllyeth's* own place, and I enter to see a human barring my way into it?" Her resolve began to crumble as she drew a heavy breath. "A human I dared give affection and trust unto?"

Venic paced his way before her, and Archane took two steps back, then halted, desperately trying to make sense of what she saw. He was ancient in his look, hair and beard nearly white, eyes and forehead lined with age, yet his eyes twinkled as they roamed her supple figure. He stopped only a hand's-width away, and touched his fingers between her breasts where the dagger point had entered. She held his hand there gently, eyes locked with his, and whispered, "You are real, therefore, I am dead at last, yes? Speak the truth of it, for regardless, I am free of the witch Mors'ul'jyn."

His smile faded slowly, yet his hand never wavered from her skin. "In part, tho' there is a price for taking of your life by your own hand."

She kept his hand upon her flesh, the sensation warm and reminiscent. "Speak of it, for I will trade it all for your touch once more."

He smiled. "Has the Dark Princess grown so soft in her maturity?" Her eyes flashed, and he laughed, then drew her closer.

She nestled deep in his embrace, buried her face, and tightened her fingers round his arms. They stood together for how long she did not know, begging in her silence the feelings there would never end.

At last he raised her face to his and kissed her gently. "There are words we must share."

Her face fell. "You will speak of my punishment for such a sin. Yet I could not remain a prisoner forever. Mor'i'jil is gone, *Ung'gu'wi* surely fallen now to war, and here I stand, shivering naked in the mists with a man who deserted and betrayed me so long ago."

"Deserted, but not forgotten, it seems."

266

Her eyes blazed once again as she drew back. "Still I am the Dark Princess and your mistress. Do not presume upon my mercy further."

He laughed and backed away, hands raised before himself in false terror.

She stood, fists clenched at her sides, and bristled.

He bowed. "Your pardon, for here you have no power and are little but a spirit. I, however…" He waved a hand, and a hooded tunic, belted with a gold medallion, formed about her body. Archane said nothing, but nodded gratefully.

"Now that I am not distracted by your naked beauty, we may parley in necessity." Venic motioned to a path that formed before them, offering his arm. She took it with reluctance, and they walked their way through the parting mists.

"I am not yet certain, but the spell may now be broken." He glanced aside to her, but she only listened, warry. "When set, you were all but dead, and my words… my incantation was, for the most part, incomplete or ill-said. Now, death has found you in a manner never contemplated."

Archane looked away. "Little choice was given. Never would I escape Mors'ul'jyn's clutches, as five years she held me with no opportunity for escape."

"Yet you found a way, a manner always with you, but never taken."

She stopped and drew away. "A way unclean and sinful! A way of cowards and those without hope or courage! A way only taken out of desperation and base depression!"

"A way at the last realized, as Mor'i'jil was taken from you?" Venic shook his head. "A way even I had considered many times, yet could not do."

"You ran! You stole the secrets of the Window of Coronis! You are a betrayer of the worst kind, and many times I wished your heart within my hand!"

He shook his head. "The Window… may not exist, or no longer exist," he replied bitterly, then shrugged. "Centuries I searched with no success, yet still I cannot be certain. Times may come that I look further, tho' have not for near a hundred years. Wherever it may be, it is too lost or too hidden for its finding."

Archane's face drew taut. "Therefore, you remained apart. I sought you in the mountains north, that we might take this land into our hands, yet was thwarted by minions of the City-State of Truth. Now they search again for Mors'ul'jyn, to cease her evil on them."

"She is evil, yet…"

267

"And why then have you not dealt with her?" She waved her arms in anger. "Surely one of your talents may cease her madness."

"Let us set this circumstance aside," said Venic gently. "Issues closer to your own heart come now to prominence. Issues of life and death."

"…What issues?"

"As said, my incantations were desperate as your solution for escape. I held your dying form and had only moments to complete the enchantment."

"Meaning?" Archane swallowed hard, knowing the words to come.

"You now may be mortal as all others in the land. This may be your one and only life remaining."

She glanced aside and closed her eyes, forced back tears and nodded. "Little can I say, and I am not surprised. Surely did I know a price would be extracted."

He nodded gravely. "Therefore, use it wisely."

Again, her eyes flashed. "Still I am the Dark Princess, *Iyllyeth's* chosen to lead the Race. Little does it matter I am not immortal. None must know, and in that secret, it stays their hand, that I would rise, no matter their intent."

"Or hold you hostage for a hundred years, as Mors'ul'jyn surely would have done."

"Then on that revelation, end her in my name! Give me true freedom from her, as she seeks to use my body for her own and seize control of Drow society!"

Venic nodded to himself. "Yes, she would do that without question, now with Mor'i'jil gone and no witnesses about. Yet I cannot."

"You disobey?"

Venic laughed. "No longer am I your subject, Archane. Our story ended two thousand years ago and more."

Archane held her peace, thinking. "Then aid me in my return. As the Houses war against each other, a bitter end will come. Hovenethra seeks to rule, as they have for many centuries."

Venic drew closer and held a hand to her face, gently. "Then find a way beyond war and conquest. Your skills as leader and mentor are yet within you. Use them."

They held each other's gaze for many moments. "How have you survived the ages?" Archane asked.

Venic grinned. "My wits, and finding compromise, my beauty."

Archane scoffed. "There is no compromise for Drow. Our way is of conquest, and you know this. *Mother Darkness* is fed by our victories."

"Times change, and with them, the gods. As said, find a way, not just in *Ung'gu'wi*, but all the land. The world."

With that, he faded, and as Archane's eyes grew wide with questions, so did the mists around her turn to light and forest.

* * *

On the Plains of Ardwel...

Steffyn rolled aside, yawning. Sleep had come at last, and as he woke, he came to know it was night, with moonlight shining through the trees. The tome lay aside, a glowing rock upon the cover, the dagger in his hand still sheathed. His stomach rumbled, hunger a fine edge upon his mind, and he gathered apples once again as he thought of tea and pastry, and the pleasures of Jyslin's company on waking. He sighed.

Return to DragonFall, find her if I may and set matters right. Tho' I cannot think Chitthra and Aeren would turn her out for complicity in my dealings. He chuckled wryly. *Yet she herself may seek my blood for all this stark duplicity.*

Sounds from beyond his thicket caught his ear, and he rose slowly, looking round. A figure stood away, a shadow in the light reflecting from the stream nearby, as having watched as he studied, slept, and woke. Steffyn waited, breathless, saying nothing, his hand digging in his pouch for his one remaining fire-stone.

"I am lost," came a female voice, a dark elf lilt within it, a sensuous contralto, nearly pulling at his lust.

Steffyn replied at last with a guarded tone. "The forest is safe enough, and there is clean water in the stream. Find comfort and take your ease for the night."

The figure came before him, hooded, dark, a pleasant scent drifting in the air about her. "Might I share your company, for I am not of the forest in most times."

He watched with care, noting deep red eyes glinting in the moonlight, and motioned to the small clearing where he had lain. "Sit, if you will. All I may offer this night are apples, tho' they are sweet and plentiful."

She knelt, drew back her hood, and shook her glowing hair loose about her shoulders. The clasp of her tunic lay open, and Steffyn glanced tender dark elf woman-flesh beneath. All his senses shouted caution, yet his eyes could not ignore her dark allure.

She ate slowly as he watched, entranced.

"May I know your name, that I may thank you?" Her ruby eyes peered from beneath her brow as she continued eating.

269

He drew a breath to answer, then caught himself. "I would ask the same of you. How does a woman become lost in a forest known well by those about?"

She laughed, a sound as music in the darkness. Steffyn shook himself, not understanding the feelings growing in his belly. *What is happening?*

She ate another apple, then made way carefully to the stream nearby.

Steffyn waited as half-full *Mina* crossed the zenith, wondering if she had simply slipped away. Splashing reached his ears, and he panicked, that she had fallen in the water. He made haste beyond the thicket, parted shrubs and watched, entranced, as she bathed herself. Her tunic lay on the river bank, and she turned as he quietly approached. Moonlight glistened from her skin, her breasts firm and full and darkly-tipped, nipples erect in the cooling stream, her legs long and tapered, parted slightly, showing soft, inviting flesh between them. Her eyes caught his and she beckoned. Steffyn found himself at the water's edge without knowing how he had gotten there, standing in nothing but his breeches.

She drew closer, her fragrance once more as a calling, knelt before him and slowly untied the cording. "I wish to show my gratitude," she crooned, as his clothing dropped away.

She rose, and bade him lay in the softest grasses. His breath came quick as she ran her hands about his body, raising his ardor to a scream. Little could he do but moan and lay his head against the river bank.

She straddled him, and he gasped as she drew him in, deeply warm and snugly wet.

What is happening? Why am I not resisting? Who is she!? What is she!?

She moved slowly at the first, eyes locked with his, her hands upon his chest. He reached for her, and she arched her back, her body as a living sculpture now within his reach. His hands found her shoulders, her breasts, her hips, and he clung with whitening knuckles as his climax rose to an explosion.

She drained his every drop of essence, and he thought to sink into the earth itself in his afterglow. She stretched her body onto his, still holding him within, and breathed into his ear.

"Who... who are you?" Steffyn only stuttered out the words, for his lips were numb and weak as the rest of him. "Why... how do you come to me and turn me to a slave?"

"Love me," she whispered in reply, nearly a command within his mind, and he found there was no resistance in his spirit.

"I... love you." What little strength remained within Steffyn's spirit crumbled and was gone.

270

"Crave me," her voice breathed into his ear, and he wrapped his arms about her.

"Obey me." Her voice was as the sweetest lash he might ever feel.

His fervor rose once more, and the last thing he recalled was the sensations of her womanhood as she brought him once again to ecstasy.

Dennis Young

BOOK TEN
WAITING FOR
THE NEXT STORM

*"Understand, Ysilrod, the chamber below may become
not only our battleground, but our tomb as well."*

Duncan Brannigan

Dennis Young

PART ONE
A TURNING TIDE

In the Depths of Drakenmoore...

The descent was treacherous, and more than once they paused for rest not planned. The passage of time was different in the dungeon, as told to Sheynon by Re', when on their quest for *Kingmaker*, yet the elf lord could not affirm it still was so.

"Doubtful," said Ysilrod, as they passed a waterskin around and ate jerked meat. He motioned to the walls, little more than dirty rock, cold and dead, a bone protruding from beneath a fallen stone. "What magics were used to make this place likely faded with Re's passing."

"Yet she did not die," replied Audrey, looking to Sheynon. "Is that not true? Her soul resides in Reena's body, therefore, she survives."

Sheynon shook his head. "The tales told by Diatus were, once the family was no more, the Cave of Bells would ring out the ending of the castle and all its lands. Somehow, with the soul of Re' departing her own body, this set the prophesy in motion." He drank, then passed the waterskin to Thalion. "Little does it matter, for we search in vain."

"Yet may find clues, Cousin," said Thalion, smiling gently. "And other than to be in our own company, what would be your wish?"

"A bath," replied Audrey with a sigh, and they laughed together as she blew dust from the holy symbol round her neck.

A tremor, and they rose as one, looking round. Another, and Ysilrod drew a parchment from a hidden pocket in his robe and held it, waiting. "If a third comes now, it is a sign."

"Might she know our presence?" Audrey drew *Mír'rë Cala'wyne* and faced the way they had tread before.

Sheynon raised his torches as Thalion stood. They waited, tense and watching, yet no further quaking came. All returned to silence.

"It would be best we move on," said Thalion. "Too much time leaves impressions in the aura of this place, and likely felt by Mors'ul'jyn."

Ysilrod held the scroll in hand. "She is alerted, tho' does not know whom or where. Even in a stolen body, she knows the labyrinth well."

Thalion looked to the tilted stairway and the darkness seen beyond it. "Take care with your pace. Do not follow closely, should a step give way."

He led them on, its *Gil Estel's* holy light glowing in the solitude.

* * *

275

Deeper into the ruin they descended, finding the path followed those years ago by Kaul and Reena, seeing signs of the Mongrel's great strength used in many places to simply force his way beyond whatever blocked their path. Stones fallen from the ceiling, weighing more than all the Companions as a group, had been split and shoved aside. Audrey wondered of it, as neither Kaul nor Reena, to their knowing, carried magic.

"*NorthWind*," said Sheynon, "Kaul's sword given in their descent by Re', taken from the body of a soldier." He ran his hands with care across a boulder's edge, cut cleanly as with a razor. "Here you see the power of the greatest weapons ever forged by mortals."

Audrey examined the cutting closely as the elf-lord held a torch nearby. She nodded grimly. "A single stroke, and surely such a weapon would feel little pause as it passed through armor." She stood and faced them all. "Take great care, my lords, for should she have guards, they will likely be so armed."

"She does," replied Sheynon. "Or at the least, did in my time herein. In the forge were three suits of *NorthWind* armor, animated, we were told, by magic. Should they have survived…"

"I may deal with them, should time come." Ysilrod patted his cloak and nodded. "Yet the warning is goodly, that we may prepare." He looked about, the stones offering shelter in the passage. "We should remain here for our rest. This is the fourth level by my count."

"Three more to the forge," said Sheynon, "and the source of *NorthWind*."

"Yet the forge is cold, yes?" asked Audrey, sitting with her pack. "Or only ruin, as all the rest herein?"

"Do not discount any possibility from the mind of Teresa Drakenmoore," cautioned Ysilrod. "While mad, her cunning knows no bounds, and she will do whatever necessary to impose her will upon the land. Even in the devastation of her family's home, her plans will move as shadows."

Sheynon turned away, and Audrey held a hand to him. He took it gently, his face a mask, and she moved closer. "I am here for you, my friend. My ear yours for whatever need."

He nodded wordlessly, and squeezed her fingers tightly.

* * *

Twice they came upon broken steps within the stairway, and twice Ysilrod used his magics to make safe their way. Marching on, the walls of the corridor narrowed, filled with even more debris. And before them lay only broken stonework, the ending of the corridor nothing now but scattered rock and ancient dust. Beyond were great oaken doors, twisted on their hinges and charred about the edges.

Sheynon held his torch aloft to show the damage done. "Rock and earth on this side only, and the doors laying in this direction, as something within sought escape."

Ysilrod motioned to the walls about and deep grooves running back along the corridor. "Marks of claws or perhaps weapons."

"Escape from what, is the question," said Thalion.

"Something with strength enough to break through stone and mortar." Audrey watched to the rear once more, then nodded forward. "Lead on, Lord Priest, that we may find the answer."

They chose their path with care, that stones lying one atop the other did not dislodge and cause them injury. Once past the broken wall, they paused at the doors, one laying in pieces on the cavern floor, the other halfway open.

"We must clear the doorway," said Sheynon, yet before he could raise a stone, Ysilrod held a hand.

"Touch nothing, Brother. We know not what may lie behind the rubble, and I would not wish your death in such a place."

Sheynon backed away with Thalion and Audrey, as Ysilrod prepared his incantations. The elf-mage gestured, and a shimmer grew within the air, between the Companions and the obstructed doorway. Then one by one, the rocks and broken masonry began to lift away, carried to each side and laid carefully upon the ground. Twice stones fell from the ceiling, and fragments glanced from the shimmer. Ysilrod kept his focus, though his brow began to sweat.

They waited in anticipation, Thalion with holy symbol in his hands, Sheynon holding torches aloft, that Ysilrod would have light to see his work, and Audrey, once more with *Mír'rë Cala'wyne* in hand, guarding as a sentinel behind them all.

At the last, the work was done, and Ysilrod sagged upon himself. Sheynon came to his side with a wineskin, and the younger brother drank deeply from it. Thalion nodded, smiling, as Audrey sheathed her weapon at the last.

"I deem it safe to enter, yet be wary." Ysilrod capped the wineskin. "Still I felt traces of magic there within, and a hint of malevolence."

"The spirit of Reena seen before?" queried Thalion.

Ysilrod knelt and drew symbols in the dirt, then laid three pebbles from the rubble across the entrance. "This will block the way for any now within, should we need retreat." He chuckled. "Do not disturb them in your haste."

"A ward," said Thalion, nodding approval. "Well thought, and you prove your worth again." He grinned, as did Audrey in return. "Doubt not the elves when it comes to belief in the Arts, Excellency. As the miracles of gods, they know the truth of it."

Audrey shook her head slowly. "Then show to me these things. My eyes must see for themselves."

They entered the open doorway slowly, Sheynon at the first, then Thalion, Ysilrod, and Audrey. What met their eyes was only more of what had been before. A tilted vestibule, ancient settee, and a suit of armor, crushed beneath a fallen wall. Rats scurried from about their feet, deeper into the chamber, through a broken doorway showing signs as seen of claws or weapons used to force the way.

"None live within," said Ysilrod, and pointed to the doorway beyond. "There surely lies the forge, tho' cold."

Audrey looked him in the eye. "A bitter place, and doubtless horrors still exist therein."

"Your point is taken well, Excellency," said Thalion. "Yet let us proceed as we may. Sooner we are beyond this heartbreak, the sooner we may reach our goal."

* * *

They studied, examined, and probed as they thought safe, noting clues among the bits of wreckage. The forge itself was little more than a tumble of heavy bricks with ancient ash and bits of bone. Two skulls were found, one likely Drow or elf, the other human.

"Others have been here, tho' not recently," said Ysilrod at the last, pointing to the ash, swept side to side to clear the firepot.

"The mad woman?" Audrey sought movement in the shadows, yet saw nothing. She turned as Thalion lit an incense wand and traced smoke about the forge ruins, holy symbol held high and chanting all the while.

Ysilrod stepped away and set a second ward within the doorway, then turned to Sheynon. "Your thoughts, Brother? Might you say of your time herein?"

Sheynon shook his head. "Never did we enter the forge itself, only the anteroom and another, for rest. We did not press the issue, as Re' insisted our goal was only *Kingmaker*."

278

"The carvings," Audrey whispered, pointing to the walls and ceiling, covered with friezes of males and females, entwined and copulating. "To represent creation in this place." She turned to Thalion. "And her deity, Lord Priest? Have you felt its presence?"

Thalion waved his incense in a corner, paused, then continued down the far wall. At last he drew the wand away, doused it with his fingers, and spoke a word; the stub vanished from his hand. He drank from his waterskin and faced Audrey. "Excellency, yes, there are impressions not of mortal guise, and this is why I said a blessing herein. We stand in a place where a god was forsaken and abandoned."

"And there are traces still of great power used," said Ysilrod as he approached. "Here is where Re' stole Reena's body, I am certain. A crime not only of necromancy, but pure selfishness and evil."

"And her spirit wanders still." Audrey gazed into what had been the forge. "In surety, and the bones may be those of Re's own body. My lords, this place cries into my heart with sadness. Whatever curse or prophesy Re' unleashed was only mercenary, thinking with the ending of the family, no more the world should carry on."

They returned to the entrance room for rest. Sheynon passed cheese and bread about, and they ate in silence for a while.

A rumble was felt more than heard, and they paused their breath, waiting. A second, then a third, and Ysilrod stood quickly. "She knows our presence and seeks more of us."

They rose, and Sheynon raised the torches, looking round, seeing nothing. "Brother?"

Ysilrod held a hand for silence. Thalion and Audrey drew their swords, watching all about. "She tests my defenses, with much care. The tremors felt before were light and only probing. These sought a way beyond my wards."

"Might they hold her back?" asked Thalion. "Should we consider escape, or prepare for battle?"

They waited, and at the last, Ysilrod deemed them safe again. "My thought is, while she knows of us, for the nonce she can do no harm."

"We did not come this far to be chased away," said Audrey. "If our quarry comes, we will meet her with faith and courage."

Thalion glanced to her aside. "Never have you changed, Excellency. Comes evil, you will meet it fairly."

"Always, Lord Priest. Always."

* * *

279

Sheynon and Thalion slept soundly in a corner, as Audrey and Ysilrod kept vigil in the anteroom. Near three days had passed since their descent, by Audrey's count, and all were tired, worn and dirty, to say nothing of their worry. Little had been found as evidence of Mors'ul'jyn's whereabouts, though Ysilrod had spoken quietly of his feelings she was near.

"And watching, or at the least, aware," he said to Audrey, as they sat opposite the open doorway.

"Tell me, why do we wait? Have the clues you sought been found?"

Ysilrod was silent for a moment, then he turned to her. "My lady, we must draw her out. Only with encounter, preferably face to face, may we defeat her. I have gleaned all I may from the forge, and little enough was found. Therefore…"

Audrey nodded, understanding. "We bait the trap. Not the first time in our adventures, yes? Tho' I am older, as is Thalion, and without experience these long years." She showed a smile. "Still, I am not without ability."

"Never would I say such," replied Ysilrod with a grin, and he passed a waterskin to her.

"My lord… I have a question of great delicacy to ask." Audrey looked to Sheynon curled in the corner. "It has come to my attention your brother no longer carries *Aráto Calidrii* at his side. Might you know the reasons?"

Ysilrod's face grew taut, and at the last he shrugged. "It is… sequestered for reasons of his own."

Audrey touched his hand. "Still he carries guilt and rage and sadness, and I understand it all. Recall, I bade him back into the light after Culwenril's assassination many years ago. Yet he grew beyond that loss to Join with Galandria and bring a family into the world. Now she, as well, is gone, yet… Sheynon is not the elf he once was."

"How would he be, Audrey? The matriarch of Elvenkind, murdered in her own castle, betrayed by the Guild of Learned, to say nothing of our own elf-brother, Steffyn Foxxe. Yet there is one thing you may not know, and I will tell it only if you swear to secrecy."

Audrey nodded. "On my heart's honor, you have my word. You and I know each other well enough, do we not?"

Ysilrod paused, glanced at Sheynon sleeping, then continued. "It was with his own blade Mors'ul'jyn slew Galandria. While in the chambers of the Guild, she gained control, as the sword had been given to the mages for enchantment. Mors'ul'jyn stole it away, and with it, killed Her Ladyship."

Audrey only stared, and tears showed in her eyes. "Dearest *Jhad*. I know not what to say, Ysilrod. I cannot…" She turned away, drawing ragged breaths.

The elf-mage let go a breath. "He asked I hide the sword forevermore, that he never see or hear of it again."

She drew away and knelt, signed herself, crying silent as she could. At last she turned, eyes red and running still. "May your great lord grant him vengeance against this woman, and by his own hand. I cannot think the pain he must bear every day."

"Nor the guilt, Audrey. Sheynon feels his duty as Joined was undone in many ways and by those he trusted on that day. And he seeks to bury reminders, else he may go mad."

"I will stand beside him and ward the blows, should I be able."

Ysilrod nodded. "As will we all."

* * *

Mors'ul'jyn had spent time huddled in her bed, even as her alarm bell rang above her. Archane dead, plans shattered into nothing, and solitude a dark, foreboding companion. Tears had fallen until there were no more left to cry, fear and rage and harsh denial nearly overwhelming her own mind.

At last she rose, called the bell to silence once again, yet in only moments, it rang once more, telling her someone, somewhere, was in the labyrinth and moving downward.

She called her cleaning cantrips, bathed herself of sweat and grime and sadness as the bell tolled out its warnings. She stepped from the waters and toweled herself mostly dry, then stood before the mirror. The reflection yet showed the form of Reena, youthful, firm, and brimming with a sensuality almost visible. Still, Mors'ul'jyn could not bring it to her mind, and at the last, donned a simple robe and cloak.

I must clear my mind of this, or never will I find a way beyond it.

She entered her workshop, summoned a scrying mist, and peered into it deeply. *Four or five, I cannot tell, for they are shielded. Did my wards in higher levels not dissuade them? How have they descended deeply into the dungeon? What have I missed in my withdrawal?*

Mors'ul'jyn stepped back a pace from her conjuring. *They are in the forge, and in my rage, I did not see them even enter the ruins above. Now I find a mage within their midst, one of power. Steffyn Foxxe perhaps, or someone else? And prayers said within the forge, tho' not to Urijah? Who, then?*

She pondered, drifting to the outer chamber once again. There upon the floor still lay the body, cold and stiffening. She snarled beneath her breath, caught herself before the anger took her senses, and turned away. At the last, she faced the ruin of her plans upon the floor and summoned her magics once again, to clear the room of death and all it meant.

The body lifted into the air, then into the hearth, and the fire rose to a roar as Mors'ul'jyn retreated to her workshop. She paced, plans running rampant, yet with no real direction. She stopped, raised her head, and nodded. *First, I will delay them, or possibly cause them to withdraw. With luck, one or two may die, and in that, diminish their exuberance to invade my domain.*

She returned to the outer chamber, faced the gleaming sentinel of *NorthWind* armor in the corner, and uttered incantations. *"Go therein, slay all who stand against you but one, female if there be. Bring her to me, and the heads of all the others. Go now!"*

The armor moved, raised its sword in quiet salute, and vanished without sound.

Now we shall see who dares invade Drakenmoore's own realm. My rage returns, and those who think themselves the better will soon find the folly in it!

* * *

Audrey had drifted into fitful sleep when Sheynon's voice screamed alarm. She rose with Ysilrod aside, the elf up and running to his brother's aid. Thalion was through the entry into the forge, and sounds of battle rang as Audrey tried to clear her mind.

Shadowed movements showed through the doorway, the ring of steel on steel, oaths and grunts and heavy breathing. She shook her head once more, drew a breath and stumbled past the dingy settee. The scene that met her eyes was of deadly chaos. Sheynon was down and bleeding, Thalion engaged with a fully-armored figure, and Ysilrod standing over Sheynon's prone form conjuring into the air. Audrey drew *Mír'rë Cala'wyne*, screamed and charged into the fray.

Her sword strike glanced from the gleaming breastplate, leaving not so much as a scratch.

NorthWind! she thought, and called to Thalion. "You cannot penetrate it, and there is no flesh within! It is her enchanted sentinel, not mortal!"

282

"Back!" cried Thalion, and as the priest held the sentinel at bay with all his skill, Ysilrod dragged Sheynon to the doorway, dropped to his knees, and incanted beside his brother's form.

Audrey charged once more, dove beneath a swing within the air, rolled behind the armored figure, and drove the sterling point of *Mír'rë Cala'wyne* deep and through the back of the knee where no armor showed. The figure staggered, yet did not fall, and Thalion's *Gil Estel* battered hard away at the full-face helm.

Audrey rose, and the figure turned, a heavy blow aimed at her head. She parried, dodged a second swing, drove *Mír'rë Cala'wyne* up and through the empty helm, then charged again, her sword embedded through an eye-slit. She drove the figure back, crashed into the earthen wall, and held it there. The figure could not raise its sword, as she pinned its arm between the breastplate and her body.

"Ysilrod!" Thalion called, and the elf-mage shouted in return.

"Hold for moments! Sheynon needs my aid!"

Thalion turned and ran to the entryway. "Go, I will tend him! Audrey needs your Craft!"

The warrior-woman let out a cry and spun away as the figure drove her to the side. It swung again, the blow only blocked away in part, and Audrey's bright blood sprayed across the shining breastplate. She grimaced, fell back, then gathered up herself and charged again.

They met in the ash and wreckage of the forge, blows exchanged and knocked away, *NorthWind* and *Mír'rë Cala'wyne* ringing in the scattered torchlight. Sparks flew in the air as enchanted steel met Dwarven forging, neither giving way.

"My lady, get away!" Ysilrod's voice cut through the clamor, and Audrey leapt aside. Something unseen lifted her and dropped her none too gently behind a pile of rubble, as a roaring blast of heat and light filled the chamber fully.

Audrey covered up her head as debris rained down about her. Twice she was struck by falling stones, and she curled herself more tightly.

Then silence.

She coughed, lifted up her head and peered above the shattered brickwork of the forge. Heavy air hung within the chamber, and scattered bits of armor lay about. She rose and limped her way through the rubble, as Ysilrod rose from kneeling. A shimmer in the air about him slowly dissipated, and Audrey knew he had formed a shield of magic about himself at the doorway.

She eased herself onto a pile of bricks, breathing heavily, a hand pressed against her side, blood leaking between her fingers. Ysilrod aided her into the antechamber, laid her on the settee, and pressed a hand against her wound.

Her eyes grew dim, but Thalion's voice was strong within her ears. "You will live, Excellency, and another story to tell your children." His hand touched her forehead, warm and welcome, and the pain, only in this moment she had noticed, slipped away as she closed her eyes and slept.

* * *

Slowly, Audrey woke from a dreamless sleep. Sheynon sat away in a corner, his arm in a sling across his chest, and a heavy bandage round his neck. Ysilrod and Thalion stood at the doorway, backs to the anteroom, talking lowly, words Audrey could not hear.

"My lords…" She coughed and cleared her parched throat, and Thalion came to her with a waterskin in hand. He aided her to rise, and she sat, then drank. "The sentinel?"

"Vanquished by your hand and that of Ysilrod." He motioned 'cross his shoulder. "Still, Excellency, you are the warrior, it seems."

Audrey looked to the bloodstained chainmail, the ragged cut across it, and the bandage there beneath. "It would seem my speed is not what it once was." She smiled wryly, and Thalion grinned in return.

Ysilrod turned. "Sheynon will survive, tho' his wounds were severe. Once he is awakened, we will depart this place."

"We cannot go without his waking?" Audrey asked.

Ysilrod looked to Thalion, and the priest nodded, then the elf-mage continued. "There is a thing he must do, that is… of our discussion earlier."

"And you, my lady?" Thalion motioned to her side. "Might you take your feet?"

Audrey rose, wincing at the tightness below her ribs, and nodded. "I will live, yet may not like it at the first."

Ysilrod had gathered up the damaged armor, set it in the ruin of the forge, and conjured a shield of magic all around it. Audrey paced gently into the chamber and looked within, marveling at the finish, now grey and colorless. "The magic is gone," she said, a note of sadness in her voice.

"All but the sword," replied Thalion, now at her side. "And this is what Ysilrod speaks of."

"I do not understand."

He motioned back into the vestibule. "For now, rest and wait for Sheynon's waking. We may have found a bit of magic of our own to give him hope and courage."

* * *

Nothing came to threaten them, and as time passed and they kept the vigil, Sheynon slowly stirred. Audrey tended him as Thalion slept and Ysilrod stood sentry at the doorway.

The elf-lord rose to sitting and laid his head against the stones. "It appeared from nothing, stepped before me as I turned, and all I can recall is pain and blood, my very own."

"You shouted warning, and Ysilrod took you from harm's way." Audrey offered the wineskin and he took it, drinking deeply.

"You and the Lord Priest battled it to submission, yes?" He grinned weakly, and Audrey laid a hand upon his shoulder.

"It was your brother's talents that saved us all."

Sheynon was quiet for a moment, eyes closed and breathing softly. Audrey stood when he opened up his eyes and took her hand. "Still, we know not where she is."

"No, yet closer, without doubt. That she would send this sentinel says she fears us and knows we hunt her. Justice will find her in the end, my friend."

Sheynon gave a wry chuckle 'neath his breath. "Justice. I cannot know the word in this time. If justice, why was it not done before? How can justice come, if those who hold it in their hands decline its use?"

Audrey knelt again. "You speak of Steffyn, yet forgave him in that time. Now you reconsider?"

Sheynon did not answer, only closed his eyes and sighed.

Ysilrod came to them and held a hand to Sheynon. "Come, Brother, as I have a gift for you. Audrey, wake Thalion, if you will."

Sheynon's eyes found Audrey's, but she only shrugged, then moved to the priest and roused him gently. They all made way into the forge room once again, to see the armor gathered in a heap.

"There," said Ysilrod, pointing to the sentinel's sword atop the pile. "Take it, as you need a worthy weapon."

Sheynon only stared as he leaned against Audrey's arm supporting him. His eyes were wide, his face filled with thoughts and emotions they all could read as an open tome. His hand slowly reached for the leather-covered hilt.

285

The sword was large, yet balanced well enough to be wielded with a single hand. Sheynon held it aloft, torchlight glinting off the edges. A fuller ran the length upon both sides, the blade tapered to a gleaming point. The crossguard was of heavy brass, and the pommel disc-shaped and thick. The *NorthWind* rune stared out from the pommel, blood-red and angry in its look.

"Take it," said Audrey. "May *Jhad* forgive me for my words, but this becomes your vengeance weapon, my lord. One worthy of your heart."

Sheynon nodded slowly and let go a breath. "Thank you, Brother. My thanks to all of you."

Ysilrod gave a slight bow. "Let us leave this place, for now I have a link to this Mors'ul'jyn and can follow her wherever she may go."

* * *

On the Road to Drakenmoore…

Near four days to Jeseriam from DragonFall, a day of rest, then pausing at the shop of Stokar before departing for the ruins of Drakenmoore. The bell above the door rang cheerily as they entered, and the old half-elf shopkeeper looked up from his counter and grinned around his ever-present pipe. "The secret lovers return to grace my presence once more."

Aeren rolled her eyes as Chitthra gave Stokar a look of disinterest. They approached, the dark elf woman's voice but a whisper. "We seek information, should you have it, of Drakenmoore and the mad woman."

Stokar motioned to customers, then to the backroom, and the women nodded. They passed through the beaded curtain to find a table set with cheese and bread and beef, and a pitcher of dark ale awaiting. Aeren chuckled, sat and began to eat, as Chitthra paced and looked about.

"Nothing changes here," the dark elf woman said, noting the simple room. "It is tho' Stokar and his shop set beyond the realm of time, waiting for questions, offering aid, or wisdom when ears and minds are closed."

Aeren poured two tankards full. "My liege has said many times, do not question blessings when shown, but give thanks for them, and repay in kind when able."

Stokar entered before Chitthra could reply. "Well met once more. Sit, and tell me of your troubles."

Chitthra's mood was dark enough, and Stokar's teasing banter sat ill upon her mind. Yet she took a chair as he did the same, ignoring the offered meal, as Stokar watched. At last she spoke, knowing there was little reason to hide the truth from this enigma of a half-elf. "Steffyn

Foxxe lives, and we have seen him. Hidden as Drow for many years, still he tracks Mors'ul'jyn, as do we. Truly, we know not where to go, and only follow comrades to the ruins, in support if nothing else."

Stokar nodded, then pointed to her with his pipe stem. "This has come full circle, has it not? A blade, forged and cursed in *NorthWind*, found to be a prison, yourself and the mad woman, as you call her, placed there by Foxxe himself. Now broken, the trail has led to me once more, where the blade was first revealed."

He mused for moments, then chuckled. "Even I did not know who she was in the beginning. Now she sets the whole of the land upon a dagger point."

"What would you have of us, my lord?" asked Aeren. "You know it all, and in five years have done nothing to assist. You claim to be a friend of elves and family Calidriil, yes? Yet tragedy and heartbreak sought Sheynon once again."

"Stokar saved the life of Earion," said Chitthra softly.

"And for each victory comes a price," added the old half-elf, and Aeren only frowned.

Stokar poured their tankards full once more. "I know nothing, other than Archane is gone from Mors'ul'jyn's holding."

Chitthra's eyes grew wide, and Aeren closed her eyes and whispered prayers beneath her breath. At the last Chitthra found courage to speak once more. "I will not ask how you know this, for it does not matter. Does she live, is my only question."

Stokar grinned. "Question not does she live, but does she live again?"

Aeren paused her cup. "Her immortality is known, as my liege herself was witness to it years ago. You say she has died again and returned? If so, where might we search?"

Chitthra raised a hand. "No matter, for Archane is not of our concern, only Mors'ul'jyn."

"Yet Archane —"

"Chitthra is correct," said Stokar, as he filled his pipe. "If Archane is alive, she will only seek her way back to *Ung'gu'wi*."

"My liege would argue the point of her importance, I am certain."

Stokar chuckled. "And lose the debate, for the Drow are no longer a threat, yes? Defeated twice, their armies decimated, and now the Houses immersed in a struggle for power and leadership... Archane will have more than her two hands may carry."

"This must be told to Thalion and the others," said Aeren. "Whatever strategy they have will likely change."

"A point to consider," said Chitthra, nodding. She looked to Stokar and smiled. "You are a true friend, my lord, and with hospitality."

Stokar lit his pipe and blew smoke aside. "Use this wisely, and see their focus is to the importance of Mors'ul'jyn. Still, she is the danger, and Archane likely returning to whatever waits in *Ung'gu'wi*."

* * *

They rode from Jeseriam side by side, all the while speaking plans and thoughts and feelings to one another. Though troubled by Stokar's words, it soon was certain their focus should remain as before, and thus, they set aside their worries.

"What shall we do, Dearest?" asked Aeren, after a lengthy quiet.

Chitthra knew of what Aeren asked, and thought upon her answer. "I have not attended my Brotherhood for some time. A pilgrimage would be appropriate, once matters are concluded."

"And then?"

Chitthra blew a breath. "You ask if my love is true and will I stay beside you. The answer is, with all my heart, yet I cannot see beyond the task ahead."

Aeren smiled to herself, a glow within her rising. "Then a homestead and garden in the sunshine? Perhaps to raise horses for the city-states or villages about?" She grinned. "Little ones?"

Chitthra laughed.

* * *

On the Plains of Ardwel...

They had walked eastward half a day, avoiding villages and roads, resting and eating what they could find. A creek ran south, and they followed against the current, twisting their way until the sun was set and ruddy *Selene* grew large above the trees. Still, Steffyn did not know the woman by her name, or why he followed as a pet, or how he might serve her further. Last in his mind, not even as consideration, was escape, for she had bound him as a servant with her charms. Her warm, exquisite, delicious charms his body cried for with every breath he took.

They found a thicket and he draped his cloak, that she could lay without touching grass or twigs or brambles, if she desired. She sat, and he knelt before her, head bowed and waiting only for her voice to fill his ears and spirit. He glanced upward, and her ruby eyes caught his, bringing forth a skip within his heart. Nearly did he cry for her words, or touch, or to feel her breath about his face.

288

"Know you of the forest in the east, beyond the river?"

His ardor rose with the words, and he nodded.

"How far?"

He tried to speak, yet his throat was parched. She offered water in a folded leaf, and he drank it gladly. "Days, perhaps eight or more afoot. Yet the road would take less time."

"Your name, what is it?"

"Stef... Steffyn. Steffyn Foxxe, my lady."

A pause, and he saw a flash of recognition in her eyes. "Foxxe. Have you a son by name of Daeron?"

Pain and sadness nearly overwhelmed him at the mention of the name. His breath came quick for moments, then at the last he calmed himself enough to answer. "He is... no longer in the mortal world."

Her lips slowly twisted to a small smile of satisfaction. Quiet passed between them for a while, then her voice aroused him once again. "How did you come to be injured?"

Steffyn's mind was nearly clear, yet the memories of that time seemed distant. He shook his head slowly, trying to recall. "I do not know... that is, I have no recollection." He touched his face, yet swollen, and his shoulder ached deeply still. "A fall, perhaps, or... I do not know."

"No matter," she replied, "yet we must find a better way."

"Horses?"

She scoffed. "I see none about, nor have we coins to bargain with in a village. Nor would we." She looked away, as in thought. "My return must be silent as a falling leaf in winter. None must know, else plans will fail."

"... plans?"

"Not of your concern. You will aid my journey, nothing more."

Steffyn mulled the answer, certain he had missed a clue. "And then?"

Again, she smiled, this time with knowing in her eyes. "Sleep. Morning we will resume our walk. Should chance come, perhaps we will find fortune."

Steffyn's eyes grew heavy, his mind dimming quickly with her words, and he lay himself in the cooling grasses. His final thought was little more than a glimmer of subservience, before darkness descended like a shadow.

* * *

Drakenmoore...

The campsite at the ruins was larger than they had thought, and as Aeren and Chitthra approached from the road, they were challenged by sentries round. At last Rohesia came and bid them in, and they led their horses to a hastily-built corral, to be tended there by grooming boys.

"They have not returned," Rohesia said, as they made way to her tent in the center of the camp, the standard of DragonFall waving in the breeze before it.

They entered and Rohesia dismissed the guards, offered cushioned chairs to sit, as servants served them tea. "Near ten days they have been gone, and still no good or ill becomes of it. They took no guards, only the four descending, and their thought was they would travel more quickly."

Aeren offered a warm smile. "My lady, you speak of comrades of the ages, never seen before or since within this land. Guards or soldiers would only be a hindrance."

Rohesia sipped. "What news of DragonFall? Was your audience granted with His Majesty?"

Chitthra shook her head. "No news of importance, and the king was busy otherwise, I am certain. Therefore, we departed, to offer what we may herein."

"What of Archane, and the events at the palace grounds?"

Chitthra exchanged a glance with Aeren before she spoke again. "My lady, there is little known, and we only wait for the safe return of Sheynon and his comrades."

"There is a tent away you may use as needed in your stay," said Rohesia. "And my thoughts are with them in the labyrinth."

Commotion from without was heard, guards running to the south where the ruins lay, voices rising in the evening quiet. They quickly took their exit from the tent, following the crowd, and in only moments spied the four companions emerging from the shattered gates of Drakenmoore.

"My liege is injured," said Aeren, and she ran to Audrey's side. Chitthra caught her, then aided Sheynon as she could, the elf worn and dirty, as were they all. They led the four to a campfire, then called a healer.

Camp runners helped Sheynon to a tent, Ysilrod nodding Chitthra and Aeren to follow, as Thalion fell in behind. Audrey rose on Aeren's arm, and they made way to cheers and lifted cups, as the camp began to celebrate their safe return.

All the while, no words were said, and they walked to the tent in quiet, as Thalion whispered to Rohesia to set guards about as necessary.

The tent flap closed, and twenty mercenaries took places round the pavilion. The sun set low, and grand *Selene* rose full and ruddy in the east, as the camp milled in curiosity.

They waited there within, all the while looks of deep concern passing between Chitthra, Aeren, and Rohesia. Ysilrod held a finger to his lips and shook his head as the healer tended each one with skilled fingers, salves and ointments with vile scents applied to wounds looking days old at the least. They drained two waterskins, and at the last a servant came with a platter filled with meat and bread and greens.

The healer bowed and took her exit, and they gathered closely in the center of the tent, eating quietly, and saying only gentle words between them.

At the last, Thalion nodded to Ysilrod, and the elf-mage rose, said a quiet incantation, and waved his hands with purpose about them all. A shimmer formed about the tent walls, then he turned and nodded to the priest.

"We are sealed within safety for a time," said Ysilrod, as he sat beside Sheynon once again.

"My Liege, my lords, we give praises for your deliverance," said Aeren softly, then let go a breath of great relief.

Thalion looked to the others, then nodded thanks. "There is much to tell, and I will yield to Ysilrod for our account."

Rohesia poured tea into the elf-mage's cup, and he drank before beginning. "Mors'ul'jyn is certainly alive and dangerous as we always knew. The forge is but a ruin, as is the dungeon itself, and for the most part, vacant. Yet we have advantage now, as I hold a way to find her."

Chitthra, Aeren, and Rohesia looked to each other, eyes wide and filled with questions.

"I shall not reveal it for the nonce, yet ask you, inform your king we soon may deal with the mad woman, and he may sleep again at night."

"A thousand thanks to you, my lord," said Rohesia, bowing in her chair. "Kaul's worries are deep and real, not only for himself, but his family."

"With all respect," said Sheynon tightly, "Kaul knows little of the fear felt by those Mors'ul'jyn truly holds as guilty for crimes against her family as she sees them."

"I… meant no disrespect, Your Lordship," replied Rohesia, flushing.

"None taken. Only a reminder, one I am certain Kaul is aware of."

"Your injuries." Chitthra spoke to calm the air about them.

Audrey grinned to Thalion, and the priest chuckled lightly. "Taken in battle for the first time in many years," she said. "The spirit is willing, yet the flesh weaker than in that time."

"You live, My Liege," said Aeren, smiling, "therefore you were victorious."

"By the knowledge and skills of my brother," said Sheynon, clasping Ysilrod's shoulder. "Even *NorthWind* is no match for the elven Arts."

They touched cup rims and drank, as the others gave a soft cheer and toast.

"My Liege, my lords, there is other news," said Aeren. She glanced to Chitthra, who nodded. "Steffyn Foxxe lives, and we have seen him."

Sheynon drew his cup from his lips, his face nearly unreadable.

"When and where, my lady?" asked Thalion.

"DragonFall," replied Chitthra, "hidden as a dark elf mage by name of Mend'rys, with a servant girl. However..."

"Where is he now?" asked Ysilrod, suddenly intent.

Chitthra did not answer, yet Aeren offered reply. "Unknown. We found him, yet he escaped, leaving his servant in our care. We saw her to their hideaway where she will be safe."

"Five years he has been missing," whispered Sheynon, "and now I find he has abandoned his former life, and for what reasons?"

Aeren again replied. "My lord, he tracks Mors'ul'jyn, seeking to make amends for what was done... or not done, as it were."

Sheynon looked to Ysilrod. "Brother, might you find him for us?"

The elf-mage thought for moments as Rohesia once more poured tea around. Aeren moved closer to Chitthra, as Audrey did the same with Sheynon. She held a hand to him, and he took it, trembling.

"Have you an artifact of his he touched or carried?" asked Ysilrod.

Sheynon shook his head. "Nothing I can recall this moment. Yet surely at *Barad Anna*..."

"Dearest *Jhad*," said Audrey, signing herself. "His wife has not seen him in more than twenty years, and now this. Abandonment and self-torture, seeking only absolution."

"Steffyn Foxxe is gone, Excellency," said Chitthra, then held her hand as Audrey's face grew taut. "He is mad with guilt and thoughts of setting right what he may with his own hands. I fear he has a death-wish, and nothing will deter him from his vengeance."

"We must find him," said Sheynon, and Audrey nodded wordlessly.

Thalion looked quickly to his cousin. "It is Mors'ul'jyn who is our goal, is it not? We have advantage, yet for how long? We must proceed as planned, else we cannot know where next she may strike. Or whom."

Aeren looked to Chitthra, then the dark elf woman spoke. "There is another revelation, given us by Stokar."

"You have seen the old half-elf?" Sheynon shook his head and chuckled wryly. "The whole of the land, it seems, becomes involved."

Chitthra drew a breath, continuing. "Archane has escaped the grasp of Mors'ul'jyn."

Her words brought silence to the tent for many moments.

Sheynon hung his head. "I know not what to say, events around us moving different ways."

"How did she escape, if you might know?" asked Audrey.

"Unknown, My Liege," replied Aeren, "tho' surely she seeks to make way to her people."

Ysilrod rose and paced away in quiet, and all eyes followed him. At last he turned. "Too many changes, Brother, and in my mind, not coincidence."

"What do you say, my lord?" asked Thalion.

"For the moment, I am not certain, but still we have a task. Let us continue as tho' things are as they were. In that time, I will find out what I may. For if plans change, Mors'ul'jyn will once again have time to consider her own movements."

* * *

The night was late as Sheynon walked the campsite in the waning blush of *Selene* and the bright silvery light of *Mina* at the zenith.

Too many changes once again, too many ways chaos seeks its hold on Ardwel as we scratch and scrabble for answers refusing to come forth. What now, Great Yarhetha'an, must we endure, as enemies of old and enemies long forgotten seek our blood once more? He sighed, pausing near a sentry line, closed his eyes, and shook his head in sadness.

"Sheynon?" He turned at Audrey's voice and gave a bow. She offered a mug of tea, and they drank together in the darkness for a while.

"What will you do, should we find Steffyn in our travels?"

Sheynon only shrugged and drank again. "What would you have of me, my lady? Five years ago I offered him forgiveness, and now I find he has forsaken everything. His wife, his kindred, even the tower established to become his sanctuary. He hides among the Drow, takes a servant, who surely is more to him than that, and seeks to change what cannot be changed, no matter his attempts or skills."

"I have spoken with Aeren of their finding of him. They had him in their power, yet Aeren begged Chitthra for his life. His escape was only due to their knowing he was once your trusted friend."

293

Sheynon drank a long draught, then coughed aside. "Perhaps they should have killed him, to end his suffering."

"And yours, my lord? Truly, Sheynon, you have done all you can for Steffyn. There comes a time when we must face transgressions as they were made. Steffyn owes family Calidriil dearly, to say nothing of Elvenkind itself. This is a debt he cannot repay, and he knows this, regardless your forgiving him."

A moment passed in silence. "And so?"

"Hold dear all around you, my friend. Let us find those guilty and exact our justice. I understand your feelings well, for once I had them of myself."

Sheynon turned to Audrey, a question in his eyes.

"Yes, long ago in Argonnian Castle, as you recall, I slew Ajax Argonnian, thinking he had killed Damien, the Overlord. Yet he had not, and my penance done was for a year. Still that sin rests on my soul, and never will it be forgotten."

"All herein have killed, for reasons great and small, my lady."

Audrey nodded. "Yet here was a time when Steffyn knew right from wrong, and chose unwisely, costing lives. Your forgiveness of him, if I may be so bold, was for your own release as much as his."

Sheynon mulled her words, nodding at the last, then gave a dry chuckle. "You speak the hard words as friend Tarnak himself, my lady. Well said."

Audrey smiled, and they touched cup rims and drank again. "Words to carry on the true and righteous fight, my lord. We are comrades, not only of the sword, but of the heart."

* * *

PART TWO
SKY ABOVE, WORLD BELOW

In the Depths of Drakenmoore…

Mors'ul'jyn stood before the conjuring mirror, trembling. Though she had no Sight within the forge, she had been confident of her *NorthWind* ability against whomever the intruders were. Yet now, that ability was gone, for she no longer felt the thread of magic between herself and the armor she had fashioned.

She paced before the mirror, little shown within it but a swirl of darkened clouds and rain, reflecting of her feelings. Archane was dead… Mor'i'jil she killed by her own hand… and now, her enemies held a link between themselves and her.

The sword, and if not destroyed, they will keep it. What now? I cannot stay awake forever to defend myself. And eventually, they will find their way into my sanctuary.

It will take time for them to read the magic in the sword, tho' less than I might think. Tho' the forge is gone, still there may be a way to know with whom I deal.

She set protections round the walls, ensuring there were no voids within the spells. Even on the floors and ceiling did she cast enchantments, that none could enter without penetrating magics learned in more than fifty years of study. Blessings, too, were set within, of *Urijah*, God of the Forge, the one who blessed the creations born of those fires. Yet not only did these protect her from those seeking entrance, but sealed her furthermore within. And with guards and wards lighting up her sanctuary, she sat once more, exhausted, drinking tea.

For the nonce, I am protected, yet cannot remain for long, as food and water, to say nothing of the air to breathe, will be consumed. Somehow, some way, I must draw them in, yet leave a way for my escape.

Arms folded on the table, she lay down her head to rest, collecting thoughts of where she might then go. She drifted into fitful sleep, mumbled words in Drow and human tongue, then woke with a start. Raising up her head, she smiled.

I must go to Ung'gu'wi, a place I may hide among so many others of ability. And perhaps I will encounter Archane again, and as planned and told, steal away her body. I may become the Dark Princess and lead the Drow! Then I will take my vengeance upon all the land, and my enemies but a sacrifice upon the altar!

* * *

295

Dennis Young

Beyond the Black Forest…

Three days beyond the forest in rain and weather growing cooler in the nights, Ry'lld and Lualyrr now found themselves in dire straits. Once highwaymen had been avoided, and now they ran before a pack of wolves growing closer with each moment. Little did they have but daggers and a broken staff Ry'lld had found set beside a tree. All they might do was run, as fatigue and desolation set heavy in their hearts.

"Ahead! A cottage!" Lualyrr shouted with what little breath she had, then turned as Ry'lld screamed behind her. Down he went, his boot caught in a fallen branch, and three swift, gray shapes descended on him in a heartbeat. Lualyrr stopped, took up a rock, and tossed it at a wolf, striking it upon the head. The animal yelped, ran away, as the others sought Ry'lld's flesh.

Another rock, another strike, and the dark elf priest kicked away the third creature, rose on shaky legs, and bolted to the west, trailing dark blood. He caught Lualyrr's hand and she pulled him along, and with the sun growing dimmer in the trees, they ran for their very lives as the pack took up the chase once more.

Into an open entryway, slamming shut the door, then looking round as braying wolves threw themselves against cottage, gnashing teeth and howling with such a din, Lualyrr screamed and covered up her ears.

A wolf crawled through an open shutter, and Ry'lld beat it senseless, drew his dagger and cut its throat before it could recover. Then he closed and latched the shutters, then another, and another, and lay his back against the shuddering door.

"Are you injured?" He called to Lualyrr as she lay upon the rough-hewn wooden floor. "Are you hurt? Speak to me!" Again, the door shook, dust from the thatched roof drifting down, and Ry'lld pressed hard against the entry, the dagger in his hand. Teeth clenched, eyes closed tightly and tears trickling down in anger, sadness, and deep-seated fear, he dug his boots harder into the floor beneath them.

Then Lualyrr was there, pressing with him on the doorway, and at the last, the wolves ceased their attack, and only cried beyond the cottage.

Ry'lld slid to his haunches, back still against the door, as Lualyrr pressed hard against him, and he wrapped her in his arms. He breathed at last, and let the fear trickle from his spirit, as she lay in his embrace, sobbing softly.

* * *

296

Ry'lld woke with a start, his back still against the door. He rose and stretched the stiffness out, then gasped at the wounds upon his side. "Never did I feel it," he said softly, noting three deep rents within his flesh, and the ragged edges of his tunic.

His injuries had been cleaned and he looked to Lualyrr sitting at the table. "My thanks." He gave a bow, and she looked to him and smiled. He noted his surroundings, a single lantern burning by the doorway, and darkness seen beyond the shutters. "Where is this place?"

"A haven for the nonce," Lualyrr replied, motioning around.

The cottage was small and simple; two rooms, the largest with a hearth. Hand-hewn chairs rested in the corners, the table set for four with wooden plates and cups. Ry'lld walked carefully into the second room, three beds there seen, one larger and two smaller. A nightstand held another lantern and a book. He glanced at the cover, yet the script was not one he knew.

"Human tongue," said Lualyrr from the doorway, "and this." She held a parchment to the light, the words faded, with letters having run as though water splashed upon them.

"You can read it?"

She nodded. "It says the family left this place, returning to the city."

Ry'lld shook his head. "What city? Of Kaul, perhaps, or another?"

Lualyrr shrugged. "It does not say, tho' it begs whoever finds it, keep the cottage as their own."

Ry'lld blinked in disbelief. "Why would... I do not understand."

She came to him softly, closely, draped her arms about his neck, careful to avoid his wounds. "It means, dear priest, prayers have been answered, tho' not as we thought they would be."

"You wish to... stay here? With me?" Ry'lld drew back to see her face in the flickering lantern-light. "I am no farmer, nor a cattle-tender."

Lualyrr nodded to the door. "There is a garden behind the cottage, and with work, we may survive. We have hunted and gathered in the forest, fought wolves and escaped torture. Surely a more gentle life would not be a terrible thing to consider. And more..." She took his hand and placed it on her belly, then met his eyes demurely.

Ry'lld's face nearly lost its darkened color and his mouth moved without sound. They stood in silence for many moments, then he drew her deeply into his arms. "Praise *Iyllyeth*," he said with reverence, then chuckled into her hair. He drew back, tears glistening in his eyes. "Will you now sacrifice me to the goddess?"

Lualyrr cast off her dirty tunic, then took his hands gently to her breasts, grinning wickedly. "With all the passion in my body, Dark Lord."

* * *

Ung'gu'wi...

The return of Aysa'lil and Kreothren from Warinethra lay as a wound upon the spirit of Ba'tula. For her clergy had been turned away, not allowed within the halls and chambers of that great House, only met by acolytes with insincere excuses for having been ignored. And with such a harmful slight, Ba'tula met once more with her Lancer Captains, orders to press the fight given with stirring words and veiled threats of punishments.

"*Iyllyeth* watches, and *Mother Darkness* will have her due," railed the matriarch of Hovenethra. "For sacrifice is demanded of us all. Glorious battle awaits in the chambers of Archane's House, by conquest or honorable death, it matters not! Go, and show the strength of Hovenethra with sword and arrow and songs raised to the glory of the Race! Find their weakness and exploit it! Bring back the heads of those who dare oppose our righteous doing!"

The Lancer Captains bowed and left her presence, muttering beneath their breath and casting glances one to the other. With rumor of Warinethra's warning, and the Houses of Karachitthra and Modennethra yet standing from the conflict, plans were few for victory.

Yet no matter. Ba'tula had spoken with her edict, and as said, only battle there awaited. It was a soldier's lot to fight and die, and should they not find worthy the words of leaders who did not fight, they would find glory for the Race, and the waiting arms of *Iyllyeth* in the Darkness of the Afterlife.

* * *

Ba'tula's senior Lancer Captain waited in a niche aside the passageway, scouts sent forth and skirmishers poised to probe the passages secured by other Houses. In time, ten soldiers made way back into the recess, to a tiny chamber where servants tended wounds and set refreshments at their sides.

"What say you, Volkirk?" The Lancer Captain chuckled as the veteran quaffed a cup of wine and a healer sewed a cut upon his arm.

"It was as they knew our coming! Ten waited as we passed, then descended on our rear ranks. Ten more to either side, and as we turned to fight, their main garrison trapped us in between. Only by the grace of *Iyllyeth* did so many live."

He slammed the cup upon the table. "This stinks of sorcery! Surely Warinethra aids the House of Iyllyeth, giving warning! Treachery is in our midst, and all because…"

His words trailed with a warning look from the Lancer Captain, who glanced to the others listening. "Say only what was done, nothing more. Let us not speak of what we do not know for certain."

Volkirk slowly calmed, then spoke. "Six scout leaders left of a dozen. Thirty soldiers surviving without wounds of near three score, and too many others being tended."

"And worse it might have been," replied the Lancer Captain. "Yet this is not a battle, but a holding action, nothing more. Holding for the return of Archane, or Mor'i'jil more likely." *And Alystin becomes the match for Ba'tula,* he thought. *What says this of our matriarch?*

"What of Warinethra?" asked Volkirk, returning the Lancer Captain's thoughts to their predicament. "I do not see the scout leaders probing there here among us."

"Here." A voice came from behind them as a ragged figure entered. She was singed about as burned, the stench of smoldering leather armor filling the room quickly. Volkirk coughed and turned his head, nearly retching. The Lancer Captain raised his chin and tensed himself for the coming words.

"All dead save my own self," said the woman. "Once within the leading chamber, we were trapped by a simple spell. They laughed as we ran burning, jeering as we cried."

Two healers came to her side, but she brushed them away. "The soldiers of Archane's House we can match, but cannot stand against Warinethra's magics! Words say Ba'tula was warned against this, yet pressed the fight! Now we stand alone!"

"Never are we alone, Latu'le, as *Iyllyeth* stands at our side."

Latu'le spat. "Send me not again into Warinethra. I am not afraid to die, yet will not burn to satisfy Ba'tula's lust for power!" With that she turned, not saluting as she left.

The Lancer Captain motioned to the healers standing silent. "Go. See to her hurts and tend her well. See she is fed and given wine." He looked to Volkirk once again. "Your thoughts?"

Volkirk only chuckled dryly.

* * *

299

In the House of Iyllyeth, Alystin met once more with the Inner Circle, Xa'lyyth, Vrammyr, Molva'yas, Narlros, and Krenasst all attending.

"Speak of our fortunes," said Alystin, as servants exited the meeting chamber and closed the doors.

Narlros sipped wine and gave a bow. "Dark Lady, as instructed, our soldiers do not press the fight, only defend the House. With Warinethra's warning, and as your wisdom has perceived, only do we protect ourselves against Hovenethra's soldiers."

"What of the other Houses?" asked Vrammyr, eating as she spoke. She was known to be a glutton with little interest beyond food and drink, and many times Alystin had petitioned Mor'i'jil to replace the old priestess. Yet still she held many favorites in the clergy, as she was eldest next to the dark lord himself.

Too many well-placed spies, thought Alystin, *too many favors yet to be collected. Should Mor'i'jil... when Mor'i'jil returns, I will ask again for his consideration.*

She shook herself back to attention as Xa'lyyth replied to the older priestess. "A point to be considered, and I will take the duty, if Narlros will accompany me."

"You have done honors to our House," said Alystin, before Vrammyr could reply. "It is time others do the same. Molva'yas and Krenasst shall prepare a mission to Modennethra, then we will confer regarding Karachitthra. It is my hope Modennethra will take up a place beside us."

"And Karachitthra?" Vrammyr drained her cup and refilled it, ignoring Alystin's hard glare. "Their House was weakened in the battles against elves and humans, yet to be rebuilt. Perhaps an opportunity therein?"

Alystin knew well Vrammyr's meaning, yet answered feigning innocence. "Surely you do not think of war against a House with ties deep and rich unto our own."

Vrammyr shrugged. "One less worry would be advantage, yes?"

"Shall you lead the charge, Dark Lady?" Molva'yas chuckled as Narlros at his side turned away, hiding a malicious grin. "Will your armor yet fit your figure, let alone your priestly robes, which, to my knowing, you have remade many times."

Vrammyr gave a withering glance to the priest as Alystin held a hand. "Enough of this. Molva'yas and Krenasst shall proceed with all haste. Dark Priestess Vrammyr will lead the Second Circle in prayer and sacrifice this day and on the morrow. Xa'lyyth and Narlros will attend me here for private words."

Vrammyr's eyes narrowed. "Words of what sort, Dark Lady? Surely the Black Web must know of what you speak."

Alystin nodded. "And once decisions made, we will confer further."

"Yet —"

Alystin raised the silver bell. "As said, enough. Mor'i'jil set my own self to rule in his stead. Final decisions shall be mine until the Dark Lord reappears."

"Or Archane herself? You think you are capable, and may lead this House?"

"She is." Narlros's voice carried deep warning. "And you are aware of precedent, that Mor'i'jil, in ruling in Archane's stead, may choose the one to lead, should he be absent." The priest looked hard upon Vrammyr, pointing his finger at the opulence of food and drink before her. "Tend your manners and your vices. Once you were worthy of the Black Web, yet now I am not so certain."

"Enough," said Alystin again, the silver bell yet in her hand. "We have no time for pettiness. This House is absent two leaders and we must be of one mind. All of us." She looked to Narlros, then Vrammyr, both of whom dropped their eyes and nodded silently. "Molva'yas, Krenasst, prepare your journey. I will instruct a Lancer Captain on escorts and protection." She looked once more around the circle. "Give prayers to *Iyllyeth* and *Mother Darkness* for deliverance."

* * *

The door had closed moments before, yet Alystin kept her counsel. Xa'lyyth and Narlros waited for her words as the others of the Black Web had taken exit. She paced before the altar, brushing hands across the onyx surface, and glancing briefly at the sculpture on the wall, its eyes glowing deeply as dark embers.

At last the priestess turned to the waiting pair. "This impasse must be broken. If Modennethra will not join the struggle, little choice is left but proceeding on our own."

Narlros glanced aside to Xa'lyyth, then chose words with unmitigated care. "Dark Lady… did we not receive warning from the sorcerers of Warinethra? Would such course of action not bring them into the fray?"

"Indeed, Dark Lord, and it is my sincere hope it does. Yet first, we will invite their leaders to a council, to hear our plea, and know our cause is just."

"And should they not accept our reasons?" asked Narlros, worry showing on his face.

Alystin drew closer. "It matters not, for in that time we will strike the blow, capture Ba'tula and her Circle, holding them hostage against further... rebellion."

Narlros began to speak, then closed his mouth, not knowing what to say.

"Dark Lady, you have shown such patience in this time, difficult more than any we have seen in years. Might your plans be hasty?" Xa'lyyth's words were quiet and filled with respect.

"They might, yes, yet I see no better course. I ask your counsel, for you both have proven well your dedication to this House. I trust no others as I do the two of you."

Again, Narlros looked to Xa'lyyth, and they bowed deeply before Alystin together.

Alystin continued. "We know nothing of Archane or Mor'i'jil, their place, their fate, or how to find them. Word comes humans of the city-state called 'Truth', and that of Kaul, search the catacombs of Drakenmoore, yet no word of either." She struggled with the human terms, cleared her throat, and continued. "Nor of this Mors'ul'jyn, the perpetrator of all that now consumes the land."

"Then we should go to them," said Xa'lyyth. "Beg aid and offer service. Dark Lady, there is no greater quest than the finding of Archane whole and safe. Our people fear the worst, and tho' your hand is steady, hearts beat quickly as this confrontation widens."

Alystin considered, paced away once more, then turned. "You know this place, these human castle ruins?"

Xa'lyyth shook her head. "Dark Lady, no, yet we know the city-state of Kaul." She shuddered with bitter memory, then closed her eyes and whispered prayers. "I would stand before him once again, tho' he defiled me and caused shame, to learn whatever might be done to reclaim the Dark Princess. Surely the humans seeking this Mors'ul'jyn will be more willing to hear our part."

Alystin looked to Narlros. "Your thoughts, Dark Lord?"

Narlros looked to Xa'lyyth. "I would stand beside her in this duty. Yet I implore you, send soldiers with us, that should we find word, we may keep Archane safe for her return." He shrugged. "And ourselves, if you will."

Alystin nodded after pondering for a moment. "Very well. Yet prepare your prayers, that you may send messages if necessary. I will not have you unarmed in this journey. Surely the humans know Archane is missing by this time, and the danger of Mors'ul'jyn. Deal as you must with

302

them." She looked to Xa'lyyth again. "They will not seek tender flesh as payment, but recompense. Bargain for the Race, yet not its safety. Archane must return, or the whole of Drow will become naught but a memory in this land."

* * *

Beyond the Black Forest…

Within Steffyn's mind there was a wall, pausing his thoughts from proceeding in directions he wished with all his spirit for them to go. Somewhere, somehow, he knew he must escape, as danger sang in every fiber of his being. Escape the sensations of subservience, the desire to simply obey without a single question, the deliciousness of her body, her charms, her touch…

There it was; his answer. For he knew, in some corner in his consciousness, it was a Charm that had been laid upon him by her touch, her voice, her very breath about his face, as she spoke close and warm and pulled him into ecstasy once more.

How to resist? How to break the Charm? How to say no to commands speaking deep within his spirit, leaving him a slave to whatever she might wish?

"Speak."

Steffyn shook himself from his reverie. Again, she touched his mind, and he looked to her through a haze of growing lust. "I… did not hear your question. I beg forgiveness."

"Say your thoughts." She knelt closely, as she always did, her hair a shroud of white against dark skin, eyes as rubies in the waning sunlight, her lips beckoning his words.

He glanced about, the forest preparing for the coming of cooler weather. He shivered. "Shelter is needed in this time. Still perhaps six days before we reach the Silver River if by foot." He glanced to his tattered tunic, then to her belted garb. "Surely we will need of clothing."

She touched his head, then rose to pace away. He thought to stand, yet could not force his legs to move, and knew it was the Charm again. Still, little could he do but understand the meaning.

"One day more, and we will travel dawn to dusk. A farm, or perhaps a village, where we may find aid." She turned. "And as said before, horses to speed our journey."

"I have no coin."

303

She grinned wickedly. "Yet you are clever, and at night a gate may come unlatched. There are more ways than even that to garner what we need."

Steffyn bowed his head. "You would steal from honest folk?"

Her eyes flashed, and nearly did he stagger, even on his knees. His breath caught heavily, and he gasped, a hand held to his chest. "Please, I mean no disrespect..."

Her face softened, yet only slightly, and the pain subsided in his heart. She knelt before him, opening her tunic slowly. His eyes sought her flesh beneath and he raised his hands to touch her.

"Morning, and you will be satisfied again," she said, a promise as her words caressed his face. "For now, find fruit and water. Return before the sun has set."

Steffyn bowed his head and stood, looking to the trees about, and began to collect whatever he could find.

* * *

They spied the cottage from the edge of the woods and paused before proceeding. Steffyn shuddered with the cold, not only of the cloudy morning, but rain hanging heavy in the air and wind from the north bringing it into the plains. He looked to her, arms wrapped about herself, uncomfortable as he, mulling thoughts as how best to proceed.

"Look!" Steffyn pointed to the cottage, seeing dark figures emerging from the doorway. Two there were, one male and one a female, and they made way to the garden where they gathered greens and other things.

"Drow." Her voice was soft and tinged with great relief. She turned to him. "You are my servant and companion. We have traveled from... what place is to the west?"

Steffyn's thoughts moved slowly. "Telveperen. Yet perhaps a village of dark elves is where we met."

She nodded. "As you say, and we have journeyed nearly for a moon and now seek shelter. Surely these farmers do not know our faces."

"Should I not know your name?" Steffyn closed his eyes, seeking clarity of his thoughts. Surely, he knew who this woman was, though did not know her face!

"You are mute and will not speak, therefore I took you in." She showed a cruel smile. "Humans shunned you, yet a kind-hearted dark elf woman gave you shelter."

Steffyn only nodded, thought to answer and found his tongue unwilling. He clenched his fists, seeking desperate release from the Charm upon his spirit.

They walked their way beyond the copse, to the road aside the cottage, and made approach. She walked as though she owned the world, and Steffyn stayed two paces to her left behind, his head bowed, hands tucked into his tunic sleeves.

The dark elves at the cottage turned as she called a greeting in her tongue. They stood for a moment, then ran to her, screaming praises in the morning light. They fell to their knees and bowed their heads, and she touched them both with gentle hands. They cried and wailed and raised their hands in exultation, as though having seen a miracle.

And it was only in that moment, as Steffyn stood alone, he realized who this enigma of a woman was and why his spirit crumbled in her presence. For the word they shouted was her very name.

Archane.

* * *

They spent the day in talking, Ry'lld and Lualyrr nearly at Archane's feet, until she bade them set a table for the evening meal. Steffyn had stood in a corner, mute as ordered, and as rain began to fall, he wandered out the doorway when Archane was inattentive.

He walked south along the road, the Charm yet within his mind, then stumbled into the copse of wood and across the stream. Naught was in his clouded mind but to walk, to where he did not know, and as the light of sunset faded, a voice upon the wind caught his ear.

"Return. Return and love me as you did before."

He moaned, collapsed to his knees, then took his head in hands. *No! Stop, or I shall go mad! Stop!*

"Return. My body aches for you!"

He tried to rise and failed, cried mutely, then knelt again and waited. Waited only for her to find him and return him to his fate.

The others came, Ry'lld and Lualyrr, raised him up and led him back into the cottage. In that time, he knew he likely would not live to see the sunrise.

* * *

Along the road to DragonFall...

"Hold!" Ysilrod reined his horse and spurred the gelding to the roadside. Sheynon, Audrey, and Thalion followed closely by

305

as Rohesia called the column to a halt. Aeren and Chitthra joined them as Ysilrod was speaking.

"There is magic on the wind, not far," said the elf-mage, and the Companions cast their eyes about. "Tho' not aware of our passing on the road. Yet…"

They waited as the sun set low, and Rohesia spoke of camping for the night. Two days more to DragonFall, and Thalion nodded silently for her to see it done. She turned her steed away, shouting orders to the column.

"What say you, Brother?" asked Sheynon softly.

Ysilrod drew a feather from his pouch, tossed it in the air and watched it drift east and to the north.

Audrey looked about, her hair blowing softly to the south. "How does it move against the breezes?"

Thalion smiled. "As said, magic on the wind."

"Ah…" Audrey nodded, grinning then as well.

"Less than a day away," said Ysilrod, "and of a power." He looked to the waning sunlight. "We may reach it by the mid of night, should we decide to ride."

Chitthra motioned to the column waiting. "I will advise Rohesia to continue to the city-state, inform Kaul of our findings, and wait for our arrival."

"My ladies," said Thalion to Chitthra and Aeren, "I beg you accompany Rohesia to the city-state and see Kaul is calmed with our messages."

Chitthra's steely eyes met Thalion's, then Aeren laid a hand upon her arm. "Jyslin waits, Dearest, and by the time we reach the city, it will be more than ten days."

At last the dark elf woman nodded curtly. "As you say. Yet tarry not, for we seek answers as do you."

"A day, surely no more," replied the priest. "See to your charge and keep his kingship calmed."

They clasped hands with all about, then turned back to the soldiers waiting.

Thalion looked to Audrey, and the baroness raised her face in eagerness. Sheynon caught Ysilrod's sly grin and nodded.

"Hurry!" Audrey cast her eyes upon the road. "By the light of *Mír'rë Cala'wyne* and *Gil Estel*, we will find our way!"

* * *

They rode away, fast as they might travel safely in the darkness, Thalion with *Gil Estel* held high lighting the path before them and Audrey at his side, *Mír'rë Cala'wyne* blazing as the sun. Wind in their hair and horses breathing heavy in the nighttime, they grinned tightly to feel the rush of adventure in their blood once more.

As *Selene* rose half-full and *Mina* set in the western sky and quartered, Ysilrod called them to a halt. A cottage lay beside the road, half a league away, lights showing from the windows. He drew another feather from his pouch and they watched it drift, following the road.

"There," said the elf-mage, "and again, there is power within, tho' little malice. There may be more than one with ability, yet no more than two."

"Is this not a private place?" asked Audrey. "A farm with no village nearby or other neighbors, might it only be a solitary sorcerer?"

Ysilrod considered as the horses caught their breath and dug hooves into the road in nervousness. Whatever the elf-mage had found, they, too, felt within the air. He looked to Thalion. "My lord, you are the one with experience of strangers. I ask your advice."

"You say no malice?"

"There is some, but it is of the reluctant sort."

"How can you know this?" Audrey hurried on her words. "I mean no disrespect, yet cannot understand."

"As when we speak with voices, my lady," replied Ysilrod. "Tone of voice, tilt of head, the stances of our persons… all is plain to me with the Craft, and I read these things with practice."

"Years, nay, decades of it," said Sheynon. He nodded to the cottage in the distance. "Let us approach begging comfort for the night, even if taken in the storehouse. If human or elf, there would be no reason to deny us, yes?"

"And if Drow?" Audrey looked to her companions.

Thalion grinned. "Then we say adieu and bid good rest."

Sheynon did not return the jest, yet looked to Ysilrod again. "Might it be Steffyn? Aeren said he escaped the city, and if wounded, might he seek shelter?"

"Near ten days ago, my lord," reminded Audrey.

"Yet there is a certain hint of familiarity about this," replied Ysilrod. He met Sheynon's eyes. "And if Steffyn, what then?"

"If Steffyn, it is good Chitthra is not among us," replied the elf-lord.

Audrey shook her head, frowning. "One of the Brotherhood, who follows Steffyn's own son, our departed comrade, seeking now his blood.

I cannot fathom the complications of our task. Never have we seen such dissention."

"Never have we dealt with Drow at our side, my lady," said Sheynon. He waved a hand. "I do not say that as it sounds, yet still, it is… difficult to accept."

Thalion sheathed *Gil Estel*. "Light a torch, that our steeds do not stumble in the darkness. Let us see what this innocent cottage holds with magic in the air."

* * *

Steffyn stood apart once more in the corner, weak from hunger, thirst, and wounds yet to heal completely. Archane lay abed, spent herself from their journey through the forest, as Ry'lld and Lualyrr spoke together softly at the table.

Soft sounds beyond the shutter caught his ears, yet he could not turn his head, nor call a warning, for Archane had left him mute once more and commanded to stand motionless. Therefore, he did nothing as his body slowly sagged upon itself and fatigue lay as a blanket on his mind.

A knock came upon the door. Ry'lld rose in surprise as Lualyrr covered Archane with a quilting, that she would not be seen. Neither moved to Steffyn, only walked to the door and opened it a hand's-width. Though he could not see who was beyond the cottage, the voices heard were plain, and even in his clouded mind, Steffyn knew them well.

Greetings were exchanged, words spoken with great consideration as the dark elf couple stood together at the entry. At the last, they closed the door once more, then held each other, trembling.

All the while, Steffyn fought the Charm, though little could he do to break it in his sorry state. Yet the voices were a calling, known well for many years.

Thalion Lahai! Audrey Vincent!

So weak he was, Steffyn did not even have the strength to shed a single tear.

* * *

"Hold your thoughts for the elves."

Audrey nodded at Thalion's words as they walked their way from the cottage. They led their horses down the road and back into the copse, meeting there with Sheynon, as Ysilrod approached.

"It is Steffyn," said Ysilrod firmly, and his brother let go a breath.

308

"Yet why would two dark elf farmers hold a mage as him?" asked Audrey, looking at them one by one.

"He is not of himself," replied the elf-mage. "Charmed, perhaps, or in a trance of some other sort. Regardless, the question is, how did it come to him?"

"There is another in the cottage," said Sheynon, and they looked to him askance. "Through the shutters I saw a figure in the bed, tho' covered, and I could not see if male or female."

Audrey posed a question. "Might it be Archane? If so, the gods are with us, as we find Steffyn and an age-old enemy at once. Justice may be done upon her for her crimes."

"First matters first," said Thalion. "Steffyn's safety, then we deal with whatever there is left."

Glances passed, one to the other, and they nodded all together.

Thalion glanced to the heavens, noting *Selene* lowering in the west. "Darkness before the dawn will be upon us soon. We will wait and enter the cottage before the sunrise." He looked them all deeply in the eye. "No killing, and weapons only in defense. We know not the truth of it, yet will find it soon enough without bloodshed."

"I will enter through the chimney," said Ysilrod, and they nearly laughed at his words. "It will be a manner they do not expect." He looked to Thalion. "Sheynon will guard the doorway as yourself and Audrey enter and press the dark elf farmers to the table. I will hold them there as we give aid to Steffyn and find the identity of the one sleeping. Still, if it is Archane…"

"Prepare then for the fight of your life," said Sheynon, and Ysilrod nodded at his side. "Tho' I will not surrender Steffyn to Archane." Sheynon faced Thalion and Audrey, jaw set and fists now clenched.

Thalion shook his head. "There will be no sacrifice, for think, my cousin. What is Archane's wish in this time? Return to her people, yes? She cannot have designs upon our land if she has no power."

"May the gods be with us, that we near the end of this nightmare." Audrey gave a sign above them all, and they joined hands and bowed their heads in prayer for a silent moment.

Thalion looked to the cottage in the distance. "Give us time to reach the doorway once again, Lord Mage. Then we will show surprise upon them as they have never seen."

* * *

R y'lld and Lualyrr, exhausted and sleeping at the table, woke with a start at the pounding on the door. Ry'lld shook himself, raised the daggers lying on the table, and called for Lualyrr to toss a blanket over Steffyn's form. Lualyrr then roused Archane from the bed quickly as she could.

"Do not allow them in," said the Dark Princess, as she slowly woke from a heavy sleep. Her strength had yet to return, and she stood slowly, thoughts running in her mind of how they might defend themselves.

"If elves or humans, we may use Steffyn as a hostage," suggested Ry'lld, as the pounding came again. The latch turned, yet the door would not yield against the lock. Archane tossed a goblet of wine beneath the threshold, incanted a simple cantrip, and flames burst, following the wine trickling without. Cries from beyond the door brought a wicked smile to her lips, and she thought what else she might do in her weakened state.

The fire in the hearth ceased, as ash and soot blew about the room. They coughed and sneezed, covering their mouths and noses, as a figure formed before them.

Ysilrod Calidriil! Archane's mind leapt back nearly thirty years as she recognized the face.

The elf-mage gestured to the door, then in burst Thalion and Audrey, followed moments later by Sheynon, guarding their backs. Ry'lld leapt with a shout, but Audrey took him to the floor, disarmed him easily, and dropped the daggers in the once more-burning hearth.

Thalion pressed Lualyrr and Archane to the wall with *Gil Estel*, then motioned Sheynon to tend Steffyn still standing in the corner, the blanket draped about his head.

"You are safe, elf-brother," Sheynon whispered in his ear. Steffyn made no reply, nor did he even look at Sheynon's face. Yet a tear trickled from his eye as Sheynon held him close.

"Release him," said Ysilrod to Archane, and the Dark Princess only laughed.

"You have him held by Charm or spell, do you not? Therefore, release him… or shall I place you under such enchantment of my own?"

"I hold him only by his love for me."

The elf-mage scoffed. "He loves you not, and you are but an impertinent temptress, your body as a lure. Truly, I could not imagine the numbers of males who have searched your warmth for pleasure and found naught but slavery in it."

Archane's face twisted into rage, yet Ysilrod only held a finger there before her. "Caution I would give, else you will find yourself without a voice."

"Ysilrod." Thalion tone urged temperance and he nodded to the table.

Audrey sheathed her sword and led Ry'lld and Lualyrr to the chairs. Archane followed, as Sheynon lifted Steffyn from the corner and laid him on a bed. He poured a goblet full and fed it slowly to him, though the elf could barely drink. Once more Archane grinned with satisfaction as she watched.

Ysilrod sat before her, eyes intent. "Should I need to break whatever incantation you have made, it will not set well for you in judgment. You have been a prisoner five years to Mors'ul'jyn, and while unpleasant in many ways, surely she was gracious in her hospitality."

Archane's brow wrinkled and she shook her head.

"Imagine how much less accommodating Kaul's dungeon might be for all eternity."

Sheynon turned to listen, a smile growing on his face.

"I am the Dark Princess, leader of the Drow."

"No," replied Sheynon, approaching slowly. "You are a prisoner of the elves for crimes against our kind. And as you claim sovereignty, stand responsible for whatever has been done in your name."

"Likely you are devoid of powers," continued Ysilrod, "else you would have taken us to task as we entered." He motioned to Ry'lld and Lualyrr, listening closely. "Something has changed in your demeanor, to say nothing of your ability. We knew you free of Mors'ul'jyn, and by the grace of gods, found both you and our elf-brother." He nodded to Steffyn on the bed. "Now we will search for answers as to what has become of the ability seen before, all those years ago."

Archane's eyes narrowed, burning as hot embers.

"Yes, you recall, I am certain, as do we."

"Ysilrod, that time is passed." Thalion laid a hand upon the elf-mage's shoulder.

"Base revenge, is this your thought?" Archane huffed a breath and dropped her eyes away.

"Release his voice and movement," said Ysilrod, warning in his voice.

Archane only raised her face defiantly. The elf-mage gestured, and she clutched her chest, gasping for breath. Down to her knees went the Dark Princess, and Lualyrr screamed, bolted from her chair, and held

Archane close. Ysilrod clenched his fist, and Archane nearly retched in pain.

"My lord, please." Thalion stood, and Ysilrod, after a moment's hesitation, dropped away the spell.

Archane knelt on hands and knees as Lualyrr cried and turned her head to Ysilrod. "This is how you take revenge? Then kill me, not her!"

"Enough," said Sheynon from Steffyn's side. "We descend into the madness they brought years ago. This moment, nothing matters but Steffyn's safety. Shall your servants become the price for your refusal?"

"Please, I beg you…" Ry'lld's voice was small and filled with anguish as he began to rise. Thalion pressed him down to his chair once more.

"She… they are not servants." Archane's voice was weak and raspy, yet she drew herself up at the last. "In truth, I knew them not until coming to this cottage."

Thalion looked to Ry'lld.

"We are of Hovenethra, one of the Great Houses," said the dark elf.

"Not of mine," said Archane, and she chuckled. "A House grand, yet coveting what they cannot have, rule of Drow, for their leader thinks only of herself."

"Release Steffyn," said Sheynon, once again.

Archane nodded, rose, walked slowly to the bed, and kissed Steffyn on the forehead. She incanted words too soft for them to hear and stepped back. Steffyn groaned, and Sheynon moved quickly to the bed once more.

"Now," said Thalion, looking to Archane and Ysilrod sternly, "we will speak of what and how to find a way beyond this place. A way for all of us."

* * *

"What now, my friend?" Audrey sat with Thalion at the table, Steffyn yet abed and the dark elves sleeping in a corner. Sheynon had curled himself at Steffyn's side, and Ysilrod knelt at the hearth, trancelike in his demeanor.

The priest poured tea before them both. "Find balance, and a way beyond this circumstance. Still, it is Mors'ul'jyn we pursue, that her plans not come to fruition."

"Too long I have been away from Ardwel to know the truth of it. Still, I trust what you and Sheynon have imparted is as known. Yet always have the dark elves been our enemies, and I cannot see how it changes in this time."

312

"Excellency, is it not time to let go the issues of the Drow?"

Audrey looked to Thalion and he held a hand before she could reply. "As we have said, surely they pose no threat to our land. They have no armies, their leadership missing now for many years, and by Archane's own admission, their Houses fallen to internal matters."

"How then is balance found?" Audrey searched for words. "I know your thought, that the *Rising Star* seeks Order above all things, and in this I cannot disagree. Yet even in Crysalon's own ending, Order was brought about for five years and more. Now again those bringing Chaos, Mors'ul'jyn and Archane, return. Are we the instruments of Order as in the past, or others?"

Thalion shook his head. "Others?"

"Aeren. Chitthra. These clergy from the Drow found only by coincidence. Even Steffyn, that we rescue him from whatever evil might have been."

Thalion sipped his tea, contemplating. "I do not think these refugees are evil, but escaping it as they may. Only, as you say, by circumstance and coincidence did Archane come upon them."

Audrey nodded, pressing forward and lowering her voice. "And this is the truth of it! The gods move in ways we do not understand! Here we are once more, with opportunity in hand, to end the struggle for all time. Archane powerless, the Drow fighting among themselves as she is absent. All left to quell the land is Mors'ul'jyn."

Thalion was silent as he thought again. "Have we the right to keep Archane from her place? Mors'ul'jyn, yes, but a sovereign leader? Is Ysilrod's threat of Kaul's dungeon but a ruse?" He chuckled. "Little do I think the Mongrel would wish Archane within his city."

Audrey nodded in reluctance at the last. "Your point is taken with all sincerity. Yet what now, Lord Priest? How do we find the balance and keep safe the land?"

Thalion laid a hand on Audrey's arm. "Never have we failed our great lords, nor shall we. The world is too tender in our hearts for us to give it up to evil."

Audrey smiled and took his hand, as so many times in years before. "Amen, together as always, and once again. Ever faithful, ever true. It is good to be in such company once more."

* * *

In the Depths of Drakenmoore…

Mors'ul'jyn prepared for her leaving of the sanctuary.

Too long I have tarried here, and perhaps Archane's death is a blessing. Now I am free again to peruse my vengeance, or whatever I see fit.

Yet she would not leave this place to those who might invade without costing them a price. Therefore, she laid her traps, some obvious that would be found, others subtle, of magic or of simple things; a snake whose venom would kill only within moments, or a nest of spiders hidden in a corner, that would emerge only when those about were sleeping, and eat their flesh and lay their eggs within. That one she had learned during her time as Archane's own body-servant in *Ung'gu'wi*, and forced to watch it as a warning.

Two magic traps were set within the doorway to her private chamber, one a simple cantrip of a slippery floor, with spikes that would emerge once the victim fell. The other was far more deadly. The scrying mirror, should it be used, would pull those round within, entrapping them forever in a formless mist where they would slowly starve.

Much like the Black Blade's prison, she thought, *tho' insidiously wicked.*

More simple ruses were set about, and at the last she gathered up her tome, a traveling pouch of items, a waterskin, and cloak.

There are places in Ung'gu'wi I recall, and I may travel there by magic easily. I will find a hideaway, set myself as a solitary mage, and wait with patience for Archane. Once I hear she has returned, I will find her, and become the new leader of the Drow.

She chuckled, poured a goblet full of wine and savored it, reflecting.

Tho' at war, surely Archane's return will settle matters for the dark elves. And should Sheynon choose to follow, he will be within a realm I rule. Then we will see how truly brave his heart is, as I cut if from his chest and hold it before his dying eyes!

Mors'ul'jyn gathered up her pack, breathed deeply as she looked about one final time, gestured as she incanted arcane words, and vanished. Naught was left but swirling dust and a hint of jasmine, sweet and haunting in the air.

BOOK ELEVEN
QUEEN OF THE
UNDERGROUND

Change must come,
Or change will come.

Elven Proverb

Dennis Young

PART ONE
REFLECTION

The City-State of DragonFall…

It took all the power of the House of Iyllyeth to send Narlros and Xa'lyyth with their bodyguard into the land, mages gathered as not seen in more than a century to work their Craft and thereby propel a hundred dark elves into the misty void. And likewise, the clergy used their prayers to keep them safe, for it was known that daemons stalked within those voids and sought those of mortal ilk, to take pleasures of them for passage, or torture them if so desired.

They arrived at nightfall and set a camp beyond the road at the edge of a growth of pines, lit fires, took their supper, and waited for Kaul or his soldiers to seek them out. Yet it was dawn before the black and crimson standards of the City-State of DragonFall were seen, with a century of riders armed and armored shouting challenge in the morning light.

Narlros stood with Xa'lyyth before the call for recognition, soldiers arrayed behind them, and a parchment extended in his hand. "For your king, as we wish honorable parley. We come with no malice aforethought, only seeking aid and counsel. We ask in the name of the House of Iyllyeth, and the Dark Princess Archane."

The column captain took the scroll and stuffed it in a pouch. "Word says Archane is no longer leader of the Drow." He chuckled. "And your woman I recognize, as our king says her pleasures were disappointing to him."

Dark elf soldiers stirred, hands on sword hilts gripping tightly, crossbows cocking in the silence. Narlros did not look to Xa'lyyth, but faced the captain squarely. "We come as it is said your king is strong. You insult us, and we take offense, yet this is not the time for redress. The land stands on the brink, for us, for you, for your king and his holdings. Bring him to us, or an emissary with authority for decisions. We ask humbly and with all respect." He bowed, as did Xa'lyyth.

The captain's face yet was hard, and his eyes roamed over Xa'lyyth's figure beneath her robes. He raised the parchment. "What says this? Tell me, or it will not be delivered."

Narlros shrugged. "Only what I have said. Other words are for his ears only, or of his appointed. Again, we ask with deference."

317

At last the captain nodded. "We will leave a line of soldiers as a sentry. You are not to cross, otherwise, it will be war. Remain here until I return with answer."

Again they bowed, and the captain shouted orders to his column. Fifty soldiers dismounted, and handlers took their steeds to the copse nearby. The remainder wheeled about, off quickly to the distant gates as the sun rose brightly and stars faded in the morning light.

"We outnumber them now more than twice," said the Lancer Captain into Narlros's ear. "Their hearts would make a fine offering this night."

"Put thoughts as such from your mind," replied the priest, "tho' I may share your feelings, know we are here not for blood, but saving of our Race. Keep watch, but nothing else. Give prayers to *Mother Darkness*, that *Iyllyeth* watches over Alystin in *Ung'gu'wi*."

The Lancer Captain nodded. "Word says she has done well, wise and patient as Hovenethra presses war."

"And again, prayers of thanks for her patience, tested by Ba'tula's greed. A worthy hand at Mor'i'jil's side in his absence is Dark Priestess Alystin." He turned and walked toward his tent, Xa'lyyth at his side. "Tend your duty," he said over his shoulder. "We have prayers of our own to give, and shelter from this withering sunlight."

The Lancer Captain only chuckled wryly, knowing well the feeling.

* * *

Kaul crumpled the parchment and tossed it aside, drained his tankard and held it forth to be refilled. "How many?"

The captain showed a questioning look as he stood before the throne.

"Soldiers! How many dark elf soldiers are in the camp?" Kaul drank again, waiting with little tolerance.

"No more than five score, Great King, and two of the priest caste is my thought. They lead the party and begged your attendance."

"Not a party of war, yet enough to keep our attention for a day," mused Kaul. "What of Rohesia? What word of their return from the ruins?"

"A rider came only on the morning, saying two days, as they had passed Jeseriam. However…" He paused, and Kaul motioned to a servant. A mug of ale was offered to the captain, and he drank quickly, then bowed. "The adventurers separated from our column, all but Lady Aeren and the dark elf woman. The rider did not know the reasons."

Kaul paused his cup. "Something then is afoot, else why not return? Only of importance would they tarry." He straightened on the throne.

318

"Tell these Drow we wait for word from our emissaries south, and once conferred with, we will advise them of our decision."

"They may not wish to wait —"

"Then damn them!" Kaul brought his tankard down, shattering it on the arm of the throne. Dark ale splashed, and servants scurried to clean the mess. "This is the realm of DragonFall, and I rule here, no others. If they depart, so be it. I have no interest in their parley. Tell them to wait or leave, it matters not to me."

The captain bowed. "At once, Great King." He turned on his heel, striding for the great oaken doors quickly as his feet would carry him.

* * *

Jeseriam…

What Rohesia's rider had not said to Kaul's captain, as he was not aware of facts and changes, was Aeren and Chitthra remained in the city of Jeseriam, sending on Rohesia and the soldiers to DragonFall. Their reasons were to confer with Stokar regarding Archane's escape, but more, of Mors'ul'jyn, as she had not been found in Drakenmoore.

"I have no thought where she might have gone or when," said Stokar, as they sat at table in the shop. The sun had set, and stars winked into the sky as *Mina* climbed the heavens, seen through the window of the back room.

"Ysilrod said of magic in the air," said Chitthra. "We were… 'encouraged' to accompany the column from DragonFall back unto the city. In truth, we have business there, yet…"

"Something they did not wish you to be a part of?" Stokar filled his pipe, reflecting.

"Steffyn?" Aeren's voice was but a whisper. "Ysilrod said of power, and surely there are few of ability to attract the notice of Ysilrod Calidriil."

Chitthra nodded slowly. "Agreed, as they know my task. Yes, Steffyn, almost in certainty."

Aeren looked to Stokar, yet reflecting. "Your thoughts, my lord? We ask your wisdom once again."

Stokar lit his pipe with a snap of his finger and blew smoke aside. "What if Archane herself?"

Chitthra shook her head. "Then all our ability would not have been enough. Her power is nearly as a goddess."

"After five years of captivity, devoid of tomes, potions, or other artifacts? Only prayers, and held in a secluded place, likely protected by the god of *NorthWind?*" Stokar chuckled. "Weakened nearly to a mortal's standing, I would say."

"We will learn once returned to DragonFall," replied Aeren, "and until then —"

A knock came upon the door. Aeren rose, drew her sword, and Chitthra pressed herself against the wall beside the entryway. Stokar only watched, amused, then stood and walked calmly to the door, lifted up the latch and chuckled once again.

In rushed Thalion and Ysilrod with a third, draped in a blanket and nearly carried to the bed. Thalion tossed the covering aside.

"Steffyn!" Chitthra nearly shouted out the name, and a look from Stokar ceased her words. Aeren sheathed her sword and knelt beside the trembling figure.

"He fights against a Charm," said Ysilrod, as Aeren wiped sweat from Steffyn's forehead with a cloth handed her by Stokar. "It may take days, for he was deeply in her power."

Chitthra watched, then looked to Ysilrod. "Whose power? What has happened since we parted?"

Thalion stood before her, begging calm. "Archane, my lady, and we have her in our keeping."

Aeren turned, stunned to silence at the priest's proclamation. Chitthra looked to Stokar, in the corner and puffing quietly on his pipe. "You knew," she said.

"I surmised," replied the old half-elf. "And both you and the Lady Aeren held the likelihood, did you not?" He turned to Thalion. "What now, Priest? How to deliver them in safety to the City-State of Truth? Your safety, as well as theirs."

Thalion poured wine from a bottle on the table and drank it down. "We will go to DragonFall. The Dark Princess proclaims to make an offer even Kaul may find tempting in its daring."

* * *

The night was late and the tavern nearly empty as Aeren and Chitthra sat at a corner table, two empty pitchers before them. Little had been said as the eve progressed, and only now did Aeren raise the subject.

"What will you do, Dearest?" She sipped what remained in her cup and watched Chitthra with a worried eye.

"You ask will I kill Steffyn in his sorry state?" She grinned wryly and shook her head. "Surely you know me better. The question is, what will

320

he do when recovered from his malady?" She drank, then looked to Aeren. "Where then is Archane, as the priest says they have her in hand? Why do we not see her in attendance?"

Aeren laid her hand gently on Chitthra's, and smiled. "Your mind was elsewhere, and this I noticed. Thalion says Sheynon and my liege guard her well, with a spell by Ysilrod cast for their protection. For the nonce, she will cause no worry."

"And now what comes of this? To DragonFall again and Kaul's throne room, to hear of bargains between mortal foes? What part of this is ours, pray tell?"

Aeren shrugged. "Perhaps none, and would this be unwanted? Still Mors'ul'jyn is free, and this is our concern. Sheynon, Thalion, and Her Excellency tend greater things. Safety of the land, of the cities and the elves, the future for all of Ardwel and beyond."

Chitthra raised her face. "And the Drow, in certainty. Archane will make no treaties without her people uppermost in mind. Whatever humans and elves may think, she tends the dark elves well, and has for a thousand years."

Aeren nodded at the last. "As said, and if conditions are set as such, my prayers would only be they are for all time. I would not wish ill on any, humans, elves, or Drow."

Chitthra met Aeren's eyes. "And what of us? Still, I must do honor to my vows, to bring those guilty of Galandria's murder to justice."

Aeren squeezed the dark elf woman's hand tighter still. "And I will stand beside you in that duty, as pledged before. Our love is strong and will not be broken."

Chitthra showed a wan smile. "Your feelings warm me, heart and spirit. I cannot say the happiness you bring."

"You have said it many times, with words, with deeds, with simple gestures. My soul sings in your company."

Chitthra raised her cup, and they touched rims and drank their last. "Let us take rest for the night. Perhaps the morrow will bring better understanding with the sunrise."

* * *

Morning dawned as Sheynon sat at Steffyn's bedside in Stokar's shop. He had arrived in the night as Thalion and Ysilrod retreated to the forest, taking watch with Audrey over Archane and the other dark elves. Ry'lld and Lualyrr had accompanied the Companions, with assurances from Thalion no harm would come to them or Archane in their journey to the city-state. Further, he had pledged once agreements had been reached between the Dark Princess and Kaul's court, they could return to the cottage and live in peace as farmers, should they choose.

Steffyn had not stirred, and Sheynon found himself at the last succumbing to fatigue, of body and–spirit. As sunlight brightened the window shade, Stokar came into the room, a pot of scented tea in hand and a serving dish of pastries. Sheynon roused himself, nodded thanks, and sat with the old half-elf.

"Two of three," said Stokar softly after moments, and Sheynon nodded, contemplating. "What now, Calidriil? You hold the fate of Drow in the collective hands of yourself and your comrades."

Sheynon drank, then refilled their cups. "Never would I have thought such, yet your words are true. What should we do with such power, is my question. Hold Archane away from her people and let them fall to war? Return her to her place, and watch them rise once more to threaten Ardwel? Or as Mors'ul'jyn, keep her prisoner all her life, hidden away in a dungeon, such as that of Kaul's?" He shuddered. "As I, you know the elven way is freedom, of the mind, the spirit, the body. Have we the right?"

"Right or responsibility?" Stokar drank, then motioned to Steffyn on the bed. "And what of your elf-brother and his doings? You forgave him, yes, but now? Chitthra will seek his blood or that of Mors'ul'jyn... perhaps both. Have you the right to claim vengeance for yourself in her place?"

Sheynon sighed and looked away. "She came to me with open heart, stating purpose, thinking I would turn her away because of it. Yet as Steffyn with Mors'ul'jyn, I could not, as her cause, while hurtful and frightening in its way, is just. I know not what to do."

"Circumstance will likely intervene."

The elf-lord nodded. "And if so, decision will not be mine, therefore. Truly, Stokar, how has the world come to this, where we fight amongst ourselves as Chaos rules the land?"

"Does Chaos rule?" Stokar chuckled. "You have forgotten the true meaning, then."

Again, Sheynon was silent for a while, drank once more, then shook his head. "Your point is made well. Chaos is not our concern, but heartbreak and loss, issues we may control, should we find the courage. Yet it is... hard."

"Always are concerns of the heart difficult, Calidriil. You will find the way, as always. You have not faltered in your destiny, nor do I think you will." Stokar laughed softly. "Not the life a simple thief might have chosen, eh?"

* * *

Ung'gu'wi...

B a'tula's Lancer Captains did not tarry further in their action, sealing off the passages of Warinethra into the central chamber, and standing guard at those of the other Houses, should they interfere. Then soldiers waiting in the corridors charged forth, attacking Archane's holdings, and quickly overrunning fortifications set for defense.

Deeper into the House of Iyllyeth, servants, merchants, and others running from the onslaught pressed against the chamber walls, or were trampled if no retreat was found. Soldiers finding clergy at their prayers, or beds filled with concubines, they slew them all, cut off their heads, and retreated quickly, carrying away their trophies as ordered by Ba'tula.

Soldiers of the House soon followed, yet trailed behind, as bodies littered passageways and the screams of wounded filled the air. Arrows flew, yet only minor spells were cast about, as they knew, should magic fill the air, the whole of the earth might bury them forever.

Back into the central chamber, and the rear guard held retreat, as a hundred Hovenethra soldiers cried victory in the depths of the Drow enclave.

For the first time in more than one thousand years, Drow had drawn the blood of their own kind within the House of the enemy.

* * *

A lystin called council once again, yet as Narlros and Xa'lyyth had been sent into the land, only Vrammyr, Molva'yas, and Krenasst attended at her side. All were shaken with the news of Hovenethra's bold venture, Krenasst most of all, as two acolytes in his tutelage and a favored concubine had been slain in the attack.

"Your mission to Modennethra is more urgent than before," said Alystin, the goblet in her hand trembling with each word. "Leave at once, yet do not go unprotected."

"And where are Narlros and Xa'lyyth? Hiding in their bower?" Vrammyr looked about the chamber devoid of food and drink, and sighed. She drew a small flask from her ornamented belt and drank.

"On a mission vital now more than ever," replied Alystin.

"Yet where?" Vrammyr pressed the question, as the others waited in their silence, passing glances.

323

"Into the land, for we have word of Archane's finding." Alystin's hand clenched within her robes at the falsehood, yet knew she must calm the matter and keep order in the House.

"Praises be to *Iyllyeth*," said Krenasst softly, as he knelt in prayer.

Vrammyr scoffed. "Has this not been before? Is this not why Mor'i'jil himself is missing? Chasing rumor about the land we are held away from and shunned within?" She drank again from her flask and tossed it to the side, empty. "Is this your ploy, to send us all away, that you hold the power yourself? Perhaps you took the old priest into your bed and charmed him with your woman's guile to leave *Ung'gu'wi*."

"Enough of you!" Molva'yas crossed the room, drew a dagger, and held it at Vrammyr's throat. "Say your apology or leave this council! You are naught but a stain upon this House!"

Alystin stood silent in the chamber as Krenasst rose and stood at her side, his hand upon her shoulder.

Vrammyr backed to the wall and Molva'yas followed, the dagger close at hand.

Alystin raised the silver bell and rang it once. Vrammyr paled, her deep skin losing nearly all its color. Molva'yas held the dagger near her breast and touched it to her robe. "Your regrets will be said, or your heart will beat its last," he whispered.

"Molva'yas." Alystin's voice was soft, but carried strength. The priest slowly backed away, and Vrammyr nearly swooned.

"I will admit," said Alystin to Vrammyr, "your words have merit, as they have often done. Yet in this time, we are certain, and seek aid from one who holds no interest other than of what he himself might gain."

Vrammyr took moments to regain herself, as none within the chamber moved to aid her. She sought to speak, yet her voice stayed absent, and at last she only bowed her head.

"Dark Lady, do you speak of this mongrel king once more?" Krenasst's voice was earnest, filled with deep concern.

Alystin nodded. "I do, and yes, again we hold out hope, tho' know our cause is righteous. Yet we cannot allow Hovenethra's attack to go unanswered. I will call our Lancer Captains to a war council, and all will be heard. Then, my dark lords, you will venture to Modennethra and seek their aid, for surely we stand in need as not before."

* * *

Alystin's Lancer Captains took no urging, and as Molva'yas and Krenasst were hastened beyond the safety of the House of

Iyllyeth into the passages leading to Modennethra, their soldiers were unleashed.

Crushing scant defenses left at the entrance corridor, and charging through a shield wall hastily assembled, ten clergy were quickly captured, for Alystin had ordained no killing beyond that of soldiers. Then just as quickly, they retreated, hostages carried past the shattered entrance to the House of Hovenethra and into the central chamber, where a brace of crossbows cut down those giving chase.

Taking refuge behind a wall of gathered stones and running down the corridors, those captured were forced into a tiny cell, held there by two wolf-like beasts and six guards.

At the last, and once secured, Alystin herself came into the chamber and stood with two guards at her side, as the clergy of Hovenethra cowered. "Stay your fear, for there is no reason," she said to those within the cell. "You will not be sacrificed, and once this insurgency is quelled, you will be returned to your home. While your mistress cares not for your lives or safety, we will not be so callous. All of dark elves must understand the reasons for what is happening."

"And what is that, false priestess?" came a voice from within the crowd. A ragged male stepped forth as the others round him parted.

Alystin faced him squarely. "Ba'tula thinks herself worthy of rule, and has the mind but not the heart for it. She craves power, not responsibility, accolades, not accountability. No matter the lives of others, such as yourselves, never will she accept her part."

"Untrue," replied the priest behind the cell bars, "for I have prayed with her for return of Archane many years. You know nothing of our mistress."

"Return of Archane, perhaps, yet should that not follow, what then? Once more, you do not understand her motives, blinded as you are by whatever she has offered."

"Ba'tula's reasons are clear! Archane is gone, Mor'i'jil as well! You speak lies within your own House to keep your place!" He spat and glared at Alystin as the others round him stirred with growing anger.

Alystin stepped closer, and her guards followed in silence at her side. "Your name, what is it?"

He raised his face defiantly. "Dhuunyl, of the Inner Circle. I am a favorite of Ba'tula and know her well."

Alystin nodded slowly. "Then tell me, will Ba'tula parley in faith for all the Race? Will she join all the other Houses to find a way beyond death for all of Drow? Or will she press the battle until *Ung'gu'wi* is filled with only blood for her own reasons?"

"Conclave was called, and in that time no decisions made! Again, you pause only to gain time!"

Once more Alystin nodded. "Agreed, and as we wait for Archane's return, is it not to the benefit of all that blood not be let? Where is the reasoning of Ba'tula, Matriarch of House Hovenethra, that war is better than prayer and reconciliation?"

Dhuunyl paused, looking round for support, as those about him murmured nervously at Alystin's words. "Strength begets strength, and endless talk shows only weakness. Therefore —"

"Therefore, Ba'tula sends soldiers to fight and die, while the House of Iyllyeth yet searches the land for Archane's place. Even now, we know she is alive and has been seen, sent emissaries to find the path, and offer prayers and sacrifice to *Mother Darkness*. How has Ba'tula's greed for power aided in this cause?"

Again, Dhuunyl paused, then turned and walked away. "Lies again, and you will feel her blade soon enough in your own heart! I will hear no more!" He knelt in a corner of the cell, facing the earthen wall. Others crowded around him, yet two approached the bars and bowed.

"Dark Lady, a word, if you will," said one, a female, young and fresh of face.

Alystin nodded, waiting.

The young one sought words, then spoke with deep respect. "You speak of the Race, not only of your House. These are words I heard as a child from Archane herself, years ago. Words not as... our mistress says. Pray tell, why is there so much dissention between your House and ours?"

Alystin paused before reply, thinking. "For reasons more than two thousand years in age and terrible to behold. If, in your brief life and study of our history, you have not heard the tales, perhaps there are those here with you who will say them. Yet heed my warning, Hovenethra knows the truth of it, and has sought through all the ages to keep it from you."

The young acolyte cast her eyes downward for a moment, the raised her gaze again. "Have you any in your knowing who would share these truths, that we might understand? I only ask for safety of all dark elves."

Alystin stepped a pace closer. A guard whispered caution, but the priestess raised a hand for silence. "Who are you, so young, yet wise beyond your years?"

326

"I am called Phaer'jss, but an acolyte and little known. I offer..." she swallowed. A male close by offered his hand, and she took it. "I offer myself, my body, my heart, as needed to bring ending to this conflict."

Alystin nearly smiled at the earnest voice before her. "Your body will not be taken pleasures of, nor is your heart in danger. Yet I will consider your offer, and perhaps you will become a way between not only the Houses of Iyllyeth and Hovenethra, but all others. Innocence may aid in understanding, as those involved have lost theirs many times in ages past. I will return with words for you."

She turned and motioned to waiting servants to feed those in the cell, then left the chamber, thoughts of hope and danger running through her mind.

* * *

The City-State of DragonFall...

With agreement between Stokar and the Companions, Steffyn was left in the old half-elf's care as they ventured to the realm of Kaul and his holdings. Rohesia and the soldiers' column had arrived the day before, and once within the city, advised Kaul of the happenings, though did not know of Archane's capture. Therefore, when the Companions arrived at the city gates, there was no confrontation, no fanfare, no thought of who the dark elves accompanying Thalion and the others might then be.

"And this is how we wish it," said Thalion to Audrey, as they wended way to the palace with no escort. "Once arrived at the gates to Kaul's regal domain, I will send a private missive."

Audrey smiled at the priest's simple wisdom. "Always do you find a way to calm whatever angst might have been brought, my friend. Tho' I wonder how his greeting may transpire, as surely he holds animosity for Archane."

Ysilrod rode to their side with answer. "There will be no confrontation, Excellency, as Kaul knows we have success, as told by Rohesia herself. We must keep our wits collected and find way into his throne room for private parley." He glanced over his shoulder at the silent figure of Archane, returning only a deep and hateful stare. "Still, tho' she is without power, she is a force, and her strength of will unbroken. Once I release her tongue, what might we hear?"

"Ill words," said Thalion, chuckling, "not for gentle company." He gave a wink to Audrey, who blushed in understanding.

327

"And what of this campsite passed, a league beyond the city gates?" asked the warrior-woman. "Word says dark elves once more come to parley. Will this not become an issue in our negotiations?"

Ysilrod smiled. "I masked Archane's sight as we made approach, then quickly scouted, seeking word of hostile intent within the camp. Finding none, I returned, yet would say of caution necessary, as we know Kaul will seek whatever advantage he may find to use. Patience and gentle words will go far, my friends."

Audrey glanced to Thalion. "Once more I stand in awe of our comrade. Let us pray the gods as well are most impressed."

Ysilrod and Thalion only laughed.

The palace gates were reached without incident, and quickly Thalion set pen to parchment, folded it, and sealed it with his signet ring. He bade the gate captain see it with his own hand to Kaul's throne room, passed a coin of gold quietly to the man, and said a blessing in the air. Though the mercenary captain only gave a huff at the sign before him, he did not refuse the gold. Thalion smiled, winked once more at Audrey. She nodded, knowing Thalion's mind more than a match for a greedy soul.

"And now, we await the pleasure of the king," said Sheynon softly, noting Chitthra and Aeren watching the dark elves closely by. "I pray his wits are about him, as the day is early."

Ysilrod chuckled. "Yet what if he reveled all the night with the return of his lady friend?"

"The thoughts of men will never cease to amaze me," said Audrey, and they laughed together in the morning sun.

* * *

They were escorted into the palace on Kaul's reply, a dozen guards beside them through the corridors draped in black and crimson banners. Looks passed between Audrey, Thalion, and Ysilrod, memories of years ago as they were prisoners themselves of Vichelli's emperor, when the city waged genocide against the elves.

The Purge, thought Audrey as they approached the throne room doors, *and a time of evil as never seen in Ardwel. I praise Jhad I was a part, to bring it to its end and see justice done. Now again we march through the place of where it ended, when Daeron, rest his spirit, crushed the evil's heart, most literally, within his hand.*

They entered, guards holding the heavy oaken doors apart, Thalion and Audrey, with Archane yet mute between them, Ysilrod and Sheynon, then Chitthra and Aeren as rear guard with Ry'lld and Lualyrr at their fore, all surrounded now by no less than a score of soldiers.

The priest and Audrey came before the throne, bowed to Kaul lounging there with Rohesia standing at his side. The Mongrel flicked his hand to a servant, and they were each offered a crystal goblet of chilled wine. They bowed again, then drank, waiting for Kaul's questions they knew would come.

Kaul rose, walked slowly to Archane waiting silent between Thalion and Audrey. He raised her chin with a finger and grunted satisfaction. "You have not ruined her look, I see. Excellent. She will make a fine addition to my harem, quiet as she is."

The Companions exchanged glances all around as they waited without reply. Kaul only laughed, and sat once more upon the throne. "A jest, and I would have thought it worthy, yet I see you have no mood for it." He met Archane's blazing eyes and chuckled.

Thalion spoke, with delicacy in his words. "Great King, we come only to parley. Archane is in our... protection, as it were, and held mute for reasons we will explain, should you wish it."

Kaul waved a hand, dismissing the priest's words. "There is no need, and in truth, you have my admiration. When last I saw her, she was but a burning corpse, headless. I must admit, her look has bettered since that time."

Once more Archane's eyes were as a fire. Chitthra whispered words of Drow into the ears of Ry'lld and Lualyrr, urging calm, knowing well Kaul's manner.

Kaul lifted a tankard from a silver tray offered by a servant at his side. "Say your words, as I have little time for parley."

Thalion nodded to Ysilrod, and the elf-mage waved a hand before Archane's face.

She drew a breath and cleared her throat before speaking. "I have escaped the one you call Mors'ul'jyn, yet was... found by those about me. In this time, there are greater matters than any I would hold against yourself or them. I... we come with offers of alliance for the nonce. Little might we do apart, but much together. Great King."

Thalion nodded to himself, that Archane had kept her wits regarding her demeanor in Kaul's presence. Yet even with her words, still he knew they must be on their guard.

Kaul rose from his throne, walked to Archane once more and stood before her. "Release her from whatever magic you hold her under. I wish to hear her true voice, as much anger there is within those eyes."

Archane's chin lifted. "I am the Dark Princess, leader of the Drow, and will parley only with honorable words. Surely you may find someone in your kingdom worthy."

Kaul's face grew taut, and he drank a draught, then laughed beneath his breath. "Should I wish, you will live your days in my dungeon." He looked to Thalion, then Audrey, both with hands upon their sword hilts. He paced his way back to the throne again, then sat. "I have no interest. There is nothing you can offer, save the old priest, your minister, before me, or perhaps only his head."

Archane now turned away, walked two steps then turned again, screaming out a word. Half the soldiers arrayed about dropped to their knees, as did Ry'lld and Lualyrr. Aeren fainted dead away, caught by Chitthra before she collapsed upon the floor. Ysilrod gathered Sheynon up as the elf-lord dropped to his knees in agony.

Thalion and Audrey drew weapons, though staggered by Archane's voice as they were, yet backed the Dark Princess into a corner.

"Never did I trust your manner, knowing it a ruse," hissed Audrey, forcing Archane against the wall with *Mír'rë Cala'wyne*.

Archane laughed, long and hearty, the truest sound she had made since their encounter at the cottage. "You cannot fathom what I hold! You are as children searching knowledge, not understanding what you seek! I know her place! I have been there, and will bargain! I have that which you do not, and you will aid me in my task!"

Audrey would not yield, *Mír'rë Cala'wyne* held breast-high before Archane.

Thalion lowered *Gil Estel*. "Excellency let us hear her offer. Let us strike a balance and aid her seeking, for it is truly why we have brought her here."

Audrey's eyes did not blink, her hand held steady as it ever was, as she stared into the fiery gaze of the Dark Princess.

Archane slowly paced her way to Audrey, took the point of *Mír'rë Cala'wyne*, and placed it o'er her heart. "You slew me once, did you not? And now we have met again, and I am in your power." She ran slender fingers across the sterling blade, her eyes never leaving those of Audrey. "Dear lady, this world never will be done of us, and I know you have come to realize that, as I. If it is truly your desire, then take my life again. It will not matter, for I will rise, and still you would wish to slay me, yes? Ever in a circle, life and death… tho' should I prevail, will your god grant you another life?"

"I will not be party to evil," replied Audrey, and Archane spun away, laughing.

"There is no evil here! There is but fear and anger and gross indecision, deeds half-done and never conviction enough in any of us to bring them to conclusion. Yet Mors'ul'jyn will be driven once again, to kill elves, to torture Calidriil unto death, to do whatever in her madness she may put her mind to. A mind, as you surely know, keen as any in this land."

Audrey closed her eyes, whispering prayers to calm herself. Slowly, she dropped her sword away, and sheathed it at the last. Sheynon and Ysilrod knelt together and exchanged glances, at last letting go their breath.

Kaul chuckled from his throne as he shook his head. "You have made my ears ring as no other woman in many years."

Archane's glance would have turned a lesser male to stone in a single heartbeat. Kaul waved a hand. "Let us hear your tale of woe and what you desire. Surely these good folk have not brought you to my city only to send you to the dungeon."

"I would ask the king to mind his manners," said Sheynon tightly, yet only for Kaul's ears. Once more, the Mongrel waved away the affront.

Archane looked to Ysilrod, now standing closely by. "Tho' you masked away my sight and hearing, I felt them, the dark elves camped near the road. I am not without ability, even in my rebirth."

Their eyes locked for long moments, and at last Ysilrod nodded. "They touch your spirit, and I understand. You have lived so long, others of your kind seek you as a moth to flame, knowing comfort there. A fascinating venture."

"Brother," said Sheynon with warning in his voice. "This is the way of Steffyn, in his succumbing to the wiles of Mors'ul'jyn's mind."

Archane smirked. "Did she capture his heart and spirit? There is nothing alike between the two of us, as I rule by feeling and ability. She is simply mad, tho' her mind nearly as a trap."

"Little difference do I see," replied Sheynon, standing now at Ysilrod's shoulder. "Yet we will set this all aside. You are in need of something from all of us." He motioned to Thalion and Audrey, then Kaul watching from the throne. "Deal truthfully or face the king's justice, as you stand before him in judgement this very day."

For only a passing instant, Sheynon saw concern in Archane's face, yet it faded quickly. She faced Kaul once more. "Very well. I am the Dark Princess, chosen of Iyllyeth in her mortal time, and have ruled the Drow

331

since coming to this land. Yet now, with happenings these years, my people struggle in my absence. The Great Houses of the Drow fight among themselves for leadership they cannot hold. Only I am chosen. Only I may keep the power."

"Yet you have no power, witch," replied Kaul.

"Great King, I beg indulgence." Thalion gave a warning look to Kaul, grinning on his throne.

"This is no time for subtlety," said Kaul, dismissing Thalion's words. "You need of soldiers willing to fight for you, as there are not enough of dark elves to turn the tide of battle for any House. How many? Ten score? Twenty? Say the number and I will name my price."

Looks passed around, from the Companions to each other, Chitthra to Aeren now standing once again, Audrey to Thalion, then to Rohesia aside the throne. The room was hushed, all within awaiting Archane's answer.

"Before I reply, there is more to contemplate."

Kaul chuckled. "You speak well for one begging service."

Archane only raised her face again. "No persecution of dark elves in your land."

"There has been none," said Thalion, before Kaul could reply. "Edicts from the City-State of Truth and elven strongholds have made it so." He caught Kaul's gentle nod from the side, and glanced to Ry'lld and Lualyrr, waiting in a corner.

"Who are they, those who wait beyond the city gates?" asked Archane, as a silence set upon the throne room.

Kaul grinned. "Your people, as said, two of your priesthood, tho' I do not know their names. A male and female, the woman of which I have sampled, yet was disappointed."

Archane took a single step toward the throne before a dozen guards arrayed themselves before it. Thalion took her arm, Audrey grasping Archane's shoulder firmly. The Dark Princess trembled at the implication, and turned away again, shrugging from the hands upon her.

Thalion faced Kaul squarely, Audrey at his side and red of face, the elves standing at their shoulders. "You would do well, *Great King*, to offer strength by softer words, else matters may grow tense within the land. There are those you would do well not to anger with your roguish manner."

Kaul's face lost its humor. "You threaten me, Priest?"

"A warning," said Audrey, before Thalion could answer. "And I see before me a lack not only of decorum, but true strength. Perhaps a lesson

332

is in order." The warrior-woman's hand gripped the hilt of *Mír'rë Cala'wyne* once again.

A heavy, nervous calm set upon the room once more, then Kaul laughed it all away. "Say again your need, Archane. I grow bored by your inaction."

Audrey faced Archane and spoke softly. "State your need in simple terms, then we may leave this den of ill-mannered feelings. Do not provoke him further, else we may find ourselves fighting our way beyond the doors."

Archane met the cooling, crystal gaze of Audrey, and at last she nodded. Once more, she faced Kaul and drew a breath. "Fifty score, that victory will be assured."

"Fifty!" Kaul huffed. "How, pray tell, shall we get a thousand soldiers into your realm unnoticed?"

"That I may provide, yet need first your agreement." Archane waited as Kaul mulled the offer.

"And what will buy my payment? Do not offer fleshy pleasures, as my harem is quite adequate."

"We will discuss this in private, Great King," replied Thalion, as Archane hesitated. "For the nonce, we ask you consider the request and we will speak further on the morrow."

They bowed, all but the dark elves, and exited quickly as they could. Ysilrod fell in beside Archane, whispered words into her ear, and the Dark Princess strode calmly beside the elf-mage. Thalion glanced across his shoulder, Ysilrod nodding gently, then taking Archane's arm. They made way beyond the palace to their waiting horses, mounted saddles and rode without the gates and into the city proper. Only then did they breathe free, and wonder what the morrow would bring.

* * *

They rode to the inn near Steffyn's hidden sanctuary, Chitthra having recalled the place it set, beyond the merchantry and in an ill-kept corner of the city. They found the path, still overgrown as seen before, and wended through as the sun set low and shadows lengthened, the night quickly growing chilled.

"Wait, as Aeren and I enter and see to Jyslin," said Chitthra to Thalion.

They entered the cabin slowly, Chitthra on her guard and Aeren with sword in hand. "Jyslin," called Aeren, and the girl roused from the table where she had fallen into sleep.

She ran to Aeren and fell into her arms. "I prayed you would return soon, as nearly did I go mad with needing company."

Chitthra held a hand as Aeren cradled the girl closely, then searched the rooms, finding all in order. She noted the sigil yet on the workshop door. "You did not enter, yes? Very well, sit, as we have news."

They took chairs and told the tale, ending with those waiting beyond the door.

"We have those with us of Drow, two you likely do not know, one of deep persuasion."

Jyslin shook her head, not understanding.

"We have a prisoner," said Aeren plainly. "And will be here only for a night, or no more than two. Others travel with us, elves and humans of importance."

"Then you should be at the finest inn, should you not?" asked Jyslin.

"Secrecy is needed in this time, and a place none know of. All we ask is your discretion."

Jyslin looked to Chitthra, then back to Aeren. "And my master? Where is he?"

"Left in trusted hands, recovering from… a bout with magic," replied Aeren. "He is well, and perhaps you will see him again soon."

"As elf or Drow?" Jyslin dropped her eyes away. "I was a fool and feel dishonored."

"None of your doing," replied Aeren. "Yet for now, we must hold away these feelings. We will call the others waiting, and we ask only you tend them well."

Chitthra rose, opened the door, and ushered in the entourage, Thalion leading, then the dark elves, Archane the last, with Ysilrod at her side and watching closely. Sheynon and Audrey had tended steeds at a nearby stable, then brushed the horses quickly. At last they entered, looking round in awe.

Jyslin stood as Archane passed her by without a glance, and nearly took a knee. Chitthra stood behind the girl, a hand firmly on her trembling shoulder, then bade her tend her duties.

"A cozy hideaway," said Ysilrod, as he led the Drow into the second room. There he set them against the wall with blankets, and cast a cantrip to keep them still and silent. Once more, Archane's eyes blazed, yet he only held a finger for her silence.

Aeren made simple introductions, omitting titles and alliances. Thalion and Audrey sat with Sheynon at the table, were served stew and tea by Jyslin, who said not a word, but only stared at the warrior-woman as she ate.

"You have questions of me?" Audrey asked, smiling softly at the girl.

"I have heard tales from my master… from Mend'rys, of a human woman in this land many years ago, a Champion. I wondered of the tales and how he knew them so well, yet never did I understand."

Audrey nodded. "Perhaps we know your master by a different name. And yes, I likely am that woman."

Jyslin nodded. "And I cannot know why or how, yet I knew this as you entered. There is a… presence, one about you as a shield. Nearly holy in its feeling."

"Audrey is a warrior," said Chitthra, gently guiding Jyslin back to the hearth for stew and bread. "My thought is, when time allows, she will speak of her travels. Until then, all herein need rest." She glanced to Audrey, speaking quietly with Thalion. "Pray this night is gentle on us all, for matters remain grave beyond this sanctuary.

* * *

Jeseriam, in the shop of Stokar…

Three days, and at last Steffyn stirred, sitting in the bed, drinking broth and searching in his mind for answers. Stokar entered through the beaded curtain and set an ornate bottle and two fine-made goblets on the table, then lit his pipe and took a chair in the corner, watching.

"You are looking less than dead at last." The old half-elf pointed with his pipestem. "Drink a bit of that and tell me of your travels."

Steffyn rose, his legs weak and hands unsteady, but he managed to pour the goblets full without a spill. He sipped. "Mead of the city-state, yes?"

Stokar drew from his glass and nodded. "Of my own recipe, fermented long and sweet." He sipped again before continuing. "You have caused much angst these years, and I wonder of it."

Steffyn shrugged after a moment. "Surely you know the tales, therefore why the bother? Reasons known will not change with retelling."

"And now? You are no closer to a resolution than before, Mors'ul'jyn yet at large and Chitthra seeking your blood. What are your thoughts?"

Once more Steffyn shrugged. "Only to rejoin the land of living. These past days have felt as a fog upon my mind."

"Five days, and likely it will take a fortnight for your recovery. Whatever spell was placed by Archane nearly was your ending, as she cared not for your living beyond her needs."

Steffyn shuddered, his memory in shattered pieces, only now sorting through his mind, bringing sadness, pain, and deep-seated hunger he knew would be long in letting go. He touched his face, the bruises from Chitthra's pummeling nearly healed.

"The knot on your nose is mostly gone," said Stokar, chuckling. "And still your wife will recognize you if the lighting done with care."

Wife! Emildir! Steffyn choked a cry, nearly overcome by guilt in that moment.

Stokar nodded. "Yes, and with the healing of your body, perhaps it is time to heal your heart. Have you given thought to what happens once the murderess is dealt with?"

Steffyn wiped his face, drained his glass, and poured another. "One step before the next, and I may not live long enough to see it. I have no thought of absolution. My choices in the past speak of my stubbornness and lack of wisdom."

He rose, walking to his cloak hanging on a nail beside the window. He felt the weight of his tome yet in the hidden pocket and saw his belt and pouch resting on the floor beneath. He slowly donned his boots, the dagger hilt showing within the sheath tucked in the left and three gold coins still sewn into the right.

"You are not well enough for travel," said Stokar, still in his chair.

Steffyn straightened and strapped the belt around his waist, noting he was slimmer by a notch. He drew his cloak about his shoulders wordlessly, thinking what to say, and wondering if Stokar would detain him.

"They have gone to DragonFall," said the shopkeeper. "There is a horse at the stable waiting with supplies."

Steffyn turned slowly. "I have often wondered how you know the things you do, yet decided years ago not to question. My thanks."

"You will live to see justice," said Stokar as Steffyn turned the latch. He only nodded as he closed the door behind himself, wondering if the words were meant as a farewell or a warning.

* * *

PART TWO
PACTS AND PROMISES

In the Depths of Ung'gu'wi…

A soft shimmer in the air, dust blowing outward from the center of the room, and Mors'ul'jyn appeared, casting cautious looks into the corners. The chamber, she recalled, was much the same; dark and filled with musty barrels and crates of moldering *something* giving off a dreadful stench. It was, Mors'ul'jyn considered, the reason it remained as it did, as no one cared to deal with such an ancient mess.

From here, she might find a niche or room less unpleasant and unused. She pulled her hood atop her head and peeked beyond the door into the corridor. Lanterns lined the hallway, guards posted twenty paces distant, then twenty more. She pondered, then cast a cantrip, snuffing out the lamps to her left, and as the guards gathered to investigate, moved quietly to her right, around a corner and deeper into the caverns.

She came upon a chamber known, and tried the latch. It opened, and she looked inside, seeing it was clear and empty, save a table, two ancient chairs, and sconces on each wall, unlit, yet holding candles. She entered.

How to procure food and drink, how to associate without being recognized? Tho' there are few likely who recall Reena as Archane's body-slave, still I must be watchful. Most important, how to find what transpires now between the Houses?

She sat and drank from the waterskin, pondering. She knew taking of a servant would be a risk, yet one likely necessary. Always were there young dark elves seeking to better themselves beyond the foundlings' crèche, who had no interest in becoming soldiers or concubines.

Slowly, she began setting of her wards, small cantrips at the beginning, on the door, the sconces, even the table and the chairs. Then spells with more power, to keep other magics from intruding, then at the last, traps that could be triggered by a single word or gesture.

How long she worked, she did not truly know, for the castings took away her focus other than upon the spells. At the last, she sat with fatigue at the table, rolled her cloak and laid her head upon it, drifting in exhaustion. Her thoughts before sleep descended was of Calidriil, and how it would feel as she made him a sacrifice beneath her blade.

* * *

337

In the House of Hovenethra...

Ba'tula listened closely as her Lancer Captain spoke the news; of the House of Iyllyeth's bold counter; of the hostages taken, yet still alive, as said by seers; of the soldiers killed in the attack, and whisperings of some who ran, not seen thereafter.

"What is this?" asked Ba'tula, narrowing her eyes at the Lancer Captain's words.

He bowed as he did before, so many times now he could not count them all. "Dark Lady, two we know have gone, one likely hiding in passageways beyond, the other unknown. Yet there are words of dissention in the ranks."

"Dissention caused by what? Our cause is just and right! Archane's hold upon the Race is no more! Hovenethra's time is come!"

The Lancer Captain only lowered his head in reply, saying nothing.

Ba'tula rose, standing regally before the soldier. "Prepare another sortie into the camp of the enemy. We will crush them and set rule upon *Ung'gu'wi* as should have been done centuries ago."

Again, the Lancer Captain bowed. "It will be done, Dark Lady. I will inform you of the victory once confirmed." He turned and took exit from the chamber, then servants entered and prepared for conference. Aysa'lil and Kreothren soon would come, Ba'tula knew, and Dhuunyl's acolyte had sent a message his arrival would be late, as a fever had kept him abed throughout the day.

More likely a concubine took away his will to rise, thought Ba'tula, sipping wine. The matriarch of Hovenethra was not oblivious to grumblings within her clergy, that without sacrifice, victory could not be assured. Further, she knew tension rose within the warrior caste, as little had they gained in their ventures. Yet it would come, and once what leadership remained in the House of Iyllyeth crumbled, Hovenethra would at last have their due.

So long as Mor'i'jil does not return, nor Archane herself. Should that come to pass before Hovenethra is confirmed by the other Houses, there is only one outcome waiting for us all; the altar and Archane's blade, nothing else.

Aysa'lil and Kreothren entered quietly, bowing deeply and taking seats about the ceremonial fire opposite Ba'tula. She watched as they passed nervous glances to each other, then around the room, empty save the trio. They poured wine but drank little, offering no words.

"Word of Ry'lld and Lualyrr?" Kreothren nearly flinched at Ba'tula's question, and only shook his head.

338

"Dark Lady, as said before, never did they return, seen last in the central chamber." Aysa'lil drew a breath. "Further…"

Ba'tula gave her a glance. "What now? More ill news, I fear?"

Aysa'lil bowed her head. "Dark Lord Dhuunyl… was captured in the attack."

Ba'tula shook her head, not understanding. "The Lancer Captain said nothing of this. You know its truth?"

Kreothren spoke as Aysa'lil turned to hide her tears. "I have spoken to his coven. Dhuunyl's acolyte Morselaus, took to the bath with favored concubines last eve. There they pleasured him in darkness, and left him satiated and happy. When called upon to rouse him, they found he had taken away his own life, and bled his last into the waters." He drew a parchment from his pouch. "This was left, his seal upon it, only for your eyes."

Ba'tula took the missive slowly, her eyes never leaving those of Kreothren. She laid it aside and looked into the fire. *What have I wrought?*

She found her voice at last. "Why would he do such a thing? Was he ill with drink?"

Kreothren shrugged. "That, of course, may be determined, yet Dhuunyl always was… passive, Dark Lady, and Morselaus and the others chosen, no less so." He hurried on at Ba'tula's piercing glare. "What is meant, he worried of war and conquest. Dhuunyl's way was of parley and mediation, not honorable combat as our soldiers do. His acolytes, male and female, were taught such. They have lost their teacher, and despair. They fear Dhuunyl will become a sacrifice beneath Alystin's blade."

"His place in this Circle was because of his tempered thought. You speak nearly as an insult against one of our own House." Ba'tula's voice was filled with warning.

Aysa'lil wiped her eyes, then her soft voice reached Ba'tula's ears. "Dark Lady, it falls to the three of us now to guide our House. Say your words and we will obey. We only wish to aid and comfort."

Once again, Ba'tula's gaze found the fire and contemplation. At last she waved a hand. "As you say, passive, and therefore, less dissention now among us. Give me your thoughts of our way forward."

"Allies?" Kreothren paused for moments. "Warinethra cautions, yet still we battle, yes? Only when confronted do they act. Perhaps their warning is only meant to give us pause, that we think clearly in our objectives."

Ba'tula nodded. "Plausible, and well said. And in not opposing us, we gain the knowledge they will not do so unless opposed themselves. This says they do not care who rules, only they are spared, yes?"

Kreothren mulled the words, then nodded. "I would agree, Dark Lady. So long as battle does not come to their own doorstep, so to say, they will not interfere."

"Might Alystin know this?"

Kreothren shrugged again. "Unknown, yet her attack did no damage we know of to Warinethra."

"Or other Houses," added Aysa'lil. "All stand aside, watching for a victor. Or a weakness."

Ba'tula nodded slowly. "So long as we remain strong in our endeavor, they will stand apart. Should we show hesitation, they may ally themselves with Alystin. Yes... I see the wisdom. What I thought would be a clash of Houses becomes only a waiting game to the others." She met their eyes with hers. "Hovenethra is therefore committed to the last. We succeed or die, all of us, in battle or on the altar. There is no other choice."

"Might we offer..." Aysa'lil's voice trailed.

"Subjugation?" Ba'tula scoffed. "Is that not what we have done for a thousand years? No more! Comes the time for Hovenethra, this day or never." She rose, as did the others. "See to your covens, give prayers and find worthy sacrifices. I will confer further with our Lancer Captains and make plans. Send messages when your preparations are complete. We must strike the killing blow before Mor'i'jil returns with more falsehoods of Archane's living!"

* * *

In the House of Iyllyeth...

Alystin sought comfort near the hearth, a goblet in her hand and thoughts deep and dark sitting in her mind. A knock upon the door, and Molva'yas and Krenasst were ushered in by soldiers. Servants followed with a meal, as the clergy stood aside, worn in their look, yet hope upon their faces.

Alystin waited patiently as the door was closed and they were alone. "My prayers have been for your safe return. Say your findings."

The priests bowed, and Molva'yas spoke with a weary voice. "Dark Lady, Modennethra sends greetings and prayers, saying their hope is for swift victory by our House. Still, they offer nothing of soldiers or aid, yet pledge no affirmation to Hovenethra's cause. They hold against involvement, that other Houses would do the same."

Alystin held her peace for moments. "And thereby seek to ingratiate themselves unto the victors." She paced away, her anger growing. "I am not surprised, yet disappointed in their reply. Still, their point is made. Should they choose against Hovenethra, what then of the other Houses? And still Warinethra's notice given to all is considered, tho' they have made no reply to the confrontations between our soldiers and those of Ba'tula's House."

"We wonder of that as well, Dark Lady." Krenasst offered wine to Alystin and she held her empty goblet forth. "To our knowing, they have done nothing to Hovenethra for their aggression, yet neither did our House suffer from our reply. I cannot know the reasons."

"What of the prisoners?" asked Molva'yas.

Alystin drank, then shrugged. "I have made no decision. Tho' tempted to release the young acolyte with a warning of harsh reprisal to Ba'tula, I cannot see the benefit. I ask your thoughts."

"Is it wise to let them live, when so many died on orders from Ba'tula?" Krenasst's voice was filled with respect, though he knew the subject must be breached.

"As said, no decision. This Dhuunyl, saying he is of their ruling council, know you of him?"

Molva'yas nodded. "A small voice within their circle, Dark Lady, said to be weak of heart."

"This is not what was shown when I spoke with him," replied Alystin, recalling the fiery words.

"Circumstance, and his life in your hands. Perhaps your very sight brings his courage forth, and he will speak his mind with one of true authority."

Alystin nearly chuckled. "More his anger would draw mine, perhaps..." She paused, thinking. "If he shows strength, others rally round him. Should he become a sacrifice, his memory then grows." She nodded. "Weak of heart or otherwise, his manner was correct. I will think on this. And the young acolyte."

Krenasst set away his goblet. "What now, Dark Lady? With Narlros and Xa'lyyth absent the council, and our numbers down a hundred soldiers, how best to proceed?"

"We wait, Dark Lord, and remain vigilant. Do not discount attack by Ba'tula's guard, for when we take our ease, she will surely strike."

* * *

341

DragonFall…

Morning came with no issues in the night, and Jyslin fed them all with the aid of Ry'lld and Lualyrr, then the trio sat aside, whispering in the corner of the sleeping room.

Thalion called a parley and they gathered at the table; Audrey, Ysilrod and Sheynon with Archane between them, Chitthra, Aeren, and the priest. Jyslin came into the room and served tea around, then retreated once again.

"We hold opportunity in our hand," Thalion began, "to find the balance and set matters as they should be for all, human, elf, and Drow. There is no better time, nor will there be, for all concerns lead to only one solution."

"Mors'ul'jyn," said Sheynon softly, then looked away. Audrey sat closely by the elf-lord and laid a hand upon his shoulder.

"Tell us where she is," said Thalion to Archane, and the Dark Princess gave a dry look to the priest.

"Where she is may not be where you presume, and were I her, I would be elsewhere."

"No riddles," said Sheynon in a warning tone. "Else we may see you in Kaul's dungeon after all is said."

Archane gave the elf-lord a withering eye. "You are the cause of this, yes? Your stealing of the artifact, given unto the clergy of the human god." She glanced to Thalion. "Lahai, your father?"

"Your knowledge is a lie," said Sheynon tersely. "Never did I agree to the taking of *Kingmaker*."

"Ah… elves are yet so honorable." Archane chuckled beneath her breath.

"Sheynon's words are truth," said Thalion, glancing round to Audrey, then to Ysilrod. "Sheynon's will was the sword should be returned, yet it was not, for reasons of… how shall I say it? Faith. Yes, reasons of faith, regarding one of piety and vision. Her name was Kaanan."

"Why then does Mors'ul'jyn hold blame upon the elves and Calidriil?" asked Archane. She glanced again to Sheynon. "A curse, perhaps, or thwarted lust for Re' in her youth?"

"Hold your tongue," said Audrey quietly, but with strength. "Keep civil, as we offer aid for all. Show us this strength you say is in your spirit, and speak with your people in your mind. Never is it too late for Kaul to decide other than to aid any of us."

The room was tensely quiet for moments, then Archane drank tea and shrugged. "Continue, Priest, as you have my ear."

"What is your offer to Kaul for his soldiers' blood? What of the Drow might he ask for?"

Archane considered, drank again, then refreshed her cup. "He wants not for concubines, his treasury is full, and his hold upon the land about is strong." She glanced around the table. "None here oppose him nor seek his lands or city, he cares not for holdings in your domains, therefore, what is left?"

"Rule of the Drow?" asked Chitthra. "It has been rumored, as surely you know."

"And said by Mors'ul'jyn herself." Archane showed a wicked grin at Sheynon's widened eyes. "Yes, and her thought was to use my body in its doing. As she did with Reena's."

"Dearest *Jhad*," whispered Audrey. "The evil therein I cannot abide. This woman must die, assuredly."

"Let us set this aside," said Thalion, drawing Archane's attention once again. "What might all herein offer Kaul for his aid?"

"Safety," replied Audrey, and Aeren tensed beside her. "For his city, his rule, his... validity as king." She looked to Thalion. "Freedom from the eyes of the City-State of Truth and their coveting of the city's return to the domain of Crysalon."

"A hard bargain, Excellency," replied Thalion, and Aeren nodded in agreement.

"For the safety of his rule, it is little enough to ask," said Archane.

"It is not your choice, therefore," replied Audrey, as she met Archane's gaze again.

Sheynon held a hand. "We bargain together, or this shall not come to pass. All must find a part, or none will be successful."

"Once more," said the priest, "what of the dark elves is offered?"

"A better choice," replied Archane, "would be I bargain with your need, and Ardwel offer in my stead."

Thalion looked to Sheynon, then to Ysilrod. "Would the elves accept such an offer?"

"As said, safety of the land is paramount," said Sheynon. "And Mors'ul'jyn the true threat in this time."

Audrey began to speak, then held her peace. Thalion caught her look and motioned her to offer words, whatever they might be.

"My concern," said the warrior-woman carefully, "is for all the souls and spirits of the land. As said by the Lord Priest, balance is imperative and must be found, else none of this will matter to our children, or to theirs."

"A notion of interest," replied Archane, with the same delicacy in her words.

"You have no family, say the tales," said Audrey. "Therefore, all the dark elves are your concern, and with that, I begin to understand your reasons."

Archane said nothing, only showed a wistful look upon her face.

"To the offer, we are agreed, yes?" Thalion looked to each in turn. "Safety for the land and all within it. A pact between the city-states, the elves, and the Drow."

"Should I sign a treaty, I would be a sacrifice upon the altar," said Archane, heat within her voice. "It is our way to conquer and give offerings."

"Therein, that may change or be redirected," said Ysilrod. "There are lands beyond the Black Forest to the east, unknown by any here. Perhaps explorer should be added to your titles."

Archane shook her head. "The Kingdom of the Sun, your realm," nodding to Audrey, "borders the forest north and east."

"There will be no insurgency within my borders," said Audrey, "yet whatever lies beyond there, I know nothing of."

"First, I must regain my place." Archane shrugged. "Else nothing herein will matter to me. Should you desire your safety, best you aid me in my cause."

"Agreed," said Thalion at the last. "Kaul's soldiers at your side, our land gains safety and what knowledge you have of Mors'ul'jyn."

Archane looked to Ysilrod. "I will need your aid to take us to her haven."

The elf-mage only showed a wry grin.

* * *

They met again at high sun in the throne room, and Kaul waved away their concerns as they were spoken one by one. He nearly laughed at their obvious confusion, then ordered a captain to his presence.

"He will follow your orders, Priest, and should you think to give control of my soldiers to Archane, I bid you fair luck. Therefore, who will descend into the depths of *Ung'gu'wi* at her side to lead them?" Now Kaul did laugh. "Surely it will keep you sleepless as you decide."

Thalion nodded slowly, the words he truly wished to say held silent. "We will confer, Great King, and find a way. Therefore, let us plan and we shall send a missive once details are final. Then, by your grace, we will meet once more and toast victory."

"What of my people waiting beyond the city?" asked Archane, giving little honor to Kaul as he lifted a cup to his lips. "They came seeking me, therefore should they not know of my living?"

"A point of order, Great King," said Thalion, hoping then to keep calm about the throne room. "If a missive from Archane were written in her hand, might you have a trusted herald to deliver it?"

Kaul mused and scratched his stubbled chin. "Very well, yet be quick! My day is filled otherwise."

Thalion bowed. "At once." He glanced to Archane and she nodded, then his eyes returned to Kaul. It was no task to imagine the thoughts within the mind of the Dark Princess.

Nearly did Thalion laugh then, as well.

* * *

At the last, and not until the passing of another day, were final preparations made complete. Orders had been given, a gathering place for the army and the Companions chosen, with time and place kept secret but for Thalion and Kaul's captain.

Ry'lld and Lualyrr were offered a choice, to remain with the dark elves in the campsite, or return to the cottage where they were found.

"We are of Hovenethra," said Ry'lld to Thalion as they spoke within the shack, "therefore would be little better than sacrifices. We will become farmers of the land. Perhaps one day, when the Dark Princess is returned to power and *Ung'gu'wi* purged of war, we will venture there again."

He took Lualyrr's hand as she came to his side. They bowed to Thalion. "We thank you for the mercy shown, surely better than we would receive from Ba'tula. We only ask safety for Archane. And for yourselves, returning her to her rightful place again."

"Keep yourselves and each other well," replied the priest. Then they were gone.

* * *

They rode out from the city, heading south once more to Drakenmoore, where, with fortune and preparedness, they would find Mors'ul'jyn in her lair. Talk was plentiful between Audrey, Aeren, and Chitthra as they rode, with lessons yet to be learned, and those now known coming to the fore.

"It is Kaul's self-importance that sits now in his mind," said Audrey, Chitthra riding on her left and Aeren on her right.

"His legacy?" asked Aeren.

"If you will. Mortality becomes an issue, and he worries how his reign will be recalled in time. What better way than as the founder of peace within the land?"

Thalion rode to Aeren's side from his place and offered thoughts. "There are reasons more practical and self-serving, Excellency, my ladies. A thousand soldiers gone are a thousand mouths less to feed within the city. More taxes, more duties now going to his coffers and not upkeep of mercenaries seeking revelry and mischief."

"Kaul's legacy," said Chitthra from Audrey's left, "is but Vichelli becoming a pit of inequity, yet I wonder if in doing so, he knows the service rendered?"

Thalion shook his head. "My lady?"

Chitthra grinned. "All the rotten eggs within the land held in a single basket."

They laughed around, and Thalion gave a bow from his saddle.

"There were times in our dealings I saw a bit of honor in him," said Aeren. "Perhaps in his maturity it rises further in his mind. We may hope."

"And pray," replied Audrey. She looked to Aeren, then motioned her horse to her side. "You have questions of me."

Aeren nodded, then spied a gathering of trees. "In private, if you will, My Liege."

They turned away, spurred their steeds into the wood and dismounted, letting the horses forage. They sat in the shade of a slender pine and wrapped themselves in cloaks, the wind chill as sunset gathered in the west.

"You worry," said Audrey, and Aeren nodded.

"Chitthra. Concern of this duty sworn against Steffyn, or Mors'ul'jyn herself. Nearly do I foresee her death."

"You must be prepared, if time comes, to let her go. Not because you do not love her, but rather that you do. Feelings, at times, require release."

"My Liege…"

Audrey took Aeren's offered hand. "Never can you hold a spirit in a cage of any sort. In your young life, surely you have learned this in your travels."

Aeren held her words for moments, then raised her face, tears glistening in her eyes. "There was a man…"

346

Audrey nodded. "I know of Hawk, and have offered prayers for his passing. I see the glow he left within your heart, and give praises for it."

"I sinned against our lord."

"How can love be a sin? Dearest Aeren, there were times in my own life temptation stalked me endlessly. Be happy in your knowing of this man, that he loved you, and you, him."

Aeren wiped her eyes. "I do not know why these thoughts come to me now. Is it only fear of losing Chitthra as I did of Hawk?"

"With certainty in part, and there is no dishonor in it. Live each day fully, give prayers for your blessings, and you will know peace."

Aeren nodded, then chuckled 'neath her breath. "Nearly do you sound as the village priest."

They laughed together for a moment, then took their saddles once again, riding on to Jeseriam, and Drakenmoore.

* * *

Jeseriam…

Ysilrod and Thalion had remained beyond the town, holding Archane and the other dark elves in their company. Thalion had cautioned against bringing Steffyn into Archane's presence, saying all would be best if the elf-mage remained in Stokar's care.

Therefore, the others stood in the back room of Stokar's shop, the air filled with pipe smoke and tension, as clouds and cold rain waited beyond the door. Sheynon seethed, as did Chitthra, yet for different reasons. Aeren stood at Chitthra's back, Audrey beside her with a hand upon the dark elf woman's shoulder. All the while they waited as Stokar sat quietly in the corner.

"You gave no direction for his keeping, therefore he was not a prisoner," Stokar said mildly.

"When last was he here?" asked Audrey, as she could not chance the others' voices being heard.

"Two days, and likely gone from the town." Stokar lit his pipe once more and blew a smoke ring. "More you should ask, where might he go?"

"Jyslin, and the city-state," said Aeren quickly.

"In search of Mors'ul'jyn is more the like," replied Chitthra after a moment. "Absolution, then escape."

Sheynon shook his head, eyes still locked with Stokar's. "Little does it matter, for we cannot follow. Our course is set."

"I can," said Chitthra. "I must. I have given vows yet unfulfilled."

347

"No!" Sheynon turned to the dark elf woman. "I do not hold you to taking vengeance on Steffyn for crimes of any sort. What was done is done, and Galandria's spirit will rest no easier for your actions… or your vows."

Chitthra met him eye to eye. "My lord, with all respect, it is not your choice."

"It is! Steffyn's transgression has been forgiven by the only one who could do so, my own self!"

"And your great lord *Yarhetha'an*, has he given blessing on your doing so?" Chitthra turned away, walking to the door.

"Stop this." Audrey's voice was soft, but held command within it. "We may hold agendas different from one another, yet first Mors'ul'jyn, then other matters, else we risk everything."

Stokar only sat, pipe in hand, watching all the while. Chitthra looked to him. "Where has he gone, as you seem to know all about us? Pray tell, what was in his mind?"

The shop-keeper shrugged. "Little of any consequence, tho' I piqued his heart a bit. If there are any dear to him, I would think them to be likely."

Aeren nodded. "Jyslin. Yet Steffyn is a mage of ability."

Stokar shook his head. "He travels on the road, or did so on leaving."

"How then did we not see him?" asked Audrey, looking to Chitthra. "How might he be caught?"

Stokar chuckled. "As said, a mage. You have one of your own within your party, yes? Ysilrod might send you to the city-state to wait."

"Assuming he goes there," replied Aeren. "Tho' likely, I cannot be certain."

"I will chance his choice," said Chitthra. She glanced to Aeren. "Dearest?"

Aeren turned to Audrey. "My Liege, I must go, as I, too, have pledged to Chitthra. Surely, should we find Steffyn, we may parley and keep him safe. From himself, if nothing else."

Audrey looked to Sheynon, but the elf-lord's eyes were locked with those of Chitthra. "Go. I pray you find him," she whispered, "for *Jhad* knows we cannot abide him in our midst. We must seek Mors'ul'jyn and end her terror."

* * *

348

Drakenmoore…

Half a day south of Jeseriam they rode, then camped away from the castle ruins, speaking in the evening round the fire, of what they might expect, or how Mors'ul'jyn would use her magics, or if any in their party would survive. Archane had begged rest, and Ysilrod cast *Sleep* upon her, then the Companions ruminated on the coming days.

"There is another possibility," said Sheynon, stoking the fire. "Might she be gone, having known we defeated her *NorthWind* sentinel?"

Ysilrod shook his head. "Therefore, I would find her, tho' I have not searched. There or absent, clues may linger, to say nothing of traps awaiting us."

"How then to be safe?" asked Audrey.

"I will enter with one other, to search for Mors'ul'jyn or ambush. Should she be there, we will return quickly, then enter all together."

Thalion shook his head. "This gives her warning, my lord. Likely we have but one chance for surprise, and surely she knows not who pursues her."

"She knows only those of ability would do so," replied Audrey, "and in that, may surmise our identities. Surely she is aware the Craft is with us, as her sentinel was defeated."

She raised a question to Ysilrod. "If you hold the *NorthWind* sword, do you not have a link? You said as such when we descended into the ruins and fought in the forge."

They were silent round the fire for moments.

"Brother, might you scry for her?" asked Sheynon, as he drew the *NorthWind* sword from his saddle sheath lying at his side, and held it forth.

Ysilrod did not take it and held a hand. "She may know then of my spying on her. If surprise is our goal, that surely would negate it."

"Agreed," said Thalion. He grinned. "Therefore, we attack en masse and blind?"

"En masse and blind!" Audrey laughed and raised her cup, as did the others, cheering.

They drank, still chuckling round, then quieted once again.

"As old times," said Audrey wistfully, catching Thalion's eye. He winked and showed a toothy grin.

"Legends all," said Sheynon, and rolled his eyes, nearly laughing once again.

"Daeron," whispered Audrey, after a moment. "A comrade as no other." Once again, they were silent in their contemplation.

"Courage as never seen," said Thalion, and Ysilrod nodded, eyes upon the fire.

"Steffyn." Sheynon's voice was filled with sadness, then he raised his face and spoke earnestly. "And in that matter, there are words I now say. You must understand, my friends, even should opportunity arise, I will not kill in cold blood." He looked to them, one by one. "I will fight should need come and defend myself, as I will all of you. And if I slay Mors'ul'jyn in combat, then my vengeance is surely taken, yet I will feel no pleasure, other than to know Galandria is avenged. Never will I dishonor her death... or her life, by murder."

"Always are you an honorable elf," said Audrey softly, then moved closer and took his hand. "In all the years we have been acquaintanced, and all the travels we have journeyed in together, never have I known one whose heart is kinder."

"At times, too kind." Ysilrod put a hand on Sheynon's shoulder. "Yet my brother seeks the balance Cousin Thalion always speaks of. If occurrence comes to make amends, so be it, yet the larger view of the world is always in his mind and heart."

"Then how, Lord Mage?" asked Thalion. "Once in her lair, we have advantage only for mere moments. We must strike quickly or surely perish."

"I will set protections round us before entering, then we shall see."

"What of Archane?" asked Sheynon quietly. "What will she do, should we encounter Mors'ul'jyn?"

"Likely she will not wish to become her prisoner again," replied Audrey, offering tea around.

"I may keep her mute," said Ysilrod. "In truth, I know not what to do other than leave her here, bound in Charm and unable to cause mischief."

"A distraction?" asked Audrey, and Sheynon looked to Ysilrod, who nodded.

"Let her decide," said Thalion. "If she holds sincere animosity for Mors'ul'jyn, a chance for revenge may be advantage to us."

"And should she die?" asked Sheynon. "Tho' I cannot believe I sit here uttering such words, are we not bound by agreement to see her safely to her home?"

Once more silence settled, then Audrey met their gazes, one by one. "Honor, friends, and we are bound to it. An enemy from our past for many years, yet now circumstance forces us together. As Sheynon, I find difficulty in these words, yet know they are true. A common foe, a common cause. We cannot proceed otherwise."

Thalion touched his cup to Audrey's and they drank once more. The elves did likewise, then they passed their looks around the fire again.

"To the morrow," said Sheynon, and they raised their cups one last time and drank them down.

* * *

They stood at the entrance once again, the morning cold and gray, with fingers of chill wind finding way beneath their collars. They waited as Archane surveyed their place, looking round.

"From where did you enter her sanctuary?" asked Ysilrod.

Archane shook her head. "Is it necessary to know? More than once we descended part way into the ruins, other times by her Craft."

"What of the time from DragonFall?" asked Thalion.

"No matter," said Ysilrod, before Archane could answer. "We would need to return to the city, otherwise, we find the leaving place here."

All the while, Sheynon and Audrey kept watch about as rain began to fall.

Archane's fiery eyes swept the entrance once again. "From here, but with clearing of the gates, it is difficult to know."

"Yet this area, and you recognize the place?" Ysilrod took a scroll from within his cloak. Archane nodded, and the elf-mage drew them close.

"What is this?" Archane nodded to the parchment and Ysilrod grinned.

"You will read the spell and take us to the lair. Once there, I will cast protections before we search." He placed the scroll within her hand.

"Yet if written in elvish, I may not pronounce the enchantment properly."

Once more he grinned. "The inscription is in Drow, therefore, you will have no worry."

Archane gave a dubious look. "Am I to trust your translation?"

"It was written by a dark elf of my acquaintance. There will be no errors." He turned from Archane's incredulous stare. "Keep weapons sheathed until I have formed wards about us."

Audrey shook her head. "My lord?"

"Traps, steel to draw lightning, Excellency," replied Thalion.

"My Brother's ability knows no equal in this land," said Sheynon.

351

Archane gave Ysilrod a hard stare. "You are clever, and would make a fine addition to my guild of mages."

Ysilrod held his tongue for a heartbeat. "I will take your words as given, a compliment, I am certain."

"Of course."

"Enough," said Thalion. "Proceed, Lord Mage, and lead us." To Archane, he said, "Read the scroll if you will, and prepare yourself for whatever may come."

Archane hesitated. "I have no weapon."

Sheynon drew a dagger and passed it to her waiting hand. "Recall who is our enemy here… my lady."

Archane took the dagger and slid the sheath beneath her belt, blew a breath and rolled out the parchment. The words, she knew, were Drow, the hand ancient, though not unknown. Briefly she wondered how it had come to an elven mage, then set the thought aside. *Too many changes, agreements I never would have considered in the past, and now I stand among elves and humans, doing bidding for my life. The only life I now possess, perhaps.*

She glanced once more around, and read the words within her mind, seeking calm and wondering of the workings of the world. Then read the enchantment in full voice, a voice commanding in its manner.

They disappeared, leaving only swirling dust and leaves in the falling rain.

* * *

On the Road to DragonFall…

They pressed their steeds hard as they might, straining to perhaps catch Steffyn in his weakened state. Yet in her mind, Chitthra knew they would not find him until they reached the city.

"His hideaway," she had said, and Aeren nodded, both nearly breathless as their horses running with the wind, as night grew upon them and they forced themselves to stop.

"First light," said Aeren as she stripped away the saddle from her steed and brushed him quickly, then tethered him to forage. She did the same for Chitthra's mount as the dark elf woman built a fire, the evening chill now upon them.

"Find a stream, if you will," called Chitthra, laying out their blankets. She set the saddles closely and sat to wait, drinking from her waterskin and thinking.

Aeren soon returned with three fish wriggling on a pointed stick. Chitthra smiled as they scaled the fish, roasted them and passed a wineskin hand to hand. Little had been said since leaving Stokar's shop two days past, yet now she knew the subject must be broached.

"What will you do?" asked Aeren, before Chitthra could say her thoughts.

The dark elf woman bowed her head and shrugged at the last. "What I must. We have spoken and given pledges to each other. Vows were made moons ago, and I must hold them." She glanced to Aeren. "My question is, what will we do after?"

"What if he is elsewhere?"

Chitthra chuckled. "That, Dearest, is a possibility, yet where else might he go? If I were him, I would gather Jyslin and run far as I might."

"Would she have him still? Recall, she saw him as elf, not Drow, and cursed him roundly."

Chitthra nodded slowly. "Yet is love not strong enough to weather ill revelations?" She looked again to Aeren. "Is ours not deep enough to stand, should I find opportunity to fulfill my vows? Once more, you promised to defend my back, should it be necessary."

Aeren drank from the wineskin and cast her gaze into the fire. "Your vows are yours to hold, as are mine. We must stand together, for what choice do we have? Else love will wither and die, a victim of circumstance neither of us may control."

Chitthra nodded once more. "Yet I know he is there. My heart says it in certainty."

"How so?"

"Were I him and you her, I would find you once again." Chitthra drew closer, and they sat side by side, arms entwining. "Truth be told, he may well know we seek him and be ready. I may not survive our next encounter, and no choices will be needed."

"There is no choice, Dearest. We are One, as elves say."

Chitthra motioned to the blankets. "Then let us take this night and make of it our own. There may never be another time."

* * *

In the Lair of Mors'ul'jyn…

They formed again in a cloud of Charm, hidden from without, said Ysilrod, and would remain so until he could complete his wards against whatever Mors'ul'jyn had set as traps.

"If she is here, alarms will be sounding now," said the elf-mage, "if not, this place will be naught but a den of horrors."

Thalion and Audrey took their shields from off their backs and held them firmly to their arms. Sheynon looked about, sharp eyes seeking movement, seeing none.

Archane watched as the scroll turned to ash and fell from her hand, then cast her gaze about the room, so familiar. "There," she said, pointing to a door aside. "Her private chambers, and never have I been within."

Ysilrod continued with his work as Thalion looked to each in turn. "This will be a test for all of us in many ways. Magic, yes, yet surely, she will send minions of many types against us. Tho' years, still we have ability and trust. Give prayers and thanks as we stand together once again."

Archane said nothing in reply to Thalion's oratory, but watched about with care. "The hearth, for I have sensed enchantment round it."

Ysilrod breathed a sigh and spoke. "Once the mist is gone, I will seal away the door to her chambers, then the hearth. This will take moments, and I will need your protection as it is done."

Thalion glanced to Audrey, and the warrior-woman nodded as they stood at Ysilrod's sides. Sheynon took a place before his brother, Archane to the rear. The mist began to clear and Ysilrod once more incanted spells. A shimmer formed at the door aside, another at the fireplace, then the room began to dim.

"Swords," said Thalion softly, and they drew their weapons, waiting for the onslaught. It came with swiftness from the corners, with ghostly forms and flashing steel-like brightness.

Blows against their shields were turned, *Gil Estel* and *Mír'rë Cala'wyne* slicing through the apparitions in reply. Those struck by Thalion's blade faded into nothing, yet Audrey's sword had no effect. Sheynon, too, wielding the *NorthWind* blade, could only parry, his counter-strikes unheeded.

Archane screamed, and Audrey turned in time to ward a blow in part. Down went the Dark Princess, blood trailing from her arm.

"Only holy steel will banish them!" shouted Thalion, and Sheynon took the fore, warding blows with uncommon speed. Archane crouched behind Audrey's stance, wrapping a tunic sleeve about her wound.

Ysilrod chanted once again, flashing blades within the air, seeking out the insubstantial forms circling round them. More ghostly swordsmen came, more flashes in the dimming light, and Ysilrod called a brightening in the room. The phantom forms vanished, those within the light, and the Companions formed a circle round Archane, still on her knees.

Now serpents from the hearth broke Ysilrod's protection, hissing smoke and fire about the room. Thalion called a storm of water, dousing all about them, the serpents drawing back.

They drew tighter about each other, and caught their breath as the specters faded, one by one. They waited, shields upraised and weapons ready, yet nothing more appeared.

Ysilrod formed another ward about them, then took a knee himself, exhausted in his work.

"Brother." Sheynon knelt beside him, offered a waterskin, and Ysilrod drank. Audrey tended Archane's wound as Thalion kept the watch about.

"This was but a test," said the elf-mage as he rose, his hand on Sheynon's arm. "They will return soon, and with greater power."

"How may they know?" asked Audrey, wrapping Archane's arm. "Are they not but conjurings with no minds?"

"In part, my lady, tho' Mors'ul'jyn would set sense about them, should we survive the first attack." Ysilrod drank again, rose and walked slowly to the hearth.

"The ornaments," said Archane, rising, moving to his side. "The pictures on the walls, the tapestries, all likely hold a threat." She nodded to the door apart again. "If she is here, she waits to scry upon us now."

"We must defeat whatever lies within this room," said Thalion, as he studied the walls and paintings hanging about. "Else we will be trapped between what remains here and what waits beyond the door."

"Touch nothing," said Sheynon, motioning to the goblets on the table. "She sets a place and thinks us fools enough to drink. Poison likely."

A rumble from the ceiling, and they quickly returned to their entry place. Ysilrod looked upward to the stones above. "We may have little choice but to enter the other room."

With that, stones began to fall around them, small at the first, then larger and more deadly.

"Go, my lord!" Thalion waved them toward the door, and Ysilrod called the ward to cover as they ran. More stones fell, and Archane was struck twice, collapsing with a cry. Audrey sheathed *Mír'rë Cala'wyne*, lifted up the Drow woman, and held her shield above them.

Sheynon's speed took him to the door before the others, yet the latch would not turn, nor could he force the entry.

"Stand back!" Ysilrod called a spell as the others knelt and raised their shields about themselves. The door exploded inward as the elf-mage was struck by debris, both from the ceiling and the door itself.

Sheynon took up his brother, Ysilrod dazed and bleeding from a dozen cuts, and they dashed in as quickly as they could. Then fell about, the floor as ice, and spikes rained down from above, piercing nearly everyone.

They retreated, only to be pummeled once again by ceiling stones.

"Ysilrod! Withdraw! Take us out!" cried Audrey, yet the elf-mage was unconscious.

"Thalion!" Sheynon covered his brother as he might, as Audrey huddled with Archane's limp form in her arms.

"Hold fast!" Thalion stood, sheathed *Gil Estel* and called a prayer quickly as he could. As the whole of the ceiling fell into the chamber, they vanished. Naught was left but wreckage, and Mors'ul'jyn's sanctuary buried in the earth.

* * *

They formed again where they had entered and collapsed around, bleeding, crying, calling out for aid.

"Thalion!"

The priest shook himself, his wounds lighter than the others, and crawled to Ysilrod, clutched in Sheynon's arms.

"Thalion! Archane is dying!" Audrey's screams roused the priest, and he looked to Sheynon's eyes, fear and pain within them.

"Keep me alive," hissed the Dark Princess through her clenched teeth. "I cannot die! I will not die!"

Thalion knelt, examining her wounds, then looked to Audrey, bleeding herself from a myriad of abrasions. "No worse than many battles," said the warrior-woman tightly. "Tend her, and I will see to Ysilrod." She rose, wincing, and stumbled to the mage.

Thalion carefully pulled Archane's tunic below her waist. Two spikes yet were in her side, and a score of cuts, some deep, laid about her breasts and belly. "I must... touch these to heal them," he said gently. She nodded listlessly, blood yet flowing freely, and he knew her heart was strong. "Sheynon, come." The elf hurried to his side. "Hold her firmly, as this will take nearly all my prayers."

Sheynon looked aside to Audrey, now crouched beside his brother. He held his peace and wrapped his arms about Archane, then nodded Thalion to begin.

356

"I will burn," whispered Archane.

Thalion gave a chuckle filled with disbelief of what was happening. "That you will not do, tho' I may need absolution afterward."

Archane's eyes met his, and she tensed, knowing what was to follow. Thalion began his chant, and the dark elf woman thrashed and cried as the healing prayer began. Sheynon nearly lost his hold upon her, weak as he was, yet found strength enough to cope.

The spikes slowly withdrew and fell aside, and Archane screamed as they tore in their release. More dark blood flowed, and quickly Thalion laid his hands upon each wound, the more serious first, then the lighter. Still and all, and even as he called upon the *Rising Star's* power to aid him, his hands were covered in Archane's blood before she began to calm.

The worst of injuries began to close, and Thalion touched her gently, searching for bones crushed or broken, finding only ribs he knew would heal. At last she drifted into healing sleep, and Sheynon could relax his hold and catch his breath.

Thalion fell aside, spent and sweating in the day's cloudy chill. Sheynon laid Archane down, covered her again with her bloody tunic, then found a blanket from his saddle and tucked it round her. He rose, then knelt again, his mind spinning still with pain, and crawled to Audrey.

"He will live," she said, swathing unguents on Ysilrod's wounds as she whispered prayers.

"And you, my lady?" Sheynon nodded to Audrey's arm, bruised, perhaps even broken. She shook her head. "You may tend it, tho' not yet. Still Ysilrod may need attention further." She looked to him. "Or yourself. What of Thalion and Archane?"

"She sleeps the healing slumber, and my cousin needs of tending. Might you see to him?"

Audrey nodded. "Keep your brother well, I will see to the others." She rose stiffly, stifling a gasp.

Sheynon looked to Ysilrod, who took his hand, eyes yet closed. "We must speak of Mors'ul'jyn," the elf-mage whispered.

* * *

Night came, and they gathered round the fire, all with aches and bruises, and bandages about their wounds. Archane slept aside, wrapped in blankets, as the others sipped broth and spoke low about the fight.

"She is not there, or surely we would have seen her," said Ysilrod. Sheynon looked to his brother, propped against a saddle and half awake.

357

"Her traps were set to kill and bury us forever," said Thalion. "Therefore, I agree, yet where might she have gone?"

"There is more," said Audrey quietly, motioning to Archane. "She begged that she not die. If she is immortal as we know, would it not be her advantage to start afresh?"

Thalion considered, then shrugged. "Who can know her mind? Yet you have a thought, Excellency?"

"Only how did she escape Mors'ul'jyn's grasp? If she did not know her place, or have ability of her Craft, what manner did she use?"

"How indeed?" Sheynon looked to Thalion, the priest drawn and weak.

"Excellency, it has been a hard day. We beg your words and enlightenment." Thalion drank more broth, then Sheynon offered to refill his cup.

"My lords, surely Mors'ul'jyn would not harm Archane, yet if so, for what purpose? I can only surmise Archane has sinned, as I would think it. She took her own life to escape, and her immortality was the price. There can be no other way."

Sheynon raised his face. "What of this dark priest, her minister, taken with her from Kaul's courtyard?"

Thalion shook his head. "Truly, I had forgotten. I have no answer."

"Dead, almost in certainty," said Audrey. "Perhaps the reason for Archane's death, that she knew then Mors'ul'jyn would use her body as she did that of the girl Reena."

"Dearest *Yarhetha'an*, the evil in her mind knows no bounds." Sheynon looked away, eyes clenched shut, avoiding tears.

"When Ysilrod awakens," said Thalion, "we must ride to safety. We are far too vulnerable in the open wood."

The elf-mage stirred, opening his eyes. "Jeseriam, and Stokar's shop. It is doubtful she knows of him or his ability."

"Brother, have you the strength?"

Ysilrod shook his head. "Sunrise." He looked to the others, one by one. "Keep Archane alive, else our cause is broken. Once with Stokar, we may consider options on Mors'ul'jyn's whereabouts."

BOOK TWELVE
PIPER'S DUE

*"Those who set storms about themselves
should not cry havoc when the rains come."*

Elven Proverb

Dennis Young

PART ONE
FIRST BLOOD

In the Depths of Ung'gu'wi…

Mors'ul'jyn eyed the scrying stone, intent upon the happenings in her sanctuary. Though she could not see it all, she knew blood had been drawn and the hideaway collapsed, trapping any left within. She blew a breath and nodded, satisfied her trail was covered, and likely no one knew where she had fled.

Her newly-found servant came to her side; a young female barely of age, and set a plate before her, then filled her cup with scented tea. Mors'ul'jyn bade her sit and talk a while, needing respite from concerns.

"Three days and you are learning well, Nullwyss," said Mors'ul'jyn. The girl smiled, saying nothing. "Now I would need you to find a fledgling mage, one with means to purchase minor spells or training. Do that, and comfort shall be ours."

"Dark Mistress, I shall. Yet before…" Nullwyss knelt before Mors'ul'jyn and drew down her tunic, showing firm breasts and tender flesh. She bared her neck, inviting a kiss or playful bite.

Mors'ul'jyn shuddered within herself, having no interest in another female. Though she knew Drow were likely to take concubines of either gender, her fingers tensed at the thought of intimacy with the girl. "For now, I need only your service," she said, holding back the tremble in her voice. "Go and do your duty, and perhaps later for pleasures or other things."

Nullwyss rearranged her dress, stood and bowed, then exited without a word. Mors'ul'jyn shook her head. *Perhaps I should have taken an older female, one seeking only safety or small comforts.*

Nullwyss had proven, in her brief time, to be a font of knowledge, knowing well the happenings within *Ung'gu'wi*; the skirmishes between the Houses, the rumors round of Archane yet alive, the Priestess Alystin now leading the House of Iyllyeth, and her adversary, Ba'tula. Mors'ul'jyn's hideaway was not within any of these places, being well away from the central chamber, down a half-finished corridor tucked beyond an ancient fallen niche. Few knew of it, and even fewer passed its way, therefore leaving her alone.

Yet I must not become complacent, as Sheynon has a brother skilled in the Craft, and others may have been involved. Steffyn Foxxe, as surmised before, or those of the Guild within Telveperen.

361

She sat again, poured tea, and reminisced about Galandria's death for the first time in years. A wicked grin came to her lips as she savored the memory of Galandria's bloody face, and the horror in her eyes as she died at Mors'ul'jyn's hand. Mors'ul'jyn knew, in time, Sheynon would suffer that very fate, and her grin widened, wondering if it would be as satisfying as watching Galandria's life slip painfully from her body. She prayed to *Urijjah* that it would.

* * *

The House of Hovenethra…

As ordered, the Lancer Captains of Ba'tula's Guard prepared attack against the enemy once more. And in the silence of the sleeping cycle, launched a wave of soldiers larger than before, crushing outer defenses, running through the corridors unhindered, killing with abandon those who stood to fight, or who ran and could not find escape.

Yet this time there were differences. Now Ba'tula had sent three mage acolytes to cast minor spells and cantrips, not only to aid in the attack, but to see responses given, and not only from the House of Iyllyeth. Ba'tula's growing confidence was bolstered by Warinethra's failure to enforce their warning, and therefore she pressed hard upon Archane's people and her holdings.

Deeper into the passageways and chambers of the House of Iyllyeth they charged. Deeper into more habitats of senior members of the Second Circle, and they killed all they saw in robes of black and crimson, knowing them to hold more power and prestige.

Into the storage chambers, cages filled with rats and other things were loosed, to poison and putrefy foodstuffs and casks of drink. Into even a prayer chamber, where three acolytes were killed and another left alive with wounds of disfigurement, to tell the tale and fill the hearts of survivors with fear and worry.

Then they sought retreat, near two score of the House left bleeding out their last, and those alive screaming in the darkness with wounds about their bodies.

Their losses were lighter than expected, and Ba'tula's soldiers sang songs of victory as they passed beyond the central chamber.

None noticed the small figure knelt aside, hiding behind a boulder as she watched. And as the screams of dying faded in the dimness, Nullwyss quietly made her way back to her mistress, to tell the tale and warn of the growing threat. She wondered, as she ran, bare feet upon the hard-packed

362

earth, what Mors'ul'jyn would do, and if she, herself, would be safer without her mistress now.

* * *

The House of Iyllyeth…

Alystin paced before the fireplace, worry in her mind and aching in her heart for the killings. The savage suddenness of Ba'tula's attack had shocked her to the core, and only by good fortune had she herself not fallen victim. Early in the prayer-time, Alystin was within the chamber assaulted by Hovenethra's soldiers, two of her acolytes killed and another maimed. Now she waited for others of the Black Web to assemble, as fifty soldiers guarded beyond the door.

Vrammyr, Molva'yas, and Krenasst entered quietly, grim of face and shaken. They bowed wordlessly, sat at the Circle, and offered small sacrificial items, going through the motions as their eyes watched the darkened corners nervously. Vrammyr was dressed more subdued than in other times, and partook only sparsely of the meal.

At the last, Alystin took her place and made the ritual offerings, then poured wine and passed the carafe to Molva'yas, and he to Krenasst. The priest in turn offered it to Vrammyr, who declined, and Alystin knew then matters were severe. They drank in quiet, all with thoughts running rampant, not knowing what to do or how to voice their words.

Alystin broke the silence at the last. "It has come to this, tho' in our patience we had hoped it never would. Hovenethra has killed now twice, without care for whom their victims were, be they servant, soldier, or clergy." She cast her eyes around the Circle, yet none would return her gaze as they stared into the fire, lost in thought.

"We must stand forth," Alystin continued. "We must meet insurgency with strong reprisal, else the other Houses will think us weak. Should that occur, the whole of the Race may become involved."

"Warinethra…" breathed Molva'yas.

Alystin held a hand. "Warinethra issued warning, and to this time, has done little to enforce it. Shall we wait until Ba'tula sends her soldiers once again? Until they probe deeply enough into our House that you or I are killed or captured? What then will Warinethra do? Will they come to our rescue, or raise us from the dead?"

"Dark Lady, no offense is hereby intended."

"Then offer your mind, for we must have it. We are the House of Iyllyeth now, until the time Narlros and Xa'lyyth are returned. By then, far too late it may be for any of us. Ourselves… Mor'i'jil… Archane."

363

"I know nothing of war," said Vrammyr, drawing her heavy cloak tight around her shoulders.

Molva'yas traded worried glances with Krenasst, then replied. "We accept your words as given, Dark Lady. Surely we must defend our House, or all herein will become sacrifices."

"Your trust is noted and confirmed," replied Alystin. I propose a meeting with our Lancer Captains and retaliation soon thereafter. No longer will we be fodder for Ba'tula's soldiers."

"What of... Warinethra?" asked Krenasst carefully.

Alystin drank, thinking. "I will send a private messenger with word, asking not for their support, only they not interfere. No longer is this the fight of any but our House and Hovenethra."

Krenasst nodded, as did Molva'yas. Vrammyr only shrugged her shoulders 'neath her cloak.

"Prepare to move your clergy and your entourage deeper into the sanctuary chambers. Alert your captains and bodyguard contingent. Set stores as necessary, see to the mages in your party, and insure traps and wards are set. We prepare for siege, and it may last for many moons."

* * *

It took the better part of three sleeping-times for preparation. Alystin's entourage was larger by far than the rest, for she now commanded those of Archane and Mor'i'jil by right. Still, matters were attended, the missive to Warinethra sent, and a reply received and worried over until Alystin found understanding.

She stood in the meeting chamber with Molva'yas and Krenasst, as Vrammyr set her duty with the acolytes. She held a parchment with no words upon it. "They have no reply," she said. "They do not speak in favor of or against, therefore, they give no blessing, nor another warning. They now stand aside, yet we have no proof, only silence."

Krenasst shook his head. "The ways of sorcerers are as no other. Still, I commend your understanding and agree. What other purpose could their silence have?"

"I will accept your words as well, Dark Lady," said Molva'yas, bowing. "Should we consider further, it may take a moon to find another answer."

"We have no time, not a moon, nor a fortnight, nor even a day. We must prepare and strike with purpose." Alystin tossed the parchment into the fire and watched it burn, nearly afraid it might release some spell or daemon in their midst. Only did the missive fall to ash, and then was gone. "I will meet with the Lancer Captain for final words. You, Dark Lords, are to keep safe and give prayers with your clergy through the night. The Dark Moon rises soon, and our campaign will begin."

They bowed once more, then departed, the door closing slowly with a nearly-silent click. Alystin paced before the fire as was her custom, waiting for the Lancer Captain to appear.

The door opened, and a servant's face showed through. "Dark Lady, word comes from beyond *Ung'gu'wi.*"

Nearly did Alystin's heart stop. She ushered in the servant, and he knelt, two guards standing at the door.

"Rise and speak. Who comes?"

"The far-speaker, Malaggos, herald to Mor'i'jil for many years."

Alystin looked to the guards, then back to the servant. "You have seen him? He is here now?"

"Dark Lady, word comes from above, in a village. Malaggos seeks entry, but was denied."

"Who denied this?" Again, she looked to the guards. "Bring your captain."

The guard on the servant's left bowed and took his exit. Alystin once more began to pace, then the door opened for the guard and captain, a female Alystin knew as Qiless. She bowed to Alystin on entering.

"Word comes of Malaggos, Mor'i'jil's herald, sent with the party to the Mongrel's city, seeking entry with word from beyond the forest. Now I hear entry is denied. What know you of this?"

Qiless shook her head slowly. "Dark Lady, nothing, for should we hear, surely Malaggos is known well and would be admitted."

"Seek his place and bring him here in safety." Alystin's fists clenched in worry and in anger. "Then send my Captain of the Corridors at once."

Qiless bowed and took her exit quickly.

"Rise and seek your quarters. Tell them you are to have wine and bread." The servant bowed to Alystin and disappeared beyond the door.

Alystin faced the guards again. "No one is to disturb me until your captain brings Malaggos or the Captain of the Corridors appears."

"Yes, Dark Lady."

The door closed and once more she was alone.

Something is amiss, known when I met with the Circle three days past. Intrigue stirs, and I must be aware, else my heart may beat its last within Ba'tula's hand.

* * *

Jeseriam, and Stokar's Shop...

Two days on, and at the last Ysilrod and Archane held strength enough to travel, soon arriving in Jeseriam. They sat in the back room of Stokar's shop once more, Archane abed and sleeping from her wounds and fatigue of traveling, Ysilrod knelt away in a corner, surrounded by a shimmer of bluish fog and blankets.

Audrey and Thalion sipped healing spirits, wondering of what now would come.

"Once healed, should we not continue to the meeting place for Kaul's mercenaries?" Audrey moved her aching arm gingerly aside and winced, then found a less uncomfortable position.

Sheynon looked to Thalion, deep in thought. "Cousin? You seem distracted on this day, or are you ill?"

The priest shook his head. "Ill of thought only, and what may happen if Steffyn is returned to DragonFall and found by Chitthra." He drank his cup and refilled it with tea. "I will send a message to Kaul's throne room, asking him to search the inns near Steffyn's hideaway. I will not say where it is, yet Chitthra and Aeren may well take a room close by."

"A prayer message?" Sheynon grinned. "Perhaps it will burn his fingers upon opening."

Thalion showed a slight smile, looked to Archane on the bed, then to Audrey. "I have pondered your conclusions of Archane's escape and find agreement. Simple answers, Excellency, and I commend your thinking."

"Therefore, we hold advantage over her," said Sheynon. "And opportunity."

Audrey gave a disapproving look. "My lord, I beg your patience. Still we are bound by honor of our agreement."

The elf-lord nodded at the last. "And as said, I will not succumb to murder, in any fashion. My apologies for such vile thoughts."

Audrey returned the nod. "What now, my lords? To the army, yes?"

Stokar entered from the shop, pipe in hand and a smile upon his face. "You are lucid enough to deliberate again, and now hold the future of the land firmly in your hands." He nodded to Archane sleeping. "How will you shape what is to come?"

Sheynon looked Stokar in the eye, uneasy with his presumption. "As said by Lady Audrey, honorably. Regardless the past, we must shape the future, but with temperance."

"You pique us, sir," said Audrey, reproof heavy in her voice. "I have often wondered why."

"To make us think before we act," said Thalion, and Stokar's smile turned into a grin. "Therefore, we seek the better way, and the balance needed for the land to remain at peace, all parties satisfied."

Stokar motioned with his pipe to Ysilrod. "The mage will understand, once wakened. He will hold the key, is my thought." He turned, disappearing beyond the beaded curtain into the shop as the bell above the entry door rang brightly.

"Never will I understand his knowing," said Sheynon softly. "Since I have been in his acquaintance, always is he one thought ahead of all."

"A seer?" Audrey scoffed. "More a reader of our hearts and minds."

* * *

The House of Iyllyeth...

Word came from the village and the guards, Malaggos was safe beyond *Ung'gu'wi*, and Alystin's corridor captain had set guards about him.

"Still there is ill news, Dark Lady," said the guard before her, as they waited in the meeting chamber. "Dark Priestess Vrammyr keeps us from descending with the far-speaker, yet we gleaned a message." He passed her a fold of parchment with a seal well-known. Alystin held her breath. "Call Molva'yas and Krenasst to my presence at once. Tell them of urgency."

The guard retreated, leaving Alystin alone once more. She sat, broke the seal, and read the message, nearly swooning as she did. Feelings great and small passed across her face, and tears began descending, of joy, of hope, of bitter sadness, and anger for revenge. She let it all escape, for in truth, she had held it many moons, too many now to count, as the House of Iyllyeth had been set into her care. Now the endgame approached, and Alystin knew she held the way to bring Hovenethra to its knees.

Time passed, and in its doing, she composed herself, took a kerchief from her sleeve, and dried her eyes. She knelt away to pray, then rose, walking to the tiny fountain in the corner, and let the cooling waters play across her hands. She washed her face, dried it once again, and took a breath, more free of fear and worry than for many days. She held the missive in her hand, read it once again to be certain of the meaning, then nodded to herself. Time now for ending of this bitter struggle had finally come.

The door opened and Molva'yas and Krenasst entered, bowing as they always did. She bade the guard call the Captain of the Corridors, then nodded for the door to be closed.

"Sit, Dark Lords, and rejoice." Alystin held the note before her. "From Archane, written in her own hand and with a secret sigil known only to ourselves. She lives and is safe, only days ago." She laid the note before them.

Molva'yas perused the message quickly, passed it to Krenasst, then burst into tears, singing praises to the ceiling. Krenasst read, then closed his eyes and wept silently. Alystin watched as the priests embraced each other tightly.

"With this blessed news comes sadness as well," said Alystin. "Dark Lord Mor'i'jil is no more, murdered by this Reena-woman, now called Mors'ul'jyn. The Dark Princess lays it all before us, and we praise her wisdom and her courage."

Molva'yas took the parchment in his trembling hands and read it once again. "She is in the company of elves and humans, Dark Lady, yet says they are of little threat. The army returns soonest, and with them we may face Hovenethra on better terms."

Alystin nodded. "Read on, and you will see Archane brings the might of Kaul, the Mongrel, with her. Soon we will hold advantage of numbers great enough to end this insurgency."

"I cringe at the thought of humans in our homes," said Krenasst bitterly, "yet if it is enough to end Ba'tula's threat, so be it. We will purge their stink with the blood of Hovenethra!"

Molva'yas chuckled, then looked about. "Where is Dark Priestess Vrammyr? Is she not party to this news?"

"She is not." Alystin sat, her voice dropping to a whisper. "The Captain of the Corridors saw fit to keep her in the village. I am told she held Malaggos from this very duty, that we would not know of Archane's words. I say to you, Dark Lords, as I trust you with this thought, Vrammyr's agenda is not as ours. I sense treachery, and will order her confined at once."

Krenasst nodded, as did Molva'yas. "Truly, I knew tension grew within her in the last moons. Think you Ba'tula has gained her as an ally? Yet why?"

Molva'yas waved a hand. "She falls in status in this House, therefore seeks another. Never has Vrammyr been other than selfish for her cravings."

"Dark Lady, I will take this duty, should you wish it." Krenasst bowed in his chair.

"And I," said Molva'yas. "We will bring her here, that you may find the truth within her tongue."

"Do so now." Alystin rose. "Say nothing of the message, and bring her here in comfort. I want no chance she may see her death waiting for her in this room."

* * *

The City-State of DragonFall…

Steffyn's journey had been difficult at best. Weak and frail, not yet recovered from the spirit-crushing dealings of Archane, he took rest more often than he wanted, knowing time against him, and likely someone on his trail.

Chitthra, as she will not be deterred. How will I deal with her, once seen again? Who will survive, and will Aeren be the one to strike the death-blow in her stead?

He rode on, the third day beyond Jeseriam, yet had not reached the villages below DragonFall, and knew he risked capture. Yet his body ached with every fall of his horse's hooves upon the road, and barely could he hold himself within the saddle. In time, he became aware of his surroundings, and realized he had ridden half the day asleep. Beyond the hills rose the gates of the city-state, and Steffyn roused himself, knowing he was safe.

He shook himself to keep alert, riding hard into the gates where guards passed him on with nary a glance or word. He rode to the stable near the inn, led his steed into the stall paid for in silver many moons ago. No others were around, not the stable master, nor the grooming boys, nor even the young redheaded girl who had fed his horse so many times. He tended his mount for moments, waiting for someone to appear, yet no one came. It was only then he realized his error, that still he was an elf, not the Drow Mend'rys known, and gave a silent prayer for solitude.

More time I need to recover, and Jyslin will care for me. Surely I may explain away what she has seen and gain her trust again. How I miss her, the small touches between us in the night…

Again, Steffyn drew a breath, deep to clear his head and heart. He glanced around, seeing no one still, then cast the look of Mend'rys on himself. His horse started, then settled as the dark elf Mend'rys stroked his muzzle gently. Sounds from the entrance, and a grooming boy and the redheaded girl appeared, hand in hand. They stopped on seeing him.

"Master Mend'rys, we thought you had left the city." The girl nodded to him, then nudged the boy to do so.

"Business of an urgent nature," Mend'rys replied, "yet I bid you now care for my steed. I may need him ready on the morrow or the day to follow. I will send a message." He tossed them both a coin of silver. "No one is to know I have returned. Seal your lips of our words."

They nodded, eyeing the coins, then set about their tasks.

He took his leave, down the pathway known, through the head-high weeds and grasses, at last coming to the door of his sanctuary. He paused, drew a heavy breath, and opened the door slowly. The central room was as he had left it. So long as his heart beat, the magic would remain. He crossed the room to the sleeping chamber. Jyslin lay in the bed alone, and he only stood at the threshold watching for a moment, then backed away, stirred the stew at the hearth, filled a bowl and sat, eating quietly.

A small sound from the sleeping room and Jyslin slowly walked to the entry, rubbing her eyes. She yawned and looked into the room, gasped, then shuddered, and Mendr'ys thought she would faint away.

"Master?"

He rose, walked slowly to the girl, and she collapsed into his arms, sobbing tears of love and joy.

* * *

Though he was weak and worn and dirty from the road, he took time to speak of his reasons for escaping, offering what he might of apology and explanation. She bade him bathe, washed his back, then dried him with slow and sensuous hands.

She led him to the bed, tossed off her tunic, and wrapped herself around him. She drew him in, then took him into ecstasy until he was exhausted.

They lay together in a tangle, coupled once again, then drifted into sleep. All the while Jyslin's hands clutched his arms, his shoulders, or held him tight against her breasts, as though he might disappear if she looked away.

Until night fell beyond the hideaway, they slept, Mend'rys waking at the last to the sounds of soft singing from the other room. He rose and dressed, then stood at the doorway watching Jyslin dance about as at the ball or in the forest. He smiled, took her in his arms and swayed across the floor, around the table, and back again. They laughed, as they had not done in many moons, and Mend'rys held her tightly, and she him.

"Master, come, and I will feed you breakfast." She twirled away, held a chair for him to sit, and brought him greens and fruit and tea and bread. She sat beside him, nudging her leg against his hip, and fed him playfully.

How to make escape, thought Mend'rys once again, *with Chitthra and Aeren soon to darken my threshold? How?*

370

Jyslin held bread before him, watching questions race across his eyes. "Master?"

* * *

Ung'gu'wi, and Mors'ul'jyn's chamber…

Nullwyss brought the news of Hovenethra's gambit, and Mors'ul'jyn sat contemplating how best to plan her doing. She watched the girl kneeling in the corner, a talisman clutched tightly, and fervent prayers being whispered. Mors'ul'jyn knew she must show strength, or the girl would be gone in heartbeats, and likely, should she be questioned, reveal all she knew.

Mors'ul'jyn rose and walked slowly to Nullwyss, then placed a hand upon her shoulder. "Calm, child… be calm in your demeanor. Know you are safe with me, and must hold our secrets dear. You will obey, you will be loyal, should you be asked of your whereabouts."

Mors'ul'jyn raised her up and to the table, sat her in a chair and watched her slowly quieting face. "Now… you are at peace, yes?" She held the talisman before Nullwyss's eyes. "This is your link to me, and should worry cross your mind while away from our chamber, you will simply hold it in your hand. Anxiousness will fade, and you will know to only say you are away from your crèche for food or drink. You understand and will do as commanded, yes?"

"Mistress, I understand and will obey." Nullwyss's eyes were nearly closed, dreamy, placid, no worry shown.

Mors'ul'jyn smiled. "Return to your duties, and take a glass of wine for yourself. Always are you safe with me."

Nullwyss rose and bowed, then set about arranging their sleeping niche. Mors'ul'jyn watched for moments, thoughts running with concern. *How will this play, with war and battle all about us? Does this offer opportunity, or only danger? I must have answers quickly, for with her freedom, Archane will find a way back into her power. I must be well-hidden in Ung'gu'wi on her return.*

Nullwyss set a pot of tea before her, then knelt in the corner once again, praying and studying a tiny book of scriptures.

Mors'ul'jyn drank and filled her cup again. *Who else might I find as an ally in this place? With Mor'i'jil gone, who rules now in Archane's stead?*

She raised her head in revelation. "Nullwyss." The girl turned, stood and bowed again. "Dark Priestess Alystin rules now in House of Iyllyeth, yes? And might you be acquaintanced of a messenger?"

* * *

371

The House of Hovenethra…

Ba'tula sat with Kreothren and Aysa'lil, as the Lancer Captain gave account of the strike against the House of Iyllyeth.

"At the least, a score slain, Dark Lady, and twice that wounded. Shall we prepare another sortie?"

Ba'tula glanced to the clergy at her side, yet neither offered words. "For the nonce, see your soldiers fed, and send concubines among them as reward. Double guards at entryways and have runners sent, should reprisal come in strength."

The Lancer Captain bowed and took his exit, then servants entered to set the chamber for prayers and chanting. Others brought a meal and wine before Ba'tula, and she nodded Kreothren and Aysa'lil to partake. They poured wine and ate slowly, all the while Ba'tula watching closely.

"You have thoughts and I bid you speak them," said the matriarch, in amicable voice and nearly smiling.

"Concerns only, Dark Lady," said Aysa'lil, reluctant to meet Ba'tula's eyes. "We hear the reports of deaths and dealings upon the House of Iyllyeth and wonder… was there not another way?"

Ba'tula scoffed. "Moons ago conclave was called, and nothing came of it. Council was recommended and rejected by Mor'i'jil, now he as well is gone, leaving only Alystin and others to guide the Race. Shall we allow her to be our mistress?"

"Rumors…"

Ba'tula paused her cup. "Only that, and lies to keep us placid. Now Hovenethra marches to destiny and our rightful place as leaders."

"Should we… when we are successful, what then?" Kreothren spoke quickly at Ba'tula's glare. "For their clergy, Dark Lady, for Alystin and their Circle? What will you do?"

Ba'tula considered. "A worthy question, and I will be magnanimous. They may join our priesthood should they choose."

"And if they say nay?"

"Then the altar waits. *Mother Darkness* will claim her due of hearts in sacrifice."

"What of the other Houses?" asked Aysa'lil, her words growing bolder with the wine.

Ba'tula shrugged. "What of them? They are unwilling to interfere, or surely would have done so by now."

"Perhaps they wait for the ending, then take the mantle of leadership themselves, our House weaker than before with losses," replied Aysa'lil.

"Should that occur, I will give you the pleasure of being first upon their altar." Ba'tula poured wine for herself and drank. "Where do these dark thoughts come from? We stand upon the threshold of victory and leading of the Race! Hovenethra is strongest of the Houses, and is worthy of the scepter!"

"Not dark thoughts, but only of concern," said Kreothren, with a bow. "We consider other outcomes as we know your days are filled."

Ba'tula set her cup away with care. "Think you I do not consider of these things? I am advised by our Lancer Captains of every sortie, every skirmish, every intrusion into Alystin's holdings. I am assured by them of victory. Do they lie?"

"No, Dark Lady, only… they may say what you wish to hear, only to appease you."

Ba'tula's nostrils flared and her eyes flashed heat. "Say why I should not send you to the confines below now. You sit in the Circle of Rule within the House of Hovenethra. How dare you speak against our destiny!"

Again Kreothren bowed, this time more deeply. "With deepest love and admiration, we say words only for your ears, that you may know us in your confidence. We only hope you will consider other possibilities and let us aid you in preparation for them."

"You hold so much within," said Aysa'lil. "As you say, we are of the Circle, and only wish to be of service."

Ba'tula sipped, searching calm and thinking. "Very well. Should these matters become an issue, we will speak further, and I will consider your words with greater care. For the nonce, know our Lancer Captains are vigilant upon the other Houses, Warinethra paramount. So long as we show no threat to them, they will not act in turn. Their warning was only that, to keep us from their door."

Aysa'lil traded looks with Kreothren, and they bowed to Ba'tula. "We thank you for your trust with these knowings. Truly, Hovenethra is on the cusp of a greater day within the Race. How shall we proceed, Dark Lady?"

Ba'tula grinned in satisfaction. "With all haste, and blood of the House of Iyllyeth on our swords. Soon Alystin will be our prisoner, and we may examine her heart closely, as it lays within my hand."

* * *

The House of Iyllyeth…

Alystin waited by the fountain as Molva'yas and Krenasst entered with Vrammyr between them and two soldiers following. The door closed, the soldiers standing between Vrammyr and the entry.

"What is this?" The priestess cast her eyes about.

"More you should ask what this is," replied Alystin, holding the note before the priestess's eyes. "A message from beyond *Ung'gu'wi*, brought by Mor'i'jil's herald, Malaggos himself, known a century or more for faithfulness. You held him from my presence."

Vrammyr shrugged. "It is nothing. I perused of it, a report saying little. Surely you do not think otherwise."

Alystin nearly barked a laugh. "How can you lie in this place? I have read the missive, and there is gladness in it." She glanced to the soldiers and motioned them to exit. The door closed with a soft latching, then silence fell for moments.

"My words were said that the soldiers considered nothing of the note," said Vrammyr. "Nearly did you give away its contents to them."

Alystin shook her head. "How could you have seen the words, as the seal was unbroken!"

Vrammyr chuckled. "Surely one as wise as you know the trick. Unroll the parchment from the center, then return it to its place."

Alystin looked to Molva'yas, who answered for her. "The message was not rolled, but folded. This is known to be the way of only one within the Circle. The Dark Princess her own self."

"You did not know of the message," said Alystin, stepping closer to Vrammyr. "You held away the far-speaker of Archane's own minister, bearing news we have waited five years and more to hear."

Vrammyr bowed her head, sweat now beading on her skin. "More lies, more falsehoods, for Archane is gone, and likely Mor'i'jil." She raised her face to Alystin. "This House is weaker for it, and yes, you do little in their stead. Hovenethra presses us, kills with stark abandon, and you do nothing. You have no courage to draw blood, let alone lead the Race."

"I do not lead the Race, only hold the seat for those who rightly do."

"Yes!" Vrammyr nearly spat the word. "And Ba'tula will take that seat away. Archane is dead! Mor'i'jil likely, too, and with those passings, the House of Iyllyeth dies now! Nothing you may do will stop it."

Alystin slowly and with care unfolded the note before Vrammyr. "Know you this hand?" She held the note to Vrammyr's eyes.

"…Impossible!" Vrammyr looked away.

"You held away words to bring peace back to our people. Why so? I can think only of one reason."

"A ruse! A trick! Never will Archane return, she has forsaken us, even should she live!"

Alystin tucked the note into her cloak and looked to Molva'yas. "Call the guards to return. Confine her to chambers, see no less than ten soldiers keep her there. Take her acolytes, that all will be accounted for. I will suffer no more traitors in this House."

She looked to Vrammyr once again. "Soon we will decide your fate, yet now there are matters more important. Perhaps on her return, Archane will be the one to hold your heart. Surely that would be a fitting end for one whose belief falters deeply as does yours."

* * *

On the Road to DragonFall...

Aeren's horse had caught a rock within a crevice of a hoof, and half a day was lost as they bargained for another. Then on the road again, and rain caused them to seek shelter in a wood, waiting out the storm as the horses foraged.

"I have a thought," said Aeren, as the huddled 'neath their tent, rain falling lightly and thunder in the clouds above. "Should Steffyn be at the hiding place in DragonFall, might we offer him to join our descent into the Drow underground? If agreed, would this satisfy your vows and allow him to live?"

Chitthra shifted in her place, thinking. "You worry of my vows, yet say nothing of your own. Truly, where is your interest?"

Aeren looked away. "I do not mean to renew the argument, and think only of your safety."

"I have fought him twice, defeated once, and won as well. This will decide both our fates, and I want no further word."

"Dearest —"

Chitthra crawled to the tent flap, looking out into the forest, then turned to Aeren. "Should you wish release from your duties, I will grant it. Yet say no more of this, for I cannot discard my pledge. My path is set."

With that, she was gone, and Aeren left alone.

She lay down, tears stinging in her eyes, knowing fear and love had driven her, once more, to broach the subject. She tossed about, then sat again and sighed, at last kneeling and whispering a prayer.

"Dearest *Jhad*, what am I to do? I love her, and cannot let her face such as Steffyn Foxxe alone. Surely there is a way other than death for one or both, or even of myself, as I have sworn to guard her back. Never would I shirk my vows to her, never would I break my word or promise. Still, why must either die for such madness we were not a part of?"

She signed herself, then sat again and drew her sword from the sheath. She took the sharpening stone from her saddle pouch and held it, thinking, then drew it down the blade, the steel ringing in the silence of the tent.

* * *

Chitthra wandered in the forest as the rain abated, pausing at a young oak tree to think. *Surely, I should not have spoken such, and I know Aeren only thinks the best of all, that they may be redeemed. So much as her mentor, yet here I stand with vows assured, and cannot break them. Yet twice I held Steffyn's fate in my hands and was paused, once by Aeren her own self! No more can I deny my own judgement, or I will fail again!*

She lingered, picking leaves from a low-hanging branch, thinking what she should do. *Drow do not... love. Yet here I stand, the love of my life beside me, and I sometimes wonder at the feeling.*

She glanced across her shoulder as Aeren came from the tent to saddle the horses once again. Chitthra turned, walking slowly to the camp, placed her hands on Aeren's shoulders from behind, and gently squeezed. Aeren came into her arms and kissed her warmly.

"Let us continue on the road," said Chitthra. "Still we have a day to ride and must arrive soonest as we may. Then, Dearest, we will consider how best to deal with this sorcerer."

Aeren touched Chitthra's cheek and nodded. "I love you."

Chitthra showed a crooked grin. "You cannot resist my charms, yes? Therefore, let us ride. The sooner we are in the city, the sooner a warm bed and comfort will find us there."

* * *

DragonFall...

Another night of Jyslin's charms, and Steffyn woke to the smells of roasting meat. He turned aside, found his undertunic and donned it with sleep still in his eyes. He padded barefoot into the central room to see Jyslin tending a loin turning in the hearth. He glanced aside, a bottle on the table, and two crystal glasses of deep red wine beside it.

Jyslin smiled. "The human Aeren gave a pouch of silver to me on her leaving, and with your return, my thought is we should celebrate." She basted the loin with spices, turning it again.

Steffyn only watched, half-awake. He sat and sipped the fruity wine, savoring the taste.

Jyslin came to him, wiping her hands clean on her apron, and knelt before him. "I understand your leaving, and hold no ill for it. You are powerful, Master, and never would I question you." She dropped her eyes for a moment, then looked to him again. "Still, I worry of your true form, an elf, and know I am not one to understand. But I must know… is your love for me still real, or am I but a harlot for your pleasure?"

Steffyn shook his head, then yawned, and they shared a quiet laugh. She held him close, and he wrapped his arms around her, sighing, knowing soon he must explain himself.

"Feed us, for you have brought the hunger from me," he said, jesting.

She nodded, returned to the hearth and turned the spit again. She carved the loin with a heavy knife and licked her lips playfully, then winked.

Steffyn pondered. Where would he go? The thoughts had been in his mind the night before, but Jyslin's charms had tempted him, his lust nearly at a roar. Therefore, he had slept the day away, exhausted from his wounds, his ride to the city-state, and the ache left within his spirit for Archane.

Jyslin placed a plate before him, the meat hot and fragrant, fresh bread beside it, still warm from the oven. She filled his glass again, then her own, and took the place beside him.

"I have a task," he said after a bite. "Still there are things to be done, and tho' I had opportunity once past, now I must steel myself to do them."

Jyslin nodded. "We will go together, Master. I will keep you well in your obligations."

Steffyn did not answer, not knowing what to say.

"They told me lies," said Jyslin, peering into her wine. "They said you have done terrible things, yet I did not believe them. I said nothing, Master, I swear, and when they left, I knew you would return." She drank, then continued. "Yet they came again, with others."

Steffyn's head came up quickly. "What others? Did you know of them?"

His sudden intensity startled her, and she drank again. "I did not know what to do, I could not keep them from this place, for you were gone, and… and…"

"Who?" Steffyn struggled to keep his voice from rising. "You must remember, for it may mean my life!"

Jyslin shook her head slowly. "Elves, and a human woman, the one you spoke of many times."

Audrey! Sheynon, and likely Ysilrod! "And a half-elf male, a priest?"

Jyslin's eyes showed tears. "Yes, Master, and others, Drow, two females and a male."

"Who?!"

Tears rolled down her cheeks. "Please, Master, I did only as I had to. Yet I could not deny the needs of the Dark Princess her own self."

"Archane was *here*?!"

Jyslin nodded, now weeping openly.

Steffyn rose, walking quickly to the sleeping room, and began to dress. He made way into his workshop, pausing Jyslin with a hand. Once within, he gathered scrolls and a pouch filled with fire-stones, another holding gold and silver. He looked about, then took two daggers, thrust them into his belt, then exited the room.

"I must leave at once. You will stay and admit no one, do you understand? Not Chitthra, not Aeren, nor any of the others. I will set a lock upon the door and teach you the hidden word to open it."

"Master, let me go beside you. Surely you will need my aid in some way or fashion."

"No!" He paused and huffed a breath. "There is danger, more than you will ever know. Whether I live or die, I cannot endanger you further."

"Master, please…"

Steffyn raised a hand to pause her words, then tossed the bag of coins onto the table. "Once I am gone, perhaps you should leave as well. I will latch the door and once you exit, no one may enter evermore. This place is known by far too many enemies."

"Master, I had no way to keep them out!"

"It matters not, what is done is done. You make your own way from this time forward."

"I cannot do so!" Jyslin held her arm before him, though in its look it now was full and strong. "I am disfigured, and of little use! I will be taken as a slave by any who might see me!"

"I think not. There is gold enough for passage wherever you might wish to go and live well."

Jyslin's eyes filled with tears once more. "I wish to go with you!"

"No. As said, danger waits, and time it is for us to part. Prepare your travel items and we will leave together. Stay at the inn this night and perhaps the next, then leave the city."

"Where... should I go?"

Steffyn shrugged. "I... cannot say. Perhaps the City-State of Truth, or a dark elf village. Surely you might find someone to take you in." He turned to gather up his things as Jyslin cried at his back.

"No! I will not go! I will be with you! I have given all I am, asking nothing! Take me with you, I beg you!"

Steffyn paused, sagging upon himself, then turned. "The elf I am is real. Mend'rys is but a mask, a disguise, a hiding place. Too long I have kept it and now must face what is to come alone." He turned to his pack once more, sorting through the contents.

"*No!*"

Fire erupted in Steffyn's back, once, twice, thrice. He staggered, fell, rolled and saw Jyslin standing over him, the carving knife in her hand, wet with his own blood. She came at him, screaming all the while, and he raised his hands to ward the blows. Two fingers flew aside as she cut his palms to the very bone, then drove the knife into his gut. Steffyn retched, choked out a cry, blood spewing from his mouth. Jyslin screamed again, cut his throat, then straddled him and drove the knife deep into his chest.

Steffyn's hands fell aside, his body now aflame. Numbness settled slowly, and he felt his heart's ragged beating. He could not draw a breath, and the sight before him began to fade.

Jyslin backed away, the knife dripping blood and gore beneath her. "I loved you and gave myself to you! You lied, you deceived, and never did you truly care! Only could I take revenge, and I prayed to *Iylyeth* I would have my chance should you reject me! Now you die, and only one thing more have I to do! I cannot live in shame! I cannot live in heartache! You have killed me as I have brought death to you!"

She held the bloody knife to her breast, tears streaming down her face. She wailed and cried, and at the last, thrust the knife into her belly. Dark blood flowed down her arms, dripping to the floor. She crawled her way to Steffyn, his life's blood a dark and widening pool beneath him. She kissed his cheek, drew his limp and now-pale arms about herself, and closed her tear-laden eyes.

The magic of the sanctuary began to fade as darkness took them both.

* * *

379

Dennis Young

PART TWO
TEARS AND RAIN

The House of Iyllyeth...

In the great prayer chamber, where once each dark moon Archane had led the assemblage in prayer and song and sacrifice, Alystin called them all; priests and priestesses, acolytes and other tenders of the Faith, Lancer Captains, soldiers, laborers, servants, and concubines. The whole of the House filled the chamber and the corridors beyond, to hear the miracle now said in rumors, spread by Alystin herself.

For it had come to her, in a flash of inspiration, a cause was needed to carry the fight to Hovenethra, one true and factual, not made of hope and dreams.

With Molva'yas and Krenasst at her left, and Narlros and Xa'lyyth now returned from the land of Ardwel on her right, Alystin, in full regalia and her acolytes chanting from the gallery, stood ready to announce the news. Even Vrammyr had been permitted from her holding, though she was flanked by soldiers loyal to only Alystin, and soon would be returned to her chambers.

The crowd mulled, anxious and anticipating, Lancer Captains speaking in low voices of what this might mean for glory in the ranks, and guards about watching for trouble that would catch their eyes.

"I come bearing a gift of gladness," Alystin began. She glanced to Molva'yas, who stifled a growing grin, tears gathering in his eyes. She held the missive in her hand and raised it. "Here, in her own hand, Dark Princess Archane proclaims she lives this day! Her return is certain, and we rejoice in our prayers to *Iyllyeth* being answered."

Only for a heartbeat was there silence of disbelief, before the chamber erupted into joyful celebration. Priests within the crowd led prayers and song, soldiers clasped each other in camaraderie and oaths shouted to the heavens, as servants scurried to and fro, offering toasting goblets filled with wine.

"To Archane's return!" shouted Alystin, then raised her glass. All around, a thousand cups were raised in answer, and they drank down their salute, then carried on the celebration.

Quietly, and to the side, Alystin led the Black Web to a private chamber, speaking with the Captain of the Guard to return Vrammyr to her chambers. They passed through the door held by a brace of soldiers, then bolted it behind them and stood, hand in hand, as Alystin led a prayer.

At the last, with the din of merriment still heard beyond the door, Alystin met the eyes of the clergy gathered round. "Your thoughts, and spare no words." She looked to Molva'yas, the senior of those attending.

"Dark Lady, we see naught but joy and thankfulness. In truth, what else might there be?"

"Deep concern and guilty feelings," replied Xa'lyyth, then she dropped her eyes away. Narlros offered his hand, and she took it tightly in her own. "All herein know of words said for years of Archane's absence, to say nothing of Dark Lord Mor'i'jil. Will Archane seek those saying disparagement against her?"

"What say you?" asked Alystin. "Tho' the youngest among our Circle, you have borne much of giving and of shame at the hands of others. What might you do in her stead?"

Krenasst shifted nervously. "Dark Lady —"

Alystin held a hand, and the priest fell silent, waiting as did she.

"I would give... absolution," answered Xa'lyyth at the last. "And pray only she will do the same for me."

"Nothing you have endured was other than for the Race and House," said Narlros softly.

Xa'lyyth gripped his hand tighter, sighing as she did.

"Therefore, you will beg this boon before her, your own circumstance as payment," said Alystin.

Xa'lyyth bowed, showing a small smile of gratitude.

Alystin once more looked at the gathering. "What of Vrammyr?"

"I have thought upon this," said Molva'yas, "and spoke with Dark Lord Krenasst at length. I shall offer argument for her reinstatement, with restrictions."

"And I will counter with words against," said Krenasst. "Tho' my argument will be weaker than that of Molva'yas. Vrammyr yet is useful, and as known, a favorite of Archane. Dark Lord Molva'yas and I will find a plea acceptable for all involved." He gave a slight shrug. "None here wish to see Vrammyr's heart in Archane's hand, I am certain."

Alystin nodded. "Well thought, yet do not discount Archane wanting a lesson to be given on her return. Yet still, Ba'tula's own heart will surely warm her hand well enough."

They chuckled round, then Alystin brought forth a small decanter of dark wine and poured their glasses full. "To Archane's return, and the end of war within our people. May *Iyllyeth* grant us favor, as we offer *Mother Darkness* the hearts of those who sin against the Race."

* * *

The House of Hovenethra…

Ba'tula listened with care as Aysa'lil spoke and Kreothren trembled at her side.

"Dark Lady, it is confirmed by our infiltrator. This day, Alystin offered word and proof of Archane's living, saying soon she would return." The priestess glanced sternly to Kreothren, who held his arms about himself in abject fear. "How might we proceed? What may we do to save ourselves this day?"

Ba'tula refilled her cup and drank, saying nothing as she stared away. *So close we were! And now, will our hearts beat their last in Archane's hands? No! I shall not allow it!*

She straightened, arranged her robes once more and looked upon her clergy. "Should this even be the truth, still we have a chance. We will send our soldiers into the House of Iyllyeth in numbers great enough to kill them all, clergy, guards, what few sorcerers they have, even their concubines and servants. We will cleanse their corridors with fire, should it be necessary. Should Archane return, nothing will be left for her to rule, then we may deal with her alone and without allies." She stood, commanding in her presence. "Go! Send me the Lancer Captains at once, that we may plan! Then offer your prayers for victory."

They bowed and hurried beyond the door. Ba'tula stood until the latch was set, then rang the service bell. Servants entered, a tub and scented waters carried into the meeting chamber. Two raised the curtains as others assisted the priestess to disrobe, and they bathed her gently as a minstrel played beyond the drapery.

Sweets were set beside her, and wine poured into a goblet. She lounged in the tub, worry in her face for the first time since Hovenethra had made war upon the House of Iyllyeth. *And now nothing there is left, save to win, or die as a sacrifice. Curse Archane for her yet living, curse Mor'i'jil for his refusal to accept a leading council! Should he have stayed, I might have found a way within his mind. Or taken him a hostage and coerced Alystin into agreement! Curse them all!*

The door creaked open and a messenger stood beyond the curtain, begging audience.

"Feed him," said Ba'tula, as she rose from the water. Servants dried her as she stood, thinking once again, then she donned a heavy woolen

383

robe and took her place at the high seat once more. The messenger came before her, bowing, then offered a scroll with the seal of Alystin upon it.

Ba'tula cracked the seal, read the message quickly, then called an acolyte to her side. "Find Aysa'lil and Kreothren, have them here once they have spoken with the Lancer Captains. Go quickly!" She faced the messenger once again. "Inform your counterpart from the House of Iyllyeth, they will have our answer within one day, no more."

The messenger bowed and took her exit.

Ba'tula nodded to herself. *And so, our decision made for us by others comes, and now we have no choice, as Alystin sends her ultimatum. The House of Hovenethra will prevail or fall from grace. May history recall us with words of righteousness, or have our names wiped away forever!*

* * *

Mors'ul'jyn's hideaway…

The mood of *Ung'gu'wi* had changed markedly in little time. Even far from the corridors and chambers, even though her tiny room was beneath the beaten path, still Mors'ul'jyn could hear soldiers marching in the pathways, chanting, singing, swearing oaths of vengeance or of glory against whatever House they opposed.

One sleep-time, Nullwyss had crawled into Mors'ul'jyn's bed, trembling and cold with sweat. Mors'ul'jyn had tossed her blanket over the girl and held her closely, though it nearly made her flesh crawl. Nullwyss's hand had laid gently on Mors'ul'jyn's bare hip, then moved upward. Mors'ul'jyn caught her, holding it away. "Sleep," she whispered into the girl's ear, then rose and paced, nearly sick with fear.

I cannot remain! They will know me, all of them, Calidriil, his accomplices, Archane… How to stay alive? Where might I go where I will be safe from discovery and death?

Nullwyss stirred, rolled in her slumber, and pulled the blanket closer. Mors'ul'jyn watched for moments, mind racing, then realized the answer lay there before her.

The girl is unknown, naught but a runaway! She glanced to her own body, that of Reena, still taut and firm and lithe, and shook her head. *A plan, and certainly a last resort. As my ability may follow wherever my mind will go, I am capable. And there Calidriil will have no warning when my blade comes for his heart.*

* * *

On the road...

Two days more, and the Companions with Archane rode from Stokar's shop, north and to the east, to join Kaul's mercenary army and make their way into the Black Forest. Still, their way was hindered by Archane's fatigue and Ysilrod's insistence of time to search with care for Mors'ul'jyn, should she have passed this way.

"Would she not have chosen magic?" asked Sheynon, as they set camp for the night, half a day beyond the forest.

"Or knew we would think such," replied the elf-mage. He wove a spell between two large oak trees, threads of light nearly invisible as a spider's web, catching colors of the setting sun as Sheynon watched. "Yet perhaps she thought otherwise, that we would think as you say, then turn it all about," Ysilrod grinned.

Sheynon only shook his head. "We may debate all the night, not knowing what to do. Better to plan both ways, is it not?"

"What ways, my lords?" asked Audrey, approaching with mugs of tea in hand for them. They paused to drink, then Ysilrod explained.

"Should she be in *Ung'gu'wi*, we will know, one way or another. Either she has passed into the forest by horse or foot, or made her way by magic. I will know soon, whichever way she chose."

Audrey shook her head, not understanding. "How will you know, should she have used magic? Are there footprints left, so to say?"

"There are, my lady, but surely she has set spells of her own for protection." Ysilrod nodded to the *NorthWind* blade Sheynon carried in his back-sheath. "Regardless her place within the depths, I may find her. On touching of the blade, and casting a spell of lore, she cannot hide, regardless her enchantments."

"As her spells leave the same impressions, yes?" Audrey smiled at Ysilrod's bow. "Still, your abilities I cannot fathom, yet know well enough to accept them as truth. *Jhad* provides, my friends."

They touched cups around, then Sheynon nodded to Archane, speaking quietly with Thalion at the fire. "This scene I never could have considered only a moon ago. As you say, the gods seem to favor us, yet still I stand in wonder."

"A meal and rest will aid your clarity," said Ysilrod, a hand on Sheynon's shoulder. They turned together and made way to the campfire as evening chill set upon the land.

* * *

385

rand Selene shone half-full at the zenith, and *Mina* climbed the eastern sky, bright and silvery as a lantern. The elves had found comfort in a hidden glade, and Audrey knelt in prayer between two stunted pines. Thalion sat once more with Archane, the dark elf woman worn from their travels, but willing to share words with the priest.

"Who rules in your stead?" asked Thalion, refilling Archane's cup with scented tea.

The Dark Princess considered for a quiet moment. "Our council, yet one among them surely as overseer. Likely a priestess of the name Alystin, bold, yet tempered in her manner, and well-placed." She paused her cup. "Mor'i'jil spoke with favor of her many times."

Thalion noted tension in her face, and chose his words with care. "We know Mors'ul'jyn took both of you from Kaul's city, in a chance encounter with another, of whom I wish to speak. Yet before, I must ask, what of this Mor'i'jil? Know you of his fate?"

Archane's eyes blazed in the darkness. "Dead at the hand of Mors'ul'jyn. Murdered, of madness in her mind and obsessive fear of everything around her. You cannot know the terror I suffered five years and more."

Thalion waited patiently as Archane's temper lessened. "Your words are taken as given," he replied, "and as humans and elves do in times as this, I offer condolences sincerely. A trusted minister is a blessing all leaders learn to share."

"Trust." Archane barked a laugh. "Drow trust few within our lives. As the world turns and opportunities arise, we take them without regard to those about us. Still… in rare times do we find those whose counsel cannot be done without. Mor'i'jil was one as such."

Thalion offered tea once more, yet Archane declined. He poured for himself, then continued. "Two days, and Kaul's mercenaries will arrive. What then is your plan?"

"Descend," replied Archane. "Seek Alystin or whoever rules, yet before Kaul's rabble is allowed within *Ung'gu'wi*, strict measures, Priest, and I will allow none but you to lead the Mongrel's army."

"And how best to coordinate with your leaders, then?"

"Few know the human tongue, therefore, it will be difficult at best."

Thalion gave a knowing nod. "I speak Drow, tho' not well. Perhaps on the morrow you may aid me in recalling certain words."

Archane gave him a glance. "I am not surprised, and likely the elves know, yes? And as we speak of battle, the mage will search for Mors'ul'jyn once within *Ung'gu'wi*, I am certain."

"His search began once we departed Drakenmoore's depths. I thought you would have known."

Archane shrugged. "Nearly was I killed, and only at the shopkeeper's place did I begin to realize the happenings. It matters not. She is there, or she is not, and if she is, surely waiting with a plan."

"Ysilrod will search with Sheynon and Audrey. What think you of this?"

She waved a hand. "Do as you will, for I would rather they find her themselves than worry others in my House of her. I have offered all I know, yet seek no vengeance at this time." She drank the last of her tea and set the cup away. "Yet if she prevails, what then? Will your god intervene?" Archane chuckled.

"Do not disparage Ysilrod, nor Sheynon, and surely not Audrey Vincent. I have traveled with them on pursuits both great and small. They are heroes of the ages."

The Dark Princess shrugged once more. "Heroes die, of battle, of misfortune, of over-assurance, to say nothing of a worthy foe. Even should your friends prevail, do not think victory will be without its due. Prepare yourself to bury one or more of your comrades, should you, yourself, not become a victim of the struggle."

* * *

The City-State of DragonFall...

They came upon the gates to the city at a gallop, slowing only when guards showed alertness and gathered before them in a line. They reined their horses at the challenge, then Chitthra dismounted and offered words too soft for Aeren to understand. For her part, she stayed in her saddle, hand on her sword hilt, watching the brigands closely as they stood about the dark elf woman.

Chitthra turned, stalked back to her horse and dug within her saddle bag. "They demand payment, silver or pleasures, and laughed when I cursed them." She found a pouch and hefted it.

"Hold, Dearest," said Aeren, dismounting. She walked boldly to the leader of the guards. She could not think him a captain of any sort, as his look was more an outlaw than a soldier. Yet she knew Kaul's mercenaries were only that, and the Mongrel himself little more.

"With all respect," she began, bowing slightly, "we ask entry to the city, as a friend in need waits for our arrival. I am the Lady Aeren Greywald of the City-State of Truth, Warden of the City, esquire to Her Excellency Audrey Vincent, and friend of Lord Priest Thalion Lahai."

And that, thought Aeren, *will gain us either entry or combat, and in this time, I do not care which, as my patience is at end.*

The leader, missing a tooth or two, grinned, looking her up and down. "I know of you," he said, his voice a rumble to her ears. He stood before her, half a head taller and likely twice her weight. He lifted a stray bit of Aeren's hair from her forehead with a grimy finger. She tensed, then found her calm as Chitthra's shadow lay across her shoulder.

"Hands away from her." The dark elf woman's voice carried naught but warning, and the brigand lost his grin.

"Silver, ten for each of us," he growled, "or pleasures in the guardhouse."

"Shall I repeat the names, those of my acquaintance?" asked Aeren. "Your great king knows them well, and should it be heard you detain our way, there may be more words for you than mine."

"Let them go, Huul," came a voice from the guard contingent. "Neither is entranced by your lack of manners." Scattered laughter was met by Huul's scowls as he turned away.

Aeren drew Chitthra back to the horses. "Go now, and quickly."

They took their saddles and were past the gates as guards jeered and called and cursed. Then on, into the city and the inn close by Steffyn's hiding place, they led their horses to the stable and bargained quickly for the groomers.

Down the alleyway, across another street, then between two close-set shops and into the heavy brush beyond, they slowed, approaching the hovel they knew was Steffyn's sanctuary.

"Hold," said Chitthra quietly, then took Aeren aside, behind a tumble of debris. She looked deeply into Aeren's eyes. "I must know, are we together in this venture? Should he be here, one or both of us may die, perhaps all within. Tell me truly, yea or nay?"

Aeren drew herself up, a hard look returned to Chitthra's stare. "Vows are never broken. My promise was to stand beside you, and here I am. Regardless our disagreement, I love you, and will guard your back as said. Never doubt Aeren Greywald's word of honor."

Chitthra nodded, and they embraced, kissed warmly and held each other once again. They looked to the door, and Aeren drew her sword as Chitthra slid silent beside the entryway. Aeren drew a breath, nodded, and Chitthra leapt, kicking in the door.

A stench blew from within, one both knew well, and caught them by surprise. They covered up their faces, nearly retching, eyes running, and entered. No longer was there a well-set room with hearth and chairs and table. Only did they see a packed-earth floor, an ancient fireplace now but a tumble of broken bricks, and little else. Aeren searched quickly as Chitthra ran into the sleeping room.

"Aeren!"

Chitthra was on her knees before what appeared to be a bloated body when Aeren came into the room. Here the stench was stronger, and Aeren sought breath by covering her face again. Sword hand trembling with her weapon raised, she slowly circled what she now could see was not one, but two, rigid in their deaths. The earth beneath was dark and filled with insects, flies buzzing round, and a rat gnawing on a hand with two missing fingers.

Aeren knelt, hoping against hope these were not the ones she feared. Garish robes of gold and purple had certainly been seen on Steffyn when fought by Chitthra, and his identity revealed. And the withered arm of the smaller body was confirmation enough that here lay Jyslin, her own hand upon the hilt of the knife buried in her belly.

Quickly Aeren sheathed her sword, took Chitthra by the arm and all but dragged her from the shack, that they could breathe, if for no other reason. She closed and latched the door behind them, took the dark elf woman behind the shanty, collapsing there beside her. They panted out their breath, then turned, looking to each other, as tears began to fall.

They sobbed, then cried, then nearly wailed, holding in their grief closely as they could, for attention was not their intent. Until shadows fell, and stars winked into the sky, they held each other tightly, sharing angst so deep, they dared not move, else they would simply collapse of heartache.

At last they drew apart, yet neither wanting to let go. They dried their eyes, stood and held each other dearly once again.

"I must give them rest," said Aeren, her voice husky, raw and ragged, little more than a whisper in Chitthra's ear. "Stand beside me if you will, for I know not the ways of dark elves."

Chitthra only nodded, and they quietly made way back into the shack. Aeren lit a candle found lying on the floor, and they knelt beside the bodies.

"Grant them rest, great lord," she intoned, voice filled with sorrow. "Give passage into your loving hands, and forgive their sins, for surely they are great."

Chitthra raised her face to the ceiling, eyes shut, and breathed a prayer. *"Plynn nind wund lil' oloth de' dosst arlyurl, zhennu Iyllyeth."* She drew her dagger, ran the blade across her hand, and held it above the bodies, dark blood dripping on them both.

Aeren swallowed, not knowing what to say, yet feeling no desecration there was given. *Surely this is a blessing. I pray it is! My heart breaks, and I know not what to do! I love her dearly, yet what now will be her path? Dare I ask? Must I now save her from herself?*

They stood, bowed to the bodies, and turned to leave.

"What is this?" Chitthra motioned to a pair of pouches on the floor.

"Gold and silver," replied Aeren, retrieving and opening the first. She tucked it into her belt and unlaced the second. "Stones of some sort, with sparkles in them."

"Fire-stones." Chitthra motioned to the bodies. "We may burn them, to cleanse their way beyond this world." She nearly showed a grin. "Yet it may take the whole of the hovel with it."

Aeren dithered, then handed three to Chitthra. "Burn them, as never should they be found by others."

Chitthra nodded. "Go to the door and open it, then prepare to run."

Aeren complied as Chitthra stepped back into the sleeping room. Fire erupted suddenly, and Chitthra ran out the door, followed closely by Aeren, down the alleyway again and into the street.

"Fire!" they cried to the folk about, running quickly as they could, heading for the stable, never looking back. "Fire!" they screamed once more, passing by a street guard. Aeren glanced beyond her shoulder as the alarm bell hanging at the corner lamppost began to ring.

* * *

They rode away beyond the gates, beyond the villages and towns, not pausing until the open plain was found. They rode into the rising sun, east and toward the gathering point, and only as the day fell about them did they pause.

Into the wood, they tethered the horses that they could forage, then quickly built a fire, saying little in their work. Still, tears descended as sniffling prayers and oaths were quietly voiced, and at last they sat, arms entwined, weeping softly as the sun approached its zenith.

Aeren brought forth a bottle from her pack, mead of the City-State of Truth, deep and sweet and strong. They passed it hand to hand and drank it dry, sang songs of loss and heartache, then fell into their bedroll, desperate for the touch of loving flesh, ravaging each other until the sun was nearly set.

Only then did they sleep, as horrors of their findings chased across their faces and through their minds. Yet still, together and alive, at last they rose as dawn approached, saddled mounts, held back their lingering sadness, and found the strength within to carry on.

* * *

They rode, side by side, following the path made by Kaul's army half a day before, traveling to the gathering place. They knew they would arrive by nightfall, though Archane would not likely wait before descending into *Ung'gu'wi*.

Campfire smoke was seen rising from beyond a ridge, and they made way to a sentry post, passed through by a mercenary known well by name of Zeqis, who hailed them on approach.

"Well met, tho' late," he jested, then cast an eye to their somber look. "Trouble, or a disagreement?"

Chitthra shook her head. "We seek the Lord Priest Thalion Lahai and the brothers Calidriil. We bring word of an acquaintance."

Zeqis motioned to the center of the camp, and a standard with a rainbow slash upon it flying in the setting sun. "They confer with the captive, Archane, planning entry to the underground." He drew closer and his voice dropped lower. "We revel at the mid of night, should you need of company other than noble." He glanced to Aeren, listening. "Always are you both welcome with your tales of derring-do."

"Your offer is kind, and we will consider." Chitthra clasped his hand briefly before riding on. Aeren touched his hand in passing.

"What now, Dearest?" Aeren's question drew Chitthra from her thoughts after moments of winding through the camp.

"First, we must give word and comfort, then whatever follows."

"I am here for you," replied Aeren quietly.

Chitthra nodded, but did not smile. "My vows are no longer possible to discharge, and I know not what to do."

Aeren drifted her horse closer to that of Chitthra. "Nothing of what happened is other than the fault of Steffyn Foxxe himself. Lord Sheynon will understand this, tho' his heart will surely break."

"Only one course is now possible, that of Mors'ul'jyn herself. I must take justice to her, yet that is the right of Sheynon."

"Then we will guard him well, seeing opportunity is his," said Aeren. "Therefore, your vows are held, and Galandria Telveperen avenged."

Chitthra glanced to Aeren, then shook her head. "Your mentor taught you well, and never do you waver. More I love you for it every day."

Aeren offered her hand, and Chitthra took it. "Undefeated," Aeren whispered, the word reaching into Chitthra's heart.

At the last, she squeezed Aeren's hand and smiled.

* * *

Thalion was in council with the Companions and Archane when Chitthra and Aeren sent word they had arrived. They took time to clean themselves of road dust, quaffed a cup and ate a hasty meal, then were led to Thalion's tent with fifty guards around it.

They entered quietly, receiving greetings from all around as Archane took a seat away. Thalion noted their solemn mood and held a hand for patience of the others.

Aeren's tears slipped down her cheeks as she found Audrey's eyes. "My Liege, my lords, we bring grave tidings. Steffyn Foxxe, friend and comrade, and his ward, Jyslin, are dead. We found them in the hideaway, two days beyond their ending, too late to intervene. We are sorry for our failure, and for your loss."

Thalion quietly drew his holy symbol from his belt and pressed it to his forehead. Audrey signed herself twice and whispered prayers, then took Aeren in her arms. They held each other as soft tears descended in their embrace.

Ysilrod came to Sheynon's side, and the elf-lord turned to his brother, face pale and lips drawn tightly. A single tear wended down his face, then the brothers clasped each other, elven words too low to hear between them.

Chitthra waited, then looked to Archane in the corner, the face of the Dark Princess showing little. She walked slowly to the chair as Archane watched with a growing smile of dark malevolence.

"*You wish to take vengeance on me for my treatment of your friend? Recall, I did no harm to him, and this occurrence is of his doing, not of mine.*" Archane spoke in formal Drow, then waved a hand. "*You are not the only ones to bear losses in this chaos.*"

"No," replied Chitthra, replying in the tongue as an equal, "*yet still, the beginnings were of your arrogance, as you sent your minister to parley with the mad woman of Drakenmoore herself. Look now at what the land has fallen to. Her doings built on yours, and your quest for hearts to Mother Darkness.*"

Archane scoffed. "*What would you know of this, a traitor to the Race? Your path of Drow ended the day you took leave of Ung'gu'wi, never to return.*"

Chitthra nodded. "*And now, I will descend into those depths, left so many years ago, and search for the one whose madness exceeds only yours. Should I find her and prevail, perhaps I will hold her heart, not you.*"

"*I am not mad, by any measure. I have ruled the Drow more than a thousand years, while those as you fade into forgotten tales. Your loss means nothing to me, nor your vengeance. We have a pact, held by honorable agreement.*"

Chitthra narrowed her eyes and dropped her voice to a husky whisper. "*You have a pact with Lord Priest Thalion and the others. I am not a part.*" She turned, and faced Sheynon once again as he spoke with Aeren.

"How... how did he, they, die? Who was responsible for their ending?"

Aeren looked to Chitthra with a worried glance, then spoke. "My lord, we know not, yet they died in each other's arms. Perhaps thieves or those seeking riches in the sanctuary, or someone having followed them in time. We simply cannot say."

Sheynon's eyes drifted to Chitthra at the last, a cold, hard look upon her. "You did not take your vengeance on him? This was not your doing, and you swear it?"

"My lord Sheynon," said Audrey softly. "My esquire will not lie for any reason."

Sheynon waited, as Chitthra met his gaze with strength. "My lord, by the spirit of *Din'daeron'dae* and my standing in the Order of *Däe Quivïe*, I so swear, this was not my doing, nor that of Aeren Greywald. As said, we found them in their death." She glanced to Aeren once again. "We gave them fire, to cleanse their way into the afterlife."

"What of his items, those in the workshop or what he carried?" Ysilrod stood with Sheynon, a hand upon his shoulder.

Aeren offered the pouches from her belt. "Only these, my lord, as the shanty was consumed by flame. Nothing else survived."

Ysilrod nodded, glanced to Sheynon, who shrugged and sighed. "Keep them, and in time they may provide as needed."

Aeren bowed.

Thalion turned to Archane, still watching with disinterest, then looked again to the Companions round. "We will sing songs to him this night. All have lost a friend, some nearly a brother, and surely the world is poorer for their passing."

"Amen," whispered Audrey, signing herself once more.

"And in the morning, we descend," continued the priest. "More there is to do, and with fortune, we may find the mad woman in our searching."

"Nearly am I certain she is there," said Ysilrod. "For I know she is not within the land at large, and where else might she go? *Ung'gu'wi* provides protection and a hiding place as no other, masked by spells and wards of sorcerers of all the Drow."

"How then may we find her?" asked Audrey, wiping her eyes, and holding Aeren closely yet.

"As you say, my lady… the gods provide." Ysilrod glanced beyond his shoulder to Archane, listening now with growing interest. "We have a distraction, do we not? One to drive Mors'ul'jyn from her hiding place amidst marching soldiers and ringing steel. One where even the cleverest of adversaries may succumb to a mistake."

* * *

They took time as promised by Thalion, to light a fire and give offerings and prayers to Steffyn's spirit, and that of Jyslin. Sheynon stood with Ysilrod beside him, Audrey at his shoulder, Aeren and Chitthra at his back. Thalion sang a song so sweetly even the mercenaries gathered round could hardly hold a tear. Though none of them had known Steffyn or the girl, still a small contingent, led by Zeqis, stood quietly to the side, ensuring the night's revelry did not interfere.

At the last, only Sheynon, brother Ysilrod, Audrey, and the priest were left at the fire, as Chitthra and Aeren gave last condolences and found their beds. Soon the mercenaries all drifted from the ceremony, and Audrey, too, said her benediction, then kissed Sheynon gently on the cheek.

Thalion stayed a while, trading small stories of Steffyn, and from time to time, a gentle smile of remembrance would come to Sheynon's face. In time, the priest said his good nights, leaving the elf-lord with his brother.

"*Yarhetha'an* grant them rest and forgiveness." Sheynon made a sign within the air and turned to Ysilrod. "Can you say how they might have died? Surely Aeren's words were false, tho' I cannot think she would lie with purpose."

"Her words were meant to spare you pain, Brother. Does it truly matter, the manner of their deaths? Steffyn was lost to us years ago, by ill decision, by doing wrong for right, by withdrawing into himself when friends about most needed." Ysilrod shrugged. "It is the way of sorcerers, to feel themselves having answers to all questions, whether wise or foolish. Nothing you or I might have done would have kept him from his path."

"A path costing his own life, and that of an innocent dark elf girl." Sheynon heaved a breath.

"Rest this night," said Ysilrod, "and the morrow will rise as always it has done. Clear your mind, for surely, we will need grace from all the gods. No matter our sorrow or our grief, none care where our steps will lead us now."

* * *

Morning, and the rains came, making streams throughout the camp, as waters ran from the forest. Thalion called a hasty meeting of the mercenary captains, then the Companions and Archane.

"Half a league into the forest, yet with storms, likely more a day," said the Dark Princess. "The village waiting will know we are delayed and set their plan aside."

"Should we wait the storm out, what then?" asked Audrey, still wary of Archane's manner.

"We proceed," said Thalion, before Archane could answer. "Should word have spread of our coming, we cannot spare the time."

"My instructions to Alystin were to create diversion, therefore, you are correct." Archane looked round to all of them. "Where is Chitthra? Where is this apprentice of yours?" She shot a glance to Audrey who began to speak, then held her peace.

"Excellency?" Thalion waited, fearing the answer he knew would come.

Audrey straightened, meeting Archane's gaze. "Gone ahead, to find Mors'ul'jyn. Therefore, our task is only as the Lord Priest has planned, to seek your seat of power. I did not detain them, nor would I." She turned to Thalion. "Forgive me, my friend, but their duty is not as ours."

Sheynon traded glances with Ysilrod, the elf-mage deep in thought. "Brother?"

Ysilrod nodded, as to himself. "Knowing them as I do, I may see them easily with the artifact, the sword. Yes, a goodly plan, and with their eyes I can find Mors'ul'jyn, should they encounter her."

"Should they live, is more your meaning." Archane shook her head and turned to Thalion. "Bold, yet foolish. The mad woman will have little challenge from them."

"Not so," said Sheynon, "for Chitthra is skilled in the ways of stealth and guile. Aeren's heart is strongest ever, and her ability second to only one." He bowed slightly to Audrey. "A formidable pair, and my hope is, Mors'ul'jyn's arrogance will be her downfall, should they find her."

"Little can we do but proceed," said Thalion. "Therefore, make ready. We leave soonest, and may the gods give us favor in the coming fight."

* * *

The House of Hovenethra…

Soldiers gathered in the mustering chambers, milling, testing one another with anxious wit and tussles, chanting oaths and singing songs, passing bottles round. A male coupled noisily in a darkened corner with a concubine, a female laid herself against a wall as another male pleasured her with supple tongue. All around, twenty score of fighting Drow prepared for what many knew might be their last night within the world.

At last the Lancer Captains called the roll, soldiers answering with pride and dignity, save the female now collapsed, panting in her post-coital bliss. Laughter made its way in the rear ranks, two lesser Lancer Captains grinning lewdly to each other.

Ranks formed, weapons were presented, idle chatter ceased, and clergy entered with acolytes around, chanting prayers to *Iyllyeth* and *Mother Darkness*, for victory, for safety of the columns, and for deliverance through valor of those dying for the cause.

Each soldier was sprinkled with waters blessed by Ba'tula, and given token coins for remembrance of battle.

All were asked "Ready are you now to die for the House of Hovenethra?", and all would shout "With all I am, I will cleave the enemy until they or I no longer bleed!".

It took time, for this was no foray in force, but nearly half of Hovenethra's army. Though more than five years had passed since the humiliation at the Castle of Lahai, Drow, as elves, procreated slowly, and only in part had all the dark elf armies been rebuilt. Still, it was no matter, for Ba'tula, as her Lancer Captains, knew the House of Iyllyeth was as depleted, and with one hundred soldiers gone into the land of Ardwel, and casualties from sorties sent before, Hovenethra's numbers were the greater. Now events would tell if they were enough; in strength of numbers, in strength of heart, in strength of courage and of fearlessness. And if, as said by legend, the waiting arms of *Iyllyeth* in the afterlife was enough a calling for war against others of their kind.

In other chambers, deeper in the House, ten score more waited as reserves, and ten more beyond their place. Ba'tula's Lancer Captains had set a plan; first wave to crush whatever might be found of defenses at the central chamber or the entry corridors to the House of Iyllyeth; second then sent as a lightning strike into the deeper chambers, half the first to join them, the others to guard their backs and form retreat, should it be necessary; third as reserves, only then if needed, or to guard prisoners, if any still were living.

Ba'tula, for herself, did not attend the battle lines, and her Lancer Captains wondered of it. Still, theirs was not to question, though many spoke in quiet words away from the ranks now waiting with anticipation. Was the Dark Mistress afraid, or was it wise discretion? While clergy certainly attended as their duty, was it not Ba'tula's duty as well, to see her soldiers on their way to victory? At the last, it did not matter, for with her blessing or without, Hovenethra would prevail, the Lancer Captains thought, and on return, should they live to see the ending, reward and praises would be theirs.

Yet true soldiers did not seek reward or praise, for victory was its own. And none, not clergy, not sorcerers, not even the Dark Mistress her own self, could ever wrest that from their spirits, live or die, so long as they served *Iyllyeth* and *Mother Darkness* with their blood.

* * *

Hovenethra charged through the central chamber, guards caught unaware at the entrance to the House of Iyllyeth, and blood flowed, darkening the earthen corridors.

Into the chambers, killing all they found, clergy, servants, they found little armed resistance, and ran deeper as alarm bells rang and Alystin's forces massed before them.

Hard into the shield wall they ran, spears seeking tender flesh, crossbow bolts by dozens whispering in the air, shortswords ringing steel on steel, shouts of the leaders and cries of wounded everywhere.

Alystin's trap had not been anticipated, and as the first wave passed by the chambers closest to the entrance, two score of her soldiers fell on the rear ranks of Hovenethra, trapping nearly half their number.

The other half fell back, as crossbows came to bear, and bolts too many there to number found armor and the flesh beneath it.

Alystin's shield wall pressed forward, pace by pace, Lancer Captains calling out the steps, drums keeping time as soldiers battled in the dimness of the lanternlight.

On it went, dead and dying filling up the corridors, boots sliding, slipping on bloody floors, gory steel seeking flesh behind the shields, bolts

397

buried in bodies everywhere. On they pressed, the soldiers from the House of Iyllyeth, when the second wave of Hovenethra came. Back into the deeper chambers, back against walls of hardened earth and rock and carvings done a thousand years ago, Hovenethra pressed, and Alystin's forces slowly gave away the ground fought for so valiantly to hold.

Pressing into the deepest chambers, and a dozen Hovenethra's soldiers broke ranks and ran through an open door. There they found Dark Priestess Vrammyr and her acolytes, and slew them all. A hand of crossbow bolts pierced Vrammyr's body, three swords sliced through her flesh, and at the last they cut away her head and carried it beyond the door, shouting to their brethren to carry on the fight.

Alystin's Lancer Captains called for reinforcements, and two score of fresh and willing soldiers fell on Hovenethra's flank. More shouts, more cries, more bolts of steel and sword-strikes traded, more death, more blood, more Drow killing other Drow, until at last, Hovenethra called retreat, backing out the corridor quickly as they could.

The Lancer Captains of the House of Iyllyeth did not give chase, for they knew more of Hovenethra's soldiers likely lay in wait. They stood their ground at the entrance to the central chamber, three hundred strong, shields held forth and spears presented, watching as Hovenethra's soldiers disappeared into the corridors beyond.

Only then did they raise a cry of victory.

* * *

One who had avoided the carnage of the corridors was Nullwyss, huddled in a niche as the soldiers passed her by. She had come into the House of Iyllyeth seeking a messenger of acquaintance, that word might be sent by her mistress to the leaders. Yet now, she only pressed her slender self against the earthen walls, hoping against all hope she would not be found and slain, or taken as a hostage, or ravaged by the victors. Little could she do as the sounds of battle nearly deafened her, and the stench of fresh-hewn bodies assailed her senses.

She prayed quietly as she might, keeping her hands tightly covering her mouth, that her whimpers would not be heard. Twice a soldier fell within her sight, once a female, throat sliced nearly through, eyes glazed and dead. The other was a male, and as he died, he reached to clutch her foot in his death-throes. It was everything Nullwyss could do not to scream aloud.

She peeked around the corner, two combatants only a breath or two away. A male buried his axehead in the chest of a woman fighter, and as she fell, her shortsword cut away his hand. The male screamed and staggered back, stumbling in the darkness. The female's eyes fell on Nullwyss just before she died. The girl stuffed her sleeve into her mouth, stifling another cry.

At last, with moments seeming days, the battle line moved back away from the deeper chambers, yet Nullwyss waited, shivering in the darkness, knowing surely there were others trailing to watch the way, and dispatch wounded enemies should they be found.

In time, she peered once more into the corridor, the cavern floor slick with darkened blood and entrails, wounded softly moaning, and ragged breathing from what seemed too many there to count. She slipped away, careful not to fall, stepping lightly over arms and legs and heads not attached to bodies. Nearly did she retch, and held bile deep in her throat as she found solid ground, then ran down the deserted corridor to the hiding place.

She turned a corner, paused, knelt and prayed once more, for breath, for calm, praises given for her safety. Then on, and at last she reached the door, spoke the secret word and entered, breathless.

"Mistress! War comes to the House of Iyllyeth!"

* * *

Dennis Young

PART THREE
DEATH UPON THE VINE

The Black Forest, and into Ung'gu'wi...

"We will find her in the realm of Archane." Chitthra spoke with Aeren as they traveled east and through the forest, talking of Mors'ul'jyn. The village Chitthra knew housed an entrance into *Ung'gu'wi*, yet would not allow those unknown to use it.

"Therefore, we wait until nightfall to descend." She looked to Aeren, riding at her side, and grinned. "Likely a human would be taken as a slave, especially one comely as yourself."

Aeren shook her head, scoffing. "Why Archane's domain? Would she not be recognized?"

Chitthra mulled the question. "It has been many years since the face of Reena was seen in the House of Iyllyeth, tho' your point is taken. Surely she hides herself, and taken of a servant to learn of goings-on. Never was she seen other than in Archane's entourage, and not beyond the House."

Aeren eyed the dark elf woman. "I am curious how you know these things of the Drow, having not lived among them for so long."

Once more, Chitthra gave thought before her answer. "Let us say, before you won my interest, I spent times learning all I could of *Ung'gu'wi* and Archane, for the Brotherhood's knowing, if not my own."

"I... accept your life before we were acquaintanced. I do not need to know of it, should you not wish to say."

Chitthra nudged her horse closer to Aeren's and offered her hand. "Dearest, I am an avenger of Elvenkind, tho' I am not elven. My choice was made years before your birth, and never does one renounce vows made as *Däe Quivie*. More now than ever, no matter our love for each other, duty must prevail, whatever cost."

"Whatever cost," replied Aeren, sadly. "Therefore, your life may end and my heart break, for duty."

"And your vows to Audrey Vincent, and your vows to me? Are they not important, that you would hold them, whatever comes?"

Aeren nodded at the last, then gently smiled, squeezing Chitthra's hand tighter. "We face duty side by side, and vows will be honored by the both of us. Still, there is a vow together we have made. Let us not forget we face the foe as One."

* * *

They tethered the horses in a hidden thicket, making way the final league on foot. They waited in the cold and darkness beyond a thatched-roof barn where Chitthra said the entrance to the Drow underworld was hidden.

"Tho' I have not been in the village for many years, and it has grown." She motioned to a circle of huts, all with smoke coming from their chimneys and lantern lights still glowing in the windows. "Twenty years, and no more than a score of new homes. Drow, as elves, do not propagate quickly as do humans."

Aeren drew her cloak tight about her shoulders. "How far below, once we begin descent?"

"Stairs, then an entryway, likely guarded, then passages leading further down. More guards once we reach the corridors proper, and be prepared to fight our way, unless…"

"Dearest?"

"A thought," said Chitthra, eyes aside. "If you are my prisoner, found in the village skulking about, a ruse may provide a bit of luck."

"Put me in irons if you must, for fighting our way into *Ung'gu'wi* surely is not wise."

Chitthra nodded. "When in the barn we will find restraint you can loosen quickly, should need come." She glanced to Aeren with a wicked grin. "The thought of you in shackles at my mercy warms my blood."

Aeren rolled her eyes, then grinned herself. "My thought was the same, yet with you restrained, and not myself."

"One of us must be free. Perhaps we may take turns."

* * *

They found ropes and looped them round Aeren's wrists, with frays hidden in her hands. Chitthra drew soot across Aeren's face and forehead, to give the look of bruises, and a small cut across her cheek with blood running down. Chitthra strapped Aeren's sword across her own back, as Aeren hid a dagger in her boot, and another 'neath her brigandine.

"Should we be forced to fight, I will shuck your sword away." Chitthra tested the tether fastened to Aeren's belt, insuring it would break with little pulling. "Stay at arm's length or more, that I may engage guards if necessary. Protect yourself, for it is doubtful any below know my abilities."

Aeren nodded tightly, heaved a breath and whispered a prayer. "A gag would be suitable, yes?"

Chitthra drew a kerchief and tied it loosely around Aeren's mouth. "Into the second stall and beneath the board-work there. Mind your boots, as the stairs are steep."

They brushed away straw and lifted up loose flooring, then descended slowly, Chitthra in the lead with a glowing rock held in her hand for light. The passageway was narrow, made for those of smaller stature than was Aeren, and more than once her shoulders dragged against the earthen walls. The steps were shallow and near a hundred in their number. At last they came to a level place with two doors at the end, iron-banded, covered with sigils and designs.

Chitthra held a hand. "We enter the House of Iyllyeth, close to a main chamber. Be ready, as surely guards wait beyond the door."

Aeren drew a breath again, another prayer said silently in her mind.

Chitthra turned the latch and opened up the door. She peeked without, seeing no one near. Quietly as they could, they slipped into the passageway, closed the door and latched it carefully. Aeren laid her back against a rocky outcrop as Chitthra knelt away in meditation.

At last they stood once more together, staring down the corridor growing dark with distance. Chitthra turned to Aeren. "I cannot know why there are no guards, other than matters may be worse than thought within *Ung'gu'wi*. Surely there will be soldiers at the final entry."

Aeren nodded, then motioned to the passage. They continued, the hard-packed earth beneath their boots slippery and dangerous. Another set of doors were seen, these stouter than the first. Chitthra pressed her ear against the clammy wood, then peered through the space between the doors. Light shone beyond, and two figures stood away, backs to the door. She turned, pointed to the door and held two fingers before Aeren, who nodded in reply. They touched foreheads together briefly, then Chitthra tripped the latch.

The guards turned at the sound. Two other soldiers, one from either side, stepped forth and brandished shortswords.

"Hold!" The soldier farthest from the door held a hand and drew his weapon quickly. All were armored and alert, and Chitthra tugged gently on the tether tied to Aeren's belt.

"I bring a prisoner, captured in the village above," said Chitthra, bowing, yet her eyes never left the guards about. Two closed on Aeren and searched her roughly, then took the tether and shoved her to the rocky wall.

"Your name!" demanded the first guard. Chitthra had now decided this was the gate captain, and bowed again.

403

"Miz… Miz'ri. My name is Miz'ri, of the village west." Chitthra stammered out the words, intent on showing fear. "I beg you let us pass, that I may take the prisoner to the holding place."

A second soldier sheathed his sword, closed on Aeren, and took her face in hand. "She is not ugly, and perhaps a bit of pleasure before you proceed." Nearly a head shorter than was Aeren, he showed no worry as he ran his hand beneath her brigandine.

His hand crossed her dagger hilt, and his eyes widened. "She is armed! A trick!"

Aeren slapped away his hand, drove her forehead into his nose, drew the dagger from beneath her armor, and buried it in the guard's neck. Dark blood sprayed about and he cried, clawing at the dagger hilt.

Chitthra dropped Aeren's sword away, leapt, spun in the air, kicking out, driving back the gate captain. She landed, crouched beneath a swinging sword, swept a leg, taking the third guard to the earthen floor. She drove her heel into his throat and he choked a cry before he died.

The fourth soldier ran toward the alarm bell hanging above the passageway. Chitthra leapt, driving her foot into his back, sending him sprawling to the floor. He rose, drew his shortsword and swung, as Aeren stepped before the blow. The blade slid down her own, slicing through the cuisse on her upper leg, and she fell, bright blood spewing in the dim-lit corridor.

Chitthra dodged the second blow, took the soldier's arm and bent it back until it cracked. He screamed, and she drove a fist into his throat. He gagged, coughed blood, and fell gasping. Chitthra took him by the hair, wrapped her thighs about his head, and snapped his neck.

The soldier with the dagger in his throat lay bleeding heavily, and Chitthra cracked his spine, a heavy boot into his back. Then silence.

"Chitthra!" Aeren hissed the word, back against the wall and blood running from beneath her armor. Chitthra stripped away a soldier's cloak, tore a strip of wool, and wrapped it round Aeren's leg. The bleeding slowed as Aeren panted heavily.

"Breathe, Dearest," whispered Chitthra into her ear. "Hear my breath and follow."

Slowly and with patience, fighting hard against the pain, Aeren calmed herself. Chitthra tightened the wrapping, tore two more, and wrapped them about the wound.

"Have you strength to walk?"

Aeren whispered prayers and opened up her eyes to Chitthra's earnest gaze. "I will walk, *Jhad* willing, and guard your back, tho' my thought is, you should hire a more accomplished bodyguard in future times."

Chitthra hugged her tightly, kissed her with unmitigated passion, then raised her up.

"Stand the bodies in their places, else passers-by will see them," said Aeren. She winced, then hobbled across the room. "Let us go, before my blood runs fully away. This may be my ending, but I will meet it with my eyes wide open."

* * *

In Another Village…

A thousand troops of DragonFall camped beyond the dark elf enclave, and as night fell and chill set about the mercenaries, the Companions gathered for words between them.

"No weapons drawn, no spells incanted," said Thalion, Sheynon and Ysilrod before him, and Audrey at the side, her eyes upon Archane as they listened. "We come to the time when trust must be the greatest. Tho' I have no doubt all herein will abide by our agreements, fear and misunderstandings grown for many years may be difficult to overcome. Therefore, we must hold it tightly in our grasp and see it quelled quickly, should it rise."

"My soldiers are disciplined, yet your words are understood," said Archane mildly.

Thalion bowed. "Their seeing you alive may be surprise enough to stay their hands from weapons. I say these words only that we are in agreement, and keep minds to the task before us."

"Caution always is warranted," said Audrey. "Your words are welcome, Lord Priest, and we hear well your meaning."

Thalion reviewed the dozen mercenaries he had chosen as his vanguard. Their descent would be as quietly as they might manage, Archane secreted to the entrance only with the knowing of the village elders.

The Dark Princess led them to a vacant hut and the hidden stairway beneath the hearth. Thalion took the fore with Archane close behind, Ysilrod at her shoulder and Sheynon with the mercenaries following. Audrey took the trailing place, watching their backs, that no one followed.

Down a hundred steps, muttered curses and quiet words as they descended the narrow stairwell. *Gil Estel* burned brightly in the darkness, Ysilrod's staff *Ringil* with its glowing orb atop, and *Mír'rë Cala'wyne* behind, all lit the way, as the mercenary army waited in the village for word to begin descent in earnest.

Two doors lay at the bottom of the stairs, and Archane called a pause before them. "There are guards beyond, therefore, only you and I will enter," she said to Thalion, then raised a hand at his unasked question. "We may hold the door, that your friends will see no ill befalls you. We are close, Priest, and I will honor my promises as made."

"Never would I think otherwise," replied Thalion. He nodded to Ysilrod and Sheynon, saw Audrey's worried faced a dozen steps above, and grinned. "Worry not, Excellency, for I have you as my companion. Surely we have faced worse than walking with the leader of the Drow as ally."

The door creaked inward and two dark elf guards emerged and brandished weapons. "Who speaks beyond the entry? Say your name and allegiances —"

The guard's voice stopped, and he gaped, then looked side to side and up the staircase at the faces seen. He raised his sword once more, then lowered it, as his eyes found those of Archane. He swallowed hard, tried to speak once more, then took a knee at the last, head bowed. He laid his shortsword before himself as his companion stood behind, stunned to silence, then knelt.

"Rise," said Archane softly, but with an edge to her voice. The guards stood slowly, eyes yet averted, as two more stood behind them, a male and female, both now staring with eyes wide and mouths agape.

Archane held a hand. "Say nothing, make no sound, for I return with tidings to end this chaos." She looked to the female guard and motioned her to step forward. "Say the happenings in *Ung'gu'wi*. Spare no words."

The guard looked from Archane to Thalion to the elves behind, then the mercenaries gathered close, and at the last, Audrey on the steps above.

Archane nodded her to speak.

"Dark Princess, we give praises to your living and return. I have given prayers each day." She hurried on at Archane's fiery stare. "Hovenethra seeks to rule and has killed many of our House. Dark Priestess Alystin holds the reins of leadership and shows patience. Word says she prepares attack with the message sent of your return."

"A wise decision," replied Archane, then looked to Thalion. "I bring allies, and tho' distrust has been among us many years, we have pledged to each other for my return. They... found me in my escape from the witch Mors'ul'jyn, and now aid in the House of Iyllyeth's victory to come."

406

The guards' eyes yet drifted between Archane and the others round. "A dozen humans will make no difference in the plans," said the female guard, then bowed. "I mean no disrespect."

"None taken," said Thalion, in broken Drow, and Archane spoke to clear his meaning. "We have soldiers in numbers waiting above. Once Archane is safely in her clergy's care, we will muster as your captains need. We seek only to aid your Dark Princess into her rightful place."

"Praises to *Iyllyeth*," whispered another guard, and all the rest followed in his words.

"Call an honor guard," said Archane, "no less than a score. Escort Alystin to a secret meeting chamber near the ancient passage fork, advise us then of her arrival. The priest... Thalion and I will meet with her, the others remaining at this station."

Thalion caught Ysilrod's hard look, and that of Sheynon at his side. "Accepted." He glanced to the elves, then Audrey, listening closely. "My safety is assured at the side of Archane. Let us all give thanks for this humble beginning to our duty."

* * *

Guards escorted them down a narrow passage, ten ahead and ten behind, Archane following with Thalion, the priest chanting silent prayers in his mind. *Guard them well, Great Lord, my friends waiting in the darkness, and may our Lady of Light smile upon our doing. Balance is our victory, the land at peace and old enemies to stand aside from seeking of our blood.*

They came to a tiny chamber devoid of even chairs. No hearth, no prayer fountain, no warmth, only cold earth and stone, and a single sconce upon the wall. Within was Alystin alone, and as they entered, she bowed deeply to Archane. She stood, her face filled with worry and tightly drawn, tears welling in her eyes. She began to speak, but could not find her voice.

"You have done well," said Archane simply, offering her hand. Alystin took it, and only bowed once more. They waited as the priestess found her calm and wiped her eyes.

"Dark Princess, I sing praises for your safe return." Alystin looked to Thalion for the first time since their entering. "Our... thanks for your assistance and offering of aid. Surely a new time for understanding." She paused and glanced at Archane once again, who nodded tersely. "Your words of Mor'i'jil... I am saddened and ashamed for what is lost. Dark Priestess Vrammyr was killed and defiled in the attack this day, yet Hovenethra suffered losses as did we."

"We will light a fire for their passing when comes the time," replied Archane. "For now, say your plans and we will find a way between us."

* * *

The guards had closed the doors at the staircase landing, and vanguard soldiers sat or stood speaking quietly, passing flasks and wineskins all around. Sheynon spoke with Ysilrod as Audrey kept the watch, for the warrior-woman knew the ways of mercenaries and their drink.

"Speak, Brother," said Sheynon as they waited in the light of *Ringil*. "Once within, might you scry for Mors'ul'jyn, or know of Chitthra and Aeren's whereabouts?"

"I have a dagger held by Aeren," replied the elf-mage. "With that, I may find her. My question is, will that be where we find Mors'ul'jyn?"

"Would it not be safer to track Aeren than our quarry?" asked Sheynon. "She cannot follow your scrying then, yes?"

Ysilrod considered, nodded once, then grinned. "You assume they are successful in their search. Yet with Chitthra a dark elf... Yes, a ruse, and surely I should have thought earlier of this. They will find entry and may be here now, before us. Chitthra is clever, to say nothing of her Brotherhood abilities."

Sheynon looked away, then back to Ysilrod. "Nearly do I pray she succeeds in finding Mors'ul'jyn. Truly, it has been many years since I took up the sword for any reason. Simply, I do not know if I can kill again."

"Think not of killing but of living, Brother. That is the best way to honor Galandria's memory. To keep her dream alive becomes your doing, and well it has been these years past. Someone will be your champion, should it be necessary."

* * *

Thalion sent word for the mercenary captain to descend, and soon enough he stood within the meeting room aside the priest. Introductions around were made, as Alystin had called her Lancer Captains to the chamber. As time passed, plans were laid before them all. Word was given of Hovenethra's challenge, and the killings done throughout the House of Iyllyeth. Faces of the soldiers, of Archane, of Thalion himself, were grim, no words needed, as all within the chamber understood what lay ahead.

"We will take the fore," said Archane's Lancer Captain, "your soldiers to our flanks, for we know not what the other Houses will do when word spreads of humans in our midst. I speak with no offense."

Mikkial, the mercenary captain, one of few knowing Drow tongue, chuckled lightly. "None taken, and we wait to see your soldiers fight. Word says of your prowess in battle, and I am only curious." He caught a look from Thalion. "Yet only in the sense of learning, nothing more."

The Lancer Captain nodded. "Once in place, we will send word. Daylight above, no later."

Thalion nearly paused to consider how the Drow in *Ung'gu'wi* knew day from night above, yet knew in fact, it did not matter. If the Lancer Captain said daylight, it was Thalion's responsibility to see Kaul's troops were readied. He faced Mikkial. "Pass the word, descent to begin on the sunrise. Alert your leaders to the hazards of the stairway."

"No torches," said Archane. "We will provide lanterns on the walls that give no smoke or flame."

Thalion bowed and showed a smile. "A touch of magic, and I am not surprised. Let us pledge anew to swift victory." He offered his hand, and Archane took it briefly.

"Victory," she replied, her eyes bright in the dimness.

* * *

In a Passage After Hovenethra's Attack…

They passed bodies hacked to pieces, blood black and dried upon the walls and floors. The stench of death lay about them as a slaughterhouse, and they hurried past, tears running from their eyes.

Chitthra slowed as Aeren called a pause, and they sat closely in a crook aside the corridor. Though Aeren's wound had ceased its bleeding, she was weak, barely strong enough to stand. Chitthra tightened the loop of wool around Aeren's leg, then took her in her arms.

Aeren laid her head on Chitthra's shoulder. "Dearest, I worry I am not strong enough to fight, yet will do my best at the least to provide distraction."

Chitthra was quiet as she held Aeren tightly. "We may fall back, find our friends and join their part."

"I cannot decide, Chitthra. So close, we are. Whatever you will choose, I follow."

Chitthra cursed in silence, knowing in Aeren's weakened state, they both might die. *I cannot risk her life, as she is wounded. Yet how do I find Mors'ul'jyn? This place is filled with passages and tunnels, and I do not know it well enough in certainty. My plan was foolish in its selfishness, and now I have endangered Aeren!*

"Pause a moment and take rest." Chitthra set the waterskin in Aeren's hands, moved aside, knelt, and closed her eyes. *Din'daeron'dae guide my thoughts, and clear my mind, that I may hear you. Deeper we have come than wisdom should have led, and now I find myself in doubt. Show my path, that I may honor vows given in your name. Keep Aeren safe, tho' it may be my ending.*

She drew three breaths, then three more, taking moments to find the peace within her spirit. With each breath a bit of tension fell aside, and sooner than she had thought, her mind was clear and without worry.

A noise from down the corridor drew Chitthra's ear. She glanced around the crook to see a single figure, a dark elf girl, making way swiftly down the passage. Her feet were bare and stained in blood, surely having taken the path from which they came.

Yet why would a girl be in the fight? Chitthra watched as the youngling looked across her shoulder, as if to see who might have followed. *A servant! Yet whose? Surely not of the ruling House, too young to be a concubine, and if she had been found, likely she would be dead or taken as a prize. Mors'ul'jyn's? Yes! Yes! Din'daeron'dae, you have shown the path, and I praise your name!*

Chitthra returned to Aeren, who tried to rise. "Stay, Dearest, as I have a sign, and surely our quarry is near. I will find the way and return once my vows are kept."

Aeren laid her head against the wall. "I will follow soonest, only a bit of rest, then once more we will stand together."

Chitthra only nodded, hoping against all hope that before Aeren's coming, the task would be complete. They embraced once more, kissed, then kissed again, laid their foreheads one to the other, and touched hands as Chitthra rose.

Then Aeren was alone.

* * *

Hovenethra...

Ba'tula raised her cup, and Aysa'lil and Kreothren did the same. They drank together, and Ba'tula closed her eyes, quietly chanting prayers, as the clergy cast nervous glances to each other.

"You have concerns?" Ba'tula held her cup, and a servant refilled it as she waited for an answer.

Kreothren bowed in his seat. "Dark Lady, we praise our soldiers' victory, yet wonder of the price."

"The price is the blood of soldiers whose place it is to fight and die for the glory of *Iyllyeth* and *Mother Darkness*. The goal is our rightful place as leaders of the Drow."

Kreothren nodded. "And we are in agreement, yet still, our Lancer Captains called retreat. If we are the victors, should we not have held leaders of the House of Iyllyeth our captives?"

Ba'tula showed a withering eye to the priest. "I do not want them captive, I want their hearts held in my hand! Alystin herself assuredly, and should she return, Archane! You question our righteousness at this late date? Had you worries, should they not have been raised before?"

"They were, Dark Lady," said Aysa'lil softly, "and you dismissed them. We begged patience, and now we sit as three, where six were before. We pray your indulgence in this time."

Ba'tula drank again, then shrugged. "We stand on the cusp of leadership of the Race, yet here you hesitate. I will hear your concerns this day, but I warn you, my hand against the House of Iyllyeth will not be stayed."

Kreothren bowed again. "Your indulgence is valued, and we thank you. With all respect, and assuming the next foray into the enemy's camp will be the last, we ask mercy for those leading in Archane's absence. In truth, they have only carried out orders given, and shown great restraint in blood and lives taken of our soldiers, to say nothing of the captives gathered. Missives have proven none detained by Alystin have been harmed. We ask…" The priest paused, drank, then continued, his voice dropping to a whisper. "We ask mediation for their lives be offered."

Ba'tula smirked. "You desire Alystin or Xa'lyyth as your concubine? Or perhaps you favor the males of the Black Circle?"

Kreothren's face colored in the lantern light. Aysa'lil took his hand and spoke. "We wish their abilities not be wasted on the altar, Dark Mistress, that is all. Recall, the Black Circle was once of all Houses, not just that of Archane. We wish to see it such again."

"You say a council of all?" Ba'tula's hand came down hard upon the table. Plates rattled in her rage. "This was proposed at Conclave and set aside by Mor'i'jil himself! Dare you raise the subject on our eve of victory?"

"Yet the difference now is Hovenethra will sit in rule," replied Kreothren. "With yourself as principal, leader of the Race."

Ba'tula chewed slowly at her meal, considering. "You say allow Alystin into our ruling clan? I cannot see advantage of such a thing."

411

"More than a council," continued Kreothren, now with confidence, "showing willingness to accept other views, and not only from the former leaders, but from all Houses. Especially those who have shown leniency themselves."

"You speak of Warinethra and their warning." Ba'tula waved off Kreothren's reply before he could voice it. "I see that only as a pretense, weakness shown from a House thought mighty. Your argument itself is therefore invalidated."

"We ask only you consider with all patience," said Aysa'lil, still with Kreothren's hand in hers. "Once Alystin's heart has beat its last within your hand, too late it will be for reconciliation."

Ba'tula's retort was interrupted by a knocking at the door. A servant entered meekly, bowing. "Dark Mistress, forgiveness is begged for our disturbing of your meal. An urgent message comes from the Lancer Captain at the central chamber."

Kreothren held a silver plate and the messenger placed the parchment on it. He passed it first to Aysa'lil, who waved a hand above it, then nodded to Ba'tula.

"Wait beyond the door, I will have a reply forthwith." Ba'tula paused for the door to latch, then broke the seal and read. Eyes wide and breath now coming short, she laid the missive on the table. For long moments she only stared away, eyes fixed on nothing, breath shallow, rapid, ragged.

"Dark Mistress..."

Ba'tula held a hand, yet discomfited and pale as Drow might be. She mumbled words neither Kreothren or Aysa'lil could understand, then turned at last to face them. She lifted up the parchment, her hand trembling as she spoke. "Archane is alive. She is here, in *Ung'gu'wi*, seen by our Lancer Captain with his own eyes."

She crumpled the message in her hand as Kreothren and Aysa'lil sat, no words to say between them.

* * *

They hurried down the central passage, guards about and heralds clearing of the way, Ba'tula, Kreothren, and Aysa'lil, fear clutching at their hearts and sweat upon their brows. They called the Lancer Captain to a corridor aside and faced him squarely.

Ba'tula held the crumpled parchment to his eyes. "Tell me of this, when and where! Should this be a lie, I will have your heart upon a spit!"

The Lancer Captain took a knee and bowed his head. "I saw her, a human at her side, or perhaps he was a half-elven. Others round her, ill-mannered in their look, and a score of guards and clergy." He raised his face, tears in his eyes and lips quivering as he spoke. "I bore a wound and lay among the dead, then from a passage likely leading to the land above, she came, regal in her look, eyes of fire and beauty never seen! In my heart, I knew it must be her!" He nearly groveled as he choked out the words that followed. "We have sinned! Archane is alive, and now retribution is in her hand!"

Ba'tula paced away, then turned, Kreothren stepping aside as she closed upon the Lancer Captain once again. "Send the soldiers! Send assassins! Kill her before this news may spread! Hovenethra must reign supreme!"

The Lancer Captain kept his eyes averted. "The assassins all have fled, saying they will not be party to murder of the Dark Princess. Still we may mount attack, as I have told no one but yourself."

"Then do so at once! Call the roll, form the ranks, take the battle to the House of Iyllyeth once more and let none be left alive!"

* * *

The House of Iyllyeth...

"My friends, there is no measure how strange this day will be." Thalion stood with Audrey, Sheynon, and Ysilrod in the meeting chamber after Archane and her entourage of guards and acolytes had departed. "We find ourselves deeply in the midst of those fought against for years, nay, decades, and now we prepare the fight beside them, held by promises made in desperation. If my heart did not know the better of it, I would say the world at last has lost its sense of what is real."

"This is real, Lord Priest," replied Audrey, laying a firm hand upon his shoulder. "The fight against evil in the world takes many turns, and this is but our most recent. Live or die this day, we know our cause is just, and will rest the better for it, whether in our beds or in the arms of those we worship." She looked to each in turn, her crystal eyes smiling. "Surely there are no others in this world I would choose to be in the company of this day."

"Always are you the Light, Excellency," replied Thalion, and they embraced, each and every one.

Audrey donned her nasaled helm, her chainmail hauberk 'neath a fitted jupon of padded silk and wool. Arms blazoned on her garb and *Mír'rë Cala'wyne* slung at her hip, once more she was the Champion they knew, alive and anxious once again for battle.

"Archane says her soldiers take the fore and our mercenaries are to guard the flanks." Thalion shrugged, looking to them all. "While I do not disagree, once joined, battle plans may go awry. Take care you are not trapped between friend and foe. Likely, no Drow will care if elves or humans fall beneath their onslaught."

Audrey nodded, then looked to Sheynon, worry on his face. "My lord, speak your heart, as you are among trusted friends."

Sheynon looked away, then to Ysilrod at his side, and the elf-mage spoke. "My brother remains with me. I have spoken with a sorcerer's apprentice, asked to remain behind the battle line. To this time, neither side has cast more than minor spells and cantrips, and as I have been told, another House has given warning against such practice. This is no place for spells, so deep beneath the sun."

Audrey's eyes found Sheynon's for a moment, then he turned and walked away. Ysilrod continued with his words, speaking quietly. "Excellency, Lord Priest, I beg your confidence. Sheynon can no longer fight, his spirit broken with Galandria's death and his inability to prevent it. My trust now is with his life, seeing him survive and return to our people as their leader. Should he fall, all of Elvenkind would be imperiled."

"My cousin bears the weight of spirts unnumbered," replied Thalion. "May *Yarhetha'an* grant him peace in this undertaking, and see his way safely back to his rightful place."

Audrey stood closely by the both of them. "As you say, and I am not surprised. Nearly is his spirit crushed on seeing matters come to this. His care is in your good hands, dear friend."

* * *

66 Leave none alive." Archane spoke privately with her Lancer Captains, a dozen senior soldiers standing proudly before the Dark Princess and her clergy. Unashamed tears streaked the warriors' cheeks, seeing Archane before them once again.

"Dark Princess, I do not understand." The senior-most of captains, half a head taller and proud in her sable leather armor, bowed before Archane. "Should we not find their leaders and hold them safe for sacrifice? Is it not to the glory of *Mother Darkness* their hearts should be offered, and examples shown to others?"

"Hearts of traitors have no value," said the Dark Princess. "Only from enemies born of other races do we offer them, or willing true believers whose courage is burning brightly. Take the Sword of

414

Retribution, execute her clergy in accordance with our scriptures. Ba'tula shall suffer the pain of Traitors' Death. Only her, no others."

Archane continued. "The heart of Ba'tula, Dark Mistress of Hovenethra, is without worth. Yet hear me, captains of the House of Iyllyeth!" She stepped back and took them all into her sight. "Take no pleasures, not bounty, no prizes, and give nothing of quarter in this fight! Kill all who oppose you, find their clergy and see their blood flows until there is no more! Fight and die for the glory of *Iyllyeth* and *Mother Darkness!*"

"For *Iyllyeth* and *Mother Darkness!*" The cry rang from their voices, nearly shaking the earthen walls about.

In turn, they bowed to Archane, then clasped each other in camaraderie and took their exit, all but her senior-most captain, who paused and turned with a final question. "What of these mercenaries? There are so many, and I cannot see to their control as we fight Hovenethra's forces."

"A worthy question. You have spoken with their leader, yes?"

"Dark Princess, I have, and garnered pledges."

Archane nodded. "Therefore, it is not your task to see their safety. Little might you do, yet should wrongs be seen by your command, you have authority to deal with them in whatever means are necessary."

The Lancer Captain nodded after a pause. "I understand, Dark Princess. Yet what of this… priest, and the human warrior-woman?"

Archane considered, then met the Lancer Captain's gaze again. "They are to be left unharmed by your command. I have pledges made that must be honored. Their safety is their own, and if stories are true of them, they will survive."

"As you wish, Dark Princess. Your will be done."

She bowed and turned, leaving Archane alone until her servants and her entourage entered quietly.

We enter a time unknown, when Drow and human and elf fight side by side. Archane accepted a goblet of dark wine, thinking. *Surely, I have never seen such in my dreams, nor even in conjurings with Iyllyeth in her mortal time. Yet still, Venic's words haunt my every moment, and here I stand, at the precipice of that utterance. "Find a way," he said, "not just in Ung'gu'wi, but all the land. The world." Truly, fate is in my hands, and with this, perhaps the only life I now possess, I must show wisdom, more than ever I have shown before.*

* * *

Word was passed down the ranks, and at the last, movement forward began in earnest. Yet before, Thalion took Audrey to the side and spoke with earnest words. "Excellency, we must show great restraint in our manner. To fight soldiers, this is well and good, yet once ranks are broken of the enemy, and Drow and mercenaries take the battle deeper, we must withdraw. We cannot be seen slaying clergy or servants or concubines, for in truth, this war is not our own."

Audrey thought upon his words, nodding at the last. "Always do you see with clearer eyes than most. I recall our last standing together, in a place much as this, a cavern dark and filled with challenge." She laid a hand upon his shoulder and smiled. "No other in this world would I rather stand beside in battle, Thalion. Should the battle-fever take me, drag me from the line if you must, and I will follow."

"Our friends will need our aid in the fight against Mors'ul'jyn."

Audrey's eyes drifted to the side in contemplation. "I pray *Jhad* watches over Aeren and Chitthra now, for even in their courage, Mors'ul'jyn is more than a match. I fear for their safety."

"They will do as they must. Chitthra's vows weigh more upon her than her very life."

"Yet in doing so, it may cost them both," replied Audrey, sighing. "We dare not let these thoughts distract us."

"Set your shield tight upon your arm, Excellency, and your sword hand firm. We are no longer young as once we were, yet still we know the way of battle, do we not?"

* * *

Audrey marched at Thalion's side, both watching round as dark elf soldiers began to sing. The beat was set for a languid pace, then began to quicken. Words unknown to either of them rang about, voices rising, weapons thrust into the air, male and female soldiers chanting, shouting, now advancing at a trot.

The warrior-woman glanced to Thalion, and he to her, their minds and thoughts the same. Slowly, and with purpose, they eased their way into the press of dark elves, ever closer, ever more with hearts now beating stronger, heading to the fore.

More than five years for Thalion, thought Audrey, *yet more than twenty for myself, since these feelings coursed through my blood. Do I have ability, let alone the courage, to face death here among the Drow? If I die this day, will my body even be recovered, sent back to husband Higar and my children? Is this right, to place my life in danger for the cause of enemies fought years ago?*

With *Mír'rë Cala'wyne* in hand, she increased her pace and Thalion followed in her footsteps. Gently shouldering her way between two Drow soldiers, Audrey found herself at the front, the standard-bearer on her left and Lancer Captain at the right. He glanced to her quickly, and she showed a feral grin. Bright teeth shown in the dimness in return, and he raised his weapon, shouting words she did not understand. She let go a warrior's cry, unleashing energies set aside so long ago.

For your glory, Greatest Jhad, I stand beside my enemies to do battle in your name. Evil comes in many forms, and on this day, it is not the dark elves at my side.

Thalion came as well, and stood now on her right, shields side by side and glowing weapons raised. As they closed upon the line of Hovenethra guards, the words of Duncan Brannigan burst into Audrey's mind: "*Live or die, it will be glorious!*" She grinned, tightening her grip once more.

Crossbow bolts flew from behind, arching above the soldiers at the lead. Then in return, and Audrey's shield caught two, then with lightning quickness, and one more silent prayer, they hit the shield wall with all the strength they had.

* * *

Down a lonely corridor...

Chitthra's breath was tightly held as she waited for the youngling to take her path once more. She glanced around a fallen stone, the girl still kneeling 'neath a lantern in the corridor, and Chitthra laid her head against the earthen wall.

She waited with a count to three, looked once more and saw the girl rise and run beyond her place. Chitthra followed quietly as she could, as there were few places she might hide, then paused against the wall as they neared a door close by a tumbled crossing.

Surely, if Mors'ul'jyn, the door is set with a word of Charm that cannot be broken by any means I have. Therefore...

She watched as the girl bent closely to the latch. Though Chitthra could not hear her voice, she knew her supposition was correct. The door opened, and the girl paused once more to look beyond her shoulder.

This was the chance Chitthra knew she now must take. She ran, wedging through the door before it closed, leapt above the youngling's squeal of surprise, and landed in a posture of defense.

Mors'ul'jyn!

Beyond a shimmer stretched across the room, behind a table set with baubles of no purpose Chitthra understood, was Mors'ul'jyn, eyes wide and mouth agape.

417

Chitthra gave her no time for reaction, dashed across the room and leapt, leg extended for a killing blow, and crashed into the shimmer.

Down and writhing, her left foot ablaze with pain, Chitthra cursed herself for her lack of recognition of the barrier.

Mors'ul'jyn stepped around the table, nearly grinning. "We meet again, and it has been some time, yes? You are in agony? Oh, my dear, I am so sorry, yet I am not the fool you think. Even here, I knew you or your companions would arrive and likely find your way. Still, now, in your haste, you become the first of many in this…" She paused and raised her hands, turning all about. "This sanctuary. Ah, but you found my servant and followed here. This says the Craft is in your midst. Who is it, pray tell? Steffyn Foxxe, or the Calidriil brother, Ysilrod? I do not care, it does not matter, for now I know your whereabouts and can plan my way."

Mors'ul'jyn looked to the girl. "Take your knife and cut her throat, but not too deeply. I want to watch her die. Do it now!"

The girl drew the knife slowly from her belt, and with terror in her eyes, closed on Chitthra slowly, lying in the center of the room.

Chitthra pushed away the pain, praying her ankle was not broken, and breathed in three times, waiting for the girl to draw closer. She snatched a foot, dragged the girl down quickly and disarmed her, then tossed her in a corner.

Lightning struck Chitthra's shoulder, lifted her into the air and threw her hard into a wall. Another bolt, and she felt her mind consumed by fire, blood running from her nose and mouth and ears. Chitthra tried to rise, but her arms and legs refused to follow what thoughts she could collect. She struggled to open one eye, seeing Mors'ul'jyn step through the ward and retrieve the knife laying on the floor. Again, Chitthra willed her arms to work, to no avail.

Mors'ul'jyn approached with care, watching Chitthra's useless spasms, then knelt beside her, grinning. She rolled Chitthra onto her back. Her tunic smoldered, stinking of burnt flesh and wool. Without a word, Mors'ul'jyn laid the blade to Chitthra's neck.

The door creaked open and Aeren hobbled in, sword upraised and shield presented.

Mors'ul'jyn turned, open-mouthed. She rose, but Aeren charged, quickly as her wound would let her. She slashed across Mors'ul'jyn as the sorceress spun away, yet dark blood sprayed down her back as she fell screaming, and clawed her way across the floor toward the magic barrier. She rose, wincing as she did, staring in confusion as Aeren raised her sword once more. "I do not know your face," she said. "How did you gain entry beyond my sorcerer's locking?"

Aeren looked to the girl kneeling by the threshold.

"Mistress... I opened the door. I heard a pounding, and thinking it was soldiers come to save us..." Nullwyss's voice trailed, and she cringed at Mors'ul'jyn's scowl.

"Stupid girl! These are assassins!" Mors'ul'jyn's eyes found Aeren's once again. She began to chant.

Aeren screamed and charged, swung and missed by less than a heartbeat, as Mors'ul'jyn spun in the air, landing beyond her reach. Again she rushed Mors'ul'jyn, who warded the blow with a conjuring, then tossed dust into her face. Aeren backed away, sneezing, coughing, her eyes running tears. Something landed at her feet, and a figure, shadowy and indistinct, appeared.

The thing hammered at Aeren's shield, broke it at the last, then launched itself at her. Aeren rolled with the blow, stood and drove her weapon into nothingness. The shadowed figure leapt again, forced Aeren to the wall, claws raking at her helm, searching for her throat. She fell, dodged aside, reached into her pouch and tossed a fire-stone at Mors'ul'jyn's boots.

The stone exploded, and the shadow vanished, Mors'ul'jyn's robe set to flame. She rolled and called a Charm, water falling from out of nowhere, dousing the fire and half the room.

Aeren charged again, and Mors'ul'jyn waved her hands once more. Wind caught them all, tossing them about. Aeren crashed again into the wall, her head driven against the stonework, breath taken from her chest, and she fell, lights blazing behind her eyes, the sword ringing on the floor.

Mors'ul'jyn rose, cradling an arm and limping to the weapon. She could not raise it, no strength left within her body, and she backed away as Aeren rolled aside, yet did not rise.

"Take the sword!" Mors'ul'jyn called to Nullwyss. "Cut away their heads! Drive the point into their hearts! Kill them both! Kill them now!"

Nullwyss quaked in fear, blood about the room and she, herself, dazed by the conjured gale, bruised about and nearly frantic. "Mistress... I... cannot..."

"Do it! Take their heads! I want them dead in my sight!"

Nullwyss cried, wailed, nearly mad as she fought Mors'ul'jyn's command. "Mistress... I am no murderer! I cannot!" She turned away, clawing at the door.

Mors'ul'jyn screamed, and lightning leapt forth from her hand. Nullwyss's body flashed in fire, vanished into dust, her final cry dying in the dimness.

Mors'ul'jyn turned as Aeren tried to rise again. "Never will you find me!" She spoke arcane words, yet nothing happened. She screamed once more and stumbled beyond the barrier again, as Aeren came to her knees, then fell, mumbling nonsense.

Mors'ul'jyn emerged, a pack across her back, turned the door latch and was gone.

Aeren crawled to Chitthra, took her in her arms and held her closely.

"I love you," Chitthra whispered, her voice a rasp of pain.

Silence came, then darkness.

* * *

PART FOUR
WE RIDE ON THE
BACKS OF DRAGONS

The Battle Line…

Not in twenty years had Audrey Vincent found herself fighting for her life. Though fit and having kept in training, the speed of dark elf soldiers half her age was a bitter challenge, and more than once nearly had she fallen victim to a feint or counterstrike. Still they battled, and for how long she could not know. Only did fresh soldiers take the place of those who fell, as she and Thalion fought side by side, neither giving ground.

Crossbow bolts flew from either side, and twice more her shield was struck. Another glanced from her shoulder, one from off her helm, and the barb nicked her cheek in passing. Hot blood trickled down her chin, and she licked it away, then pressed hard against the shield wall once again.

Audrey killed all who dared cross blades with her, each with a single stroke of *Mír'rë Cala'wyne*, heads rolling free beneath the front line of Hovenethra. A dozen backed away from the human woman shouting praises to a deity the Drow knew nothing of, wielding a sword burning as the very sun itself. None pressed the fight against her, and soldiers from the House of Iyllyeth streamed around Audrey to crash against the wavering shield wall.

All the while the Drow shouted curses, oaths, and chants of battle. Though Audrey did not know the tongue, little doubt was in her mind of what the words were saying.

Shouts from behind, and she and Thalion were pulled to either side, and nearly did they lose their feet. Then a cry, and a brace of soldiers with a battering ram drove into the shield wall, scattering defenders. Crossbow bolts and arrows flew, soldiers fell, and others took their places, yet all the while the ram forced its way deeper into Hovenethra's central passage.

Then came more soldiers, the mercenaries from DragonFall, shouting language Audrey had no misunderstanding of. Hard they pressed, steel ringing against steel, and Audrey's greatest fear was not of combat, but being trampled by their undisciplined advance. She knew the seemingly unending flow of mercenaries was only that because of the narrow passage confines. All she could do was press herself against the wall and let them pass.

Thalion, when last she saw him, was opposite her place, and she prayed he did not fall beneath the deluge of heavy boots. Holding *Mír'rë Cala'wyne* aloft, its blazing light reflecting from the passing arms and armor, at last she saw a glimmer from the other side.

Gil Estel! He lives, and my brother-in-arms sends a signal. Praise Jhad we have been delivered from a fight that is truly not our own!

Slowly Audrey backed her way toward the passage entrance, watching all the while as *Gil Estel* did the same. At last she caught a glimpse of Thalion, worn and wounded, and once clear of Drow and mercenaries still running toward the battle, she crossed, and caught him as he staggered to the rear.

"Sheath your weapon, Lord Priest, for our day is done." She slung her shield across her back, noting three crossbow bolts lodged within the heavy wood. She broke them away, slid *Mír'rë Cala'wyne* into her scabbard, and raised Thalion on her shoulder. Blood leaked from beneath his hauberk, and a shoulder pauldron showed a heavy dent.

"My friend, you are doubtless a worthy target for our enemies," Audrey whispered with a laugh, "yet we must retire before they beat the senses from your body."

They sat aside the entrance, at the last moving to the central chamber, where near a hundred dark elf soldiers guarded others dressed in ornate robes.

"Clergy, and likely sorcerers," said Thalion, as Audrey raised his chainmail and pressed a hand against his wound. He took her wrist lightly. "Do not pray for healing in this place, Excellency. I will live as the cut is shallow." He showed a wry grin. "We must look as tho' we have fought for Archane's return to power, and blood will be a goodly sign in her eyes."

Audrey's gaze locked with his for long and heartfelt moments. "My thanks," she said at last, "for never in my most hidden desires did I know how much I have missed this. Always did I feel I would meet my end in battle, as so many of our friends."

Thalion laid his hand on hers and shook his head. "The world is not cruel enough to take such a bright and glowing soul as yours in any manner other than of a long and worthy life, dear lady. And as you, my spirit sang to stand at your side again, swords raised and valor calling. My thanks, as well."

He rose with a quiet gasp, and they slowly made their way across the central chamber. Thalion staggered a bit as dark elf eyes watched with care, noting Audrey's blood-splattered face and armor. She helped him through the guards about, back into the House of Iyllyeth's passageways, and they sat again, passing a waterskin between them.

"We must find Sheynon and Ysilrod," said Thalion, nodding down the corridor. "Our task for Archane is done, and now we face the true enemy in this time."

"I fear for the lives of Aeren and Chitthra. Mors'ul'jyn may well be the death of all of us."

Thalion drank and laid his head against the earthen wall. "Cousin Ysilrod is her match, Excellency, and surely prepared for whatever she may bring. Let us offer prayers as we prepare ourselves for the final confrontation."

* * *

The press of dark elf soldiers and mercenaries became a flood of deathly steel into the House of Hovenethra. Those with no escape were crushed beneath the tide, and the corridors soon became a killing ground. Branching passages were sealed away for only moments before Archane's forces broke through any who defended, and chambers with no exits became the final stands for many hard-pressed spirits.

On it went, songs of battle in dark elf voices fading deep within the passageways, replaced by cries of pain and wounding, and the silence of the dead. Far into the most private places, soldiers of Archane found harems, servants' quarters, kitchens, and storage chambers. Those of Hovenethra who had no part in battle still became its victims, their bodies hacked to pieces by the passing hordes.

Deeper yet, and what few sorcerers were met offered scant resistance, though for frantic moments, Archane's Lancer Captains struggled with discipline in the ranks. Then followed Kaul's mercenaries, who had no fear of magic, and overran the few wizards and apprentices remaining. Naught was left but spells and cantrips emptying their powers into bodies left headless in the wake of near a thousand humans caring not who fell before them.

The stairway up was found, and while many thought their safety was assured, the mercenaries followed into the village, and chased down all who ran or stood against them.

Archane's senior Lancer Captain led a troupe of elite soldiers, scouring the deepest prayer chambers, the altar room, the council enclave, even the bed chambers of Ba'tula her own self. They found secret passages and followed them, where some fell to traps of magic, or of heavy spikes that pierced their armor, or blades from the walls slicing off their heads. The Lancer Captain called them back, then led them deeper yet, finding other rooms with hidden entries. There they came to Kreothren and Aysa'lil, protected by their honor guard. The fight was swift, a dozen dead of the Lancer Captain's soldiers, yet all were slain of Hovenethra. The priests were backed against a wall, crying for *Iyllyeth's* protection, and there the Lancer Captain took their heads, quickly and as called for by dark elf ritual. She ordered her soldiers to stand as witnesses, then drove sacrificial daggers with the seal of House Iyllyeth upon them into the bodies' hearts, that all would know their deaths had been as law decreed.

Onward to the ending of the passage, and carefully they searched, knowing somewhere in the corridor Ba'tula likely hid. At the last they called a sorcerer, who found the secret entrance, and the soldiers charged within, met by a dozen firing crossbows. Down went six, then six more, but at the last, numbers proved too many for Ba'tula's guards. The Lancer Captain's soldiers killed them all, then she raised up the screaming matriarch and drew the Sword of Traitors' Execution. She cut each side of Ba'tula's throat, the strokes three breaths apart, and dark blood spewed within the chamber. Three breaths more, and she chanted the holy Words of Retribution, as decreed by dark elf law. She cut away Ba'tula's head with the third and final stroke, and drove a sigil dagger deep into her still-beating heart. The cry of victory within the chamber, now filled with blood and bodies, was nearly deafening.

Thus was ended the House of Hovenethra, adversary to the House of Iyllyeth for more than a thousand years.

* * *

A Frantic Search…

Thalion and Audrey traced their steps back through the corridors, seeking Sheynon and his brother. Deeper they strove, until at last a gathering of robed dark elf figures came into view, Ysilrod and Sheynon in their midst.

Thalion took them to the side, spoke of the battle and its likely ending, then paused for the elf-mage to say his findings.

"None yet, as I waited for your safe return. Understand, should I scry with the *NorthWind* sword, likely Mors'ul'jyn will know it, and take whatever safeguards she may have." He looked round to them, Thalion with pain lingering as he clutched his side, Audrey with blood and sweat dried upon her face. Ysilrod chuckled. "More than once I have seen you thus, yet now older, the amusement no longer can be found, yes?"

They smiled, chagrined, and shook their heads, as Sheynon showed a look of worry on his face.

"My lord, your thoughts," said Thalion, gently as he might. "Our quarry must be close, or your brother would not tarry in this place."

The elf-lord looked to Ysilrod, who gave a heavy sigh, then spoke again. "I cannot find sign of Aeren or Chitthra. Surely they are in *Ung'gu'wi*, yet somehow masked, and this is a concern."

"Might Mors'ul'jyn no longer be within Archane's domain?" asked Audrey.

"Or, with fortune, no longer living?" Thalion nodded Ysilrod to continue.

Sheynon held a hand. "Where might they be? I can only surmise Mors'ul'jyn seeking solitude in this place, and therefore deeper in the catacombs. Yet if not here, then where?"

"Wherever she might find safety," replied Ysilrod, "tho' Drakenmoore no longer a possibility, she still may move unhindered in the land. A solitary dark elf would raise no suspicion, is my thought."

"We must search, if not for Mors'ul'jyn, then Aeren and Chitthra," replied Audrey, rising and pointing to the passages away. "Deeper, if we must, but still, if you cannot use the *NorthWind* blade, of what use is it?"

Ysilrod nodded at the last. "Your point is true. Let us search, and if no sign of the others can be found, I will scry."

* * *

Deeper into the corridors they went, passing few about, only doors closed and bolted from the inner side, as though none would risk the soldiers of Hovenethra who might have come. Twice they found an open door, and twice no trace was found of Aeren or Chitthra, and a lone concubine scurried by as they took exit from the second chamber.

Then on, and down a passage ill-finished in its look, a half-completed wall and debris piled in a hollow. Down a sloping path, slick with blood and entrails swept aside in haste, the passage stinking as a battlefield. A stream of water leaked from above, and Sheynon caught a glimmer in the distance.

"Light, as from an open entryway, perhaps a hundred paces past a gentle curve." He looked to Ysilrod. "Preparations, Brother?"

"Closer, then we shall see. Thirty paces, no more, and I may sense her presence, should she be there."

They paced slowly toward the light, weapons drawn and pressing themselves against the earthen wall. They paused, and Ysilrod spoke soft words, then a scene formed before them of an empty room. He turned and shook his head.

"Let us see with our eyes," said Thalion. "Mors'ul'jyn's power is great, and protections may hide her well."

They moved on slowly, and twenty paces from the light they could see the door, bent and twisted on its hinges. Sheynon pointed to the passage floor beside his boot. "Blood, and dark. Drow blood, yet why here?"

Ysilrod bent to look, a glowing rock within his hand. He touched the blood with an ungloved finger and laid it to his tongue, then looked to Sheynon. "It is hers."

"Into the room, quickly." Thalion drew *Gil Estel* and ran for the light. Audrey followed, *Mír'rë Cala'wyne* in hand, as Sheynon rose and followed aside his brother.

The scene which met their eyes was not as they expected. Beyond the door and in a corner stood a single table and two chairs. Fine dust lay about the room on every surface, and unfamiliar items were scattered, broken on the floor.

"Aeren!" Audrey ran to two figures in a corner, sheathed her sword, and bent to take them in her arms.

Thalion came to her side and knelt. Chitthra lay in Aeren's deep embrace, her body burned and twisted. Aeren's head was bloody, her skull crushed at the back, and both her shoulders surely broken.

Thalion's hand found its way with care beneath Aeren's tattered brigandine, to lay above her heart. He listened, lips moving in a silent prayer, then drew his hand away. "My lady... they are gone." Thalion looked to Audrey's crystal eyes, a wild look growing now within them.

The warrior-woman held the bodies tightly, rocking, sobbing, somewhere in her throat a scream of vengeance seeking to escape.

Sheynon knelt and took Audrey in his arms. Ysilrod stood behind her for long moments, watching closely in the room, then walked carefully to the table, touching nothing on the floor. He found a talisman resting on the table, cast a protection on his hand, then lifted it to study. Quiet filled the chamber, only the sounds of Audrey's tears and Thalion's Rites of Passing could be heard.

"We must go, as I have found her." Ysilrod started for the doorway.

426

"I will not leave them here," said Audrey, across her shoulder.

"We will return, my lady, you have my word," replied Thalion.

"Our duty now is vengeance for them," said Sheynon, rising. "No matter what may happen, the vows made by Chitthra are now my own to carry."

"She is injured, tho' not badly," said Ysilrod. "She seeks the stairway up, yet does not know its place."

"Then we must hurry," said Audrey as she stood and took them all within her glance. "I beg you, do not stand in my way once she is found."

* * *

Mors'ul'jyn limped down the passageway, her left arm ablaze with pain and right leg trailing blood. More than once she dropped away her pack, then grimaced as she bent to pick it up, nearly swooning as she did.

Further on she struggled, knowing surely her hideaway had been found and the bodies there within.

Tho' if Drow, little will they think of them, that Hovenethra was the cause. Yet if Sheynon or his accomplices… I cannot be found! I cannot die here, in the realm of my enemy, or at the hands of vengeance following in the form of Calidriil! Curse them! Curse them all!

She paused at a doorway, beat upon it and leaned against the ancient wood. Slowly the door opened, and a youngish face showed from within.

"The stair! Which way, where is it?" Mors'ul'jyn gestured and made motions with her hands, as fingers climbing upward. The youngling's face showed puzzlement, then pointed to a passageway aside, ascending. The door then closed, and Mors'ul'jyn heard the latch turning as she took up her pack once more.

The passage rose before her, up and up and up, then at the last, a set of doors came into view.

Glory to Urijah, I am saved! No guards, and surely it is due to war with Hovenethra. Give me strength, Urijah, to climb into the sunlight once again.

She beat upon the door, yet there was no answer. She sat away her pack, lifted up the bar with her one good arm, and turned the heavy latching. The door creaked on its hinges, and she took her pack in hand and pried it open further.

Hands from beyond the doors took her by the shoulders. She screamed as she was thrust against the wall-work, the pack falling from her arm. A spear point pressed against her chest, shields to either side. Lanterns round lit the space, a landing as it seemed, stairs going upward

427

so high she could not see the top, and before her, faces, one of which she knew too well.

Archane!

The Dark Princess showed a wicked smile. "Welcome. We have been waiting for a while and I prayed your thoughts would bring you here. Now we may bargain once again, yet this time for your very life."

* * *

Sheynon ran with Audrey at his side, Ysilrod close behind, and Thalion trailing with his wound.

"Left at the next passage!" shouted the elf-mage, "then right at the forking. Keep close eye for guards about, or traps set."

They paused as Ysilrod caught them up, and they waited with little patience for Thalion to join them.

"I will lead," said Ysilrod, "as I may cast protection from whatever may be encountered. If traps or magic, I can turn it aside, if nothing else."

Thalion at the last came to them, panting in his discomfort, sweat upon his brow, and his wound once more leaking blood. "Do not… wait for me. Go as needed, and I will be there as I may. I surely cannot fight… tho' may provide a prayer of protection, should it be necessary."

He knelt, and Audrey went to her knees beside him. "Take time, Lord Priest, and pray for your healing if you must. We need you now, and *Gil Estel*."

Thalion waved her away. "Too much time, Excellency. Hurry, go, I will follow soonest. Do not fail to stop her."

Audrey kissed his forehead, made a sign, then rose, running on, Ysilrod before her and Sheynon at her back. Thalion caught up his breath, then trailed them quickly as he could, holding in his side wound with a bloody hand.

* * *

Archane stood with soldiers gathered at her back. She paced closer, as burly guards held Mors'ul'jyn's arms aside. Mors'ul'jyn winced in pain, praying for focus, that she might incant a simple spell, yet exhaustion lay upon her spirit as a shroud.

How to escape? How to live beyond the next moment? How foolish could I be, to enter Ung'gu'wi knowing Archane would appear in time?

"What price will pay, those who follow? Are you worth more to them alive than to me?"

"They want my death!" Mors'ul'jyn screamed. "No difference might it make if you hand to them my body, cold and dead!"

"I thought to let them find you, then knowing you are clever in your ways, I could not chance your escape, as this would likely be our final parting." Archane grinned with malice. "To them, it is vengeance for a multitude of things I may know little of, nor do I care. To me, it is much more between us only, and yet, even then, you may serve a greater purpose."

Mors'ul'jyn's eyes looked wildly about, as she pushed away the pain within her arm, and once again sought effort for a simple cantrip. Her gaze was drawn once more as the Dark Princess stepped away.

"Here is that greater purpose," Archane said, holding forth a jewel-encrusted dagger, two points of light within the hilt as glowing embers. She nodded, and the guards stretched Mors'ul'jyn onto the cold earth floor.

Mors'ul'jyn screamed and thrashed, her arm nearly white-hot with pain. *No! Not a sacrifice! No! I cannot die gutted as an animal! Nooo!*

A noise aside, and the door swung open. There stood Audrey Vincent, Ysilrod and Sheynon at her shoulders, and Thalion closing quickly.

Mors'ul'jyn kicked the guard at her left leg away, wrenched her right hand from a startled soldier, reached into her cloak, and tossed a bag into the air. Dust scattered on a shouted word, and all about fell with watered eyes, sneezing, coughing, clawing at their throats. She called a spell and rose, fleeing up the stairway without touching steps.

Audrey followed quickly as she could, squeezing through the narrow confines. Sheynon at her back and Ysilrod flying overhead, they closed on Mors'ul'jyn quickly. Another set of doors loomed before them all, then a flash of light, a roar of sound, and splinters, dust, and earth and rock cascaded down the steps. Audrey crouched under her shield, Sheynon diving beneath her arms, as stone and shattered wood fell around them.

Soldiers followed, and somewhere within the ringing in her ears, Audrey heard Archane's voice chanting words she did not know. She rose, pressed Sheynon up before her, then trailed behind far enough to keep the dark elf soldiers from overtaking him.

"Go, my lord, go! Reach the surface, take her with your brother! More than a match you are together! Take honored vengeance for Galandria! The right is yours, Sheynon! Go!"

Sheynon ran, following Ysilrod, who cast a ward should Mors'ul'jyn turn and fight. Yet she did not, and the final doors lead to the outer world and freedom, should she reach them first.

Mors'ul'jyn called the fire, the doors exploding outward into the sun. Scattered there before her were twenty dark elf soldiers waiting. She screamed, flew through their number as they fought to gain their feet. Over and above, into a copse of wood nearby, she landed, collapsed, nearly fainting in exhaustion. She rose and fell again, her wounded leg weak and burning, turned at sounds behind her, and saw Sheynon standing twenty paces distant. In his hand was not the *NorthWind* sword, but *Aráto Calidrii*, his own blade, the one Mors'ul'jyn had stolen with which to slay Galandria.

"Where is my weapon!" she screamed. "Give me a weapon and I will cut you down as I did your faithless wife!"

The *NorthWind* sword appeared at her feet, and Mors'ul'jyn took it in her uninjured hand. "I am hurt, I am a woman, I am not a fighter! Is this honor in your eye?"

Sheynon shrugged. "Your use of magic against Galandria was unfair, was it not? Your use of the Guild of Learned in the fortress was to find your way into our home as an assassin, yet you speak of honor?"

Mors'ul'jyn motioned to Ysilrod with Sheynon, and Audrey now standing at the shattered doorway. In only moments, she knew Archane would reach the top and not hesitate to kill her, regardless Sheynon's words. "And if I slay you, your brother will take vengeance on me!"

"Not so," replied Ysilrod mildly. "That honor will be the Lady Audrey's, no other."

All the while, Mors'ul'jyn's injured arm lay quiet beneath her cloak, as her hand dug into a secret pocket. She dropped the *NorthWind* sword, sagged slowly to her knees, and bowed her head, hands before her now, and clenched.

"Make no moves," said Thalion, as he came to the top of the stairway. "Do not approach her until our numbers are greater."

Soldiers began to gather, formed a circle about Mors'ul'jyn as she knelt. Moments later, Archane stood beside the priest, watching carefully as a crowd of villagers grew in the distance. More soldiers came from below and drew a cordon about the Dark Princess, some closing about Thalion as well.

None moved, no orders given, no sounds but the breezes blowing deadfall all about and whispering in the barren trees.

"Stand, tho' slowly, and hold your arms away," ordered Thalion at the last.

Mors'ul'jyn shook her head, eyes still upon the ground. "I cannot raise my left arm, as it is injured, as is my right leg. I am in pain and not fit for fighting."

Sheynon stood away, *Aráto Calidrii* yet raised and ready, Audrey at his side, *Mír'rë Cala'wyne* in hand. Mors'ul'jyn placed her right hand on the ground as if to rise, filled it with dead leaves, and drew a breath. She stood.

Her voice filled the forest round, and trees began to sway and shudder. The ground beneath the gathered crowd split and cracked and opened as a maw, villagers and soldiers sliding into breaches in the earth wide and deep enough to swallow them.

Mors'ul'jyn rose into the air, scattering the leaves as she rose, her left hand tossing glittering dust about. In only moments, the entrance to the stairway began to crumble. The ground swayed and swam nearly as an ocean, yet Sheynon kept his eyes on Mors'ul'jyn.

"Bneir'pak ilta harl!"

The shout from Archane caught Sheynon's ear as he nearly fell, holding balance as he could. A dozen crossbow bolts flew, two striking Mors'ul'jyn's body, and she gasped, then fell to the earth, writhing in her pain. The ground about ceased its shaking, and Sheynon bolted for the figure on the ground. Mors'ul'jyn rolled to her back, raised a hand, and fire sputtered from her fingers, yet the spell was weak and faded as she grimaced.

Sheynon screamed a cry of vengeance and drove *Aráto Calidrii's* slender blade into her heart, leaned upon the hilt, and pressed until the crossguard laid against her ribs.

Blood sprayed as Mors'ul'jyn's eyes went wide in harsh surprise. Sheynon dropped to his knees, his face a hand's-width from her own. "For Galandria. And for myself, as well."

Still Mors'ul'jyn struggled, until Audrey came to Sheynon's side. A whisper of steel within the air, and *Mír'rë Cala'wyne* descended, taking off her head. Still, Sheynon's eyes did not leave those of Mors'ul'jyn, watching as she died.

He collapsed, tears flowing in terror and relief, guilt and fear and absolution years in coming, now consummated at the last. Audrey took him in her arms and held him dearly. They cried into each other's shoulders, friends and comrades as seldom seen within mere mortals, worlds lost and won and shared together, victories and losses, valor sung, and heartaches then endured. Never had it seemed to end... until that very moment.

Ysilrod came to stand beside them, then Thalion as well. Archane remained at the shattered stairway entrance, soldiers yet arrayed about her. At last she nodded to herself in satisfaction, saying nothing. For the nonce, words were not important.

* * *

They took no chances with their doings, and Archane ordered a pyre built half a league beyond the village. They bore Mors'ul'jyn's body in a wagon, gathered tinder and dry wood from the forest round, and laid the body on a slab of heavy bark above it all. As the Black Forest was Archane's domain, Thalion offered her the torch to light it all ablaze. Archane accepted graciously, even nodding to the priest, wordlessly acknowledging that vows and promises had been fulfilled, and a new day might come from chaos, after all.

Archane lit the tinder, and as the western sun set below the far horizon, the mortal remains of Mors'ul'jyn, known once as Teresa Drakenmoore, and also the dark elf girl called Reena, were consumed by fire, burning brightly as stars winked into the sky.

Drow voices sang in harmony, for Archane's clergy had joined the entourage, as villagers watched, not fully understanding what had been seen, yet knowing the Dark Princess ruled her people, as legend said would always be.

Sheynon stood with Ysilrod beside him, Audrey on his left, and Thalion at her side. Comrades and companions many years, friends bound by feelings too deep to say in words, they only watched, for what would they say? Yet as the fire burned, they clasped hands tightly, and more than once, and from each one, a tear descended.

Evil, for the time, and by their hands, had once more been banished from the world.

* * *

It took time, but by the sunrise, and *Grand Selene* traversing the sky, the fire drew down and finally burned itself away.

Ysilrod had fashioned a special urn, saying he would take possession of the ashes, and see they were taken to a place where no one else could ever find them. "I take no chances with magic powerful as hers," he said to Sheynon. Archane stood aside, listening, a knowing look within her eyes. "Never will she be allowed to return in any form, tho' it will take a moon or more for final preparations."

Sheynon nodded as Archane approached and spoke. "You fear her ability, and you are worthy for it. Trust not any who know the Craft as she, for somewhere, somehow, her essence still exists. Give her no place to focus it. Scatter her ashes far and wide, into the sea if you may, away from earth and living things." She paused, looking to Sheynon's nervous eyes. "I have no reason to lie, as nearly did she take my life. Yet her will was strongest ever, and it is said in many tongues, life finds a way. Do not let it become so in her existence."

The brothers traded glances, then bowed slightly to Archane. "Your words hold wisdom," said Ysilrod at the last. "We thank you for your aid in bringing this encounter to an end."

"Perhaps, once the land is rested, we may speak again," she replied.

Sheynon gave a nod of understanding. "As you say... once rested."

* * *

The bodies of Aeren Greywald and Chitthra of *Däe Quivie* were soon recovered, brought beyond *Ung'gu'wi* and placed within magic wrappings given by the clergy of Archane.

Alystin, with Narlros and Xa'lyyth at her side, conferred with Thalion and Audrey in the cooling eve, a day beyond the immolation of Mors'ul'jyn's body. Though none of the Drow spoke the human tongue, Thalion's knowing was enough to share the meanings of their words.

"Praises for the safe return of Archane, and your aid in doing so," said Alystin. *"These wrappings will keep the bodies of your comrades whole, until such time as you decide their final ending."*

Thalion spoke the meaning quietly to Audrey, and the warrior-woman nodded to the dark elf clergy. Audrey's face held no feeling, and her eyes focused somewhere else away.

"We will depart once speaking with the Dark Princess," replied Thalion in Drow tongue. *"She has asked our attendance before our leaving, and we abide her wishes."*

Alystin glanced to the others there beside her. *"Should you allow, we would know your thoughts on future... meetings. Surely with this happenstance, matters of all the land become more closely linked."*

Thalion glanced to Audrey, knowing well the meaning in Alystin's words. *"We will, with all respect, consider your words, and agree, future times may need of... cooperation."*

Alystin smiled. *"Again, our thanks for your understanding. Fare well."* They bowed in unison, and Thalion did the same, nudging Audrey to return the gesture as she would. The clergy took the stairway down, disappearing in the darkness.

Thalion and Audrey turned to the wagon offered by the village elders. "Lord Priest, I would know the meaning of the final words between yourself and them."

"Politics, Excellency, and the offer of continuation."

"They wish to become our allies? That I have difficulty in believing."

Thalion sighed. "If not allies, perhaps no longer adversaries."

Audrey huffed a breath. "Until I hear words from Archane's own lips, never will I believe Drow may change in any manner."

Thalion smiled. "Miracles do happen, and in our time, we have seen a few. Perhaps a new one sits upon our horizon."

* * *

Morning two days on, and as the Companions prepared their leaving, Thalion spoke with the mercenary Zeqis, and the tale of Aeren and Chitthra's ending.

"I did not know them well. We reveled more than once, and always did they carry honor between them." Zeqis laughed. "Something many of Kaul's soldiers know little of."

"Yet you speak well for a ruffian." Thalion showed a grin, and Zeqis returned it broadly. "You remind me of another I was acquaintanced to, yet briefly. A large man, one of Kaul's captains as I recall, by name of Hawk."

Zeqis nodded as his smile slowly trailed away. "He fell in battle, I am sure you know, fighting… Archane. The tale says he slew her, yet here she stands before my very eyes." He nodded to the brace of soldiers and robed figures surrounding the Dark Princess.

"His sister, Raven, resided in my city two years, a friend and confidant of Aeren."

"And this was our way of meeting," replied the mercenary. "Many years ago, I traveled with Hawk and his sister in the south. Raven was of uncommon manner for a woman, and we shared many pleasures, yet the call of battle was her truest love."

"Know you of her whereabouts?" asked Thalion. "If so, perhaps a message to her of Aeren's ending, as they were close."

"I will learn, and as a duty to both, see it delivered."

"On arrival at Kaul's city, I will prepare it for you."

Zeqis nodded once again, and Thalion took his leave, walking slowly to Audrey, standing at the horses. "The sun rises, Excellency, and with it, hope again for all the land."

Audrey's melancholy still lay upon her mood, yet she gave a smile and nodded to Sheynon and his brother standing away. "We speak in company with Archane before our leaving. Have you prayed for knowledge of her words?"

Thalion grinned. "Never would I pry within a woman's mind of what words or thoughts she might impart. It may frighten me unto death, should I even understand the meanings."

"Truly, Thalion, let us hear her now, that we may wend our way home to morn our losses in favored company. I fear what my children will think of Aeren's passing, as she was a sister to them all."

"Her death was with honor, Audrey, and you know this. Not only her vows to you as her mentor and a mother-figure, but to Chitthra. Surely they are together in the heavens once again."

"Archane awaits our pleasure," said Ysilrod, as he and Sheynon quietly approached. The elf-mage nodded across his shoulder to the party waiting by a cottage.

"Let us hear her out, then leave this place," added Sheynon. "The walls of *Annatar Yarhetha'an* will not be seen too soon."

They walked their way to the Dark Princess and her entourage, and bowed on their approach. Twenty guards laid hands upon their weapons, then Archane gave a simple sign, and all but four withdrew. "Come this way."

She led them to a field surrounded by a growing of young pines, the grasses dormant, brown and yellow, but the trees still green and vivid. Their steeds and the wagon waited in the distance as they stood in morning sun, and while there was trepidation in the Companions' hearts, Archane, they knew, was unarmed, and the soldiers carried only shortswords.

"Trust grows," whispered Thalion to Audrey, and the warrior-woman nodded wordlessly.

Archane paused and turned to face them, her soldiers ten paces at her back, attentive, yet calm in their demeanor.

"We thank you once again for your part in this," said Archane quietly, the words meant only for their ears. The Companions bowed in unison.

"And our thanks to you," replied Thalion. "It is our hope matters in your realm may calm at last."

Archane showed a crooked grin. "In time, and with necessary offerings, matters will calm, it is my assurance."

A moment passed, and as Thalion began to speak, Archane raised her chin, giving them a look of bold imperiousness. "As I rule," she said, struggling with the words, "no longer will the Drow be a threat to Ardwel and its peoples. However, should matters change within *Ung'gu'wi*, I have no thought what then will happen. Until that time, our realms," she looked in turn to all before continuing, "will be at peace. This is my vow, and I hereby pledge to honor it."

Another moment passed, one broken only by breath held close by the Companions, now released slowly and with great relief.

"We pledge as well," said Thalion, "and I speak for all in Ardwel, in the Kingdom of the Sun, in the Northern Realm of Stormguarde. Hereby, we are at peace." He bowed, as did they all, and Archane returned the gesture.

Never had they seen her bow to anyone.

* * *

On the Road, and Home…

They rode out with little fanfare, no cheering crowds, no music, no flower petals in their path, only twenty mercenaries who knew of Chitthra and Aeren by association or by reputation, and asked to travel as an honor guard.

A day, and they were beyond the Black Forest, another and they were at the crossroads leading north and south, then westerly on into the realm of Kaul and DragonFall. They paused at evening and sat at the fire, when Thalion raised a question.

"Where shall we set them free, my friends?"

Audrey paused her cup, looking to the priest. She cast a glance to Sheynon, who looked to Ysilrod, then shook her head. "I had not thought, other than to take Aeren back to Vincentholm. Yet your question holds a question of itself. What of Chitthra? The Brotherhood?"

"None I know can say where their hidden village is," replied Sheynon. "Brother?"

Ysilrod paused in thought. "Even in his time with us, Daeron spoke little of his village, as it was a secret. I would not know where to begin a search, and I would say caution to anyone so thinking. Lord Priest?"

Thalion looked to the waning sunlight and *Mina* high above. The Star, he knew, would rise in the east, and by the mid of night, be at its zenith.

436

"They traveled, fought, and loved together. Who would send them into the afterlife apart?"

Audrey mulled the question. "They came into the land as we, those many years ago, to carve their names into it, however reluctantly at the first." She glanced to Sheynon, who only chuckled. "Your point is taken, and with wisdom once again, my friend, you see the clearest of us all."

"A pyre on the open land?" Ysilrod nodded, then smiled gently. "An elven way, most assuredly, and serving of their manner."

Sheynon nodded to the mercenaries camped around. "Strong arms are in number here. The wood is filled with fallen limbs, and I spied an old fallen oak when gathering for our fire."

"Symbol of the forest and everlasting strength," said Audrey, a wistful look within her eyes. "Should I have met my end in Ardwel, I would ask to rest in such a place forever."

Thalion stood. "Then let us be about it. Still the night is young."

It took them time, and by the light of *Mina's* silvery face, they built the pyre in a dormant field. Four mercenaries known to Chitthra, with Sheynon and Ysilrod at their sides, bore her body to the standing, and set it at one side. Four more raised Aeren's form from the wagon, and with Audrey and Thalion leading as the bearers, placed her close to Chitthra.

Thalion sang a song of loss and love, of raising hope, and life then ever-lasting. Audrey followed with the song sung when burying Duncan Brannigan at the entrance to the lair of the great dragon *Ancanar*, so many years ago.

Sheynon spoke words of holding vows, of loyalty and promise, of standing fast and never losing faith. Ysilrod spoke gentle words, of love, of sharing, of standing side by side, and the word once Aeren was heard to utter in his presence; *Undefeated.*

Three mercenaries offered stories of merriment, of jesting and of simple words between them all. Few eyes around were without tears in time, and as The Star rose to its zenith, Thalion offered benediction, and bade Audrey light the northern side. The torch was touched to tinder, then passed to Sheynon on the south, Ysilrod the east, and Thalion, the west.

They stood vigil in the cold of night, the fire and memories warming them as the sun began to rise and they watched the final embers burn.

By mid of day, the ashes cooled, and they scattered them about the land, singing praises to the sun, the moons, the *Rising Star*, *Almighty Jhad*, and *Great Yarhetha'an*. Sheynon spoke a name they knew of well, that of

Daeron Foxxe, *Din'daeron'dae*, commending Chitthra's spirit into his loving hands.

Then they rode, finding solace in a roadhouse as so often done in days gone by, and filled the common room with laughter, song, and stories of grand adventure.

While it was not the best of days they had ever known, surely it was one in which no other company could have been cherished as was theirs.

* * *

DragonFall...

They paused in Kaul's city, and the mercenaries bid adieu, taking to the taverns and the brothels quickly. The Companions made way to the palace grounds, and were ushered into Kaul's presence.

Quickly he noted there now were only four, where on their leaving, six had been seen. Audrey shook her head gently as she looked him in the eye, and her gaze spoke much to Kaul, who only nodded grimly.

Words were few, and in truth, unnecessary, as none were in a mood for banter, and Kaul, himself, suffering from another night of revelry.

"We leave with this," said Thalion, as the elves and Audrey stood at his shoulders. "For the nonce, and with hope forever more, the dark elves are no more a bother. The pledge from Archane, now in her rightful place as ruler of the Drow, and we stand before you, witness to her words."

Kaul glanced to Audrey. "You heard with your own ears, yes?"

"Great King, I did. And as I confirm, Lord Priest Thalion speaks the truth."

Kaul nodded, satisfied, then grinned. "As I know, never would you lie, therefore, I accept this pact. What of dark elves in the land?"

Thalion glanced to Sheynon and Ysilrod. "They are subject to laws as any other, as the land is One at last."

Kaul pursed his lips, took a tankard from a servant and sipped a draught. "As you say. And now, home for all of you?"

"Yes, Great King," they intoned, then bowed together.

Their exit was made quickly as decorum would allow.

* * *

They stood beyond the city walls together in the morning light. Dressed in traveling garb and cloaked against the coming winter season, words seem to fail them all.

"Once before we bid fare well, years ago in Vincentholm," said Sheynon. "Never did I dream to see you once again, dear lady, and now I fear I never shall for the second time in my life."

Audrey held back a tear and nodded. "Never is a long time, my friend. Still we are alive, and years lay before us, unknown as a new day's dawn. I so swear, we will meet again before I leave this life."

"A promise by Audrey Vincent is as good as done," said Ysilrod with a smile.

She took Sheynon in her arms, kissed his cheek and made a sign before him. "May *Jhad* always bless you and keep you. Your great lord is strong, but never is there too much strength to watch over the name Calidriil."

"A warning there, I hear," said Ysilrod with a smile, then he embraced Audrey tightly. "Fare thee always well, dearest lady. Your life shines in Ardwel as a light."

"*Take care of Elvenkind,*" said Audrey in High Elvish. "*Keep faith, and always know you have my love and admiration.*"

They paused, only gazing at each other for a silent moment. Sheynon turned to Thalion. "You, my cousin, we will see in closer time, as Ysilrod's Joined, Caramir, is soon to bring their child into the world. Word will come, and by chance perhaps we will see your family at your side."

Thalion bowed. "With all my heart, it will be so." He looked to the brothers, side by side before him. "Take best of care wending your way home. Blessings on your House."

They took their saddles, Ysilrod and Sheynon riding west, Thalion and Audrey preparing to ride north to the City-State of Truth.

Audrey watched as the elves found the road and soon were lost in the villages below DragonFall. "Four days to your home now, Lord Priest, and near a moon before I see Vincentholm and my family again."

"Might you stay the winter? Travel in the mountains can be treacherous, as we know well."

Audrey looked away for moments, then turned to Thalion. "Have your daughters learned of swordplay yet, my friend?"

* * *

Annatar Yarhetha'an a Moon Later, and One Last Huzzah…

Ysilrod burst into Sheynon's study, wide of eye and panting. "Twins, my brother, twins, as yours! Male and female, healthy, and Caramir is well! Two more of Calidriil enter the world this day!"

Sheynon closed the book upon the reading stand, crossed the room and took Ysilrod into his arms. The elf-mage cried into his brother's shoulder, shaking as if seeing of a ghost. Sheynon led him to a leather chair, poured brandy in a crystal glass, and nearly fed it to him.

"I... I cannot say my happiness, I cannot know how to say my feelings, I cannot... breathe..."

Sheynon laughed and held his brother once again, and slowly Ysilrod began to calm. He sat back in the chair, sweat upon his brow and a grin upon his face.

"Was it thus, when Lae'rion and Laera'nna were born?" Ysilrod downed the brandy, and Sheynon refilled the glass, then poured another for himself. He stoked the fire, then drew a chair closer to his brother.

"It was, and surely as with all elves, we rejoice in new lives arriving. So few we are, tho' our number growing."

"In time, our kind will be overflowing, Sheynon. I have seen it in my studies."

"Crowded into cities?" Sheynon shook his head. "Surely not of elves. Coronis is the only place in Ardwel where elves prefer walls to forests."

"A thousand years, and we will fill the land."

Sheynon raised his glass, then offered a thought. "A thousand? Perhaps we should take lessons from the humans. They seem to have no trouble creating offspring."

"Value is best, brother, over great numbers," jested Ysilrod.

Sheynon was silent for a moment. "Have you considered names?"

Ysilrod shrugged. "Caramir has thought upon it, yet no decisions made. Finding of the right name is important, yes?"

"I have a thought," said Sheynon, sitting back. "Chitthra for your daughter, Daeron for your son." He looked to Ysilrod, who smiled.

"Worthy, and certainly a possibility. But what of Aeren?"

Sheynon cast his eyes away, northward. "That I will hold for the first-born to Audrey Vincent's children."

NA'ATA TA'NA'NYA ILYE MÁN...

All Good Things...

EPILOGUE

The Mists of Time...

Mors'ul'jyn burned. When her mind was not wrought with pain, it seemed always had she burned. Never did she recall not burning, her body disappearing into flame, her mind at the very last disintegrating into white-hot agony.

Then, it would all begin once more. The flash within her heart, and she felt it blacken into ash. Then her innards, and outward to her skin, up into her face, the fire burning all away, her lips, her teeth, her tongue, and at last her mind exploding in unimaginable pain.

Then again, never ceasing, allowing not a moment's respite.

Until now.

Others gathered round, and only for an instant could she see them before, again, her eyes burned away, her mind afire, her very thoughts burning into nonexistence.

"Who are you?" The words had barely formed before her face erupted into flame. Then again, as her eyes were offered a tiny bit of recognition. "Reena?"

"Yes, Reena."

The girl stood before Mors'ul'jyn, whole and beautiful as she remembered. Then fire would come again, yet when she caught another glance, more figures were arrayed. *Chitthra? Aeren? Steffyn Foxxe and Jyslin? Nullwyss? Mor'i'jil? Ma'chen'der? How do I know the names of those never met before? How do they exist herein, unburning?*

"Why are you here?" Another flash of fire, as Mors'ul'jyn felt her heart begin to burn once more.

Reena only smiled.

"How do you stand apart, in a place where torment is the only way?"

Reena shook her head. "Oh, no, we are only here in part, as we exist in other places, where the afterlife awaits us in its manner. Places much less... unpleasant. We gather here only for a purpose."

"Then... why? What do you want of me?"

Reena's smile became a look of stark reprisal. "Nothing of you, for truly, our endings at your hand are why we gather. We only wish to watch you burn for all eternity."

* * *

Ung'gu'wi, and Five Years On…

The House of Iyllyeth had prospered, and the villages within the Black Forest grown in size and number, as many of the Drow sought to shed their underground existence. In the former House of Hovenethra, a new movement had begun, one asking questions of the outer world, the sun, the moons, the stars, and how dark elves might find their way in places other than caves and caverns, as had been done a thousand years or more.

Many of tradition called them back, yet when Archane gave her blessing, those voices calmed, not from fear of deep reprisal, but otherwise. For in time, the Dark Princess began to seek the light of day, and soon others, those younger and inquisitive, followed.

Three years past, a human male appeared in a village, asking audience with Archane, and said his name was Venic, an acquaintance from "old times", as he had said. Those who knew of tales and rumors of the Other Time and Place showed skepticism, though when met, Archane seemed to fall within his charismatic charm.

In time, he became her consort, and whispered words were heard about, though none within the House doubted his calming way was seen upon Archane's demeanor.

On a day filled with glowing sunshine, in a Black Forest village far east of the land called Ardwel by elves and humans, Archane fell ill. Healers were summoned from *Ung'gu'wi*, clergy offered prayers that night for her swift recovery, then on the sunrise of the day to follow, an ancient Drow woman came to the side of the Dark Princess. She cleared the cottage where Archane lay resting, then came from within and ordered Venic summoned with all haste, and did not leave until the human soon arrived.

Venic appeared, and the ancient woman gave him a knowing look upon her exit. He entered the sleeping chamber where Archane sat in a rocking chair, wrapped in a woolen blanket.

"Dark Princess, I came quickly as I might." Venic knelt at her side, and she held her hand for him to take. He pressed her fingers to his forehead in ritual greeting, one she had taken on return from her long absence to her people. He looked into her eyes. "The ancient one gave no word, and I have worried of your malady."

"It is no malady," said Archane, a small smile playing on her lips. "Recall the task set before us by Iyllyeth herself, those centuries ago? Now it comes to stark fruition, and I wonder of its doing."

Venic thought for moments, then shook his head. "I do not understand. Yet I am certain you have words of explanation."

"No malady," Archane repeated. She drew the blanket aside, her glowing nakedness before him. She placed his hand upon her belly gently, and for the first time in his life, Venic saw a smiling of pure joy upon her face.

His jaw dropped open.

Her smile grew wider.

He took her in his arms and never did he want to let her go.

She led him to the bed. "Take your pleasures of me now, for soon I shall be too round for you to have your way with."

Still he could not speak and only stood, gazing into her fiery eyes. Eyes filled with life and love and happiness. "This is... a miracle," he managed at the last.

"Your doing, my lord."

She grinned with malice... or was it only mischievousness he saw? "Perhaps you will instruct me now on how this has happened."

ABOUT THE AUTHOR

Dennis Young's writing experience began somewhere around the third grade and has continued since. Once through the grueling trials of school (grade, high, and college level, surviving all with a flourish) he found an outlet for his imagination in the world of fanzines and fan literature. Writing for friends, family, and once in a while actual publication, his appetite was only whetted.

Working in the international construction trade, he found outlets in technical writing, business plans, and other professional works for over 30 years.

In the early 2000's he began assembling *The Ardwellian Chronicles*, and in 2006 published his first book, *Secret Fire*. This was followed by *Dark Way of Anger*, the second in the series, and he shows no sign of stopping, as *Secrets of the Second Sun* was released in 2010, Book Four, *Kaanan's Way*, in 2012, and Book Five, *Blood Secret*, in 2016. The Saga is now complete, with the release of Book Six, *Breath by Breath*, in 2018.

It is rumored in writing circles his mantra is *"Working on The Ardwellian Chronicles and Hope I Live Long Enough to Finish"*.

With stories of family relationships and blood-oaths taking precedence over all, *The Ardwellian Chronicles* offer stirring tales of high adventure and challenges to test the mettle of the bravest souls and spirits.

www.ardwel.com

Made in the USA
Columbia, SC
05 February 2018